Praise for The Kiminee Dream

"Richly written, full of magical realism and deeply atmospheric, *The Kiminee Dream* is as much a love letter to the interconnected lives of small town residents as it is a testament to how inexplicably linked our lives are, no matter how far removed."

—Kristin Fields, Author of *A Lily in the Light*

"Laura McHale Holland, knows a thing or two about the beauty to be found in characters from America's heartland. They are always quirky and some are on magical, profoundly personal quests. And if their fellow travelers include pets, wildlife and even the landscape itself, it all makes for a hypnotic and endearing story. The turn of *The Kiminee Dream*'s final page feels like the end of a much-needed visit home."

—Rayne Wolfe, former *New York Times* staff writer, *San Francisco Chronicle* columnist, and author of *Toxic Mom Toolkit*

"More than a delightful visit to the heartland in a simpler time, it's easy to confuse *The Kiminee Dream* with a tale of Midwest charm and quirky characters—sure, it's got all that—but there are twists and turns that take you to a dark side that you don't see coming. Laura McHale Holland sheds the stereotypes (while still squeezing plenty of whimsy out of them) with a tale of larger than life characters in a small town."

—Ransom Stephens, author of *Too Rich to Die*

"The little town of Kiminee, Illinois, population 1,257, has always had something magical about it. Why, if you listen closely, you can even hear the Bendy River, which flows alongside this burg, burbling to the tune of "You Are My Sunshine." But the residents of Kiminee also have a few skeletons secreted away—both real and metaphorical.

Cozy up with this novel when you have a few hours; Laura McHale Holland has crafted a page-turner. Once you enter this world, you won't want to leave until the last mystery is solved."

—Michel Wing, author of *Body on the Wall: Poems*

"While containing quite a bit of melodrama, *The Kiminee Dream* remains a deeply poetic and riveting novel, full of family secrets and the complex relationships right underneath the cheery façade of American normalcy."

—Royal Young for IndieReader

The
Kiminee
Dream

The
Kiminee
Dream

a novel

Laura McHale Holland

ISBN paperback: 978-1-7336683-3-0
ISBN ebook: 978-1-7336683-2-3
Library of Congress control number: 2019917395

Cover design by Kathy McHale, www.mchalecreative.com
Interior design and layout by JETLAUNCH.net
Author photo by Moira Holland

For the fine people of Illinois—
past, present and future—
one and all.

Some of Kiminee's finest —
and not so fine

Abby Louise Chute   High school sweetheart of Tam-Tam's son Bram. Keeps a flask of liquor in her pocket.

Aunt Truly   Storyteller and sage of indeterminate age who travels far and wide on foot when not at home in Windy Wood.

Barb and Jeff   Owners of The Good Luck Cafe. Befriend Velda when she's down and out.

Blanche and Ray Foley   Twins as close as twins can be. Born a year to the day before their sister, Carly Mae.

Bram Parlo   Tam-Tam's second son. The love of Abby Louise's life.

Carly Mae Foley   The Foley's third child, extraordinarily gifted especially in art and music.

Damon Foley   Velda's husband. Father of Blanche, Ray and Carly Mae. Math teacher and summertime mailman.

Doris Lowry   Betrayed widow and mother who falls on hard times.

Dusty Lambert   Budding journalist and Five 'N Dime clerk. Becomes a Jewel Tea salesman.

Earl Wiggs   Lifelong friend of Damon and Velda. Mailman who later becomes chief of police.

Emily Skrillpod   Jasper's wife. Raised in an orphanage. Becomes ill whenever she comes to Kiminee.

Georgia Webb   Head nurse at Dry Gulch Asylum for the Criminally Insane.

Gracie Parlo   Tam-Tam's daughter. Missy's girlhood friend.

Harlan Parlo   Tam-Tam's husband. Someone to steer clear of.

Jasper Skrillpod   Art dealer who discovers Carly Mae and becomes her patron. Estranged from his family since childhood.

Juke Parlo

Tam-Tam's eldest son. Goes steady with Missy in high school, but follows his father's footsteps into crime.

Leon Ames

A really bad dude.

Marcie "Missy" Lake

A town matriarch. Niece of Maurice T. Brewer. Mother of Velda Foley. Grandmother of Blanche, Ray and Carly Mae.

Maridee Pratt

Lifelong best friends with Missy and Tempest. President of The Suzettes.

Maurice T. Brewer

Long-time chief of police. A powerful man in his day. Missy's uncle.

Maxine

Jeff's cousin and Velda's lover. Moves to Kiminee with Barb and Jeff.

Mick Deely

Musician and music teacher.

Mrs. Henchley and Dr. Croll

Two scheming educators associated with Lily Park Academy.

Ned Burton

Director of Dry Gulch Asylum for the Criminally Insane for a short time.

Randy Tarr

Member of feuding Tarr and McDuggin clans. Kindhearted down deep.

Ray and Blanche Foley

Twins as close as twins can be. Born a year to the day before their sister, Carly Mae.

Tam-Tam Parlo

Kiminee's eldest resident. Widow of outlaw Harlan Parlo. Mother of Juke, Bram and Gracie. Has it in for Missy.

Tempest Binsack

Lifelong best friends with Missy and Maridee. Treasurer of The Suzettes.

The Suzettes

A philanthropic organization founded in the mid-19th century.

Velda Foley

Missy's daughter and Damon's wife. Mother of Blanche, Ray and Carly Mae.
A restless soul.

Prologue

In the town of Kiminee, the end was never the end, sorrow left supple scars and wishes cracked reality. This was true back in January 1936, when a teenager forced too soon into womanhood darted through a moonlit winter night, exhaling moist clouds into biting air. Clad in a sleeveless, cotton nightgown and slippers worn thin, the young fan of radio dramas, black roses and Bing Crosby's mellow baritone didn't wince at the cold. She ran on, eyes glazed with fever, dewy skin blemished.

At the riverbank, she vaulted over snow-covered boulders onto solid ice. With arms outstretched and face tilted skyward, she glided. Voice wavering, she rasped a lullaby her mother used to sing in a city where coal dust muted the horizon. Her heart thrummed. Tears flowed. Blood slid down her thighs.

She kicked up her feet. Gone were the slippers, replaced by skates of purest-white leather with gleaming blades; gone was the nightie, replaced by a costume with sequined rainbows and silver fringe. She leaped, spun, landed. Ice cracked. She rose and fell again. The brittle surface groaned. She leaped higher, higher—each time a creak, a crack. Into the air she twirled once more. When she touched down, a fissure welcomed her. She plummeted, lips closed, eyes smiling.

When she embraced her maker that bleak Illinois night in the depths of the Great Depression, all residents of the community nestled along the river's curves were asleep. Except for one. And for decades to come, they knew nothing of her brief life and demise.

Except for one.

Chapter 1

*C*arly Mae Foley came into the world much like any other babe in 1953. She wailed when a doctor spanked her bottom. Her woozy mother, Velda, croaked, "There you are," and then passed out. Damon, her father, raced from waiting room to nursery when he learned his newborn had arrived. Carly Mae's brother and sister, Ray and Blanche, flaxen-haired twins born one year to the day before her, dumped bowls of Cheerios from high chairs. They spoke in a secret language their grandmother, Missy Lake, mistook for babble as she pulled out her address book and dialed all her friends from her kitchen wall phone.

Soon Kiminee, Illinois—a town that had just grown from 1,256 to 1,257—was abuzz with the news, for whenever a new child arrived people and animals alike set aside their differences to celebrate as one joyous whole. It was the Kiminee way. Mothers jigged around kitchens. Children cartwheeled through the town square. Fathers belted out show tunes in their fields. Pigs played kick the can with bobcats; chickens dined with hawks; rabbits napped with coyotes. For little Carly Mae, even the Bendy River got in the act, burbling a tune that sounded a lot like "You Are My Sunshine" while crawdads came out of hiding to march in formation along the banks. While everyone always returned to normal in a day or two, interest in each child's development remained keen. And it wasn't long before the auburn-tufted addition to the Foley family became something of a celebrity. "A wonder," "genuine genius," "one in a million" and "uncanny" were used to describe the little baby boomer, because in every developmental area, she did nothing but astound. She sang before she talked and danced before she walked. She read *Charlotte's Web* at age two, mastered multiplication at three and did long division in her head at four.

At five, she taught herself to tap dance up and down walls like Fred Astaire. When she turned six in July of 1959, she set up a lemonade stand that, in one summer, raised $70 to help families devastated by an inferno hundreds of miles away. The conflagration had killed scores of students. She'd learned of the tragedy months earlier on the TV news, and the thought of all those children who would never again run barefoot through grass made her heart quiver with grief. She posted signs to that effect at her lemonade stand, which could be why so many people gave her 10 cents for 5-cent lemonades and told her to keep the change. It also helped that the Illinois State Fair gave her a booth near the entrance on the busiest day of the year.

On a sunny Saturday when she was seven, Carly Mae was discovered. It happened while she was painting portraits of Buster, a thirty-pound, tricolor husky-sheltie cross with a lopsided grin and only one ear. The dog had arrived on the Foley family's doorstep as a scrawny pup the day Velda and Damon brought Carly Mae home from the hospital. He looked like he'd been mauled by a bear, with gashes all over his body and one little ear torn off, but his eyes were bright and his energy high, so they let him in, tended to his wounds, and joked he was likely descended from the husky-sheltie pups that, according to local lore, had survived a drowning generations ago. He soon became the babe's constant companion and co-conspirator—a good thing since the twins were only mildly interested in their sister at the time. As the subject of her paintings, Buster was helping Carly Mae raise money for a new cause, the Touch of Kindness Rest Home, which was in danger of being shut down due to a leaky roof. She sold poses of her imperfect pooch on the sidewalk in front of the Kiminee Five 'N Dime for $1. There she caught the eye of Jasper Skrillpod, an art dealer passing through while on the hunt for antiques with his wife, Emily.

"Whoa! Look at that little girl painting right out there on the sidewalk." Jasper's unusually large brown eyes opened wide as he braked his Willys wagon. "I've got to check her out. Look at her red-brown Heidi braids. And do you see that dog? What a Norman Rockwell scene."

Emily fanned herself with a flyer for a pancake breakfast she'd picked up in a nearby hamlet. "Do we have to stop? I don't feel well."

"You were fine just before we pulled into town. I wonder what happened." He brushed sandy blond bangs off his forehead.

Beads of sweat formed at Emily's temples and the nape of her neck, moistening her dark brown hair. "I don't know. I'm just overcome with nausea. It came on suddenly."

"I don't have to meet our little Picasso right now. We should go to the motel."

Knowing how much her husband loved introducing new talent to the art world, Emily decided to rally. "Maybe it'll pass if I just sit here while you go."

"Are you sure? I don't want this to bring on bad dreams tonight."

"You worry too much. I haven't had a nightmare in ages. Go on, go."

"Thanks, love." He leaned over and kissed her cheek. "I owe you one. I'll only be a minute." He exited the vehicle and strutted to Carly Mae. Five minutes later, he returned with a 7-Up. "Didn't see any Vernor's or Canada Dry inside, but this should help." He handed her the drink through the passenger window. "It looks like your color's coming back a bit."

"Thanks." Emily took a sip and closed her eyes. "I think my stomach has settled down some, and this is bound to help." She sipped again. "So what did you find out?"

"That sweet little girl, Carly Mae's her name, she'd love to see if I can sell her paintings, but I need to get parental permission. The mom's helping with inventory at the store, and Dusty, the young man working the cash register, said he'd fetch her."

Behind him, Velda stepped out of the Five 'N Dime. She straightened her pedal pushers, tucked in her sleeveless blouse, then patted down her disheveled brunette waves and stomped over to Carly Mae. "What's going on? You need my permission for some crazy thing?" she said to her daughter.

Carly Mae looked up from the canvas and frowned at the only mother in town who was always difficult to track down. "Where were you this time?" She dabbed a bit of white on Buster's ear.

"Now listen here, Carly Mae, you may be smart as a whip, but you have no call to question my whereabouts."

"I think the mother just arrived." Emily pointed toward Velda. "She's the spittin' image of Natalie Wood—well, a disheveled Natalie Wood."

Jasper turned his head and said, "Right you are. ... Bear with me, can you? I'll be quick as a wink."

"I'll do my best." Emily closed her eyes again and sipped more soda, relieved it was going down.

Twenty minutes later, Jasper returned and loaded five canvasses of Buster into the back of the wagon. "Sorry it took so long. That woman sure took some convincing. It was one question after another."

Emily wiped her palm across her moist forehead. "I've been okay so far, but I really need to get out of here and lie down."

Jasper slid into the driver's seat and started the engine. "We could cut the whole trip short and head back home."

"You wouldn't mind?"

"Of course not. You'll be home in case this turns out to be the flu coming on, and I'll get back to the gallery with these paintings. I don't know why, but I think they'll be a big hit."

They hurried home to Chicago, and within one week, Jasper sold all five paintings at his gallery for $25 apiece, keeping 70 percent of the proceeds for himself. Carly Mae's art soon became so popular, he sold her paintings at $75 a pop as fast as she could create them. He raised Carly Mae's cut to 50 percent when her dad, Damon, complained. Carly Mae earned more than enough for the rest home's roof, so she funded new bay windows in the rec room, as well.

Several months into her art career, however, Carly Mae discarded painting in favor of playing a violin she found in her grandmother Missy's attic. Family lore goes that her great, great grandfather had marched it to and from the battlefront during the Civil War. He even hid it high in a hickory at Gettysburg, and retrieved it when the three-day bloodbath ended.

"Why are you throwing away your art for a squeaky violin?" Damon asked. "You've never been particularly interested in music."

"I don't want to be some famous painter, Daddy. I only want to be me," she said.

Jasper, who envisioned championing Carly Mae all the way to international acclaim, pleaded with Damon to convince her she simply had to keep painting. "People who have gifts most of us can only dream of have a responsibility to use them," he urged.

Damon backed up his daughter. "She's seven years old, a child. I'm not asking her to do anything except live by the Golden Rule. And who knows? She might be a gifted musician, too."

Velda sided with Jasper, but Carly Mae locked herself in her room and practiced the fiddle when her mom scolded her about the newfangled acrylic paints going to waste in the hall closet. Ever patient with his unpredictable wife, Damon got her to stretch out on the couch, massaged her perfect size six feet and asked her to try to remember what it was like to be a little girl. Ray and Blanche, precocious in their own right, took time out from preparing for a chess tournament to take their sister's side. They believed she should be able to do what she liked without everybody making a big fuss about it. Nevertheless, a fuss was made. Throughout town, from every curve and swimming hole along the Bendy River, each cornfield and every meadow, each business and every home, people had passionate discussions about Carly Mae, for she was the butter that anointed their morning toast, and while they knew she was Velda and Damon's daughter, they felt she was their very own.

Chapter 2

On a day so muggy grasshoppers wilted in shadow and clothes refused to dry on the line, eight-year-old Carly Mae and her violin teacher, Mick Deely, paused on his front porch and watched tiny balls of hail fall to his lawn and melt. Her weekly lesson completed, she was eager to get home to practice the riff she'd just learned.

"Hail! Wow!" Carly Mae jumped onto the stairs and held out a hand, stretching to catch some.

Mick pointed upward. "Best not leave now, little one. The sky's turning green, a sure sign of a twister. We should take shelter."

Carly Mae regarded the sky with awe and leaped onto his front walk to get a better look. "It's like a giant emerald!" She raised the violin case above her head. "Hear the hail hit, Mr. Deely? Isn't it something?"

"Come back up here, dear," he said. "It's dangerous."

She ran down the path instead. "Buster might be scared. I have to find him."

"No it's not safe! Your dog can take care of himself." Mick lurched forward and winced. Earlier in the day, he'd pulled a muscle while trimming his boxwood hedge and could not give chase.

When she reached the sidewalk, Carly Mae called over her shoulder. "He's my best friend in the world. I have to go."

With instrument in hand, Carly Mae raced, sneakers barely hitting concrete. Tall oaks and elms, which had formed a placid canopy moments ago, thrashed in winds that slapped the perspiration off of her face, arms and legs. She hugged the violin to her chest and opted for a shortcut. Torn petals whirled as she zipped through a backyard edged with prize-winning roses on her way to an open field that, if crossed diagonally, would take her to the edge of her yard. A roof shingle landed at her feet as she bounded into the meadow and breathed in the scent of cut grass. A lone bike tire careened toward her, then veered away. A chopstick stabbed the grass. The world around her roared louder than thunder, which always made Buster cower under the dining room table. Where is he now? Carly Mae wondered. Her heart pounded hard against ribs that felt tighter by the second. At the far side of the field, a dark funnel bore down. A mess of objects flying toward her threatened: a pin-striped umbrella, saddle shoe, record turntable, garden hose, teddy bear, queen of diamonds, hula hoop, trash can lid, address book. She braced herself to blast through.

When she awakened in a hospital two months later, Carly Mae had no memory of what happened after the violin case, wrested from her grasp, snapped apart, releasing the old fiddle to soar up, up to the viridescent sky.

The terrible twister of 1961 unfurled a torment that slapped people's hearts long after the winds wheezed down. To see so many lives upended in an instant made some Kiminee residents think red was black and old was new. It was as though the gods of antiquity had turned into morons who smash their best china against the wall in fury, except the deities didn't reach for dishes, they throttled homes and bridges and dreams through a swath of the community's core.

Twenty houses were leveled, including the home of Damon's parents, who had been found in each other's arms, crushed beneath what appeared to have been their enclosed back porch. One babe was torn from his mother's arms and dropped into the Bendy, where miraculously, he floated on his back until found two miles down river by a search party led by the mayor, Bill Pratt, whose combination garage and workshop had been lifted whole and deposited in a cornfield owned by local farmer Race Burlington. Trees had fallen on the police station, smashing in part of the building, but the feeble police chief, Maurice Brewer, had crawled under his desk and been spared.

Dusty Lambert found the violin. The sole reporter for the Kiminee High School newspaper, he was taking Polaroids as soon as roar faded to whisper and the last flying hats, golf clubs and whatnot settled to the ground. It was when he paused toward day's end that he saw strings against polished wood dangling from a hickory branch. He retrieved the instrument and gave it, scratched but otherwise unharmed, to Carly Mae's music teacher, Mick Deely, for safekeeping.

Meanwhile, Carly Mae's mom, Velda Foley, crept dazed and naked from Grant Modine's root cellar. He emerged shortly, in the buff, as well. Town gossips had long suspected the two had been having an affair while she was supposedly helping him with inventory at the Five 'N Dime, which he owned. This was proof enough for most. Grant darted toward his house, half of which still stood. Velda pulled a star-patterned lap quilt from rubble in the yard, wrapped it around her torso and tottered to the sidewalk. Meandering in a daze, she soon came upon her husband's mailbag. It was torn, holding a few letters and bits of junk mail that hadn't been snatched by the funnel. Damon Foley taught eighth grade math during the school year and delivered mail in the summer, giving him extra income, and the regular mailman, Earl Wiggs, a chance to visit relatives in Kentucky. Undelivered mail from that day showed up around town for years, but Damon simply vanished.

The twins, Blanche and Ray, turned up chasing fireflies after sundown near a swimming hole where they'd gone to cool off that afternoon. Their clothes were rumpled, their bodies bruised, the pale blue irises of their eyes rimmed with tinsel-like silver. Worst of all, they reverted to communicating only in their secret language. Nobody could understand what they were saying.

Jasper was conducting a series of presentations on twentieth century art at museums and colleges along the East Coast when he learned of the calamity. He could not get away, so he and Emily brainstormed by phone about what they could do from a distance. The next morning, Emily tucked an envelope containing $1,000 cash into a carton of Band Aids, gauze, rubbing alcohol and other first aid supplies, and sent it via bonded messenger to Kiminee's mayor, Bill Pratt. About three hours later, Bill thanked the driver for making the trip from Chicago safely and in good time, bid him farewell and began doling out money. His first donation was to a crew of volunteers who had been medics in World War II. They'd rented a helicopter at considerable expense and were low on fuel.

Carly Mae was located later that afternoon under a pile of wood on top of which an upside down rabbit hutch balanced—bunnies still inside and alive. Buster had been there barking the whole time, but everyone thought he was making a fuss over the trapped animals, which weren't a high priority for rescue crews. As soon as Carly Mae was freed from debris, the volunteer medics loaded her gently into the helicopter and headed for a hospital in Peoria, thirty-five miles upstream from where the little Bendy and great Illinois rivers converged. Missy and Velda wanted her treated at the closest hospital in Havana, ten miles downriver from the Bendy's mouth, but it was already overwhelmed with dozens of patients who'd arrived by land, river and air with all manner of broken bones, lacerations and even a few severed digits.

Just before the helicopter lifted off, Buster sprang up in an attempt to board, but he didn't get quite high enough. The dog tried to launch again, but Dusty jumped, too, and caught him in mid-air. When they landed, Dusty hugged the howling canine and whispered in his silky ear that Carly Mae was in good hands now. He didn't have to worry. Buster wasn't having any of it. He wrenched free and ran into the woods. Meanwhile, Velda, sporting dark circles under her eyes for the first time in her life, held the twins close. She braced against the draft from the helicopter as it lifted Carly Mae away. She cried out, "Oh, forgive me, forgive me. It's my fault, all my fault. I brought this on."

People might not have approved of Velda's affair, but they surely didn't think she caused the woe the twister had wrought. Neighbors tried to soothe her, but she shied away from their kind words and soft touches. And in the following days, she stopped living in the here and now. With her home flattened, her husband presumed dead, his parents in the morgue, one child barely breathing, and the other two incoherent, she didn't rally; no strength arose from deep within to save what could be saved. She retreated to her mother, Missy Lake, and her childhood home, which had been spared. She settled onto the living room couch where she recited, hour after hour, the names of all the states and their capitals, something generations of kids in Kiminee had to memorize to pass fifth grade.

Pushing sixty, depleted and left to make decisions without Velda's help, Missy called upon her cousin, Beulah, who ran a soda fountain in Cedar Rapids, Iowa, with her husband and grown children. Missy asked Beulah to take Ray and Blanche in for a few weeks while she and Velda got their bearings. Beulah agreed. After arriving in Iowa the twins kept to themselves. They huddled in a back booth in Beulah's shop, their hair almost white now, creating an even greater contrast to their olive skin, as they whispered a secret language in an equally secret world. Some customers whispered that the two children could be dangerous and should be institutionalized. Beulah didn't believe a word. She cheered her temporary charges with hot fudge sundaes, root beer floats and plenty of hugs. Gradually, they returned to normal, their excellent command of English restored.

In Peoria, Carly Mae lay immobile, her right leg and arm in casts, her mangled left hand hidden in layers of bandages. Before she awoke from her coma, word got out in Kiminee that she would never play fiddle again. Everyone lamented because Carly Mae's playing was mesmerizing, even for folks with hearts prickly as thumbtacks. For instance, at Touch of Kindness, Carly Mae played folksongs popular at the time of the Civil War. Members of the

McDuggin and Tarr clans lived there—in opposite wings. They'd had a feud going, like the Hatfields and McCoys, dating back to when one family chose Union blue and the other Confederate gray. Yet somehow Carly Mae's music touched them so deeply, they began a slow, sweet reconciliation that spread beyond the halls of the old-folks home. Former sworn enemies held hands and wailed the day they learned of Carly Mae's plight. And the whole community vibrated along, grieving just as hard for the loss of Carly Mae's music as for their own broken homes.

While still coming to grips with life in the terrible twister's wake, Missy, with Velda in tow, approached Father Byrne in the day room at Touch of Kindness. The long-time priest at Old St. Michael's parish, now retired, dozed in a recliner by a picture window facing sunflowers eight feet tall, and growing, that bent toward each other and tittered, as though passing along a joke, flower to flower. Missy pulled up two chairs by his side and helped situate Velda, who was faint because she'd been eating barely enough to sustain a muskrat.

"Why do you suppose them sunflowers Damon planted for these ailing folks didn't get uprooted and whisked away?" Missy plopped down and glowered at the view. "Seems unfair that Damon got taken, and his folks got crushed by their own home, and those things are still here, big as you please."

Father Byrne stirred, opened his eyes, peered at Missy and Velda, then gazed outside. Velda slumped in her seat.

Missy touched his arm. "Hello, Father. You wanted to see us?"

"Did I? Hmmm. My memory is like a bridge over the Mississippi. But big chunks are missing every dozen feet or so. You ever driven over the Mississippi? Imagine getting stuck there. You can't go forward and can't go back without falling in." He looked down and patted a yellow blanket on his lap.

"If you don't mind, father, Velda hasn't been feeling well, so if you could try to recall why it was so important that both of us come, you know, while Velda, in particular, is still reeling from the tornado and all—"

"Oh, oh, I do remember. I shoulda given you this a long time ago, but I … " His eyes drifted back toward the sunflowers. "Look at 'em now. They're dancin'; I'm sure of it."

"Father?" Missy leaned toward him.

"Oh, yes, yes." He lifted the blanket, stretched forward and placed it in Velda's lap. "This was your very own baby blanket. And pinned right there was your very own ring. Maybe not your ring, exactly, but somebody who knew you."

Velda brought the offering to her face and sniffed, then lowered it to her lap and stroked the weave with reverence.

"What do you mean, her baby blanket and ring?" Missy grumped. "She was wrapped in a pink-and-white one when Uncle Maurice brought her to Grover and me."

"Let me explain—"

"No need," Missy interrupted. "Uncle Maurice already explained it all. He said her dearly departed mother crocheted the receiving blanket herself. I have it tucked away in my attic. He told me and Grover she and her husband died in a terrible car accident. The baby was thrown deep into a field of alfalfa and survived, miraculously, but there were no relatives to take her in."

"Ah, yes, that story." Father Byrne said, then coughed several times.

Velda folded the blanket into a little square, ring on top. She rubbed her index finger around and around what looked like sterling silver. It had a Celtic trinity knot and circle design.

"I think you're quite confused, Father. It's no story," Missy insisted. "Uncle Maurice went all the way to Kane County to pick our baby up because an old friend of his ran the place where she was being kept. He took care of all the paperwork for us." Missy's voice hitched. She dug through her purse for a lemon drop, popped it in her mouth and continued. "Grover and I had waited so long. She was our little miracle." Missy placed her palm over her heart.

Father Byrne's eyes closed and his chin dipped, almost touching his chest. His head rolled to the side and rested against his shoulder. Then he opened his eyes and tried to straighten himself, not quite succeeding. "Ah, where were we?"

"That silly blanket and ring," Missy said, putting her hand down.

He focused his rheumy eyes on Velda. "The thing is, darlin', I was the one who found you. It was the dead of winter. You were just a wee lonesome babe someone left on the church steps wrapped in that very blanket, with the ring pinned exactly where it is now. Freezin' to death, you were. It's lucky I happened to step outside—"

Missy leaned back in her chair and fumed. "This is preposterous!"

Suddenly energized, Velda sat up straight for the first time since the twister. "Let him finish," she said.

Father Byrne continued addressing Velda. "I brought you inside, held you close to warm you up, and the first thing I did was call Maurice. Since he was chief of police, I thought he'd know what to do. He took control right away, said Missy and Grover could provide the perfect home. Pretty soon, he went with your grandmother Jolene— bless her soul—to buy a sweet little bag of baby things. He told me to dispose of that." Father Byrne pointed to the blanket. "Somehow I could never get myself to do it."

Missy put both hands on her knees and squeezed. "You're saying my mother went along with a lie and never told me? Let me think the adoption was done through legitimate means when it wasn't? I find that hard to believe. No, not hard. Impossible!"

Father Byrne turned toward Missy. "Maurice didn't want the child to know she'd been abandoned." His voice grew faint. He coughed up phlegm and spit it into a handkerchief, then continued. "He thought it would be easier on her if she believed she'd lost her loving family through tragedy. Jolene agreed, and I figured there was a certain logic to it."

"Why come up with this cockamamie story now, after all these years?" Missy demanded.

"I'm close to the end of my life now. I don't see the harm in letting Velda have a little piece of her heritage. Not much to hold onto; it's something, though. ... But you can't tell Maurice. He'd stomp right in here and shoot me if he found out."

"We don't go near Uncle Maurice anymore," Velda said. Her big brown eyes showed hints of her former allure. "His temper has grown in direct proportion to his shrinking memory. If you're stuck, he's hangin' over the water by the beams of a washed-out bridge."

"Why he still constitutes our police force of one I'll never know." Missy shook her head, then grinned at her daughter, tickled by her apparent recovery.

Father Byrne chuckled, but then succumbed to a coughing fit that increased in intensity by the second. Missy and Velda huddled over him, attempting to help, patting his back, offering water, wiping his nose, which was running like a spigot. Della Burlington, referred to by many as Florence Nightingale, managed to calm the situation and coax him to his feet. "I think he's had enough visiting for today," Della said. Then she noticed the blanket in Velda's hands. "Oh, did he give you that?"

With quivering lips and eyelids fluttering, Velda held it to her cheek. "It was my baby blanket."

"I wouldn't put much stock in that." Della waved her hand dismissively. "Yesterday, he tried to give it to Irma McDuggin, said he thought it belonged to her boy Ralph—the one who died of whooping cough, poor thing, before he was even a year old—told her she left it behind at the hospital. Irma said he was daft, that she'd never seen it before let alone wrapped one of her children in it."

"Well, I'm keeping it," Velda declared, snapping her mouth closed in an effort to calm the flurry of feelings rippling through her. "He looked me straight in the eyes just now when he spoke. And I, I believe him."

The attendant shrugged and escorted Father Byrne out of the room. Velda and Missy followed.

"I'm gonna get copies of this ring made for the kids," Velda said to Missy. "It's so hard with the twins back from Iowa but Carly Mae in Chicago and Damon swept away. I don't know how to comfort my own children, and all this disruption? It's all my fault—"

"You did not cause the twister, but I'm glad you're speaking up, real glad, even if you're talking nonsense," Missy said. "Let's go home so I can get some food into you. I expect you're ready for your favorite: chicken and dumplings."

Velda breathed in through her nose and vibrated with a manic sort of energy. "I can smell it already." She turned toward the window. "Damon's talking to us through them. I just don't know what he's saying."

The sunflowers swayed, then bent toward a doe and fawn nibbling apples from a bushel basket. "It is my fault our family's broken, but this will bond us, don't you see?" She held the blanket to her chest and squeezed so tight she almost cracked her ribs. "It's a sign. It was meant to be.

Chapter 3

*V*elda snuck away the day Mick Deely knocked on Missy's front door, violin in hand, eyes fevered with grief. He handed the instrument to Missy, who tucked it back in her attic. Seeing this struck Velda like an ice pick in her heart. The pain would not go away. In a hastily scribbled good-bye note, she said everything she saw made her feel guilty—the steep bannister she slid down every morning when she was small and fearless, lilacs by the front porch that bloomed year round, her deceased father's long-forgotten shaving kit in the medicine cabinet—at every turn, she perceived not beauty, but blame. Even the rings she'd special ordered for her children weighed on her. Instead of creating the bond she'd hoped for, they reminded her she'd never know whose arms had brought her into the world and why she'd been left to freeze to death, saved only by chance by a priest with insomnia. After weeks of stewing about this, she couldn't bear it anymore.

Before dawn Velda gobbled a slice of Missy's award-winning blueberry pie and then slinked out the back door of her childhood home. With no plan other than to outrun the sorrow and shame that dogged her, she crept toward the Bendy. She followed the water's path as it meandered along until she came upon a shack used by fishermen. There, she subsisted on sardines and stale Saltines left behind on a shelf. She might have remained and paced the warped boards until the food ran out, but echoes of laughter growing close spurred her to move on. She hid in a stand of dogwood until nightfall, then made her way to the nearest road. She walked until sunrise, found a spot of barren earth behind a boulder and spent the day listening to birdsong and the occasional car motoring by. She continued hiding during the day and walking at night until she was far enough from Kiminee to not be recognized.

A light rain fell the first day Velda stuck out her thumb for a ride. A souped-up jalopy came her way, engine belching, and screeched to a stop. She ran to the passenger side door.

"Where you goin'?" the young man at the wheel asked.

She had no idea, but Earl Wiggs came to mind. He was visiting out-of-state relatives for the summer and had missed the terrible twister entirely. "I'm headed to Pikeville, Kentucky, to see my friend Earl," she said. He had been one of Velda's two best friends since grade school. The other was Damon Foley. This was long before she and Damon fell in love, long before Earl became Kiminee's mailman. A determined debater who made it to state finals as a high school senior, Earl had a way of making sense of senseless situations.

"Hop in. I can take you as far as Springfield," the driver said, stubbing out a Winston in his ashtray.

"That'll do. Much obliged." Velda opened the door and climbed in.

After Jasper finished his lecture tour, he visited Carly Mae in Peoria every week. Afterward, he often pushed on to Kiminee to check in on Missy. She fed him homemade treats like pound cake, pineapple upside-down cake and blond brownies, while they talked about Carly Mae's progress and the twins' struggles to adjust to life with their home, parents and sister all gone. At one point, Carly Mae slipped back into a coma, and Jasper resolved to get Missy's permission to transfer her to a state-of-the-art hospital in Chicago.

"They've got some of the best pediatric specialists in the nation," he said. He used broad gestures, barely able to contain his emotions while describing a new wing with surgeons and orthopedists known for their success in repairing children's growing bodies. His desire to help was so strong, a family of squirrels stopped gathering acorns and climbed up the ever-blooming lilac to watch through Missy's window.

"I expect I can't afford no fancy doctors," Missy replied.

"She deserves the best care poss—"

"I appreciate your concern. Truly, I do, " Missy interjected. "But like I said, I don't have money to pay none of them specialist type doctors, and to tell the truth—"

"I'll pay for her treatment, rehab, everything, whatever the cost," Jasper said.

"Why would you do that?" Missy wrinkled her brow in puzzlement.

"Naturally, I hope she'll paint again, but I also realize I can't count on that."

"You've got other ways to spend your money, I'm sure," she hypothesized.

"I see raw talent in that girl, the kind that comes your way once in a lifetime, if even that. I want to encourage her and provide support, no matter what she ultimately pursues."

"I don't know. She'd be so far away—almost 200 miles from here to Chicago."

"She might not be far away in miles now, but in terms of being able to come back to you and live a full life, she's far, far away."

"You've made a good point there. I guess me and the twins, we don't have her at all." Flummoxed by this realization, Missy had to sit down. She put her head in her hands and then said, "Okay, then, draw up whatever papers you need to. I'll sign."

Jasper stood. "Carly Mae will be in good hands. I promise you."

"I sure hope you're right. I'm putting my faith in you."

Missy walked him to the door, where he gave her a hug before he stepped onto the porch, causing the inquisitive squirrels to scamper off, chattering.

Long on the road and nowhere near Pikeville, Velda took a sip of coffee from a sturdy white mug and rubbed a bump on her forehead. Banana crème pie taunted her from behind beveled glass. She swallowed, glanced out the window and imagined the semi rumbling into the parking lot was a dinosaur suffering unquenchable hunger for things it couldn't name. Returning her gaze to the pie, she swiveled her stool side to side, sipped again and held the bitter brew under her tongue. She had to go slowly. Fifty cents was all that remained of the cash she took from Missy's French purse when she left Kiminee several weeks prior, and she was more confused and directionless than ever.

Feeling grimy to the core, she'd woken up below a viaduct and couldn't recall, at first, how she'd gotten there. Now she wanted to forget all traces of her struggle to pry away thick fingers that had gripped her neck, the sound of linen ripping, the shame and terror of violation that had returned mercilessly as she scrabbled to higher ground and stumbled toward the cafe.

A chime sounded at the door. A burly man in jeans and short-sleeved plaid shirt stepped inside and took the stool next to Velda. "Hey there, Barb," he called to the waitress.

Barb ambled over, carafe in hand, and filled a mug for him. "The usual, Jeff?"

"You bet," he said.

She called to the cook, "Two eggs over easy, home fries, grits, short stack with bacon and sausage."

Jeff noticed Velda staring at the crème pie and said, "And give the little lady here a piece of your homemade goodness."

"Oh, no, no!" Flustered, Velda took a gulp of coffee.

Barb lifted the lid off the pie. "Don't be silly. By the looks of you, you could use more than pie, hon." She cut a slice, put it on a plate and slid it to Velda, along with a fork.

"I couldn't." Velda shoved the dish toward Barb.

The waitress pushed it back. "It's too late now." She gripped her love handles and winked at Jeff. "I've already gobbled more than my share, and Jeff won't have room for dessert after he chows down."

Velda's eyes welled with tears. She covered her face with her hands. Jeff grabbed a napkin and tapped her arm. She took her hands away, gave a weak smile, then accepted the napkin and dabbed her eyes.

"Just about everybody who comes through here has been down and out at some point along the road," Jeff said, as memories of his first visit to the café came to mind.

"Ain't that the truth," Barb added. She picked up a damp cloth and wiped the counter.

"Is it that obvious?" Velda's voice wobbled.

"Let's just say that Barb and I have a sixth sense about this sort of thing. First time I stopped in here, I had two bucks to my name. I ordered coffee just like you, and Barb here gave me a piece of pie. Mmmm. It was chocolate crème, best I ever had."

"There you go, butterin' me up again," Barb teased.

"You know I'd marry you in a minute. Just say the word," he said, hand on heart.

"Nonsense," Barb muttered, scrubbing where she's already cleaned.

Jeff turned his attention to Velda, who continued to eye the pie. "Anyway, I thought I'd just landed in heaven, but that wasn't the end of it." He rubbed his bottom lip with thumb and index finder. "The man sitting on this very stool said his company was hiring. He took me to his home, told me to clean myself up, even asked his wife to pick out some of his old clothes for me. Then we went to his headquarters and he gave me my first big rig driving lesson. I've been long haulin' for him ever since."

Unable to resist the sweet banana pie smell any longer, Velda took a bite. "Oh, this is good. ... I haven't had pie like this since—" A sob cracked her voice mid sentence. She downed more coffee.

Barb topped off her cup, and said, "Since you ate your mama's, right?"

Velda nodded. "Rhubarb is my favorite—" Her voice faltered again. She pushed her plate and cup aside and leaned down to the counter, head against her arms.

Jeff tapped her shoulder. "You okay?"

Velda sat up. "Just got a little dizzy, I guess."

"Let's get you to a booth. You'll be more comfortable." He helped her down from the stool, escorted her to a booth and sat across from her.

Barb brought over her coffee and pie. "There you go. ... I guess you've figured out that I'm Barb and this here's Jeff. We've got time if you want to talk—not meanin' to force you or anything."

"Sometimes it helps just to tell your story," Jeff said, "especially when you're here at the Good Luck Cafe."

"The Good Luck. Really? I've heard of you guys. You're located near Mattoon, right?"

"Yep, this town is Bright Corners; Mattoon's just up the road a bit."

"You, you are living legends."

"Oh now, we're just regular folk doin' a little good here and there," Barb said.

"How could I have missed your sign? It's like a beacon of hope for down-and-out travelers." Embarrassed she was one such traveler, Velda looked down at her lap.

"Say, Barb. I think you're right about our friend, here, needing more than pie. Give her my usual, too."

Barb went to the counter, called in the second order, returned with a bright red squeeze bottle of ketchup and plunked it on the table.

"So who are you?" Jeff asked Velda. "And what's your story?"

Velda looked up at him, then out the window. "Oh, I'm nobody and I don't have much of a story."

"Everybody's got a story," Barb said, sliding into the booth next to Jeff.

Velda regarded the two friendly faces in front of her and felt a little something soften inside. "My name is Velda, Velda Foley."

"Pleased to meet you, Velda," Jeff said.

"Velda Foley's a right pretty name," Barb added.

"Before that I was Velda Lake, and before that I was a little baby somebody left at Old St. Michael's church. I just found out that last tidbit."

"Ah, a secret uncovered. That can be tough," Barb said.

Velda leaned her head against the back of the booth and closed her eyes. While leaves fell from majestic oaks outside and were blown by the wind into groups like tiny whirling dervishes circling the parking lot, Velda said she'd always felt something wasn't right about her origins. Barb and Jeff listened attentively.

"Order's up," the cook called.

"Be right back." Barb hastened to the counter and returned with two plates loaded with eggs, bacon and pancakes. "So where were we?" she asked when she put the plates on the table.

Velda said she wasn't surprised when her folks told her she was adopted. She was seven and had always felt out of place. But she'd just found out the story they told her, that her birth parents had died in a car crash and there were no relatives to care for her, wasn't true. She had been dumped on the church steps in the dead of winter. "I used to dream of leaving when I was young, finding some big city, maybe, where I would belong," Velda said. "But then when I was sixteen I was bamboozled by a gorgeous guy staying at the Binsack Hotel for a spell."

"Binsack Hotel. Where is that?" Barb asked.

"Kiminee, a little town along the Bendy River, which you've probably never heard of. It's just another little tributary working its way toward the mighty Mississippi."

"I've heard of the Bendy. There's good fishing there," Jeff said.

"Yeah, and the Binsack was a favorite among the fishermen," Velda said.

"Was?" Barb raised an eyebrow.

Velda explained that Eddie and Tempest Binsack used to run the place, but then he died and Tempest didn't want to manage the business alone. "Now that big old building in the heart of town sits empty," she said. "I expect she'd sell it for a song, too, since two of her kids moved to some suburb outside of St. Louis. The third, Gloria, has a small dairy and has this notion she's going to make cheese so good it'll put Wisconsin to shame. Like that'll ever happen."

"You never know," Jeff said.

"So there's a big empty hotel building blighting your downtown?"

"Yeah, there's a cafe on one side of the ground floor, well, there used to be."

"We should buy it," Jeff said. "Get hitched and drive on out of here."

Barb frowned. "Leave the Good Luck?"

"Well, the state is making our little highway into a super highway with on and off ramps, and they don't plan to have an off ramp here at Bright Corners. If they do that, what will happen to the Good Luck?"

Barb shook her head, not wanting to envision the demise of her cafe. "Won't happen. Folks here will fight tooth and nail to have an off ramp. Travelers need opportunities to stop for gas—"

"And pie," Jeff said.

"Definitely pie," Velda added.

"So, back to this gorgeous guy …" Barb gestured toward Velda.

"Oh, he said he loved me and we could get married and promised to take me all around the world with him. I was a fool. I fell for it, broke up with my boyfriend, Damon Foley. But Mr. Gorgeous moved on when he learned I was pregnant. Not long after that, some lawmen came looking for him. He was nothin' but a no-good riverboat scoundrel, fleecing people right and left, which wound up being the end of him, 'cause he got caught cheatin' at cards. A fight broke out and he wound up shot dead. Them nice detectives came back afterward and told me about it, said I didn't have to worry none about him comin' around to pester me. So the rat was gone for good only a few months after he skipped out on me."

"That's tough all the way around," Jeff said.

"How did you manage?" Barb asked.

"Well, Damon saved the day. He was nineteen and already in his third year at Northwestern, on scholarship."

"Up there in the Windy City, huh." Jeff said. "I like rollin' through there."

"Yeah. He was a math whiz who could have had a real career. But he took me back and married me, knowing he hadn't made me pregnant because we'd never done more than petting yet. He enrolled at Western Illinois University, a good school but a step down, just before the twins were born. Then exactly a year after their birth, we had another child, a marvel of a girl."

"Wow! A mother of three by the time you were seventeen? That's a big deal," Barb said.

"I tried to make it work, really, I did," Velda said as tears welled in her eyes. "But I ruined my family. Damon's gone missing, my kids are split apart, and I'm to blame." She brought a fist to her mouth and bit down hard.

"Say, take it easy, there," Jeff said. "You're gonna draw blood." He pulled a handkerchief from his pocket, rolled it into a ball and handed it to her. "Squeeze this instead."

"You're being too hard on yourself," Barb said. "Your kids must be missing you something awful. We could help you fine your way home."

Velda worked her fingers around the handkerchief. "They're better off without me. I bring trouble wherever I go. I'm never going back."

After a long pause, Jeff said, "How 'bout this? I'm takin' a load of bottle caps to Indianapolis, and I have a cousin there who would be happy to take you in for a while. She just joined this church called The People's Temple, and they're known for takin' in lost souls and helpin' 'em turn their lives around. I know it's not Kentucky, where your friend is, but it's part way there. You'd have a bed and clean clothes and probably some work to do, too, while you think things over."

"That's too much. You and Barb have already fed me, and I've talked your ears off. I should just catch another ride."

Jeff pulled enough bills from his wallet to pay for their breakfast and leave a big tip. "Why put yourself in danger again? Take a helping hand when it's offered to you."

"Yeah, that's what the Good Luck Café is all about. Jeff'll look out for you. Just get back on your feet and keep in touch," Barb said. "You'll always be welcome here."

Half an hour later, Jeff sang Johnny Cash tunes as the truck chugged along the highway. Velda drifted into sleep. She thought she might have imagined the Good Luck Café, but she was too worn out to care where she'd been and where she was going next.

Chapter 4

G ripping a platter crowded with a pitcher of lemonade, three glasses, a plate of macaroons fresh from the oven, and embroidered napkins, Missy Lake entered her dining room. The summer of 1963 was rapidly drawing to a close, and she and her best friends since kindergarten, Tempest Binsack and Maridee Pratt, had been organizing school supplies for Kiminee's students. With feet wide apart and knees bent, she pushed aside a stack of canvas book bags to clear a spot on the table and placed the tray between her friends, who were seated.

"Oh, those macaroons smell good." Tempest lifted one with plump fingers with nails polished a shimmering coral. She popped it, whole, into her mouth, then reached for a napkin and dabbed her generous lips, leaving a trace of coral lipstick on the cloth.

"Wish I could wear that shade," Maridee said to Tempest.

"Nothin's wrong with your powder-puff pinks; they go with porcelain skin," Tempest said.

"Fish-belly skin is more like it. I can't even tan." Maridee gestured, palms up, to expose the fair skin of her inner arms. "And my hair turned prematurely white, so I have to spend a pretty penny on Clairol every month." She poked at her limp locks. "Bill complains about that, believe it or not. I look at your deep olive skin and curly black hair, and I'm so jealous. And your curves, my, my. I'm just skin and bones. If I had an ounce of your beauty—"

"Enough of that talk," Missy said. "We have the gifts God gave us, plain and simple. I'm right there bland in the middle, and—"

Tempest cleared her throat. "You're about as bland as a mouthful of Red Hots."

Missy squinted at her. "I am what I am. You are what you are. We can't change it."

Maridee tucked a wayward strand of golden blonde hair behind her ear and glanced out a picture window facing Missy's backyard, where Blanche, Ray and Carly Mae played croquet. "Look at them, three peas in a pod."

"You'd hardly know Carly Mae spends so much time away." Tempest grabbed another cookie.

"If she'd had her way, she'd be with that group from St. Michael's right now. They're probably pulling in to Washington, D.C., at this very moment, you know, for that big civil rights march," Missy said. "I put an end to the idea of Carly Mae going along straight away. It's not like I'm against the cause, but the twins are junior counselors at the day camp. They couldn't leave for some grand bus ride to the East Coast, and I didn't want to cut short the already limited time Carly Mae has with them."

"That wouldn't be an issue if she lived at home full time," Tempest said.

"Easy for you to say." Missy lifted the pitcher, poured lemonade into a glass, and slid it toward Tempest, liquid sloshing over the top. Then she grabbed a napkin and wiped up splatters with such force it rocked the table."

Eyes wide, Tempest leaned away from the table. "No cause to get so upset."

Missy stopped scrubbing and looked from Tempest to Maridee, then sat down. "You're right. I'm sorry." She patted Tempest's hand.

"It's just that it gets hard without their parents around. I had to make a decision when she was released from that fancy hospital. She needed physical therapy, which wasn't available around here. When Jasper suggested she stay with him and Emily and work with some of the most skilled specialists in the nation, well, I decided, for her future health and mobility, it was the best choice. She had to continue her education too, so they enrolled her in that private school, Lily Park Academy, and she's taken the place by storm. She's in all kinds of advanced courses we don't offer here." Missy poured a glass of lemonade and held it out for Maridee. "No spillin' this time, I promise."

Maridee accepted the refreshment. "Thanks. It's just the thing for a hot afternoon stuffing school bags." She waved a spindly arm at stacks of pencils and sharpeners, watercolor sets, crayons, notebook paper, Elmer's glue, scissors with rounded tips, and the canvas book bags silkscreened with a blurred scene of Kiminee. In a corner were several bags already full.

"Looks like we're about halfway done," Tempest said.

Missy surveyed the table and smiled. "It goes so much faster when we do it together."

"Oh, no! A croquet ball's rolling down the slope toward the trees. It's headin' for the river." Maridee pointed to the yard where Missy's grandchildren whooped, screeched and knocked into each other as they chased the wayward ball.

Missy chuckled. "They'll catch it long before then. … Them kids. How I love 'em."

Maridee sipped her lemonade and got a far off look in her eyes. "They're ten and eleven already, at the tail end of childhood."

Missy hummed a couple bars of the song "Toyland." Maridee and Tempest joined in. They sang a verse before their voices tapered off.

Tempest pressed a napkin at the corners of her eyes. "That song always makes me sad, you know the line, 'Once you cross the border you can ne'er return again.'"

"Amen," Missy said.

Maridee caught Missy's eye. "Now, please don't take this the wrong way. I think you're doing a fabulous job with all three of them. Surely I do, but I have to ask, since the subject already came up, are you sure you're doing the right thing sending Carly Mae back to Chicago? Haven't those therapists done all they possibly can?"

Tempest joined in. "After two years, it seems almost permanent. She's missin' out on all the day-to-day closeness she could have with Blanche and Ray."

"She wasn't any closer to them before the twister than she is now," Missy said. "The twins, they have their own world. Nobody really gets all the way in. It's like that with twins the world over." Missy grabbed a bag, threw in a watercolor set, pack of crayons and scissors, and passed the bag to Tempest.

Tempest put the bag aside. "Hold on a sec," she said. "We're having a refreshment break, remember?"

"If she lived here full time I think her bond with the twins would deepen, even if she might feel like a third wheel sometimes," Maridee said.

Missy leaned back in her chair. "I've been over this in my head time and again, and talked it through with you two last year, I might add. She's thriving at that Lily Park school—with tuition paid in full. What enrichment do we provide? New school bags for the students every year? My heart fills with joy when they're all here, but I'd send the twins up north, too, if Jasper had room for them. They're mighty bright, too, you know."

"I know, I know." Maridee said.

"Look at them dive for the ball!" Tempest brushed curls off her brow; they bounced back down.

The three women watched as the children threw their mallets aside and tumbled, entwined, toward the edge of the yard, where Blanche soon hopped up, holding a yellow wooden sphere high above her head.

Ray wrestled it from her hands and burst away. Carly Mae followed and tackled him. Soon the three were entwined again, roughhousing on the lawn. Buster ran up from the river and pounced on top, dripping water on them. The children rolled apart, and their laughter mixed with Buster's yips carried into the house.

Tempest ran her fingers over the art on the bag Missy had handed her. "At least the children of Kiminee will see Carly Mae's artwork every day," Tempest said. "I think that's why our club voted to silkscreen her watercolor on the bags this year—so we could all remember her."

"I'm glad you talked her into submitting a painting. How did you do it? She's been concentrating on math to the exclusion of everything else since she left that rehab place, right?" Maridee said.

Missy shrugged. "I told her all math all the time isn't healthy. Besides, she's an artist at heart. Since she can't play violin anymore because of her messed up left hand, which all that physical therapy couldn't fix, not yet anyway, I thought she might return to painting. I spread her old acrylics and watercolors out on this very table, and sure enough, she couldn't resist. Ray and Blanche joined in. What a fun afternoon it was."

Tempest studied the artwork. "I think it's the best design ever."

"I love the colors," Missy said. "They're joyous."

"Like the real thing, but better." Tempest tapped the bag in her hand for emphasis.

Maridee leaned in. "Sometimes our hometown looks just like this from the little rise past the Charles Street Bridge. I've seen this gold, and, oh, that luscious blue. Even those purples are right."

Missy scratched an itch on her chin and watched the children take turns whacking balls. "I'd best call them in to have some of these before we eat them all up."

Tempest, who had been reaching for another macaroon, pulled her hand away.

Missy rose up, groaning, and pressed her palms to her lower back. "Lordy, do I ever feel older than my fifty-six years."

"I hear you," Maridee said, rubbing an elbow. "My arthritis gets worse by the day."

Tempest looked again at the children. "Oh, to tumble across a lawn like those youngsters again. That would be something."

"They look so happy, don't they?" Maridee said.

Missy gave a quick nod toward the window. "It's sad but true that when push comes to shove, I'm the one responsible for them. Velda flew the coop, and Damon, dear Damon … heck, we'll probably never know what became of him. I could be wrong about sending Carly Mae back for another year, but I must stand by my decision. It's the best I can do right now." She left the room and headed for the back door to call her grandchildren in.

Several weeks into the 1963 school year, a thirty-pound, tricolor husky-sheltie mix ran across a patch of lawn and slid to a halt in front of a high-rise building on Chicago's Lake Shore Drive. Thunder clapped. Rain splattered. The dog howled and gave a lopsided grin. In the Skrillpod's co-op apartment high above, Carly Mae opened her bedroom window, stuck her head out and saw Lake Michigan, the great inland sea, was choppy. Rain pelted her face as she peered down to the sidewalk and saw him wagging his tail, head cocked, his one and only ear perked to attention.

"Buster! Buster! You're back!" she cried out.

He barked and leaped high as the lowest branches of plum trees lining the walk. He touched down lightly and bounded up again, going even higher.

"Hold on, boy. I'm coming." Carly Mae spun around, dashed out of the room and almost bumped into Emily in the hall. "Oops. Sorry, M—" The girl bit her lip. She'd almost called Emily "Mom," something that had happened a few other times recently. Emily was only a few years older than Velda, had the same dark eyes and wavy brunette hair, and did everything her classmates' own mothers did for them, but Carly Mae felt these near slips were an inexcusable sign of disloyalty to her family.

"No problem, kiddo," Emily said. "Did I hear you shout Buster's name?"

"Yeah, he's down on the sidewalk. I'm gonna go get him."

"When did he leave Kiminee this time?"

"How should I know?" The child snapped, looking as though she'd bitten into a lime.

Ignoring Carly Mae's snide tone, Emily said, "Be sure to wipe his paws before you bring him in."

The two entered the living room, where Jasper was hanging a painting by a local artist of a giant, Chicago-style hot dog slathered with mustard and loaded with pickled serrano peppers, onions and lettuce.

"Hmm, makes me hungry. Can we eat out at Dave's tonight?" Carly Mae asked as she zoomed through the room. "And can Buster stay this time till Thanksgiving?" She pulled the door open and rushed off without waiting for answers.

"Buster's here again?" Jasper asked Emily. "Why can't they just keep him indoors or on a leash or tethered or something?"

"We might be able to get the co-op board to let him stay," Emily said.

"You know that won't happen. I've run out of ways to try to convince them." Jasper stepped away from the painting and cocked his head. "Ah, it's drooping a little to the right, isn't it?"

"Looks fine to me," Emily said. "She'll be disappointed."

Jasper sidestepped to his wife and put an arm around her. "A kid can't have everything she wants, no matter how wonderful she is."

Emily leaned her head on his shoulder. "You're right, I know. But it's not easy to see how she suffers without that dog."

"Maybe we should rent an apartment in Hyde Park when Carly Mae starts the University of Chicago program next year—a place that allows dogs. What do you think?" Jasper kissed the top of her head.

"Not a bad idea," Emily replied. "Not a bad idea at all. She's still so very young. I don't like the idea of her spending so much time commuting to and from the South Side just to go to class, and I sure don't like the idea of her living in a dorm. We could rent a nice little place for all of us near the school. I think I'd like the Hyde Park neighborhood."

Below, Carly Mae ran out the door and down the path toward Buster, who barreled toward his girl and sprang into her outstretched arms. She pranced in a circle around and around, as rain splashed down. Little silver stars sprayed from her heels each time her feet hit the ground.

Chapter 5

*I*n the wings of Lily Park Academy's auditorium, Carly Mae gave Jasper Skrillpod a hug before racing across the stage to the podium. A tiny riot of nerves, she stepped onto a stool so she could see the audience as she accepted a gold-plated trophy from the headmistress, Mrs. Henchley. Six weeks shy of her eleventh birthday, Carly Mae had just accepted the school's highest award: Student of the Year. She was the first eighth grader to receive this honor from the prestigious K-12 school. It had previously been reserved for graduating seniors of outstanding merit.

Carly Mae looked toward the back of the room and saw her grandmother, Missy, flanked by her brother, Ray, and sister, Blanche. Occupying seats in the last two rows were twenty-five friends who had split the cost of hiring a bus and driver to travel from Kiminee to Chicago for the occasion. She grinned at the sight of loved ones from home. Mrs. Henchley lowered the microphone before returning to her chair in a row on stage reserved for dignitaries.

Carly Mae began her speech by thanking her teachers and academy administrators; Jasper and Emily Skrillpod; her family, including her missing mother; her classmates; and all her hometown friends, both those who made the trip to the big city to see her graduate and the ones who couldn't get away. She then talked about her presumed-dead father. "My daddy loved everything about mathematics, every part of it. He'd talk sets, differentials, polynomials, theorems—you name it—breakfast, lunch and supper. I was bored by it when I was little, but then the twister took him away. As soon as I found out he was gone, I pledged right then and there to make friends with mathematics in my daddy's memory. It's thanks to the wonderful Skrillpods, who paid all my medical bills, and then took me in and have treated me like a daughter every minute of every day for the last three years, that I have made an almost complete recovery. It's also thanks to them that I've been able to attend this academy.

"Some of you will think I'm crazy, now, when I say my daddy's still with me. In those times when I'm feeling so sad I can barely lift my head, or when I'm puzzling over a problem that simply makes no sense, he comes to me. I can see him clear as I see all of you. He's wearing his tweed fisherman's cap, which he hung on a peg by the front door, and favorite work clothes grown soft and thin at the elbows and knees, the ones he put on when he puttered in the garage or fixed things around the house. He speaks in that gentle voice of his and points me to what I need to do next. His message usually isn't clear to me right away, but if I sleep on it, what he's said starts to make sense. Without my daddy's help, I would not be up here today."

Missy reached into her pocketbook, pulled out a hankie and dabbed her eyes. Ray wiped his nose on his shirtsleeve. Blanche lifted her skirt's hem to dry her cheeks and chin. Several other people in the back rows rooted through purses and pockets, and passed out tissues to outstretched hands. Other audience members did the same, row after row, until all eyes, shimmering, conveyed a communal compassion.

"So I stand here now and have to tell you I am grateful to be Student of the Year. I'm also grateful University of Chicago is eager for me to join their program for gifted children in the fall. I know you would all cheer me on if I went there. The Skrillpods are even planning to rent an apartment in Hyde Park so I can have a home with them close to the university as long as I need it. But my heart and my daddy are telling me to go home, home to Kiminee. I know it seems to make no sense, but that is what I want to do."

Gasps arose from the audience as Carly Mae stepped off the stool and ran to Jasper in the wings. "I'm sorry, Jasper, so, so sorry," she blubbered.

He hugged her close and said, "Emily and I had no idea you were so homesick."

"I must be a giant disappointment after all you've done." She swiped at snot running from her nose with her left hand, revealing her pinky and ring finger still stiff and bent despite three surgeries and countless hours of physical therapy.

Jasper pulled a handkerchief from his pocket and handed it to her. "Nonsense. You're overflowing with emotion right now. Everything will work out, my dear and precious little girl."

Mrs. Henchley, face flushed, fanned herself with the graduation program and regarded the tittering audience. Dr. Croll, a consultant for the University of Chicago seated beside her, sputtered, "Whatever are we going to do now?"

"Keep your voice down," Mrs. Henchley whispered. "We'll have cake and coffee and pretend everything's fine, for now,"

He leaned closer and spoke softly. "No other student has brought the academy the kind of attention that she has. It's been a perfect, symbiotic relationship. I can't believe she's fool enough to snub a once-in-a-lifetime opportunity."

"Don't count her out yet. We'll get Jasper to work on her."

"What if he doesn't want to? He's not exactly a by-the-book guy. He believes in all that child-centered progressive education nonsense. The man might actually think going home would be good for her."

"Jasper has an Achilles heel like everyone else. We'll find it and make use of it if we have to."

He raised an eyebrow. She rose and stepped to the podium, wished all the graduates well, thanked attendees for celebrating the conclusion of another fine school year, and invited everyone to enjoy refreshments in the cafeteria across the hall. The Lily Park Academy band struck up the school's alma mater as people stood up, stretched, and trickled out of the room. Twins in hand, Missy rushed in the opposite direction, toward Carly Mae sobbing in Jasper's arms.

The day Carly Mae Foley came home to stay, the whole of Kiminee took on a golden hue, from the cumulous clouds overhead to the giant oak tree shading Missy's front yard, to the train set chugging in the window of Chester Dillard's hardware store, and the gravel crunching beneath Mick Deely's feet as he hobbled to his brand new Dodge Dart. Even Bendy River twinkled gold as it burbled by. A crowd had gathered at Missy's in anticipation of Carly Mae's arrival, and almost everyone brought a favorite dish to share.

On two picnic tables covered with red-and-white checked cloths, the feast lured all comers, including ancient Tam-Tam Parlo who, most folks believed, lived on air and water in a ramshackle home alongside the forest edging the Bendy and spitting distance from the best swimming hole. She dug a gnarled fingertip into a bowl of onion dip and gave a smile that revealed more gaps than teeth before she licked the goop off. This caused heated debate about whether she could really live without food. As far as anyone saw, she passed up the rest of the fare, which seemed a considerable feat to some. Others said her singular ability to forego food was nothing compared with the twenty-some years she survived as Harlan Parlo's wife. Long gone, he was still known as the meanest man east of the Mississippi.

There was homemade dilly bread fresh out of the oven; white, rye and pumpernickel, too; thin-sliced turkey, ham and bologna; American and Swiss cheese slices; three kinds of potato salad; Jell-O with mixed fruit and creamy lime Jell-O parfaits; grilled chicken legs marinated in Earl Wiggs' secret sauce; traditional lemonade and lemonade with lavender; and cakes and drinks to suit just about everyone's taste, including competing batches of moonshine brought by members of the Tarr and McDuggin clans, who were situated at different tables to avoid a confrontation. While their feud had cooled since the days Carly Mae had played for their elderly kinfolk at Touch of Kindness, many of them were still wary of getting too close.

Along with food, musically inclined residents brought instruments. Some were homemade contraptions; others were more conventional fiddles, banjos, harmonicas and such. While a few diehards continued to nosh on the feast at the tables, others began plucking and strumming. Those without instruments danced on the lawn and in the street. They were the first to herald the approach of the Skrillpod's Willys station wagon. As soon as Jasper killed the engine at the curb, he sprang from the vehicle and sprinted to Missy and gave her a hug. Carly Mae and two school chums followed and soon formed a huddle of preteen effervescence with the twins, Blanche and Ray.

This alone would have been enough, but then a series of barks and yelps arose just before Buster appeared running full speed across the lawn toward Carly Mae. No one had seen the tri-color, husky-sheltie mix for the past month. They all feared he'd met with foul play on a trek from Kiminee to Chicago to chase after Carly Mae. It seemed if he wasn't with her, he was looking for her. Now there he was, his long hair shimmering as he navigated the crowd like a contestant in an agility trial. Carly Mae spun around just in time to open her arms as Buster leaped up. Their embrace full of plenty of licks, kisses, wiggles and tears caused so much joy to flow through the gathering that the most skeptical of the Tarrs and McDuggins winked at each other across the tables.

Through all of this, Emily Skrillpod remained in the passenger seat of the Willys. She looked bound and braced for a dunk in the river like the women of Salem accused of witchcraft long ago. When Jasper noticed Emily's condition, he returned to coax her out. With his help, she emerged, but then fainted as soon as her pumps met the pavement. Jasper lifted her in his arms and carried her into the house. Missy followed and directed him to a spare bedroom at the back of the home where Emily—whose mysterious illness, which struck her only when she came to Kiminee, was now common knowledge—could rest far from the noise out front.

Meanwhile, the festivities continued. And it turned out there was more to celebrate than Carly Mae's return. When the music wound down and the sun lowered, creating a pastiche of purple, orange, red and yellow in the sky, Jasper stood on Missy's front porch and asked for everyone's attention. He said that if Carly Mae could not bear to be separated from her hometown any longer, he would bring the best of Chicago's educational opportunities to Kiminee, not just for Carly Mae but for all the students in the community.

"I've also been talking with administrators at Riverwood, the little community college just a stone's throw from here. They're struggling financially, and I'm sure we could form a mutually beneficial relationship with them. It could mean that every child here who wants a higher education could get at least two years in—on scholarship, too."

Carly Mae's former violin teacher, Mick Deely, moved from the back of the gathering, stood in front of Jasper, and said, "Supporting our Carly Mae, a precocious talent who just might take the world by storm, is one thing, but why should we trust you, an outsider, to do right by all of us? It's such a tall order. I'm fearin' you've got some angle we just can't see."

Grant Modine, who owned the Kiminee Five 'N Dime downtown and had taken heat over his dalliance with Velda Foley, pressed toward the front of the crowd and said, "Wait a minute now. Look at what Jasper and Emily have done for Carly Mae. He didn't ask for anything in return. So what if maybe he thinks he's better than us and expects he can make money off of helping us. Is that so bad if we all prosper? Everybody here knows I've done things I regret and can't ever take back. I don't want turning down this opportunity to be one of them. How many kids in America's backwaters can get a world-class education? Think about that. Think about what he could do for all our children."

Several side conversations broke out. Most folks spoke softly to those on their right or left. Grant motioned for Mick to join him in a corner of the yard. Mick hobbled over and leaned against the old oak, arms folded. Grant danced his arguments to life, arms gesticulating, head straight then cocked then straight, weight shifting side to side. Tam-Tam, who'd been seated in a section of the yard where a couple rows of chairs were set up for the weary or winded, stood and crept past other seated party-goers. When she reached Missy Lake and Earl Wiggs, who were planted at the end of the row, she said, "Scuse me." Then she stepped on Missy's foot as she went by.

"Ow!" Missy cried out and pulled her feet under her chair.

"Watch where you're goin'," Earl said.

Tam-Tam ignored them, a slight smile on her face as she ambled away from the party.

"If I may, I'd like to say a few more words." Jasper spoke into a hand-held microphone Dusty Lambert had handed him so his voice carried to the corners of the yard. Everyone quieted down. "My interest began with Carly Mae's paintings, true, but then my feelings for her grew into a parental kind of love. Emily and I would have adopted her if we could have. That wasn't possible, and ... well ... bear with me, if you will, because much of what I'm doing goes back into my past, you see, I had what you might call a reckoning. I'm not sure that's the right word for it, but I learned some things about the tobacco industry that had brought immense fortune to my family, and I inherited enough to keep me set for life. But while I prospered and was able to study art and establish a thriving gallery and do just about anything I wanted, people were being harmed by addictive tobacco products made by a company in which I owned stock, a company my father founded. I did some soul searching, and I no longer hold those shares. I've been investing in things I believe in, and those investments have gone well overall, though investing does come with risks. I want to use my wealth to do good in the world. I'm dedicated to Carly Mae no matter what, but why not help all of you, too, while I'm at it? Why not do some things right here in Kiminee that could have a lasting impact? It could go beyond schooling. We could have cottage industries to create good jobs, solid opportunities."

"Like a cheese-making operation?" Tempest Binsack volunteered, thinking of her daughter Gloria, who had a passion for all things cheese related.

"Why not?" Jasper replied.

After further side discussions, some quite heated, and with a "we'll see" sort of attitude, people gave approval to Jasper's school idea, but then muttered about him in checkout lines, at Little League games and in church pews. Everyone was skeptical, especially about Emily, who seemed aloof and not at all behind Jasper's do-gooding. Some even suspected she faked being ill when she came to town.

Chapter 6

Steel-blue shoes on teal floor, Damon Foley paced in monochrome madness. The walls were robin's egg blue streaked with cracks of indigo. The bed frame and desk were cobalt, the sink bluish gray. His navy jumpsuit covered skin with undertones of deep blue-green. Faint sapphire rays flickered through a sole window, barred. He was living a three-dimensional Picasso nightmare in Dry Gulch Asylum for the Criminally Insane.

How many years had he been walking this floor? How many conversations had he had with the director and a trickle of psychiatrists, caseworkers, orderlies, nurses and guards, trying to convince them he was not who they thought he was? When would they realize he was a good man with a wife and three children who needed him?

A bitter stew brewed where anguish, terror, rage, resignation, indignation, regret, apathy and sorrow clashed. The stench of buried dreams rose and slithered up walls. Ridicule echoed down corridors. He was quiet, his azure tears spent for now.

An attendant pushed a squeaking cart down the hall, stopping at doors to slide trays through narrow slots. The cart paused at Damon's door; he grabbed his meal: blue-black minute steak, baby blue mashed potatoes, wilting lettuce in shades of gray-green. Next to his plate, a piece of folded yellow paper startled like sun after an eclipse. He opened it and read the message. "Head honcho retiring this year. Chin up. I believe you." No signature. It could have been a hoax; cruelty thrived in this place.

He folded the note, put it in his pocket and walked to his cot. Palms pressing on a coarse, cyan blanket, he lowered to his knees, and prayed to be returned to the little town along the Bendy River he recalled in vibrant, multicolor hues; to read bedtime stories to Blanche, Ray and Carly Mae; to kiss Velda's sweet lips once again.

Down the hall, Georgia Webb, head nurse at Dry Gulch, settled her bony bottom onto her swivel chair and paused, smirking, to rub her fingertips along polished teak arm rests. She pulled a Paper Mate ballpoint from her desk drawer and wrote a note in the man's file. "Patient still divorced from reality, sees everything in shades of blue, refuses to answer to his name or take responsibility for his crimes. Will suggest upping his doses with the new director when he arrives."

Later, she filed the paperwork in her matching teak credenza under A for Leon Ames and headed home to a man she craved so completely she peeled off garments on the way to her bedroom and entered wearing only a garter belt, hose and white nurse's cap.

Chapter 7

Carly Mae, fourteen years old and precocious as ever in the summer of 1967, helped Emily stack overstuffed cardboard boxes in the back of the Willys wagon. This was after several humid days spent hauling and sorting odds and ends from the Skrillpod's co-op building's storage area. A breeze from Lake Michigan riffled their summer clothes, blew their hair up and cooled their necks as Emily closed the rear hatch.

"Thanks so much for your help this past week. I'd never been able to get these things on their way to Kiminee without you." Emily gave Carly Mae a hug, savoring the bond she felt with the girl.

"Aw, it's nothing." Carly Mae snuggled into Emily's embrace. "We might not be blood related, but we're family all the same."

"I feel that, too," Emily said.

Buster, who had been sniffing around a row of blossoming rose of Sharon bushes, bounded up. Carly Mae opened a door to the back seat, and he flopped across the threshold, panting. "There you go, buddy." The teen scratched the top of the dog's head before closing the door.

"You're growing so fast. I can't believe it's been three years since you returned to Kiminee. Soon you won't want to spend so much of your summers up here with us."

"I'll always want to spend time with you. Plus, there's this math genius teaching at Northwestern right now. I could maybe study with him next summer."

"That's sweet, but it's okay if you choose your peers over Jasper and me, or even over your studies. That's what a lot of teens do. It's normal."

Carly Mae poked Emily's arm. "I wish you'd spend as much time in Kiminee as Jasper."

Emily felt a hint of nausea rising and swallowed hard. "Nobody's been able to figure out why that town makes me so ill. I've been to one specialist after another."

"Some folks back home think you're faking it. They say you don't really want to be with us."

Curious, Emily raised an eyebrow. "What do you think?"

"I know you're not faking anything."

A gust off the lake blew several papers out of a box at the condo building's front porch. "Uh oh, look! We forgot one." Emily broke away, ran to the container and closed it.

Carly Mae chased the papers and nabbed them as they blew down the sidewalk. She passed a full block of high rises before catching the last one. When she returned, Emily was squeezing the forgotten box into the back of the wagon. Carly Mae handed her prizes to Emily—except for a black-and-white photo of a dozen children and a nun in front of an imposing brick building.

Carly Mae pointed to one of the girls. "She's smiling just like my mom in an old portrait Grams has. I think it was her first holy communion."

Emily glanced at the picture. "A lot of us smiled like that, you know, mouth closed, trying to look demure."

Carly Mae flipped the photo over. "It says, 'St. Angela Merici Children's Home and School Glee Club, 1939.'"

"I used to love to sing."

"You went to school there? Where is it?"

"It's a ways southeast of here, maybe 100 miles or so, near the Indiana border."

"A children's home—that's like an orphanage, right?"

"That's exactly what it is."

Carly Mae offered the photo to Emily. A blast of wind blew it from her hand. The picture twirled into the air, plunged down and hit the concrete, where Emily pinned it with her sneaker. Carly Mae swooped, clutched the battered card stock and offered it to Emily again. As the wind picked up, Emily took the photo, tucked it in and closed the hatch again.

"Let's get going." Emily sidled toward the driver's door, wind slapping her skin. "I want to get to Kiminee with time to spare before this campfire you and the twins have planned. I'll need to stretch out and sip Vernor's until the first wave of nausea passes. I must say you keep yourselves busy in Kiminee. You've always got something going on."

"You're gonna love the stories. There's this one about Crazy Man Wilson. No matter how many times I've heard it, my tummy still does flip flops just thinking about it."

"Oh my, I'll go from nausea to fright. Not sure I'm looking forward to it."

"It'll be fun. We all know there is no bad man lurking in our woods."

The two settled into the Willys. Outside, wind blustered, rattling the vehicle's windows. Emily started up the engine.

"Can we go see your old school on the way?" Carly Mae asked.

"It's in the opposite direction—too far out of our way." Emily backed the vehicle onto the street and merged into traffic. "And, honestly, I'm not sure I'd want to go even if we had time. It's a sad place for me. I wasn't mistreated or anything like that. Some of the nuns were actually very nice, especially Sister Anne Marie. She read us stories sometimes and had this way of listening with her eyes open wide, like she really cared. But she was so busy, and all of us kids there were lonesome as could be, longing for families we didn't have. It's hard to think about those times."

"Oh, gosh, I get it. I wouldn't want to go either."

Buster nuzzled and scratched a tattered blanket, circled a few times, then groaned as he settled in for a long nap.

Missy Lake and granddaughters, Blanche and Carly Mae, strutted one block from their home to the Kiminee town square. "Land sakes," Missy said. "I can hardly believe you girls are fourteen and fifteen already. Veritable young ladies, you are, and you'd better mind your manners. I don't want you embarrassin' me."

"Oh, Grams, we know how important this is to you," Blanche said.

Miffed, Carly Mae challenged her grandmother. "When have we ever embarrassed you?"

"It's just my nerves talkin'; don't take it personal." Missy nodded to Carly Mae. "Hope has spread here like fairy dust since you came back. I've got no complaints. You're both doin' the town proud. Ray, too."

Missy's three grandchildren attended Kiminee Academy, which Jasper Skrillpod established shortly after Carly Mae's return three years prior. They also took classes at nearby Riverwood College, which Jasper had been fundraising for through his Chicago connections. So Carly Mae and Blanche had plenty of schoolwork to do, but like teenage girls everywhere, they gabbed for hours on the phone and socialized at every opportunity.

"How long will this be?" Blanche asked.

"You'll have time to meet up with your little crowd at the Five 'N Dime—if that's what you're worried about."

Each girl agreed when she was barely old enough to talk that she would join Kiminee's Suzette Society when the time came. According to Missy, that time was today.

Trees lining the street blushed with fall colors supplanting summer's shades of green. The sisters had begged to wear cutoff jeans, casual shirts and sandals on what they thought would turn out to be the last balmy day before fall's chilly tentacles gripped their bones, but Missy had insisted they "look decent" for their induction into the club.

The trio marched diagonally across the green. Missy wore a dress of royal blue. Poking out from a hat to match were tufts of salt-and-pepper hair. Her white-gloved hands carried a platter of Ritz crackers topped with Velveeta. Her shoes, lace-up orthopedic clodhoppers, were polished to a black sheen. The girls, in gold shifts sewn following a Simplicity pattern, sported Thom McAnn flats that were already scuffed, though they had purchased them only a week ago. Carly Mae's shining auburn locks and Blanche's pale yellow tresses hung long and free. Blanche held a fresh pound cake, still warm and wrapped in aluminum foil. Carly Mae tripped but quickly regained her balance while grasping a pitcher sloshing with grape Kool Aid.

"Watch where you're goin' there. It's Waterford crystal you're carryin'," Missy warned Carly Mae.

"Whew! That was close," Blanche said to Carly Mae, who held tight to the pitcher.

They stopped at a storefront. In display windows on either side of the door were quilts, handkerchiefs, aprons, pillows, jewelry, pottery, jams and jellies, and various sundries—all handmade in Kiminee. The wooden sign hanging from a wrought iron holder said "Suzette's" in script.

The society's president, Maridee Pratt, stood at the entrance. Balancing a plate of chocolate fudge on one palm, she held the door open with her foot, and waved the trio inside. "You must be so proud," Maridee whispered to Missy as the girls rushed into the shop.

"Slow down there, Miss Carly Mae. That pitcher is fragile," Missy called out.

The girls continued apace, giggling.

"Remember when we were that young?" Maridee said as they proceeded toward the meeting.

"Why dredge up the past?" Missy marched ahead.

The interior was replete with additional handcrafted items, including furniture carved with intricate leaf and flower patterns. In the back room, they joined others in an area set up with three rows of chairs. They shuffled dishes around to make room for their snacks on an already loaded table against a wall. The ladies always make sure they had plenty of treats left over to give away.

After a fair amount of chitchat and nibbling, Maridee stepped to the podium and called the meeting to order. When all were settled, she said, "First, on this auspiciously warm autumn day, we want to welcome Blanche and Carly Mae Foley, two remarkable young ladies, who will be a credit to our organization."

"Here a … here, new b, blood," Abby Louise Chute shouted from the back row. Her face was flushed, and her breath was so laden with alcohol even the mice in the walls could smell it.

Maridee ignored her and gestured, palm up, to the inductees. "As you know, girls, you have great big shoes to fill, as do we all. Our proud tradition of community service began long ago when Charles and Fleur Kiminee lost their little girl, Suzette. From the shock, dear Fleur passed away. With no one to take care of the remaining children or keep his house, Charles came apart. And it's an unfortunate fact he grew too fond of the bottle. It wasn't right for his kids to see him like that."

"He's not the only one a little too fond of the bottle." Missy whispered to Tempest Binsack seated to her right, but her words carried and sliced like a razor.

Maridee broke the ensuing silence with a cough and resumed her talk. "So the womenfolk of the town stepped in, taking turns minding the children, cleaning up and cooking good, hearty fare. Charles came to himself, and it was just a few years later that he married one of those women, the fine Dorothy Binsack. She is a distant relation of our very own Tempest, whose kin, I believe, also hailed from Louisiana, just like Charles and Fleur."

She pointed to Tempest, who fiddled with her collar and said, "Dorothy's in the family tree somewhere, but let's not fuss over me."

Maridee coughed and cleared her throat. "So the Kiminees were taken care of, but the volunteers had come to like their work and didn't want to stop. No, it was more than that. They didn't just like it; they felt the absolute power of it. They saw the awesome, thunderous force of love put into action."

"Yeah, tell like 'tis, Maridee-dee!" Abby Louise stood, wobbling, then crashed back into her seat.

Missy craned her neck to look over her shoulder. "Shhhhhh! This isn't a revival meetin', Abby."

Maridee wiped her fair brow with a hankie. "And so the Suzette society was born. Since then we've helped families in crisis and neighbors maybe just a little down on their luck." She paused and scanned the room.

"Don't forget to mention how we've aided all them soldier boys startin' from the Civil War all the way through the Korean War," Tempest said.

"Yes, of course," Maridee replied. "And we've just sent our first care package to Dave Deely, grandson of Mick Deely. He's joined the fight against communism in a far-off place called Vietnam."

"Vieh whaaa?" Abby called out before pulling a flask from her pocket and taking a nip.

Missy turned around again. "Honestly, Abby Louise, isn't that quite enough disruption for one meeting? We've got business to tend to."

"Business, yes, our new members." Maridee smiled at Blanche and Carly Mae. "So are you ready to join this long tradition? Are you ready to be instruments of love?"

Blanche and Carly Mae nodded.

"Then step up and get pinned," Maridee said.

Blanche tripped over Carly Mae's feet as they sidestepped their way to the aisle. At the podium, Maridee fastened a dainty black-eyed Susan pin on each of their dresses. The members applauded heartily as the girls returned, blushing, to their seats. Maridee soon turned the meeting over to Tempest, the treasurer and store manager, and took a seat.

Tempest waddled to the front, financial report in hand. "I'm not gonna go into great detail, 'cause you can just look at this yourselves if you want to know the particulars." She held up the pages. "I just want to say I was skeptical when Jasper suggested we expand our activities beyond our usual home visits and care packages and stuff like that, and open a store that would not only raise money for community needs—as we see fit, naturally—but also provide income for some very talented craftspeople in our midst. It helps, of course, that Maridee and her fine husband, Mark, who own this building, have given us free rent guaranteed for five years. That's immense."

"It's good for us, too," Maridee interrupted. "The building was boarded up and run down. Our society has done my family a big favor with this project, so it goes both ways."

"That may be," Tempest said, "but we sure appreciate it, 'cause I'm proud to report that we're in the black. Our little venture is in the black!" The room erupted into a harmony of cheers. When things quieted down, she continued, "Yes, yes, it's grand, simply grand. But now we have the matter of Tam-Tam Parlo, who said she stopped by and asked to sell her dolls here, and she was turned away. Anybody remember that?"

The room was silent as the moon rising.

"Who was working that day?" Tempest asked.

After a long pause, Missy said, "I was. We already sell Varnie Black's apple dolls." She pointed to a corner display case. "Tam-Tam's can't compare. Did you know she makes her doll heads out of Elmer's Glue and flour? And there's …" She grabbed her skirt and kneaded the fabric. "There is something off about them. Unsettling, you might say."

"There's no rules 'bout wha … what dolls should a … be made." Abby Louise rose and stumbled toward the front of the room. "Whadya have agin Tam-Tam, anyways? She's our oldest rezdent. Why shouldnwe give er a hand? Let 'er contribute, too?"

Maridee almost knocked over her chair as she rose to intercept what was turning into a walking disaster. She took the flailing woman's arm to steady her. "There, there."

Abby Louise broke free of Maridee. "Lemme go!" she shouted.

"Okay, then, Abby dear. Please sit back down," Tempest said. "No call to get all worked up. We're the Suzettes, after all, with common goals. Who wants to study the pros and cons of selling Tam-Tam's dolls before the next meetin'?"

"I'll talk to her," Maridee said. "I'll see if her goods pass muster." She then took hold of Abby Louise's arm and escorted her toward the coffee urn at the snack table.

There were general murmurs of agreement in the group.

"Okay, let's see a show of hands. All in favor of revisiting Tam-Tam's offerings next month?" Tempest surveyed the rows.

Most everyone in the room raised a hand.

"All opposed?"

Missy raised her hand several inches but then put it back in her lap.

"Okay, that's settled." Tempest returned to her seat.

With that, the formal part of the meeting came to a close. Maridee helped the wobbling Abby out the door, while other members had another go at the feast on the table. Finally, as Tempest gave a little groan and loosened her belt, the last drops of coffee were consumed, and conversations wound down. Carly Mae and Blanche slinked toward the door. Missy glared at them, clapped her hands to gain the group's attention, and announced that her granddaughters would be delighted to carry any leftovers to Touch of Kindness Rest Home just a few blocks off the square.

"Dang, we were almost out of here," Blanche muttered to Carly Mae. The sisters proceeded to the table where they scooped, sorted, packed and stacked an abundance of gooey, crunchy treats.

As autumn waltzed toward winter in 1967, folks around Kiminee commented on how they'd never seen such a graceful transition, each day a barely perceptible drop in temperature, a few more leaves turning color while others fell to the ever hardening ground. Children buttoned sweaters for the walk to school, then jackets as winds nipped their noses, then parkas when the first flurries filled the air. By the time Christmas vacation came, foyers were cluttered with boots wet with melting snow, scarves and mittens tossed onto tables, coats hung willy nilly from hooks in rows.

On the coldest days children played board games, dug out half-finished paint-by-number and wood-burning kits, and begged to bake cookies without supervision. Their elders leaned back in well-worn chairs, some smoking tobacco, others knitting last-minute stocking presents. It was in those times that the adults would converse about goings on in town, and invariably they'd remark on how the Foley children, now teens, were thriving in Missy's sometimes brittle but always fiercely loyal care. They'd mention that no matter how low the temperature dropped in the days before Christmas, Missy stopped in at Chester Dillard's hardware store, which housed the post office in the back, manned by Chester himself. She asked if any packages had arrived for her grandchildren, hoping Velda had thought to send even a small gift for them to share. Chester would go through the day's deliveries and look up with sad, basset-hound eyes. She would blink, thank him for checking and head back empty-handed into the cold.

On Christmas Eve most able-bodied townsfolk went caroling, then ambled home, got into their jammies and put milk and cookies out for Santa Claus. This ritual wasn't just for children. Everyone, young and old, rich and poor, big and small still loved the idea of Santa, and most secretly hoped to meet him one day. In Missy's living room, Blanche, Ray and Carly Mae gathered on the floor at her feet. Faces washed, hair and teeth brushed, jammies on, they looked up with loving eyes at Missy, who read "The Night Before Christmas" aloud. Though in their teens, they couldn't imagine a time when they wouldn't want to gather at their grandmother's knee to hear her read this poem.

When Missy uttered the final words, "Merry Christmas to all and to all a good night," she closed the book and smiled down at her grandchildren. They yawned and stirred, content that they would have sweet dreams before rising in the morning to tear into the brightly wrapped presents under the flocked and decorated fir tree in the corner.

Before they could rise, she asked them to stay put. From beneath a red and green afghan covering her lap, Missy pulled a yellow baby blanket, which she unfolded to reveal three jewelry boxes. She handed one to each and said, "I figured your mom would want you to have these by now. She had 'em made for ya, and I believe you're old enough to take proper care of 'em."

As the teens admired their sparkling silver rings of matching trinity knot and circle design, Missy told them about the now deceased Father O'Brien's confession. She said it called into doubt the story Missy's uncle Maurice Brewer had told long ago about Velda's family dying in a car crash up north somewhere. Little Velda might have been abandoned right here on the steps of Old St. Michaels, wrapped only in the little yellow blanket now stretched across Missy's lap, with a ring pinned to it—a ring just like the ones Carly Mae, Blanche and Ray were examining with delight.

Velda's children wore their rings to bed that night and wished fervently Santa would dispense with the presents under the tree and bring back what they wanted most: their mother and father.

Chapter 8

After the last pop, Georgia Webb turned off the burner. She pried open the expanded foil bulb with long, red fingernails, poured Jiffy Pop into two Melmac bowls, sprinkled each serving with salt and sashayed into the living room, where her lover sat, fuming, on the couch. She placed the bowls on the coffee table. He seized one and hurled it at the TV. Plastic crashed against the screen as popcorn sprayed into the air and bounced onto the rug.

"You burned it again, dammit," he growled.

"There, there, sweetie, honey-lamb, nothing to worry about. I'll get you something else." She eyed him with caution as she retrieved the bowl and angled around the room, scooping up the spilled snack.

"I don want nothin' else," he spat. "I'm sick an' tired a this dump, sick an' tired a your bony ass."

"Sweetie-pie dearheart, you don't mean that. You know you can't do without me," she purred. "Besides, we'll be leaving just like we planned. It's just gonna take a little longer than I expected."

"You think I'm batshit? You think I don read the mail? The windfall you were s'posed to get from that old coot came through all right. I read all about it."

"Mr. Thurber, yes. What a lovely man he was. I meant to talk to you about that."

"Yeah, real nice guy. He left you all a $150. How are we gonna start a new life on that?"

"There's more coming, darling pie-pie. It's just that his kids contested the will, accused me of all kinds of things they'll never be able to prove. Once this whole mess plays out in court we'll travel the world, live like royalty."

"It's been years, years a livin' in the sticks, hidin'. I'm sick a these Saturday Night at the Movies on TV. I'm sick a tendin' your stupid summer garden, huntin' rabbits for sport—sick a makin' macrame plant hangers so you can sell 'em on weekends."

"With the canning we do, that summer garden helps feed us all year, and those plant hangers are selling like crazy. I'm building up our nest egg bit by bit."

"You been stringin' me along."

"Would you rather be back at Dry Gulch?"

He lurched from the couch, pulled her toward him and wrapped his fingers around her throat. "Don you say one more word 'bout Dry Gulch, ya hear?"

"I'm sorry, honeybun," she squeaked out, and gasped for air "You know I'd never want you stuck there again. Come on, I saved you, didn't I?" She rubbed her body against his and ran her nails up and down his spine.

He loosened his grip.

"Come on, lovey-pie. You know how much you want me."

He groaned. She pulled off her dress, the only clothing she'd had on, and slapped him in the face with it. He shoved her to the floor.

"That's it, sugar-lamb. I'm here," she said.

He unbuckled his belt.

Georgia Webb scratched crimson polish from her thumbnail as she approached Dry Gulch's new director, Ned Burton. Long, brown waves obscured his face as he wrote in a file on his desk.

"You wanted to see me, Mr. Burton?"

He looked up and pushed his copper-colored wire-rimmed glasses back toward the bridge of his nose. "Ah, Nurse Webb. Have a seat."

She sat on the hard wooden chair facing him and continued to scrape polish off while he returned to writing. "What is it? I need to finish prepping this afternoon's meds. I don't have all day."

He looked up again, raising one eyebrow, then finished the note and put the pen down. "This won't take long. I want to know what you think about Leon Ames. I've got his file here, and there are some discrepancies."

"The man's a nut case, obviously."

"Many of these notes were written by you. And I'm curious." He thumbed through papers in a folder and tapped his index finger on a messy page with lots of text crossed out. "Take this, for instance." He turned a document toward her, so she could read the writing. "Why did his medications change so dramatically after the twister in '61? It was a major disruption for everyone, but he's the only one whose medications changed."

"Darned if I know. You'd have to ask Warren Raines, the director at that time."

"You know I can't do that since he passed away last year."

"Well, it'll just have to remain a mystery." She scratched the last bit of polish from her thumb and started in on her index finger.

"Why do you suppose there isn't one note in here written by Warren? Other records from that time have plenty of his notes."

"I wouldn't know." She gripped the arms of her chair. "You know everything got disorganized at that time. Some records were lost completely. I'd expect discrepancies to be normal."

"I suppose you're right."

"Can I go now? It's time to dispense the meds."

"Yes, of course."

She rose from the chair and lurched toward the door.

"Uh, one more thing," he said.

She kept walking

"His shoe size. It was a 13 when he arrived."

She halted and looked over her shoulder. "So?"

"It's a 9 now."

"Don't you have anything better to do than dig around in old records, especially from the time when the twister hit? The men here need you now."

He straightened papers in the folder and closed it. "I see your point. But still—"

"I have to go." She faced forward again and raced down the hall to the nurse's station, where she addressed a woman sitting at the desk. "Sherri, I'm suddenly sick to my stomach. Must have been something in my lunch. Can you finish up the meds for me?"

Without waiting for an answer, she ran out the door, got into her car and sped off, careened down country roads, and screeched to a halt in her driveway, heart thumping so hard her neck throbbed. Color returned to her face as she peeled off garments on the way to her bedroom. She was down to her garter belt, hose and white nurse's cap when she stepped inside, expecting him to be on the bed, waiting for her. But he was not there.

"Honey? Sugar Bear? Where are you?" She looked under the bed, behind the curtains, in the adjoining bathroom. "Lambkins? Come to Mama, now." She searched the entire house, but the man she had risked everything for was gone. In her kitchen, she pulled out a step stool so she could reach the top shelf of a cabinet above the refrigerator. She grabbed a teddy-bear cookie jar and carried it down. She opened the lid and found all the bills she'd tucked inside were gone.

Their nest egg, their future, their grand escape. Gone. His promises, his vows. Her lover, the real Leon Ames. Gone.

She curled into a fetal position on her living room couch where she gnawed on her nails and blubbered until, late in the evening, she finally fell asleep.

In the morning, she ironed her white uniform until no hint of wrinkles remained, then ironed it again before finally dressing and stomping to her car, keys digging into the palm of her hand, nails bitten down to red and swollen skin.

Chapter 9

All of Kiminee feared the worst when an arctic blast hit the town with sub-zero temperatures and five feet of snow on the first day of March 1968. But people overcame their shock at the onslaught, neighbor helped neighbor dig out, businesses reopened, children returned to school, and the land rippled to life in spring. By the time final exams rolled around in June, the storm seemed a distant memory for students eager to escape their desks.

The Foley teens raced out of class on the last day of school. A fragrant breeze blew by, and the three siblings spun in circles, eyes closed, faces turned toward the sun before ambling the academy's curving paths toward home. They had an adventure planned for their first free Friday afternoon in months.

Carly Mae tapped Blanche's shoulder playfully. "It is daring to start off summer vacation by heading somewhere Grams doesn't want us to go, and it's about time we find out if those tales of polkadot fish at Tam-Tam's swimming hole are true."

"We're glad you're coming," Ray said. "Grams would split a gasket if she found out, but she must know deep down that orange carp with purple spots, and green ones with blue spots would draw us there eventually despite all her warnings about the dreaded Tam-Tam."

"I don't get what Grams has against her. She seems harmless enough." Blanche tucked a lock of flaxen hair behind her ear.

"It's a mystery to me," Ray said.

"Grownups. They're like from a different planet or something," Carly Mae said.

The trio locked arms and walked in step until they reached the academy's new library building, which was all glass on two sides. Rows of tables, usually filled with students and stacks of books, were all empty.

"Wow! Look how deserted it is," Carly Mae said.

"Yeah, nobody wants to hang out there now that school's out," Ray replied.

Carly Mae noticed movement at the mezzanine level and slowed down. Jasper was speaking with a woman and man near a wall of windows. He gestured with rapid, angular arm movements.

"I think I know those people with Jasper." Carly Mae pointed. "I'm gonna see what's up."

Blanche squinted at her. "Carly—"

"I won't be long. Promise." Carly Mae ran up the steps, through the entrance and bounded up the stairs, two at a time. She slowed as she drew close to where Jasper and the couple appeared to be arguing. Sensing they might not want her to hear, she tiptoed closer, hidden by shelves stuffed with books on the Civil War, a perennial interest among Kiminee residents, many of whom were descended from members of the Union Army's 103rd Illinois Infantry Regiment. She peered through a small gap in the volumes and saw Mrs. Henchley and Dr. Croll from Lily Park Academy in Chicago.

"It's unconscionable you wouldn't answer our calls and made us drive all this way," Mrs. Henchley scolded.

Carly Mae let out a soft gasp, then froze, holding her breath, hoping the sound hadn't carried.

"You'd better honor our contract, or you'll be such a laughingstock, even the dull people of this town will send you packing," Dr. Croll warned.

Jasper extended his arm, palm flexed up as though bracing against an attack. "Now I never agreed—"

"You don't seem to know what you agreed to, my man," Mrs. Henchley spat. "And it's about time we put an end to this insane charitable venture of yours, something that's only aggrandizing you as far as I can see."

Jasper lowered his arm. "Excuse me?"

Carly Mae's fingers and toes tingled as she drew in a breath.

"Don't pretend you didn't read the fine print when you brought Carly Mae to Lily Park or that you don't know how much Lily Park depends on you for recruitment and fundraising." Dr. Croll squeezed Jasper's shoulder. "You can't be that stupid, but then, your father didn't bring you into the family business. He knew all too well what a loose cannon you are. But the fact remains that because you bear the Skrillpod name—your charismatic, titan-of-industry father's name—you draw interest and support. So does that infernal Carly Mae, unfortunately. Imagine a girl silly enough to reject the world-class education we offered her—and advisers like you daft enough to go along with such a bad decision."

Jasper brushed Dr. Croll's hand away. "I've given more than enough to your academy. You were on the verge of bankruptcy when I approached you about enrolling Carly Mae. I saved your bacon!"

Dr. Croll lifted a document from the table. "The agreement is spelled out in black and white." He waved the paper in Jasper's face. "You agreed to fund the Lily Park endowment for ten years, as well as contribute through specific fundraising and academic efforts. You were also tasked with grooming Carly Mae as our ambassador, our grand success story. But you abandoned us."

Carly Mae held her breath to stifle a gasp at the thought of Jasper grooming her for anything.

"That's not true. It's not how I remem—"

"Oh, please. Lying doesn't become you, Skrillpod," Mrs. Henchley huffed. "The most galling thing, the thing I cannot stomach, is that interest in your upstart school is growing in our community. Four students asked to transfer this month alone when word got out you're building dorms for out-of-town students. We won't allow some hick experiment of yours to compete with our renowned Lily Park. We won't have it. And we'll crush you."

"Now, hold on a minute. Carly Mae has good memories of her time at Lily Park. She might be inclined to help you if you'd just let things play out naturally. And I can't, no, I won't pressure her." Jasper's voice quavered and cracked. "It's pointless to try." His lips quivered as he wiped moist palms against his thighs.

The tingling moved up Carly Mae's legs and arms. She tensed her muscles and relaxed them, but it didn't help.

"Look at yourself, Jasper." Mrs. Henchley waved her finger at him, like a lecturing parent. "Desperation doesn't become you."

"Yes, good fellow, don't lose your mind over this," Dr. Croll added with a chuckle. "Of course you already have, haven't you, lost your mind, that is? Imagine what would happen if that got out."

Color drained from Jasper's face. He gripped the edge of the table to steady himself.

"Ah, I see our message is sinking in." Mrs. Henchley straightened her hat, lifted white gloves from the table and put them on. "I think we can go now. Remember this well: we are counting on you. Besides, we'll pay you a handsome share of the funds you raise if you return with the girl. You really have no alternative now that your investment in that crazy packaged salad business went bust. You can't merely write us a check to shut us up. Are you really willing to lose everything?

Over this?" She swept her arm in a gesture meant to encompass the entire town.

The tingling invaded Carly Mae's chest and abdomen. Tears filled her eyes.

"Indeed, it was a harebrained investment. If you had any real smarts, you'd have the money to pay us what we're due." Dr. Croll's eyes crinkled with cruelty as he grinned and lifted his chin. "Who in their right mind would pay a premium for a bag of pre-washed lettuce? I suppose you thought you'd make a killing. Well you didn't, but that's not our problem, and you can't just shove us under the rug. You either fundraise for our endowment and return with that girl—or we'll expose your history of mental imbalance to all those friends you think you have in Chicago."

Jasper's deep brown eyes pulsed with anguish. "The lettuce business was just a little ahead of its time. Besides, I do have other resources. I'm shifting some accounts—"

"Enough! We've lost patience with you. You're out of time," Mrs. Henchley growled.

"You know what you have to do," Dr. Croll said before stepping away from the table with Mrs. Henchley.

The tingling reached Carly Mae's head. She stifled a sob and quietly snuck back down the stairs as the continuing conversation grew fainter. At the ground floor, she burst through the door and sprinted toward home, vibrations coursed through her head to toe.

"Imagine what all your art patrons and society friends will think when they find out you tried to emancipate yourself at fourteen, claiming your father had kidnapped your mother, who apparently was a seal that could take human form?" Dr. Croll let out a guttural, mocking laugh. "And then you forced your father onto a ledge at knifepoint twelve stories up on Michigan Avenue, trying to get him to confess to this absurdity? Think of where you'd be now if he had fallen?"

Jasper fisted his hands. "Whoever fed you information about what I did or didn't do in my youth was breaking the law. Those records were sealed."

"If you don't want that story out, bring that girl back to Chicago," Dr. Croll said. "We'll welcome you both with open arms."

"You have to accept that we have you over a barrel, so to speak." Mrs. Henchley smirked and put a gloved hand over her mouth.

With eyes downcast, Jasper muttered, "I'll see what I can do."

Jasper's tormentors left the library arm in arm, she tittering in delight at his pain, he with a satisfied smirk on his face, believing he had bested Jasper and gotten himself out of a jam.

Back at Missy's, Carly Mae sprang right to her room, slammed the door and plopped on the bed, waking Buster from a nap. The dog yawned and cocked his head, one ragged ear sticking up. She pulled him close and burst into tears at the notion that Jasper would even think of using her. Nuzzling into his furry mane, she blubbered, "Jasper isn't who we thought he was. He's been using me."

"Carly Mae?" Blanche tapped on the door. "What's up? Are you okay? … Can I come in?"

Ray came up beside Blanche, banged on the wood and called out, "Carly, Carly-o, Carly Mae, Carly, Carly-o."

"I, I just need … to be alone f, for … a while," Carly Mae sputtered, struggling to regain control of her body.

Perplexed, Blanche asked, "Don't you want to sneak around Tam-Tam's forbidden cabin anymore? Don't you want to see the fish?"

"Just go without me," Carly Mae declared.

"What's gotten hold of you?" Ray hovered, his nose an inch from the door. "Carly Mae?"

The twins waited in silence for a couple of minutes.

"She thinks she's the only one with feelings," Blanche griped under her breath.

Ray sidled to the stairs. "Our little prima donna," he whispered before stepping down.

Blanche followed, chuckling. "Lady Godiva."

Carly Mae held tight to Buster, tears penetrating his thick, tricolor coat as the vibrations gradually faded.

Lulled by sunshine and the river's burble, Blanche and Ray slumped side by side, heads down, fishing rods loosening in their hands. A splash broke the reverie. Blanche opened her eyes and saw Tam-Tam in oversize rubber shoes, trying to keep her balance on a steppingstone near the opposite bank. Wrapped in canvas apron loaded with way too many garden tools, the old woman wobbled, chomped on the stem of her corncob pipe and looked with longing down river. Drifting away were faded margarine containers and scratched Tupperware bumping out of a mesh bag. Blanche poked Ray, who startled awake. Seeing Tam-Tam's belongings bobbing, the teens dove in after them. Tam-Tam kept an eye on the youths as she stepped gingerly from stone to stone. The twins nabbed all of her containers, put them back in the mesh bag and greeted her when she reached the shore.

"Thank you kindly, kids," Tam-Tam said when she stomped onto solid land. "Don't like to be losin' stuff."

"It's no trouble." Ray handed her the bag and backed away.

Blanche backed up, too. "Yes, glad to do it."

"Eee gads, you'd think I'm a witch the way you act, all scaredy pants and timid like. I won't bite." She held up the dripping bag. "Come along. I gotta put these things in the shed for future sprouts and such. Then I got some treats in the kitchen I expect you'll like." Tam-Tam ambled toward her garden shed.

The twins exchanged glances, excitement in their eyes at the prospect of spending time with Tam-Tam. They'd never spoken more than a few words with her at community events before Missy had steered them away, warning that Tam-Tam was an unsavory type of person, someone to avoid.

"You don't suppose she has a great big oven in that cabin, do you?" Blanche said under her breath.

"Well, dear Gretel, even if she does, you'll push her in, right?"

The two giggled and continued after Tam-Tam, who opened the toolshed door, took off her sunhat, put away her other belongings, then motioned for the the twins to follow her to her ramshackle home.

All lanky limbs and repressed fluster, Ray and Blanche followed her inside. It was dusty and cluttered with stacks of newspapers and magazines; cardboard boxes overflowing with tattered clothing; and an array of dented toasters, broken mixers, and other odds and ends in various states of decomposition. Tam-Tam lit a floor lamp by the refrigerator and a kerosene lantern on the table. It was a cloudless summer afternoon, but the light was needed because the trees around the home were so thick only a dappling of sunlight came through the leaves.

Tam-Tam shuffled to the kitchen area and returned with a plate of brownies and two glasses of lemonade. "Dig in. They's fresh today."

The each took a nibble of brownie and washed it down with lemonade.

Ray took a bigger bite. "These are good!"

Blanche held up her glass. "And the lemonade, too."

Ray rubbed slender fingers over initials carved into the tabletop. "Who are JP, BP and GP?"

"I bet the P's stand for Parlo," Blanche said.

"Best not poke your noses in where they don't belong." One side of Tam-Tam upper lip lifted, then settled back down. "What brought you here anyway, after all these years avoidin' me like the plague?"

"Um, the main thing was the polkadot fish," Blanche volunteered. "We wanted to see if they are real. I mean, what a sight they must be."

Tam-Tam waved dismissively. "Can't believe everything ya hear. They's all kinds a tales 'bout what goes on in my neck of the woods."

"Life would be boring without stories," Ray said.

"Guess you gotta dream up stuff to get through the boredom of a long, hot summer." Tam-Tam patted his shoulder.

Ray flinched and she snapped her hand back.

Blanche took another swallow of lemonade. "We won't be bored at all. In fact, I'll be quite busy since I'm a Suzette now. Carly Mae and I might even work in the store. It needs a lot of organizing with so many volunteers coming and going."

"Damn store. They won't sell my dolls, and it's on account of your grandmother—not that I blame you kids or anything." Tam-Tam kicked aside a plastic laundry basket full of faded bath toys as she made her way to a curio cabinet filled with figurines, framed photos, miniature furniture, dolls, charms, arrowheads and other knickknacks. She peered inside, opened the door and pulled out two dolls. Returning to the table, she handed a female in a wedding dress to Blanche and a man in tuxedo to Ray.

When Blanche saw the doll's face, she stiffened and fumbled, almost dropping the doll. "How did you get the face to look so … so human? She looks like … like pictures I've seen of Grams, and the dress is just like the one up in the attic."

Ray leaned toward Blanche to get a good view. "You're right. That's a little … weird, well, a lot weird, really." He offered the male doll to Blanche. "This one doesn't look like anybody I know."

Blanche took the male and handed the female to Ray. "I don't recognize him either." She passed the doll to Tam-Tam. "Who is he? Anybody we know?"

Tam-Tam patted the doll's dark hair. "That's—no, never you mind who that is."

"He must be the JP or BP or GP, right?" Blanche brushed her fingertips over the letters.

The old woman scowled at Blanche then looked out the window above her sink. When she turned her focus back to her guests, she let out a gasp and pointed to a ring with Celtic trinity knot and circle design on Blanche's finger. "That's one pretty ring you've got there." She took on an accusatory tone. "Where'd you get it?"

Blanche put her hands in her lap and fidgeted. "Um, our mom had one made for me, one for Ray and one for Carly Mae, um, before she took off. Grams gave them to us last Christmas."

Ray held up his hand. "They match the one our mom has. "

Tam-Tam grabbed hold of Ray's arm, pulled him close and squinted at the ring. "Looks mighty familiar." She squeezed his hand hard.

Ray pulled away. "Jeez, what a grip. That hurt!"

"Where'd your mom get hers? In a pawn shop?"

"It was pinned to her baby blanket," Blanche said.

Ray rubbed his hand. "It connects to our heritage. That's what Grams says."

"Your heritage huh? How could she know? She's talkin' through her rear end," Tam-Tam growled.

There was an awkward moment of silence before Tam-Tam snatched the bride from Ray and walked her treasures back to the cabinet and tucked them in.

Gathering her courage, Blanche probed, "Why not make a doll that looks like Maridee or Tempest or Varnie? Why pick Grams?"

"I have my reasons." Tam-Tam returned to the table and lifted the now empty plate and made her way toward the counter by the stove, kicking aside shopping bags overflowing with junk mail on her way.

"Those brownies sure were good. Carly Mae's gonna be upset she missed out on this adventure," Ray said.

"Is she scared to upset your grandma? I know very well Missy don't want you here."

"Scared?" Blanche shook her head. "No, it's nothing like that. She's just a little bent out of shape today."

Tam-Tam returned to the table and smacked her lips. "Well, sorry to hear that."

"Are there really purple fish with green polka dots in your hole?" Ray asked.

"Orange with purple, too?" Blanche chimed in.

"Like I said. Don't believe everything you hear.»

Blanche couldn't stifle her curiosity. "What about people saying you can live on air and water?" she asked.

"Questions, questions, too many questions," Tam-Tam said. "You twins is like peas in a pod. Is your sister like that, too? I reckon she's quite a bit different, from everything I've heard. See, I ain't the only one people talk about."

"Of course, she's different. Ray and I, we're twins," Blanche said.

"Could be more to it than that," Tam-Tam said.

Blanche pinched the spot above her nose between her eyebrows. "She's a wonderful sister except every now and then when she acts like nobody in the world could possibly understand her. That's irritating. Right, Ray?"

Ray stared into the kerosene lamp.

"Ray?" Blanche tapped his arm. "Ray?"

He shuddered. "What if Carly Mae's not really our sister."

"Well, this is the first I've ever heard anything like that come out of your mouth. Why ever would say that right out of the blue? It's downright creepy." Blanche stood up.

"She is different from us," Ray said.

Blanche edged toward the door. "We're twins and she's not. End of story." She placed her hand on the knob. "We should go."

Tam-Tam curled her lip and cackled, exposing the gap where an incisor and eyetooth should have been. "Ask that no-good grandmother of yours what she thinks.»

"Are you coming with me, or not?" Blanche said to Ray. "Snap out of it!"

Ray blinked then trained his eyes on Tam-Tam as he rose from the chair. "I don't know what just got into me." He joined Blanche at the door.

"Aw, I'm just pokin' to find out what you're made of." Tam-Tam leaned on the table.

"Uh, thanks for the brownies," Blanche said. She exited, grabbed her fishing rod and the beat-up tackle box she and Ray shared, and ran down the path toward the river.

"Yeah, thanks." Ray rushed to catch up with Blanche, snatching his rod before he took to the air, skipping the stairs in a leap that would have been the envy of the celebrated Soviet ballet dancer, and 1961 defector, Rudolf Nureyev.

Tam-Tam moseyed out the door and called, "Come back soon."

At a bend in the river out of Tam-Tam's view, brother and sister stopped, put down their fishing gear, and removed their sandals.

"What did you mean about Carly Mae not being our sister?" Blanche dipped her feet into the water. "Where on earth did that come from?"

Ray waded in. "It hit me when I stared into that lantern. I remembered a snippet from before, something someone said about our dad not really being our dad. Nuts, huh? It was before the twister, so it's kind of fuzzy."

"We shouldn't have come here," Blanche said. "Grams told us not to."

Ray stood tall and declared, "We're almost sixteen now. We can make our own decisions."

Blanche entered the water. "Those dolls are so weird—Whoa! Look behind you."

"What?" He spun around.

"The fish …"

Swimming toward them were dozens of polkadot carp in an array of bright color combinations.

Ray dove under, then resurfaced.

"Look how fast they go, like a carnival ride." Blanche said.

They stood still as the fish circled them several times before darting away.

"Now it's like they were never here." She gazed into water so clear, she could see a hangnail on her big toe.

"We might have to do some sleuthing about her, you know, about us," he said.

Blanche hit the surface with her palms, sending a wave of water into his face. "Sleuthing, my eye!"

He blasted her back. Their laughter carried to Tam-Tam's porch, where she eased into a squeaky swing. She lit her corncob pipe, inhaled, leaned back, exhaled and rasped, "Take that, Missy Lake."

Chapter 10

*C*arly Mae awoke to morning sunlight warming her face and fierce grumbling in her tummy. She'd missed both lunch and supper the day before and was famished. After changing into shorts and T-shirt, she padded barefoot out of her room, Buster at her heels. Once downstairs, she let the dog outside, then shuffled toward the kitchen. Familiar voices mingled with the smell of pancakes on the griddle. Buoyed by the bloom of a new day, she was hopeful she'd be able to break the news to her family that Jasper couldn't be trusted and figure out how to wrestle the town from his grasp. She slowed, however, when she heard snippets of a disturbing conversation—the second in as many days.

Missy, Blanche and Ray didn't notice her listening, mouth agape, at the doorway. She had reached the threshold when, after incessant needling from the twins, Missy admitted Damon wasn't the twins' birth father. Velda had broken up with Damon, who was away at college, when a riverboat gambler detoured up the Bendy to escape from a handful of passengers who claimed he'd cheated them. He seduced lonesome Velda, promised her a life more lavish than she'd ever dreamed, and then abandoned her when he learned she was with child. Ever devoted to Velda, Damon came home to marry her and claim the twins as his own.

"So we have a different dad? Where is he now?" Ray asked.

"Did he ever look for us?" Blanche chimed in.

Missy shook her head. "I'm sorry to say, my darlings, he was killed in some fight over a card game. He'd been cheatin' again. I'm not even sure you were born yet when that happened."

With anxiety clogging her throat, Carly Mae stomped into the room and glared at Missy. "When were you planning to tell me all of this?" She turned her wrath on the twins next. "And how long have you kept your suspicions from me?"

"Oh, my dear, it's not what you think." Missy moved with arms outstretched toward Carly Mae.

Later, if the four people in that room could have changed that moment, every one of them would have. But how could they have predicted what was to come? This was lamented in whispers throughout Kiminee in the tense months that followed.

Carly Mae shunned her grandmother's entreaty. She blasted through the house, sprang onto the porch, down the steps, and across the lawn. Missy was next through the door, followed by Blanche and Ray.

"Come back here right this minute, Carly Mae Foley!" Missy called.

The crushed teen turned to face her grandmother. "Why should I? You're just like Jasper, hiding things we need to know." She spun around, leaped onto the sidewalk and sprinted away.

Confused by Carly Mae's extreme reaction, Ray plunked down on the stairs. "What does Jasper have to do with this?"

Missy took in a deep breath, trying to slow her pounding heart. "Search me."

"Why is she so worked up anyway?" Ray continued. "She's not the one whose father isn't really her father."

Missy patted the top of Ray's head, leaving flour fingerprints in his blond hair. "Don't go sayin' that. You know as well as me that Damon's your dad, blood or no blood."

Blanche leaned over the railing and watched her sister's ponytail swing as she trotted away. "I think it's cause we didn't tell her as soon as we came back from Tam-Tam's yesterday. We should have woken her up before we went to Grams."

"That's not fair." Ray's voice rose in pitch. "She shut us out, remember?"

"What's done is done, I guess." Blanche rubbed a solitary tear that dribbled from her eye.

"It wasn't my place to tell any of you about your biological father. It was up to your parents," Missy said, wiping her hands on her apron. "It certainly wasn't up to Tam-Tam to put ideas in your head."

Blanche continued to watch Carly Mae recede. "I wonder where she's going."

"The black-eyed Susan field," Ray said. "She'll lean against the old willow at the pond, most likely."

"Sure is a long ways out." Blanche scratched a mosquito bite behind her knee."

Missy peered at her grandchildren. "See what comes of consorting with Tam-Tam? I told you not to go there. I knew she'd get you snooping into things better left alone."

"What about the truth?" Blanche accused.

"Hold your horses, girl. Truth is one darned complicated thing," Missy said.

"I can't believe you're going on like a huge heap of manure didn't just land in our laps." Blanche scratched harder.

"No need to talk like that. We'll figure it out when Carly Mae gets back." Missy pointed to Blanche. "And stop that itchin'. You'll only make it worse. Now, if you'll excuse me, I have pies to finish." She shuffled back inside.

Blanche sat next to Ray. "Maybe Carly Mae feels all alone. All alone in this world."

"As I see it, there's no such thing as a half sister or brother. You can't cut yourself in two." Ray squirmed, then squinted at Carly Mae's shrinking figure. "Man alive, her feet are gonna be sore when she gets home."

Carly Mae jogged nonstop until she reached the willow. Chest heaving, she slowed and approached the edge of the pond. It was surrounded by acres of black-eyed Susans. In the distance were a rundown farmhouse, barn, chicken coop and silo. Everyone in Kiminee knew the lore, and it was common for folks to stop there and contemplate when they had things to sort out. Fleur Kiminee, matriarch of the town's founding family, planted the flowers to ease her sorrow when her youngest child, Suzette, was snatched by bounty hunters seizing anyone they could pass off as an escaped slave. Fleur was Creole, originally from New Orleans; her husband, Charles, was descended from French trappers who journeyed to Illinois in the eighteenth century. Back then, the name was spelled Kimine and pronounced *key-mean*, but somewhere along the line, people started pronouncing it *ki-mi-knee*, so Charles changed the spelling to match. Charles and Fleur were proud of all their children, especially their little girl. Unlike her brothers, who had straight brown hair, olive skin and tawny eyes, Suzette had skin the color of milk chocolate, midnight eyes and black hair cascading in ringlets down her back.

When he learned Suzette had been taken, Charles rounded up a group of neighbors and attempted to track the mercenaries—to no avail. Fleur became obsessed, working sunrise to sunset tending her beds of black-eyed Susans. She stopped caring for her home and family. Her shoulders grew hunched, her fingers blackened by dirt. Charles found her body floating in the pond at 5:05 one afternoon. As he pulled her out, the flowers' petals turned from yellow to red and took on a translucent glow that made his heart stop momentarily. A few days later, he left on horseback in a renewed search for Suzette, but couldn't find her. He repeated his search year after year, but never found a trace of his daughter.

The buildings where the Kiminees had once worked and dreamed had fallen into disrepair, but Fleur's flowers continued to proliferate; neither grass, nor herb, nor any other flora or fauna were among them. And locals swore they gleamed when in bloom like rubies at 5:05 each day.

Carly Mae picked up a flat rock and skipped it, just like her father taught her and the twins to do long ago. She found another rock and skipped it, too, and studied the ripples until the surface calmed. The faint sound of a motor broke the silence. She looked over her shoulder and saw a familiar brown Jewel Tea truck chugging toward her.

When the vehicle pulled to a stop, Dusty Lambert climbed out and waved to Carly Mae while brushing wrinkles from his uniform and adjusting his hat. He was the high school's star reporter, the one who found Carly Mae's violin after the terrible twister touched down. He still hoped to become a journalist one day, but his dad, who had worked for Jewel for three decades, suffered a stroke when Dusty was a freshman at University of Illinois. Dusty's mom, a new widow with no outside job experience, had three other children to raise. Dusty returned home and took over his father's sales territory.

Twenty-three and enterprising, he was affectionately known as the Jewel Tea Man. He sold much more than tea and coffee—everything from kitchenware in an autumn-leaf pattern to strawberry toothpaste and potato chips in tins. For many locals, his visits were the highlight of their week. He knew how to spin a yarn and make people laugh, so they ordered little things they didn't need just to keep him coming back. Missy was one of his regular customers. Carly Mae, Ray and Blanche enjoyed seeing new items he demonstrated in their home week to week. Unbeknownst to Missy, he always added a few small items to her orders and paid for them out of pocket. It pained him he couldn't bring the Foley children's parents back, but he could at least give them a treat every week.

Dusty joined Carly Mae at the pond. "What are you doin' all the way out here?"

Tension in her gut eased with his approach. She saw compassion in his brown eyes whenever they spoke. "It's a long story." She skipped another rock, then picked up two more and handed one to him.

"Out with it, kiddo." He tossed his rock. It skipped four times before sinking.

"Great toss!" Carly Mae threw hers with a deft flick of her wrist. It skipped four times, too.

"Say, you're good at this." He stared into the calming water, then turned toward her. "I've got plenty of time—only two more customers left today, Varnie and Leolia, right up the road."

His kindness broke through reservations she had about sharing what she'd just learned. "Blanche and Ray, they have a different dad than me." Her voice cracked as she struggled to continue. "Damon's not their real dad."

"Blanche and Ray?"

"Grams didn't plan to tell us. She's kept it secret all this time."

"To be honest, plenty of us have wondered where they got that light hair and pale blue eyes," Dusty said.

"I thought it was recessive genes or something. This is bad, really bad. I was already an outsider, 'cause of the twin thing. I swear, they can read each other's thoughts."

Dusty put an arm around her. "But you know you're still family, right? Things don't have to change just because of this."

"I guess." Carly Mae drew a line in the dirt with her toe.

"Say, you know, I have some booties in the truck, new item this week. I'll get you a pair. They're cool. They fold flat, small enough to stick 'em in your pocket."

Carly Mae looked up and giggled despite the tears sliding down her face. "In case you're ever out on the road and happen to need new footwear?"

Dusty chuckled on the way to the truck, where he riffled through his inventory and found the booties. He was closing up when a man emerged from woodland across the road. He was dressed in frayed and wrinkled shirt and pants ripped at the knees and streaked with grass stains. His mud-brown hair stuck out like feathers at his ears, and a matching beard and mustache gave him the look of a giant feral cat. He pointed a pistol at Dusty. "Gimme yer keys."

Neither Dusty nor Carly Mae had ever imagined an encounter like this. To her great dismay, Carly Mae froze, horrified. Dusty felt like his blood had turned to molasses. He struggled to speak.

"Say, now, I don't want trouble." Dusty drawled, as he wiped moist palms on his pants. "I've got folks to see up the road, folks who depend on me."

"Oh, is that right?"

"Yes, sir, it is." Dusty stood straighter in defiance.

"Let's see how all them folks like this." The man fired.

Hit in the chest, Dusty called out to Carly Mae. "Run, run!"

As he fell, the booties flew up and soared into the willow. Jolted into action, Carly Mae sprinted, screaming, up a largely overgrown gravel road toward the farmhouse.

"Best quit runnin' right now, girlie, if you know what's good for you."

Carly Mae raced ahead. The assailant fired. Gravel sprayed her feet and legs. She stopped, worked her Celtic ring to her fingertip, and flicked it to the ground as she turned around.

It was in the arms of Earl Wiggs that Dusty Lambert whispered, "Thank you life; thank you love," before his last breath rattled away.

With it went the wind. Until Dusty was laid to rest in Blessed Heaven cemetery, no tree branches swayed in all of Kiminee, no leaves shivered, no stray papers bounced along sidewalks, not one porch chime jingled. Electric fans created not the slighted breeze.

Finally, as the coffin inched below ground, Dusty's mother keened with a ferocity that broke everyone there into sobs, creating cacophony that awakened the sky and brought torrents. People wailed and swayed in their black clothes, rain pelting them for a good hour before, one by one, they left, uncertain what to think or do now that their community had been breached by murder. Maybe kidnapping, too, though there were differing opinions on why Carly Mae was missing.

When he learned about Dusty and Carly Mae, Jasper put old Mick Deely in charge of the academy's summer program, which was a series of age-appropriate music workshops, and took to his bed. Within a few days, his skin took on orange undertones, and circles of deep purple formed under his soulful eyes. Emily, overcome with nausea in air she said suffocated her like an overbearing grandparent, did her best to nurse him, but to no avail. He remained abed.

Earl Wiggs spent most of his time at the police station in the aftermath, often sleeping in a cell instead of going home. He was determined to solve Dusty's murder and find Carly Mae. He had joined the force the year of the terrible twister. When Kiminee's ancient, half-blind, toothless peace officer, Maurice T. Brewer, finally turned in his badge and limped to Touch of Kindness Rest Home, where he passed away, wheezing and cursing. The next day, Earl, who had studied criminal justice in junior college, stepped in. Folks didn't mind that Earl's qualifications were thin. They agreed he took to the job like butter on pancakes. He had an ulterior motive, too. As a police officer he had resources to search for his childhood friends Velda and Damon. He was one of the few who didn't believe Damon was dead, and he thought Velda could be convinced to come home if he could just find her.

Velda, Damon and Earl had formed a bond the day Earl joined the sixth-grade class at Bentley Elementary. His family had just moved to Kiminee from Kentucky. At recess, some classmates made fun of his kinky locks and mocha skin. That's when the teacher, Miss Egan, stepped in. "You know our town's founding family was French and Creole, and their daughter, Suzette, was most likely sold into slavery, right?" She surveyed the children bunched around her. "You can't tell by looking at me, but I am one of their descendants. I take any judging of people by their skin color personally."

The name-callers looked down at the grass under their feet, up in the clouds—anywhere but in Miss Egan's eyes.

Then Damon spoke up, "My last name's Foley, but I'm not just Irish. That's my dad's side. On my mom's side we're Welsh, Danish, Illini and African."

"That's, that's, wow!" Velda jumped up and down. "My mom's got some Illini, too, and a little Chickasaw, a lot of English, some French, and she's not sure what else."

The class troublemaker, Bud Tarr, sneered. "That says zero about you. You could be from Mars for all we know, since you're adopted."

Damon lurched forward to stand nose to nose with Bud. "Watch your mouth!"

Quick as a father fox protecting a pup, Earl stomped to Damon's side. "Yeah," he challenged.

Miss Egan pointed to Bud, Damon and Earl. "Settle down, boys, or you will be staying after school to write lines for me." Then she spoke to the whole class. "We've got a unit on the Civil War coming up this month. It'll be good for all of us."

The bell rang, signaling the end of recess. Damon, Earl and Velda walked back to class together and remained close ever after.

Without them, Earl felt lost. He prayed every night to Saint Anthony of Padua, the patron saint of lost things and missing people, for help in finding his friends. After Carly Mae disappeared, he added her to his prayers. He investigated every lead, no matter how small. On his list of stops was the old Kiminee property. Rumors were circulating that a band of young people with scraggly hair, beads around their necks, rips in their filthy jeans, and a penchant for dancing in circles were squatting there.

Meanwhile, Buster stood with ear cocked, dust taunting his black nose, humidity seeping through tri-color fur to flaxen skin. Blanche and Ray, sleuthing on their own, found the canine sentinel while retracing Carly Mae's steps. They called him; he pawed the gravel. They coaxed him with velvet voices as they approached; he wouldn't budge. Blanche patted his head while Ray tugged his collar; the dog growled, pawed the gravel. No matter what they did, he refused to move. They ran to the butcher downtown, brought back a meaty bone and dropped it in front of him. He ignored it, pawed some more.

At last, Blanche's gaze shifted to the gravel, and she saw the ring with Celtic design that matched her own and Ray's. She picked it up and ran with her brother to the police station. She handed the treasure to Earl and told him it was a sure sign Carly Mae had been taken against her will—maybe by whoever killed Dusty. Earl scribbled notes on a yellow pad as they spoke. When they finished giving their report, he told them he hoped they were wrong, hoped Carly Mae had simply run away, hoped she just longed for adventure in a more interesting place than Kiminee, Illinois. But his worried eyes conveyed no such hopes; in his heart, Earl Wiggs knew the twins were on to something.

Randy Tarr steered his turquoise Chevy pickup off the highway, through a fallow field and parked behind a stand of birch by the old Kiminee family property. He clasped an Antonio y Cleopatra cigar smoldering in the ashtray, took a long puff and stubbed it out as he exhaled, filling the cab with smoke. He coughed, grabbed his Winchester 94 from the passenger side, muttered, "I'll get you sons of bitches," and existed the truck.

With weapon slung over his shoulder, Randy crept up an overgrown path leading toward the back of the property. Sweat beaded on his face, neck and arms as he made his way to a rosebush hedge that surrounded the backyard where the Kiminee children once played. Usually wild and tangled, the hedge was clipped. "I'll be damned," he said. "Little fuckers playin' fix-up think they can waltz in and take over."

At a break in the hedge by a garage freshly painted red and sporting a mural of giant ears of corn on one side, Randy entered the yard and slinked across the newly mown lawn to the main house. Not one board creaked as he climbed the stairs and crossed the porch. He tried the door. It was open. He stepped into the kitchen where his stomach growled at the scents of tomato, basil, garlic, oregano and Italian sausage. He stood tall, then made his way on polished oak boards toward drum thumps, guitar licks and howling vocals coming from the front of the house. At the living room doorway, he paused, inhaled marijuana-scented air and listened to voices singing along off key, "Like a rolling stone, like a complete unknown, no direction home."

He counted to five and burst into the room, rifle drawn. "Where is she?" he demanded.

Two young women on a Persian-style rug, grabbed each other and hid under large pillows. A cat leaped over a couch by the window and crouched against the glass. A long-haired man by the turntable that was playing Dylan's *Highway 61 Revisited* album held up his hands and said, "Um, where is who?"

Randy lurched forward and pointed the Winchester at the man's head. "You know who, you useless squatter."

"Hey now, I'm no squatter. This is my place."

"Sure, and I'm President Lyndon Johnson."

"I don't know who you're looking for, fella, but—"

"Carly Mae. I'm looking for Carly Mae. What did you do with her?"

"You think we took the Foley girl?" A woman with thick eyeliner above and below each eye peeked out from beneath the pillows.

"I don't think. I know." He pointed the rifle at her.

From behind him a timid female voice said, "Uncle Randy? … Uncle Randy, is that you?"

Randy spun around. "Rosalie?" His rifle was three inches from his niece's chest.

Realizing the intruder was indeed her very own uncle, Rosalie scolded him. "Oh, my God! Put that thing down. It's not deer hunting season."

He lowered the weapon. "What're ya doin' with a bunch of squatters? I thought Bud raised you better than this. You're supposed to be babysitting my Cindy. What's going on?"

A little girl peeked out from a blanket in the corner of the living room. "I'm here, Daddy."

"What on earth?" Randy's face and ears reddened as he questioned his niece. "You brought my baby here of all places—to the vermin who took Carly Mae?"

"Vermin? Honestly, Uncle Randy. Sometimes I wonder how we can possibly be related." She gestured to the man at the turntable. "Meet Willie Holt. He teaches English lit three days a week at Western. His great uncle, Matthew Kiminee of Cahokia, left him this home and all the land around it in his will. The old man never had children of his own. Haven't you noticed all the nice things Willie's done already?"

"But Carly Mae—"

"Nobody was here the day she was taken. Everybody was at a music festival all the way down in Carbondale. If you'd bothered to check with Officer Wiggs, who's already been here asking loads of questions, you wouldn't have flown off the handle like this."

"Oh shit." Randy shoved the rifle into Rosalie's hands.

She forced it back. "I don't want this. No guns for me. Nuh uh."

He ran a hand through his thinning hair then motioned to his daughter. "Cindy, get over here."

The girl complied. Randy grabbed her hand and said to Rosalie, "You haven't heard the last of this. Not by a long shot. Wait till I tell your mom and dad what your idea of babysitting is. Bud will go through the roof." Then he tugged Cindy, sprinting, out of the room, down the hallway, through the kitchen and out the back door. They jumped off the porch. Cindy landed safely. He twisted his ankle when he hit the ground and limped all the way back to his truck.

In the living room, Willie said, "That was wild!" He took a toke of marijuana and passed it to Rosalie.

"Sorry," she said, inhaling deeply. "I think he meant well."

This struck her friends as hilarious. They were overcome with belly laughs. When the frivolity died down, Rosalie let out a little chortle, and the room filled with giggles and hoots again. This continued until, finally, Willie said, "Let's eat."

They barged down the hall and stampeded into the kitchen, where talk of Randy Tarr's grand entrance dominated. While they gobbled a spaghetti feast, they exaggerated his bulk, the rumble of his voice, the thunder of his footsteps. In retellings, details were added: the Winchester went off, windows shattered, a chandelier fell from the ceiling, he was wrestled to the ground but regained the upper hand before escaping by breaking through a kitchen wall. By the end of the evening, Randy Tarr was the stuff of Kiminee legend.

Chapter 11

Sister Ann Marie rubbed her lower back, yawned and flicked on the light in her office closet. Lining the walls were eight wooden file cabinets, four drawers each. For weeks, she'd been alone in the building, listening to its groans, hums and squeaks while searching through empty classrooms, forgotten dorms and alcoves. She'd located documents, discarded duplicate and extraneous information, and saved each child's essentials: date of birth and birth parents, if known; date of arrival; date and details of adoption, if applicable; grade and test reports; and graduation or transfer date. These records, some dating to the mid-nineteenth century, were destined for the Ursuline Academy in Springfield. In a matter of months, St. Angela Merici Children's Home and School would be closed for good.

"One drawer left in this closet," Sister Ann Marie muttered as floorboards creaked underfoot. "Don't fret." She tapped the wood with her toe. "Someone will buy you, and you'll have a brand new purpose."

She leaned down, rolled open a drawer and removed several hanging files, which exposed a layer of crinkled manila paper at the bottom. She took out the rest of the files, then pried out a lumpy, 10" x 13" envelope and carried it to her desk. She set it on her blotter and rubbed a hand over the surface. In the bold print of her former mentor, the dearly departed Sister Mary Margaret, was the name Ellyanna.

The weary nun sat down, unfastened the clasp and reached inside. She pulled out several pages of school records; a stack of notes on index cards bound with rubber bands; a rumpled handkerchief; a beaded, red change purse; and an unopened letter addressed to Ellyanna Lowry. She skimmed the school records, then slowed down to read the index cards. When she finished, she read them again while fingering her rosary and moving her lips in silent prayer. Finally, she replaced the rubber bands and reached for her letter opener. But then the banker's lamp on her desk flickered like a strobe light. She blinked, pulled back her arm and regarded the lamp. "Okay, okay. Not mine to read."

The lamp resumed its usual, steady glow. She leaned back in the chair, swiveled to face the window and stared at a verdant lawn, petunia beds and cornfields beyond as minutes ticked slowly by on the wall clock above the door. Then she spun back to face the desk and thumbed through her Rolodex. When she spotted Jasper and Emily Skrillpod's card, she stopped and picked up the phone.

Chapter 12

Stiff after hauling a load of avocados from Salinas to Indianapolis, Jeff stretched his limbs, ambled to his cousin Maxine's door and rang the bell. Half of the chimes hissed and squeaked, giving what was once a sweet melody a spastic feel. The Victorian cottage was on New Jersey Street a block from where Peoples Temple founder Jim Jones had mesmerized locals with his utopian visions before packing up and moving, along with most of his congregation, to California.

Jeff waited a while without a response before trying the bell again, then grinned when Maxine opened the door.

"Hey, Jeff. You're a sight for sore eyes." She brushed thick red bangs from her eyes; they swung right back. Once coiffed and sprayed to beehive perfection, Maxine's tresses now flowed freely well below her elbows. "Come on in." She backed up to make room for him in the foyer.

He stepped over the threshold and was greeted by a pungent smell. "Whew, what's that?" He gave her a hug.

"Patchouli. I would think you'd have run across it by now with all the travelin' you do, cuz." She shuffled toward to the living room. "Anyway, sure am glad to see you."

Ferns and spider plants hung from the ceiling in the hall and at the entrance to the room. Jeff ducked several times to avoid knocking into them. "I don't really get around much, just stick to the road and try to get home as quick as possible to Barb."

"Sure am glad you two finally got hitched." Maxine sat in a thread-bare recliner and pulled at a tuft of escaped stuffing at a seam on the arm, then motioned to the couch, which was a folded futon covered with a paisley-print spread. "Have a seat."

"Ah," Jeff said, easing himself down. "This sure is low to the ground. Not like the couch Grandma gave you for your home on Walker. This whole place is different, real different."

"I gave my house and everything in it to the church. No way to undo that. Can't cry over split milk. I'm a renter now—and a free spirit."

"There's something to be said for that. You don't get blindsided by bureaucrats who decide to route a highway around your town."

"Bright Corners is cut off now?"

"Yeah, and businesses are closing left and right."

"Will you guys be all right?"

"Who knows?"

"You can always stay with me, wherever I go."

"I appreciate that." He lifted a paperback from a pile of books and magazines on the wicker coffee table. "*The Teachings of Don Juan*, huh." He thumbed through the pages. "I heard some talk about this on the CB. The guys all think he's a fraud or nuts or both, but then the whole world seems nuts these days."

"It's a best seller! Do you think everybody who likes his message is crazy?" She slapped both hands on the chair, sending dust right into her face. She leaned forward and coughed. "This old thing might not have been such a good find."

"Do you need some water?" He put the book down.

"Nah, I'm fine." She stood and circled the room, then sat down beside him. "So what brings you here in the middle of the week when it's not anybody's birthday or wedding or a holiday barbecue or anything?"

"I was hoping Velda would be home."

"She's asleep in the back. We had kind of a wild night."

"In midweek?"

"We stopped in for a drink at the Whistle Stop and were in a booth, thought we had privacy, but before you know it, a guy breaks a glass on Velda's head.

"But why would someone—"

"It was bleedin' somethin' awful. We had to go to emergency—"

"But why crack Velda on the head, I—"

"She couldn't sleep a wink last night. It's not like the wound was all that bad once it was cleaned up either, no concussion or anything. Heads just always bleed to beat the band, don't they? And those people. At the hospital. They got carried away, I think, and did the stitches too tight. That's why she was so miserable." Maxine leaned against Jeff. A tear slid to the corner of her mouth. She licked it off.

He put an arm around her. "I'm really sorry. But I still don't get it. A whack out of the blue like that."

"Out of the lavender maybe."

"Huh?"

"Never mind. You're too square to know anything about being queer."

Suspecting Maxine was pulling his leg, Jeff shifted position so he could see her face. "Queer? Come on."

Maxine looked away, focusing on her lap. She intertwined her fingers and rubbed her palms with her thumbs in a frenzied rhythm. She could pretend she was joking or stick with the truth and risk her big, lovable, clueless cousin's condemnation. She quickened the pace of her fidgeting. "Yeah, queer, okay? We were snugglin' and kissin' in the booth, and this great big man with medals pinned all over his jacket beaned her. Almost got me, too."

Jeff covered her hands with one of his to still the movement. "You and Velda are an item?"

Sensing curiosity, not judgment, she continued. "We started out as roommates after we parted from Jim Jones and his giant messiah complex, but then love just grew. We're not exclusive."

"Velda's still married, you know."

"We're bi."

He raised an eyebrow. "You mean you're—"

"We're bisexual. We love men and women, both."

"Oh, Lordie."

"Not at the same time, no orgies."

"That's reassuring." He smirked.

"No need for sarcasm."

"I'm sorry. I'm just concerned. That's all. You're not kids, you know, like those dropouts flooding to San Francisco. You're mature women."

"It's not just kids chasin' dreams to the Haight-Ashbury."

"I suppose you're right. How did the reverend take it? The idea of you two—"

"There was nothin' between us before he left town. I expect no church would be okay with us now."

"It does seem to fly in the face of the Good Book, but then, I must confess I've read little pieces of it and surely heard plenty of readings in church, but I've never read the Bible much. I can't say for sure what it really teaches about stuff like that." Jeff raised his arms above his head, stretched his legs alongside the coffee table and yawned. "It seems much of it is open to interpretation."

"Like life itself." Maxine eased herself up and ambled to the window, pulled aside a beaded curtain and peered out. "That's some rig you've got. Your home away from home."

Jeff looked toward the window. "Sure is." He cleared his throat, turned his head toward Maxine and asked, "So when do you think Velda will wake up?"

"Hadn't thought about it." She continued to look out the window.

"It's really important."

She swiveled around and squinted at him. "That doesn't sound good."

"If ever there was a time for her to return to Kiminee, it's now. Her family needs her."

"Oh, well." She shrugged. "The kids would be better off with their mom, naturally, but no one can convince her of that."

"I guess the news hasn't reached as far as Indianapolis."

"News? It drives us nuts, everything bad all the time, so we don't get the paper, don't have a TV."

"Carly Mae's gone, probably kidnapped. And the local Jewel Tea man is dead, probably killed by whoever took Carly Mae."

She paced the room. "Oh, no, oh, my, oh, shit!"

"Come here." He stood and opened his arms wide.

She slid over and snuggled into his embrace. With her ear against his chest, she listened to his strong heartbeat and took several long breaths. "Should I wake her up?"

"Maybe not just yet. I guess an hour or two won't make much difference."

Maxine looked up into his face and saw the wrinkles above his nose and around his eyes had deepened. "So, are we okay? You and me? You seem—"

"I'm all worried and jumpy, but it's because of what I have to tell Velda, not because of … you know."

Maxine let go of her cousin and backed up a few steps. "Let's get dinner ready. Lots of veggies to chop. It'll keep us from frettin' ourselves silly."

He bent over, touched his toes and rose, face flushed. "What are we having? Porterhouse? Tri tip?"

"In your dreams, cuz, in your dreams. You're about to make your first vegetarian feast." She took his hand and the two strode into the hall and toward the kitchen.

Meanwhile, Velda slept beneath a tie-dyed sheet, her body warmed by late-afternoon sun. Through an open window, a breeze carried the whiff of rose petals from Maxine's yard mixed with hamburgers grilling next door and fumes from a multitude of vehicles traversing the city. Velda dreamt on, unaware of the upheaval awaiting her.

The earth shuddered through all of Kiminee when Jeff's red semi rumbled and grumbled toward Missy's home. The elders residing at Touch of Kindness rest home gripped armrests and bed rails. Grant, at Kiminee Five 'N Dime, slapped and bumped down aisles, trying to keep needle packets, spools of thread, buttons, greeting cards, shoelaces and polish, costume jewelry and bins of penny candies from clattering onto the scuffed wooden floor. Chester Dillard did the same with nails, curtain rods, nuts and bolts, locks, paint cans, and so forth at the hardware store. Students at the academy hid under their desks. Animals in fields stood frozen in fright. The coleus on Earl's desk rolled leaves to stem and bowed. Owls awoke from their daytime slumber and who-who'd like beaky foghorns.

Some folks thought the commotion was the onset of Armageddon; others were sure the Russians had messed with the atmosphere and created a new kind of thunder strong enough to penetrate soil and rock. A few assumed a heretofore-unknown geologic fault had growled to life. Whatever the cause, everyone in town was soon on the move, eager to see what was going on. A brilliant double rainbow greeted them, though no drops had fallen and no clouds were adrift in the pale blue sky.

It wasn't long before a crowd gathered at Missy's, awestruck by the sight of the vehicle, which had grown longer and louder as it made its way through town. By the time it grunted and hissed to a halt at Missy's curb, it was about 10 percent bigger than it used to be.

When things finally calmed, Jeff and Maxine creaked open their respective doors. But Velda scrunched herself into a little ball in the back of the cab. "Close the doors. I'm not ready. I can't," she blurted loud enough for people closest to the truck to hear. "If I'd stayed, Carly Mae wouldn't have been taken. She'd still be here. No one will ever forgive me. "

People pressed toward the truck, attempting to get within earshot. Two teenagers even vaulted onto the engine hood and saw Maxine reach back, pat Velda's arm and say, "Of course you can. We talked about this. And I'm here for you. We'll live here permanently if need be."

Jeff pounded the windshield and shooed the teens away. With gleeful whoops, they jumped down, and soon everyone knew who was in the truck and what they were doing. The minutes ticked on and on and on some more. It seemed an eternity that Jeff and Maxine worked to coax Velda outside, but only two members of the cheese co-op left the scene, and that's because a curious cloud of smoke rose from their processing plant, and they feared something had gone wrong with their signature Kiminee cheese, which was created by Tempest Binsack's daughter Gloria and sold like crazy at both Suzette's and the Five 'N Dime. The rest of the group stayed put like ticket holders at a raffle, hoping their numbers would soon be called.

Then Maxine opened her door wide and leaned out.

Maridee Pratt gasped at the sight of her glorious red hair. "My goodness. She looks like a goddess," she whispered to Tempest, who was gaping at the sight of the svelte, young stranger.

"A veritable siren," Tempest whispered back.

Maxine climbed down and held the door open for Velda, who emerged moments later—to a series of gasps observers could not repress, because the Velda they saw reaching for Maxine's hand bore little resemblance to the Velda they knew and loved.

"Wha's up with that hair stretchin' below her shoulders like a big ole patch a crabgrass? And look at that beaded headband 'cross her forehead," Abby Louise said to Tam-Tam, who gripped her arm for support.

"She ain't no Indian. Band looks downright silly on 'er," Tam-Tam griped.

Nearby Maridee confided in Tempest. "I swear she's lost her sense of style. I mean, look at that thin top with spaghetti straps and no bra. No bra! Missy will be fit to be tied."

"That skirt's a conundrum, too," Tempest replied. "Looks like it's made from a bunch of old men's ties sewn together."

With so many eyes trained on her, Velda quivered as she walked up the path with Maxine. Jeff was close behind, followed by several people trying to get near enough to hear what they might say.

Moments later they reached the porch, and Missy flung open her door. If anything about her daughter's appearance shook her equilibrium, she didn't let on. She just grabbed Velda so tight everyone could feel the squeeze, even those muttering across the street about who Velda's new friends might be and where she'd been.

When Missy finally released Velda, she waved to the crowd and said, "My baby's home. Thank the Lord!" She ushered Velda and Maxine inside, but Jeff stopped at the door, shook Missy's hand, and said he had to get right home to his sweet wife, Barbara, at the Good Luck Café.

"Nonsense," Missy declared. "You're not leavin' here without a good meal in ya, and at least one picnic basket of goodies for the road, including a couple slices of pineapple upside down cake fresh baked today—one for you and one for your missus."

"But—'

"No buts, fella. You brought my girl—and my grandkids' mother—home. That makes you an honorary member of our clan. Come on in and meet everybody." She took hold of his wrist and pulled him across the threshold. She pointed to the living room and said, "Have a seat."

He hesitated. "If you don't mind, I'd like to use your phone to call Barb. She'll want to know we arrived safely and that I'll be staying for a meal."

"Sure thing." Missy motioned for him to follow her down the hall. When they reached the kitchen, she pointed to the phone. "Help yourself."

He picked up the receiver, which was still warm from Missy's last conversation, and dialed home.

Meanwhile, Velda and Maxine hesitated at the edge of the living room, where Ray and Blanche slouched on the couch and regarded their mother with as much enthusiasm as they would toe fungus.

Velda stepped forward tentatively. "Um, hi kids."

"Gee, nice of you to stop by, Mom." Blanche sneered and jutted out her chin.

Ray grabbed a potato chip from a bowl on the coffee table, dunked it in onion dip, popped it into his mouth and chewed slowly.

Some snoops who had crept up to a side window to watch the reunion said Blanche looked like her grandmother in a particularly snippy moment. Others said she was just being a surly teen, and who could blame her for not running to hug a mother she hadn't heard from in six long years? As for Ray, people wished he'd at least said hello. After all, his tone of voice might have clued Velda in about how he was feeling.

Sensing tension in the too-quiet living room, Missy called Blanche and Ray. "Time to set the table."

They shot up, trotted past Velda and Maxine, and helped Missy set the table and spread out serving dishes of pork roast, peas, mashed potatoes, gravy, and iceberg lettuce and tomato salad.

Missy returned to the kitchen just as Jeff was about to hang up. "Okay, hon. Don't wait up. It'll be pretty late," he said to Barb.

"Wait! I want to talk to her." Missy pointed to a lime Jell-O and mandarin orange concoction on the counter. "Take that in, will you?" She held out her hand for the phone.

Jeff handed the receiver to Missy, took the Jell-O salad and headed for the dining room.

"Tell everybody to start without me. I'll be right in," Missy said.

Ten minutes later, Missy sat down at the head of the table and caught Jeff's eye. "That sure is one fine lady you're married to. She told me about the trouble in Bright Corners, with business being way off since the highway was re-routed. I said things were boomin' here, and I'd be happy to have you spend the night so we can take you around and see the opportunity that awaits should you decide to move the Good Luck Cafe to Kiminee."

"Why, I don't know, ma'am, it's—"

"Your Barb thinks it's a grand idea. So, as far as I'm concerned the matter's settled. The Binsacks have a building you could get for a song. You've got to see it."

Throughout the meal, Velda attempted to engage Ray and Blanche in conversation, but they just offered quick yes or no answers. No amount of cajoling on the part of Missy, who more than anyone had equal sympathy for her daughter and her grandchildren, could get them to open up.

When Jeff was finally ready to leave the next afternoon, his heart was warmed by the welcome he'd received, his head was full of ideas for what he and Barb could do with the old Binsack building, and the cab was packed with enough homemade goods to last a week—all prepared by people grateful he'd brought Velda home. It seemed everyone was happy she had returned except the two who mattered most. At the curb, Jeff squeezed Velda's upper arm, leaned in and whispered in her ear, "Give it time; the kids'll come around."

Jeff climbed into his oversize truck, started the engine, waved, shifted gears and lurched away. The semi roared and belched, jolting all onlookers. The vehicle rumbled off, growing quieter and smaller with every foot as it headed out of town. Velda turned to the twins, who stood behind her and tried to put her arm around them. They shrank away like children suffering through Lilt home permanents, then stomped toward the house.

In the weeks following Velda's return, Blanche and Ray gradually warmed to her, which came as a big relief, not just to the family but to the entire town. And optimism gave the walls in Missy's home a golden sparkle when she dipped into her savings to buy Velda a doublewide mobile home and place it on the lot where Damon and Velda once lived with their children. Velda and Maxine packed up their few possessions and moved right in. Believing their mother could leave again at any time, Blanche and Ray remained with their grandmother. They did, however, accept Velda's invitation for lunch outdoors in what used to be their backyard.

Velda carried a platter of fried bologna and onion sandwiches on Wonder bread from kitchen to picnic table. "I don't see why you two can't spend the night here and try it out." She put the food on the table, where Maxine, Blanche and Ray sat.

"There is no good place for us to sleep," Blanche complained. She took a sandwich, passed the plate to Ray, lifted the top slice and squeezed French's mustard on her food.

Velda sat down. "We've got a trundle bed all set up for ya."

"A trundle bed? Come on. We're not, like, six years old anymore." Ray served himself and passed the main dish to Maxine, who took a sandwich, then put the plate down by Velda's place.

Yeah, we'll come over and stuff, but this ... it just isn't home," Blanche said.

With her elbows on the table, Velda rested chin on fists. She stared past the yard and across the field to the hickory tree where Carly Mae's fiddle had lodged during the terrible twister. She didn't eat, nor did she utter another word during the meal and cleanup afterward. She didn't even say goodbye when Blanche and Ray left.

Once they were alone, Maxine wrapped her arms around Velda and held her tight. At first Velda remained silent, but gradually her muscles relaxed, she nuzzled into Maxine, and cried. She cried for her missing daughter and wary twins, her missing husband and broken home. She remembered childhood foibles and teenage drama, people she'd loved and lost and dreams that had faded away. She cried on and on for things small and large until, long after sunset, there were no more tears. Velda yawned and rubbed her eyes as a mosquito dove toward her shoulder. She swatted it away and said, "It's okay. The twins are doin' fine, all things considered. And I can focus on finding our Carly Mae," she said.

That very day she signed up to volunteer several days a week at Suzette's to keep her finger on the pulse of the community. This didn't set well with a few members. The always-tipsy Abby Louise refused to work shifts in the shop with Velda and lobbied to have her kicked out of the organization.

"Have you seen the two of them practically sitting on top of each other on that swing built into their fancy custom porch? It's way too fine a feature for a double-wide anyway," Abby Louise said to Maridee when they were straightening shelves in the shop after closing.

"Why on earth do you care?" Maridee replied. "Keep your nose to yourself. They're not hurting you."

Abby Louise tried to get Tempest worked up one afternoon when the two bumped into each other in the Five 'N Dime's notions section. "Sometimes Velda and Maxine peck each other on the lips, you know, after dark when they think only fireflies is watchin'," she whispered.

"Oh, for goodness sakes, don't you have anything better to do?" Tempest threw two spools of thread into her shopping cart and wheeled away.

In Doc Redfield's waiting area one afternoon, Abby Louise came out of an exam room, saw Velda and paused by Rosalie Tarr, who worked the reception desk three afternoons a week. "Oh my, my, it stinks in here. Better clean out the riffraff," Abby Louise said, then sashayed toward the exit.

"You got no call to say that," Rosalie replied before the door closed behind the woman's ample backside.

Velda didn't hear either of them. She was reading an out-of-date magazine article about a quilt made for the centennial celebrating the end of the Civil War. It was created by folks from all over the Prairie State whose families had quilted for generations, but the design was untraditional, consisting of thirty squares, each of which depicted a scene from Abe Lincoln's life. Color photos on the pages showed several of the squares: Abe studying by dim firelight as a lad, walking miles through snow to return a penny to a neighbor who had overpaid him, debating Stephen A. Douglas, winning the presidency, bidding farewell to Illinois, writing to his beloved stepmother, giving the Gettysburg Address, issuing the Emancipation Proclamation, signing the Thirteenth Amendment—then his assassination and the slow-moving funeral train returning him to Illinois.

Velda got it in her head that the good people of Kiminee could make a quilt about Carly Mae to help raise awareness and money to at least pay long distance phone charges Earl Wiggs and volunteers at his office were piling up from calling all over the nation in search of possible leads. Velda was so excited at this prospect, she bolted from her chair.

"Don't go leaving on account of that old bat," Rosalie said. "She don't know from nothin'."

Velda tore out of the office, not absorbing Rosalie's words at all.

By nightfall she had enlisted several people to help, including three of Willie Holt's housemates at the old Kiminee estate. Squares—embroidered and appliquéd, bright colored and muted, realistic and abstract—soon piled up at Suzette's, the ad hoc donation center. They depicted scenes like the lemonade stand Carly Mae made to raise money for fire victims; her acrylic paintings of Buster; fiddle recitals at Touch of Kindness, where she held the Tarrs and McDuggins spellbound and softened their feud; her graduation speech at Lily Park Academy; Buster leaping into Carly Mae's arms; lilacs blooming outside her bedroom window in February; the twins, Carly Mae and Buster posing on Missy's front steps; Dusty standing beside his Jewel Tea truck; the field of shimmering black-eyed Susans.

The Suzette's took turns stitching the quit together, and Missy fashioned the border with a Celtic trinity knot design, inspired by Velda and her children's rings. When the quilt was finished, Velda marched over to Jasper's and spread it out on his bedroom floor, where he was still abed. She tugged on his arm, and with Emily's help, coaxed him to rise and have a look. She told him of her plan. As his eyes shifted from square to square, color returned to his cheeks. He wobbled out of bed, stretched and then did a little barefoot jig.

"Let me bring this to Chicago," he said to Velda. "I can display it in the gallery, and then take it to New York. I have some contacts at the Metropolitan." The old Jasper was back.

"Wow! That's more than I could have hoped for." Velda wrapped her arms around him. Emily joined her. After a long hug, the three broke apart. Jasper went to the bathroom to shower. Emily and Velda folded the quilt and tied it securely with long strips of velvet Emily had picked up at a garage sale and kept in her crafts room.

Chapter 13

Tam-Tam whisked a spider web aside as she entered her toolshed and pulled a string to turn on the bare bulb that illuminated the space. While slipping out of her sandals and into a pair of rubber garden shoes by the door, she tugged a canvas apron from a hook and tied it around her waist. It had several pockets and loops loaded with gloves, trowel, weed puller and hand clippers. She then donned a straw hat with plastic fruit glued to the band, tied it under her chin and stepped back into the yard. The door squeaked closed behind her.

At the edge of her overgrown yard, she picked up a flat of pansies, placed a small watering can on top, and followed a short path leading to the Bendy, which wrapped around and circled through Kiminee. Balancing the flowers and can in her hands, she hummed the old tune "Bicycle Built for Two" as she made her way across the river, stepping on flagstones her husband, Harlan, had placed there to make a crossing decades ago. That was before he fled after a deadly shootout with the law, never to return. The last stone wobbled when she placed her weight on it. She almost fell into the rushing water but regained her balance and finished crossing to the densely wooded side of the river, the side where no one lived.

She followed a narrow path a short distance from the bank and reached a clearing about twelve feet square edged with bushes brimming with black roses. In the center was a mound of emerald green ivy. Tam-Tam padded to the ivy, pulled out her clippers, snipped several tendrils and threw them to the side. She continued clipping until only a small amount remained at the edges of a rectangle of granite laid flat on the ground.

"There you are. It sure has been busy in our little town since that Jasper Skrillpod opened his academy. Been good for everybody, I s'pose I have t'admit." Tam-Tam patted the stone. "Folks is all full a energy like you never seen in these parts. Some fancy-ass teachers moved in to work at the school, but everyone seems to like 'em and their kids. And dairy farmers—Gloria Binsack, the Burlingtons and Tarrs, a few others—started up a cheese co-op with Skrillpod's help, not that I know what a co-op means, exactly, but it's doin' real well, so I hear."

Tam-Tam pulled up weeds as she spoke, slowly revealing a bed of coal-colored earth framing the stone. "And there's this big project goin' on to sell our local crafts. A storefront, too. Imagine that. Now, I have me some ideas about that, you know. I make beautiful dolls that have left some fussy folks speechless 'cause they're so true to life, I guess you'd say, and so they won't sell 'em. Well, in truth, it's really just one person who objects to them dolls, and she's been a big thorn in my side forever. I can't tell you how much that gnaws on me. But why burden you with this? You been gone from this world for so long. I should let you rest in peace. I don't know what keeps me comin' here. It's not like I even knew you. You was just like a January thaw—here today, gone tomorrow."

Weeding done, Tam-Tam dug holes for the pansies and patted the flowers into their new home. Several times she returned to the river, dipped the watering can in and carried the liquid back to water the flowers surrounding the headstone with no name. When the flowers were soaked, she spread the ivy clippings and weeds around the base of the rose bush hedge.

"All set now nice and pretty here for you. Peaceful, I'd say." She refastened the tools to her apron and headed back home, taking extra care not to lose her footing on the wobbly stone as the sun set.

Once inside, she put pork and beans on the stove and then settled into a rocker on her rickety front porch. She packed her corncob pipe with Edgeworth Ready Rub, lit it, inhaled deeply and rocked. "Nothin' else to do," she muttered. "Couldn't save her, didn't know she needed savin', after all."

Chapter 14

In the breakfast nook of their Lake Shore Drive luxury co-op apartment, Jasper opened the *Chicago Sun Times* while Emily served her brunch specialty: Greek-inspired omelet with feta cheese, spinach, onions, kalamata olives and an assortment of spices she would never divulge.

Jasper took a bite. "Delicious, my dear, as always."

Emily carried her plate to the table, sat down and watched Jasper, who chewed slowly, savoring every pinch of flavor. "I'm so glad the quilt brought you back to life," she said.

"I used to think it was the olives that did the trick, but now I believe it's the balance of the whole, all the flavors combined. I can never get it right when I try to make this."

"Oh, you." Emily sliced her entire omelet into rectangles slightly bigger than postage stamps. "What's on your mind?" She consumed several pieces in rapid succession.

"I can't stop thinking about our Carly Mae, how scared she must be."

"If she's still alive." Emily buttered a piece of rye toast and handed it to Jasper.

He accepted the toast. "Of course she's alive. We have to believe that."

"Yes, of course. You're right." She buttered another slice for herself. "Oh darn, the coffee." She straightened her back, preparing to rise.

"I'll get it, hon. Enjoy your meal."

"Thank you." Emily relaxed and resumed eating.

Jasper sashayed to the kitchen counter where the percolator, two blue-and-white Wisconsin Dells riverboat mugs, matching porcelain sugar bowl and creamer awaited. He poured the coffee, added a touch of half-and-half and sugar to each and returned to Emily. He placed the mugs on the table, sat down again and opened the paper to resume reading.

Emily sipped her coffee and thumbed through the *Ladies Home Journal.* For some time the crackle of turning pages was the only sound. Then Emily looked out the window to her right toward Lake Michigan and said, "You know, Mrs. Henchley called several times when you were ill, but she was a bit cryptic. What does she want?"

"Oh that—it's a matter for lawyers. Ted Mignan's on it."

"Don't shut me out, like I'm too delicate to know when there's trouble."

Jasper put the paper down. "I'm sorry. I didn't mean to imply that. I just don't want to give you more worries while Carly Mae's missing."

"I'm stronger than you think."

"If you must know, then, Henchley and Croll surprised me in the library the last day of school and made threats. They must be desperate if they drove all the way from Chicago to Kiminee to harass me for more money. Croll waved around a contract he said I signed, but it contained language I was certain I would never have agreed to. I saw Ted yesterday afternoon, and we looked over the document he's kept on file for us, the one I signed when we enrolled Carly Mae at Lily Park, and I was right. There is absolutely no language in our lawyer's copy that matches what Croll and Henchley claim I approved. I was shocked by their duplicity. I didn't want to tip my hand and reveal my suspicions when they confronted me. I told them I'd see what I could do, which really meant, I'll see my lawyer, and you'll hear from him. Then Carly Mae disappeared the very next day, and I fell apart. I'm so sorry for doing that to you."

"Oh, Jasper, you don't have to apologize. I managed to nurse you in Kiminee and stave off the nausea very well. In an odd way, it was good for me to do that." Emily gazed at waves lapping against the sandy shore then out at the great expanse of water. "I've never seen the lake so empty on a calm day. There are no boats."

"That's odd." He held a hand up to shade his eyes from the sun as he looked out. "I guess everyone's off to a slow start today."

Emily brushed a stray hair behind her ear. "There's more to it than the contract, though, isn't there? Mrs. Henchley said there are things I should know about you, things from your youth that you keep hidden."

Eyes wide, he stared at her. "What sort of things?"

"She said to ask you."

He drummed his fingers on the table. "I can't talk about it right now. If you'd come with me to New York—"

"I can't. Don't you remember? Sister Ann Marie? St. Angela Merici Children's Home and School?"

"Ah yes, it's closing. It's coming up soon."

"Not soon—tomorrow. I have to visit Sister Ann Marie today or never."

"Couldn't she mail whatever it is she has for you?"

"An envelope. She wants to hand it to me in person."

"Must be very important." He surveyed the room and paused at a wall of nineteenth century postcards with black-and-white photos on the front and notes in ornate handwriting on the back. They'd found the relics on drives all around Illinois and neighboring states. "Remember when we moved in here? The way it stormed that day? Our fledgling postcard collection was almost ruined."

"Emily pushed food around her plate. "How young we were."

"You said you didn't deserve me because you grew up in an orphanage. I told you that was hogwash, that I'd always love you, that you belonged to me no matter what."

"Why not come with me today, then?" Emily left the table, stopped to look at the postcards for a moment, then entered the living room and stood at a window that stretched almost wall to wall. The floor plan was open, so she could see Jasper when she looked to the side.

Jasper swallowed his last bite of omelet and stretched in his chair. "It's simply not possible."

"Can't the quilt wait a day? You'd like Sister Ann Marie. She was the only one who really cared about me. Most people in her position probably wouldn't bother with old papers stuffed in a forgotten file cabinet."

"I can't do that. My plane leaves for New York in less than three hours. And I'm having dinner with the Metropolitan's board this evening. Carly Mae's quilt might end up on display there." He got up, walked to the window and put his arm around her.

"You always do aim high." She leaned into him.

"Look, there are some fish or—what are they?—bobbing way, way out. See?" He pointed.

"No, I don't ... oh, wait, yes, yes, they're mighty big for fish. What a sight!"

"I do wish I could go with you today." He kissed the top of her head. "I really do."

"I know." She snuggled closer and sighed, listening to his heartbeat. "When I was little, I used to ask for my big sister, Lolly."

"You never told me that."

"The sisters assured me I just had an active imagination. They convinced me I made her up because I was lonesome."

"A sister. Imagine that."

She put her hands on the window. "Look at those, whatever they are. They're coming closer."

"Probably sturgeon."

"I don't think so. Oh, my, it can't be! I think it's a pod of seals coming toward shore."

"No! Really?" He put his nose against the glass. "Seals don't inhabit Lake Michi—" He stepped back. "But, my God, that's exactly what they are!" His throat was suddenly dry as he considered a notion about his mother he'd discarded long ago and the threat he'd gotten from Dr. Croll and Mrs. Henchley. "I might not have imagined it."

"What are you talking about?"

"You're not the only one who got bullied, badgered or coaxed out of believing something you knew was true, although I must say, my story is much more far fetched than yours."

"I don't get it."

"There's so much I've never told you—never told anyone—about my early years."

"Tell me now."

"I can't. I just … I'm not in the right frame of mind. I'm focused on getting to New York with the quilt. I just can't switch gears. But I promise I'll tell you when I get back."

She pulled away. "You exasperate me sometimes. I don't know what to think." She returned to the table, stacked the dishes and took them to the dishwasher.

"Please, just bear with me for a little while longer. I'll explain it all. I will." Jasper turned back toward the window to gape at the seals heading toward the shore. "I've got to pack now." He swallowed hard and padded to the bedroom.

She turned on the radio and let Glen Gould's recording of *Bach's Toccata in F-Sharp Minor* soothe her as she cleaned up the kitchen.

After a long drive from O'Hare Airport, where she watched Jasper's flight to New York lift off, Emily drove to St. Angela Merici Children's

Home and School. Her mouth was salt-flats dry as she sat on a straight-backed, wooden chair facing what used to be Sister Mary Margaret's desk. The nun once ran the institution like a dictator. Anyone who landed in her office was in for demerits that could mean loss of privileges for months. Not that it mattered much. The place was at the edge of a town two blocks long and surrounded by oceans of corn and soybeans. The only weekly outing was to the general store, where the old man behind the counter grouched at Emily and her friends, telling them not to touch one thing.

But that was long ago. Sister Mary Margaret was no longer alive; the children she ruled were long gone. The nun at the desk, Sister Ann Marie, had always been quick to offer a hug or piece of pithy advice, a welcome contrast to her superior.

Sister Ann Marie smiled at Emily. "It's good to see you."

Emily relaxed into the chair, recalling how Sister Ann Marie would often stay up after lights out, whispering with the girls about God and boys and the meaning of life before tiptoeing from the dorm to her own tiny room at the end of the hall. "It's good to see you, too. It's been too long."

"I've been following your life, you know, when something you and Jasper do hits the news."

"I'm sorry I haven't kept in touch."

"It's to be expected. Leaving a place like this, most of you never look back. We did our best, but there's no way to fill the void where a child's family should have been. Some are bitter that we couldn't do the impossible."

"I've never felt that, not for a minute."

"Orphanages are a thing of the past now anyway. We kept the school going as long as we could after the orphanage closed, but now that's over, too. After today, I don't know what will become of the place."

Emily gestured to stacks of boxes against a wall. "Must be a lot of work going through it all."

"I've been at it for months on end, and that's how I came across this." Sister Ann Marie held up a manila envelope. "It was in the back of the closet underneath records from the thirties and forties." She offered it to Emily.

Emily leaned forward to accept the envelope. The name Ellyanna Lowry was printed on the front. She sounded it out in her mind and a twinge of loss struck, which confused her. "What is this?"

"It should have been given to you when you left. I'll never know why Sister Mary Margaret hid it away."

"So this has to do with me?" Emily set the envelope in her lap and ran her fingers over the lettering. "Ellyanna Lowry," she said aloud. "Ellyanna Lowry," she repeated with a growing sense of familiarity. She looked up at the nun. "Was that my name?"

Sister Ann Marie nodded. "Go ahead. Open it."

Emily shook her head. "Ellyanna is such a beautiful name. Why did you change it?" She blinked back tears.

Sister Ann Marie sniffed in two short breaths, attempting to prepare herself to explain the inexplicable, justify the unjustifiable. "Sister Mary Margaret always changed the ones she didn't consider to be good Catholic names. Apparently, Ellyanna wasn't wholesome enough."

Emily unfastened the envelope clasp and lifted the flap. She pulled out several pages of school records clipped together; a beaded, red coin purse; a stack of handwritten notes on index cards; a handkerchief; and an unopened letter addressed to Ellyanna Lowry. She laid them all out on the desk and patted each item several times before removing the rubber bands holding Sister Mary Margaret's notes together.

She read the top card, dated February 7, 1936: *Child found in chapel, said her daddy told her to stay, handed me the note stapled on back.* Emily flipped the card over and unfolded the attached paper. It read, *To Whom: Ellyanna cries nonstop for her mommy and big sis, Lolly, and the baby doll. I tell her they're gone for good, but she won't stop the bellyachin'. So I hereby give up all rights to the brat. I'm not cut out for this. She'll be four in August, the fifteenth, I think. Yours truly, Just another bum down on his luck.*

Emily's face reddened. "Lolly? You mean I didn't make her up? All this time she was real?" She cupped her hands over her ears, which had grown uncomfortably warm.

"It appears so. I-I didn't … know … about this," the nun stammered.

Emily folded her hands in her lap and looked into the kindly nun's moistening eyes. "My father doesn't sound like a good man."

"We don't know the whole story. It was the Depression. It's best not to judge."

"I suppose you're right, but it's hard not to." Emily picked up the next card, dated May 9, 1936: *Child continues to ask for sister Lolly and her mom. Staff members assure her she doesn't need an imaginary sister now because there are so many children here to love. Has nightmares and wakes up with skin ice cold to the touch. Talks about a baby doll named Daphne Sunshine, but never touches dolls in the playroom. Is generally well behaved and answers to the name Emily, but still says her name is Elly or Ellyanna. No adoption requests yet.*

With a mix of anger, fear and sorrow, Emily glanced through several more cards with similar entries. One dated August 15, 1938 caught her eye: *Received phone call yesterday from a Doris Lowry, who slurred her words, may have been inebriated. She said she had been disabled due to a beating she'd gotten from her boyfriend more than two years ago and was just getting back on her feet. He ran off with her daughters, Lolly and Ellyanna, who were fourteen and three at the time. She's been calling every orphanage and children's home she can find to see if anyone has them. Ellyanna is her boyfriend's child; Doris was married to the older girl's father, but he died in an industrial accident when Lolly was eight. The woman rambled on about her abusive boyfriend. I said I might be able to help her and asked her to meet with me. We set an appointment for 1 p.m. today. She never showed. She didn't leave a number where I can reach her.*

Heart quickening, Emily fanned herself with the card and gaped at Sister Ann Marie. "Wow! I had a mother who wanted me, and she mentioned Lolly, too. This is so, so …" Tears flooded from her eyes as she returned her attention to the cards and leafed through several more. She stopped at one dated September 18, 1940: *Doris Lowry called, asking if I knew anything about her daughters. She spoke much more clearly. I asked her to meet with me today at 2 p.m. She agreed, sounded enthusiastic. It's 5:40, and she hasn't come.*

"Why didn't she come?" Emily asked without looking up. "Why?" She thumbed through more cards and stopped at one written on February 22, 1943: *The Lowry woman called. We set another appointment. Again, she didn't show, but she did, at least, call back to say she wouldn't be here. She said she hadn't recovered from her injuries and couldn't work yet, so she was living hand to mouth, sometimes on the street. She said her daughters are bound to be better off wherever they are than they would be with her. I told her she might need only a little help, but she sobbed and insisted she would make life worse for them if she found them.*

A note stapled to the February 22 one was dated March 1, 1943. It was brief: *Received a letter from Doris Lowry today with letter to Ellyanna (Emily) enclosed. No return address. She asked that if I do know where Ellyanna is, to give her the letter when she turns 18.*

Emily slammed the stack of cards down and picked up the letter. "So this is from my mother, a woman named Doris Lowry?"

"I believe so," Sister Ann Marie replied.

"And I was supposed to get this when I turned eighteen? That was sixteen years ago, sixteen years! Almost half my life! Emily grabbed the handkerchief to wipe her face. All four corners were embroidered with black-eyed Susans. "This … is … all …" She dropped the cloth and gripped the arms of the chair. "I'm … so … woo … zzzy." She slumped over, head on desk.

Later, she woke up in the convent. Not recalling at first what had occurred, she breathed in a familiar institutional smell, saw the crucifix on the wall, the beige paint and thought she was back in school. Then she saw Sister Ann Marie perched on the edge of the bed and blinked. "What happened?" she asked.

"You're awake. Thank God." Sister Anne Marie patted Emily's hand.

"Oh, my, I guess I—" memories of the meeting returned.

"Yes, you passed out. Luckily, Clarence, our handyman, was here to help me."

"I, um, do you know what time it is? I should get going."

"Not a good idea in your condition. Just spend the night with me, dear."

"I wouldn't want to impose, and besides, I'm sure I'll be fine."

"You'll be doing me a favor on my last night here. You can have this room. I'll be right next door—and I have plenty of grub for supper."

"Is that pot roast I smell?"

"Yes, it is."

"I suppose there's no rush. Jasper will be in New York for a couple of weeks, and a hearty meal might be just what the doctor ordered."

Sister Ann Marie's eyes twinkled. "You youngsters always did prove that the way to a girl's heart is through her stomach, just like the fellas."

Chapter 15

*A*fter a month of bumping beside her abductor down country roads, subsisting on snacks from Dusty's Jewel Tea truck, staples stolen from unlocked farmhouses, and occasional fish caught in streams, Carly Mae stood on the porch of a dented trailer. The man who had upended her life stood inches behind, holding a gun to her back. Dozens of broken wind chimes jangled from elm tree branches creaking in the breeze. Encroaching weeds stretched high as the roof.

"Go ahead. Knock like I told you," he said. Carly Mae wiped a sweaty palm on her shorts, made a fist and rapped, knuckles on metal. He jammed the gun into her spine. "Louder. You ain't no mouse."

Carly Mae knocked harder, then took a breath.

"Keep goin'," he growled.

Before she knocked again, the door banged open. A lanky woman loomed at the threshold, her dyed-blonde hair piled high, a Mini Mouse T-shirt squeezing tight against heaving chest, and black shorts uneven, one side hemmed above the knee and the other below. "Leon Ames, you sonofabitch," she spit out.

"Aw, Mindy, don be like that. We just need —"

"Don't go tellin' me what you need. I watch the news shows." She recognized the girl standing before her, despite the greasy hair, soiled clothes, nails bitten to the quick and bags under the eyes that made her look less like herself and more like a feral cousin of the teen whose photo had been flashed repeatedly on the TV news.

"S'got nothin' ta do with me."

"You think that truck behind you is invisible? Leave now, and I won't say nothin' to nobody."

"Now, I'm gonna ask you nice. The girl needs a bathroom and some freshenin' up. You could help with that. I got big plans for this here pixie. I'll cut ya in."

"You ain't settin' foot inside, you lousy, stinkin'—"

"Move!" Leon shoved Carly Mae into Mindy, who knocked over a potted rubber plant as she fell to the floor.

The teen cried out, "Bu, Bu Buster! Buster!" as she tumbled on top of the spitfire woman.

Leon clomped inside, closed the door and locked it. "Get up. Get up!" He waved the gun.

The two rose, brushing dirt from their clothes. Leon grabbed Carly Mae and hauled her to a tiny bathroom and pushed her in. "Hurry on up if you know what's good for you."

With a mishmash of thoughts crashing through her mind, she pushed the door closed, pulled down her garments and readied to pee. When she was done, she remained on the toilet, attempting to calm her racing pulse. She scanned the room in search of a weapon, anything to use against the monster pacing the hall.

He banged on the door. "Time's up. Get out now or I'll bust this door down."

Certain he would follow through on his threat, she snapped into action, washed up and came out.

He shoved her to the kitchen area and pushed her into a chair at a built-in table. He then gripped Mindy's arm and tried to force her into a chair, too. Carly Mae gritted her teeth to still the chattering.

The terror she'd held at bay by holding herself statue still in the van had broken loose, and she didn't want him to see.

"Let go of me. I gotta fix that plant." Knowing from her days as his girlfriend that she'd fare better if she acted unfazed by his threats, Mindy pushed Leon away and scuttled to the mess by the door.

"All right. All right." He followed her. "So, Mindy, what do you have for us to eat?" He rubbed the gun barrel up and down her arm. "We've been livin' on slim pickin's, compliments of Jewel Tea."

"Uh, I've got the fixin's for sloppy Joes." She righted the plant, swept up the soil and dumped it back in the pot.

"Stop fussin' with that stupid thing, woman. I'm starvin'. I'm tired of lookin' through trashcans just to survive. Get my drift?"

Mindy patted the dirt down.

"I said I'm starvin'." Leon lunged at her.

She held a palm up. "Okay, okay. Hold your horses."

Carly Mae leaned forward. Her chair creaked.

Leon spun around, pointed the pistol at her and bared his teeth. "You, stay still."

"Lay off the kid. She's terrified enough, for Christ's sake." Mindy stomped to the stove and set to work. The room filled with the smell of braised hamburger. Before long, she plunked down three servings of a soupy concoction on Wonder Bread hamburger buns. Carly Mae took a bite and gagged. She put her fork down.

Leon slurped like a child devouring ice cream. He burped when he was done and patted his stomach. "Just as good as I remember, my pet."

"Don't call me pet. You have no right, you low-life—.»

He tapped the pistol sticking out from his pocket. "Watch your mouth, or—"

"Or what? You'll kill me like you killed that young man in Kiminee?"

Carly Mae felt something cold nick her heart and stick there. She gasped as the world blurred before her eyes, and the creative brilliance, which had always flowed through her with ease, receded behind what felt like a wall burning colder than dry ice. In an instant, with so much shifted within, she no longer felt sure of who she was.

Mindy turned to Carly Mae. "Oh, I'm sorry, kid. I thought you knew. Your friend didn't make it."

"Why'd you have to go and say that. You're gonna ruin her," Leon said.

"You've done a fine job of that already," Mindy said. "I can only imagine what she's had to live through with you."

"Get off yer high horse. I haven't laid a hand on 'er. This little one's gonna be worth her weight in gold. All I hafta do is doll her up and get her to a connection down in Cahokia, man by the name of Rufus Deems. And like I said, you help with that, and the sky's the limit. We can enjoy the amenities here for a little while, and then take off in your Jeep." Leon slid his chair away from the table, got up and strutted to the kitchen. He opened the refrigerator door. "No beer?"

"Don't drink much these days," Mindy said.

"Gimme yer keys," he said. "Gotta get some booze."

"You're outta luck. It died on me ages ago. Not worth fixin', so Cameron says. You remember him, right? Knows everything there is to know about cars. He said the engine's shot, and the transmission's wrecked—not to mention the chassis's bent, so the right front tire blows out every ten miles or so, that is, back when the thing was runnin'."

"He ain't that great. I can work on engines, too, probably better than him." Leon stomped over, grabbed his ex-girlfriend's T-shirt with one hand and rammed her, chair and all, against a wall. "You never were good for much. Gimme those keys."

Mindy staggered up and sidled toward the door. "How did you get so mean?"

"Don't go tryin' to run away."

"The keys are hangin' right by the door, like always." She hooked them with her index finger and flung them to Leon. "I'm tellin' the truth. The Jeep's dead. See for yourself."

He threw the keys into the air, caught them and put them in his back pocket. "I'm gonna do just that. First, I gotta tie you gals up." He rummaged through drawers and cabinets until he found rope and a carving knife. He sliced four long pieces and bound their feet and hands. "I wouldn't try nothin' if I was you," he warned before stepping out. The door banged closed behind him. "I don't want to have to shoot ya," he called.

Carly Mae tried to wiggle free, but the knots tightened with her movements. "Ouch! What kind of knots are these?"

"Relax," Mindy said. "The harder you pull, the tighter they get." She lurched up, hobbled, to the kitchen, worked a drawer open with her fingertips and clasped a knife. She struggled to the couch, stuffed the knife into a space between two cushions, nodded to Carly Mae and said, "This will come in handy. It might take a while, but he'll slip up, let down his guard at some point. Then I'll strike."

"But the van is low on gas, and the Jeep doesn't work, so we have no way to escape."

"I've got this little' foreign job, a Triumph TR3A convertible, British racing green, hidden in an old barn out back. Runs like a dream. Sometimes, I swear, it even glides a few inches above the road instead of on it, which is the absolute best when I need to travel in icy winter conditions. Leon doesn't know a thing about it. Let him think that dead Jeep is all I have."

"I can't believe this is happening." Carly Mae scrunched her eyes closed and counted to ten, hoping the world would look normal when she opened them again, but it didn't work. She slumped in her seat.

"Don't worry none. I know how to handle him."

Mindy struggled back to the table and sat down moments before Leon, face flushed, barged inside with such force the entire trailer shook. Animal figurines fell from shelves and clattered to the floor.

"It's just like you ta have a busted car. I need to figure a ways outa this predicament." He snatched a closet door open, breaking it from its hinges and tossed it down the narrow hall. "You gotta have some liquor stored in here. " Like a dog digging a hole, he ripped clothes from their hangers and sent them them flying. "You don't wanna be stuck here with me and no booze."

"Settle down, will ya?" Mindy said. "I have some Jim Beam and Seagram's in the bedroom closet, and Boone's Farm, too, under the bed."

He stormed over and grabbed Mindy by the neck and shook. "You know better than to hold out on me." He knocked her to the floor and stomped to the bedroom.

Mindy pulled herself up, shaking off a clump of air plant that clung to her sweater.

"Are you okay?" Carly Mae leaned toward her and blinked, trying to focus, but Mindy's features remained a blur.

"I got banged up so much as a kid my mom used to joke my bones must be made of steel. I never had a fracture or even a crack. I don't plan to now neither."

Carly Mae kicked off a glass beagle minus two legs that had landed on her foot, and then whispered "Is Dusty really dead? You're absolutely sure?"

"Afraid so."

"If I hadn't been there, he would have been way up the road when that, that maniac came along." She felt dizzy, as though her heart were pumping poison instead of blood.

"Chin up," Mindy said. "He ain't as smart as he thinks he is."

Chapter 16

Jasper hummed "Good Day Sunshine" as he unlocked and opened the co-op apartment's front door. He pulled in a dolly that carried the Carly Mae quilt, along with his luggage and new paintings he'd acquired during his time in New York. After leaning his cargo against the foyer wall, he called to Emily. She ran from the kitchen to greet him. They embraced like lovers reunited after a long war.

Emily led the way to the living room couch. "Sorry the Metropolitan wouldn't show the quilt." She sat down.

He joined her. "At least, lots of folks admired it at a little gallery near the Chelsea Hotel, and we even got some big donations."

"Do you think you'll take the quilt some other places?"

"Velda wants me to bring it back to Kiminee so the Suzettes can show it off. I think we should do it before the Democratic National Convention begins. Protesters are already flooding in from all over because of Vietnam. It'll be a mob scene."

"We'll have to remember to bring plenty of Vernor's to settle my unruly tummy. And some good books for when I get too faint to go out and about."

"Ah, that reminds me. I have just the one." He sprinted to the dolly, opened his suitcase, pulled out a book and returned to hand it to Emily. "It's a collection of stories by Alice Munro. She's a new writer everybody's raving about in New York."

Emily read the title aloud. "*Dance of the Happy Shades.* Hmmm. Sounds intriguing. ... You think of everything."

Jasper patted her hand and nodded toward a bulky manila envelope, which was on an end table. "Did you read it yet?"

Emily reached for the package and slid her mother's letter out. "Last night, finally. I think just knowing you'd be home today made it easier to take a look." She handed it to Jasper.

In silence, he read words scrawled in blue ballpoint pen. *Dear Ellyanna, if ever you want to find me, go to Joseph, the jeweler at Kedzie and Belmont. We've kept in touch ever since he let me pay off a purchase in installments a long time ago, and times when I get evicted, he lets me forward mail there. Love you with all my heart, Mom.*

"You could be on the verge of meeting your mother."

"I never dreamed such a thing could be possible."

He set the letter aside and took Emily's hand. A warm mid-afternoon glow filled the room. "It's that magic time of day, you know? When it feels like the sun's telling us everything is possible." Jasper kissed her fingertips.

"I know just what you mean."

He looked out the window toward the sparkling lake. "Those seals still out there?"

"Oh gosh, yes, even more of 'em. They're a regular phenomenon now. People are coming all the way from Australia and Japan to see them. We should go have a look ourselves."

"If I do that, I might dive in with them and never return."

"Oh, my love. Your mother ... I'm sorry. I should never have suggested we have a look. How thoughtless. Her suicide was so tragic."

He scanned the horizon. "Everyone assumed she'd drowned, but they never found her body."

"Are you ready to talk about it now? You said you would."

"Let me unpack and unwind a bit. How about at supper? I have a yen for deep-dish pizza."

"Are you thinking Uno's?"

"Yes, ma'am."

"We could walk. There's a lovely breeze today."

"A stroll with my sweetheart? What a fine idea." Jasper rose and strode to the dolly.

Emily gazed out the window toward the beach, where sightseers with cameras crowded against the fence of a recently erected observation area. They jostled for position, eager to catch a glimpse of the seals improbably diving and barking only yards away.

Jasper wiped a dribble of tomato sauce from his chin and put his napkin by his plate. "That was good." He patted his tummy.

"You shoveled it down, hon. I'm afraid you'll get indigestion." Emily took a bite of pizza and chewed slowly.

"I know. I guess I'm just nervous about the past—talking about it, that is." He drummed his fingers on the candle-lit table. "I don't know where to start. It's all so absurd, really."

She stretched forward and squeezed his hand. "Just begin anywhere. Your thoughts will come." She let go and relaxed back into her seat.

He rubbed his jaw absentmindedly and said, "I think it all started because I didn't fawn over my dad, the great Wicklogan 'Wick' Skrillpod."

"Oh yes, he was in the papers a lot. Everybody in Chicago, and probably all of Illinois, knows his story, the icon who parlayed a small cigarillo company into a dominant force in U.S. tobacco. The mayor and aldermen all treated him like royalty." Emily took another bite of pizza and then pushed her plate to the edge of the table. "I'm full. I can't possibly finish."

Jasper glanced at a streetlight shimmering outside, then looked at Emily. "You know, he came through the stock market crash of '29, two years before I was born, with only minor losses. It's like the Depression never came to our great big home. My brothers followed him around like a little school of fish, but I didn't trust him. If he said it was going to rain, I left my umbrella at home. If he wanted all of us play badminton on a Saturday afternoon, I disappeared into the basement and looked through mildewed volumes of folktales."

"Why were you so down on him?"

"I didn't know then, and I don't really know now. I had some notions in my head, probably because of those old stories I read. I was taken with one in particular about these women who could turn into seals, or maybe they were seals who turned into women. I don't remember exactly."

"Interesting. So, how did that affect your feelings for your dad."

"Well, one night, when I was just shy of ten years old, I went downstairs for a drink of water around bedtime. I overheard my dad talking with my stepmom, Monique."

"What were they talking about?"

A waiter came and refilled their coffee cups. They thanked him and each added a touch of half and half and sugar.

Deep in thought, Jasper clinked his spoon against the ceramic cup as he stirred. "Basically, my dad was complaining. He said he had everything under control except for that one boy, the one in the middle. I moved a little closer to hear better, knowing he meant me. Monique said that I was fine. I just traveled a different road."

"That was good, right?" Emily took a sip. "Oooh, too hot! Don't drink it yet."

Jasper lifted his cup and blew on it, making ripples in the mocha-colored liquid.

"Yes, she was loving and kind, and brave to marry a widower with five strapping boys. She encouraged my dad to talk to me. He brushed her off then, but later, he barged into my room when I was reading *Treasure Island*. I was startled and had to move my feet out of the way fast so he wouldn't plop right on them."

"That must have rattled you. What did he want?"

"He attempted to make small talk, but all I could do was mumble one-word answers to his questions. I kept my face in my book. Finally, he said, 'There's been a rift between us ever since your mother's death. It seems to only widen no matter what I do.'

"I kept looking down at the book and said, 'She didn't die.' I didn't plan to say anything like that. It just came out. He said that was ridiculous, but instead of backing down, which would have been the smart thing to do, I said it again, louder.

"It must have taken guts to stand up to such a man. What did he do?"

"He got a sad look in his eyes, and said, 'Oh, my dear boy. I had no idea you were so divorced from reality. Your mom left a suicide note. She was not in her right mind.' He mentioned how he found me wandering along the beach that morning and suspected I'd seen her go in the water and become traumatized. I just wanted him to shut up, and again, I didn't think. I blurted, 'I know what you did.' This was even though I had no idea in that moment what he'd done, if anything, or what I was going to say next. And then I glared right into his eyes."

"Oh my."

"He shifted his weight on the bed and said, 'You think I had a hand in her demise?' I kept my eyes trained on him and repeated, 'She's not dead.' He looked at a mural of fairy tale characters on my wall, sighed and said, 'I see I can't fix this by taking you out for an ice cream sundae or a movie. We have to get you some help. I can't let you succumb like your mother did.' This got me agitated, and I said, 'I saw her put it on—' and he cut me off saying, 'It's been almost four years, son. You've got—' I don't know what he was going to say next. I cut him off." Jasper took a sip of coffee.

"How?" Emily asked.

He met his wife's searching eyes and continued, "I said, 'The seal skin. It was in the attic.' As soon as I uttered those words, his temples throbbed. He made fists with both hands, then opened them, wiggled his fingers and said, 'Don't be a fool, lad, you're talking nonsense.'"

Jasper took a sip of water, then continued. "I wish I'd left it at that, you know, just kept quiet, but I said, 'I found it. The seal skin. I was looking for something to play with in the attic and knocked it off a shelf, and Mommy came to the doorway. She scolded me for making a racket, but as soon as she saw the skin, she grabbed it and ran to the lake. I didn't know it meant she'd put it on at the water's edge, turn into a seal and leave us. I promise I didn't know.' And with that, I burst into tears."

"That must have softened him a little."

"Are you kidding? His face reddened more, almost like his skin was burning, and he spat, 'Stop your blubbering. You're almost ten years old. Act your age.' I put my fist in my mouth to muffle a sob. He rose to his feet, all 6'1" of him towering over me, and said, 'I don't know what it's going to take, but we'll put an end to this rubbish. You simply can't believe that women can turn into seals. My God, I had no idea you were so far gone.' And he stomped across creaking floorboards to the door, where he paused and commanded, 'Now turn out that light!'"

"What did you do?"

"I switched off the lamp and listened to his footsteps recede two flights to the ground floor. Then I tiptoed to the window and looked out toward Lake Shore Drive and the dark expanse of water beyond. Leaning against the sill, I whispered, 'I won't be like him, Mommy. I promise.'"

Emily lifted her napkin to catch a tear escaping from the corner of her eye. "You must have felt so alone."

"I was on a plane to Switzerland a few days later. I remember well because it was my tenth birthday. I was headed for a boarding school. And I wasn't allowed to return home for four years, not even for Christmas or summer vacation."

"That's ... that's ... so extreme."

"When I finally came home, I fought to become emancipated, but my dad won the case, and he was furious. He enrolled me in a boarding school in Kentucky for teenagers with mental heath issues. He kept me there till I graduated at seventeen. Then he brought me to his office and said I could work in the file room for the summer. I didn't want to spend my summer anywhere near him. Something inside of me snapped. I grabbed a fancy knife that was hung like artwork on his wall and rushed him. I held it to his throat and forced him onto a ledge. We were twelve stories up, overlooking the civic center. I told him to admit that my mother really was a sea creature and he trapped her by stealing her seal skin when she came ashore with others of her kind to dance."

"Did he admit anything?"

"No, a crowd had gathered below, and police were already stomping up the stairs. I was hauled off to jail. But he pulled some strings and got me out the next day. He also had all records of the incident destroyed, or so he thought. After that, we agreed to part ways. I expected he would disown me, but he gave me what I would have received had he died at that time—a fortune, really. I thought all traces of that knife incident were gone and my school records all sealed. Doctor-patient privilege and all that. But somehow Croll and Henchley got hold of them, and they threatened to make it public."

"That's unconscionable."

"It must have been their idea of insurance in case I wasn't fooled by their altered contract, which I wasn't, of course. Not only did they want more money from me, they wanted me to withdraw support from Kiminee Academy and bring Carly Mae back to Chicago."

"They must be desperate. I doubt they'd follow through on their threat, because their shenanigans with the contract would come out, too, right? But if they are depraved enough to bring up your past, I'll stand by you, and so will plenty of others. People love you for your great big heart. Nobody will care about what you did or didn't do as a teenager."

"Oh, my love, I should have trusted you with this sooner, and for that I'm truly sorry. But before Croll and Henchley threatened me, honestly, I had concluded my notions about my mother were merely the product of an overactive imagination."

Emily replied. "It could have all been your imagination, but then again, at this very moment seals appear to be quite at home in Lake Michigan. Isn't that virtually impossible? If that can happen, maybe you'll meet your mother again one day."

"My mother died at her own hand long ago. I didn't want to accept it, and my dad made it worse by sending me away." Jasper squinted at the flickering candle for a moment. Then, with wide eyes exuding possibility, he looked up and said, "Ah, but you, on the other hand, you might be on the verge of meeting your mother."

"What are the odds are of finding her? She wrote that letter so long ago."

They held hands across the table, each comforted by the other's presence, each absorbed by missing pieces of the past they might not ever find.

In the driver's seat of the Willys parked at the curb, Jasper lit a meerschaum pipe and felt a swell of pride as he watched Emily approach an apartment building that looked like a neglected stepchild. The basement and first floor windows were boarded up with decaying wood covered with graffiti. Scraps of newspaper, food wrappers and other detritus cluttered the gutter and blighted the sidewalk and anemic lawn. This contrasted with a mid-March day so brisk Chicago's air was fresh as sheets sprinkled with rose water and dried on a Kiminee clothesline.

After weeks of warring feelings that made her feel like Jiffy Pop on a stove, Emily had finally decided to search for her mother. With Jasper's help it had taken less than a month. Feeling confident she had conquered her fears enough to handle this puzzle piece from her past, Emily rang the bell to the right of the door. Soon, a feeble buzz sputtered as the lock released. She waved to Jasper before stepping inside to race up steps upholstered with frayed floral carpeting in muted shades of mauve and green. In the dim hallway, dust on the bannister and light fixtures emitted an eerie chartreuse glow. She stopped at a door on the second floor, where an eviction notice was thumbtacked at eye level. With stomach aflutter, at what that might portend, she removed it just before the door opened.

A scrawny woman in a pink housedress with pale turquoise trim greeted her with a wide smile that revealed a row of browning teeth. Both women regarded eyes so similar to their own it gave each one a tingle up and down the spine.

Emily extended a quivering hand. "Doris?"

Doris leaned forward and pulled Emily into a hug. "Ellyanna." Three calico cats jumped from a tattered couch and rubbed against the women's legs.

Emily pulled back a few inches to look again into her mother's eyes. "They call me Emily now."

"Of course, you told me that on the phone. Well, come on in. I hope you're not allergic to cats." Doris backed up, wobbling as she made room for her daughter to step inside.

"As far as I know the only thing I'm allergic to is Kiminee."

"What did you say?" Doris stumbled and bumped into the couch.

"Kiminee, a little town southwest of here."

"Oh, oh ... oh ... did he? Could he have?" Doris plopped onto the couch.

Emily approached. "Who?"

Doris put both hands on her head and groaned.

Emily suddenly felt protective as a mother bear. "What can I do?" She rested her fingertip on Doris' arm.

The woman, wrinkled and swollen far beyond her years, pulled into a fetal position on the cushions. "I'm so dizzy. I can't ... seem ... to ..." She closed her eyes. The felines leaped up and tucked in around her. Drool dribbled from her mouth.

Emily shook her mother's shoulder and called her name. Receiving no response, she darted to the open parlor window and shouted through the screen, "Jasper! Come quick! It's Doris!" She spun back around and spotted an olive green phone, which was partially obscured by papers on a counter between the living and dining areas. She rushed over and dialed 9-1-1.

Pride turned to panic as Jasper jammed his pipe into the ashtray, exited the vehicle and raced across the street.

Emily flung the door open when he reached the flat. "She's passed out."

"Like mother, like daughter." He strode in, leaving the door wide open.

"Not even close. This is bad. I called an ambulance."

"Good. I left the downstairs door ajar just in case." Jasper kneeled at the edge of the couch, lifted one of Doris' hands and placed three fingers on the inside of her wrist. "Her pulse is weak; it's good that help is on the way."

At the sound of footsteps coming up the stairs, Emily and Jasper looked toward the door. A man in uniform entered. "Um, good day," he said.

Emily swooped toward him. "Thank God you're here! I think she's had a stroke." She took his arm to escort him to Doris. "How did you get here so fast? We just called a minute ago."

He pulled away. "You've got the wrong idea, ma'am. I didn't ... I have an eviction to do here. This lady's had plenty of warning, and today's the day. I have to put her out on the street."

Jasper pursed his lips and glanced out the window, then addressed the man. "Listen, officer, this is my wife's mother. We didn't know where she was until today. An ambulance is on the way and, if you'll permit, I can settle any back rent due on this apartment right now."

"I'm afraid that's not possible. This is the end of her tenancy."

"Can you give us till the end of the day?" Emily's voice rose in pitch. "We'll get her off to the hospital and then come back and clear the place out. Can you do that?"

The man studied their faces. "You wouldn't believe how lenient the landlord's been with this dame, but you look like honest folks. Okay, you've got till 5. Then the door locks, and that's final." He left the apartment and clomped down the stairs. When he reached the ground floor, an ambulance pulled up to the curb.

Chapter 17

*O*ld Man Winkler entered the Good Luck Cafe shortly after sunup—a time when truckers used to converge on the cozy spot, laughing and slapping each other on the shoulders in greeting. Chomping on a smoking cigar, he brushed leaves from his jacket, unbuttoned it and sat at the counter. A life-long resident of Bright Corners, he ran Heart's Desire Adventure Camp, a summer camp on land adjacent to the cafe. He'd been friends with Barb's parents, who turned over the cafe to Barb when they retired and moved to Florida ten years ago.

"Whew! Autumn 1968 is getting off to a strange start with so many leaves whirring about." He balanced his cigar in an ashtray, took off his cap, slapped it on the counter and ran a hand over his balding head.

Barb poured him a cup of coffee and looked out the window. "Strange, indeed."

From the kitchen came the sound of Jeff whistling the tune "Falling Leaves."

"He must be lookin' out the window, too," Barb said. "Do you want the usual?"

Old Man Winkler took a gulp of steaming coffee. "Guess so."

"It's chocolate crème today." Barb served him a slice.

He picked at his pie while she busied herself checking and rechecking ketchup and mustard dispensers, napkin holders, and salt-and-pepper shakers, despite knowing everything was fully stocked.

"Mighty empty in here." He downed more coffee.

"Why remind me? I'm not blind, you know." She returned to the area behind the counter, where she used to hold court with travelers sharing news from far and near. She filled a carafe with strong brew and refreshed Old Man Winkler's cup.

He took a drag on his cigar and blew out, filling the cafe with a pungent tobacco smell. "You really should take me up on my offer. I've got camp reservations rolling in for the summer, and it's only October."

"You sure hit on a winner with Heart's Desire Adventure Camp," she said.

"It's enough to keep me and the wife all winter long. The in-laws and Jeremy, that crackerjack cook you trained, they have to find other work in the off seasons."

"I'm glad Jeremy found seasonal work with you. I felt bad we couldn't employ him anymore, and I'm happy for your success. I just wish some would rub off."

"The old Good Luck has run out of luck. Who besides me would pay even a penny for this place?"

Barb turned and put the coffee pot on the warmer. "We're thinkin' on your offer." She wiped moist hands on her white apron. "I know it's generous. And there might be an opportunity for us in a little town called Kiminee."

"Kiminee, huh. Ain't that on a little tributary to the Illinois?"

"Yes, the Bendy River, it meets the Illinois a ways north of Havana."

He tucked a few dollars at the edge of his plate, stood, lifted the still-smoking cigar to his mouth and puffed. "I know this is hard for you, but don't think too long. I'll have to lower my price soon, because I might get the Johnson farm. They're thinking of pulling up stakes and moving to Kankakee, where they have family—a cousin or something. If they accept my offer, I'll have less need for your place, though the facilities here could be quite useful." He buttoned his jacket and sauntered outside.

After putting Old Man Winkler's money in the cash register, Barb wiped down the clean counters and tables again. Then she grabbed her purse from a cubby below the counter and called to Jeff, "I'm goin' for a walk, hon."

Jeff stepped out of the kitchen, cleaning rag in hand. "Where to?"

"Winkler got me rattled. I need to clear my head." She patted her purse. "I've got the electric bill in here, needs to be mailed anyway. I can go to the post office."

"We should talk."

She blew him a kiss and walked to the door. Before exiting, she turned and said, "I know. I know."

She maneuvered through leaves piling up in the parking lot, then stepped onto a road checkered with potholes. The gutters were clogged with leaves. She walked past the recently abandoned Standard Oil station toward a farmstead with weather-beaten house and barn; remains of a picket fence drooped along the edges of what was once a yard. She approached a cluster of buildings where Patsy's Flowers and Gifts, Bright Corners Insurance, and Beauty and the Barber all used to have a steady flow of customers. When she reached Bright Corners General Store & Post Office, the lights were off. A sign on the front door said "CLOSED. Nearest post office is in Effingham."

Barb leaned against the door, both hands on the glass, head down. She caught her breath as leaves piled up around her ankles. When she turned around, she faced the main street of the deserted town where she was born and raised, and in the distance, the shining Good Luck Cafe sign calling her home.

As October mornings nipped and nights grew long, leaves all over Kiminee fell like giant snowflakes in red, gold, yellow and brown. Day after day, they drifted down, yet no branches became bare. Each leaf that broke away was replaced by another in a brilliant sunset shade. The new growth remained a day or two, then fell with the rest. On and on this went.

People stared out their windows at the spectacle, but no one lifted a rake. What was the point? they reasoned. Everything in Kiminee slowed almost to a halt. The market sold out of TV dinners because people were too mesmerized by the leaves to cook; unable to bike through the leaves, paperboys stopped attempting deliveries; shops downtown opened late and closed early because people needed extra time to battle their way to and from work. The academy reduced school hours because it was taking so much longer for students to walk to class.

One afternoon Missy Lake battled her way home from the police station, where she manned a hotline set up for leads about Carly Mae. The phone rarely rang. The leaves were so high they covered her front steps when she reached her house and were about a foot deep on her porch. School children, shoulders slumped, heads down, waved to her as they waded along, struggling to get home. Missy batted and kicked her way through her yard and called to the children. "Come help me for a sec, will you?"

She motioned for them to follow as she cleared a path to her garage, opened the door and pulled out four rakes, the tines a little bent from years of use but still serviceable. She kept one and handed out the others and said, "Follow me!" She raked the leaves in her front yard into a pile. The youngsters joined in, and the pile grew. When the mound was huge, she threw her rake down and jumped in. The children followed, shrieking and laughing, the first sounds of joy heard in the town since Dusty's death and Carly Mae's disappearance.

People came out to see what was going on, and pretty soon everyone was raking and jumping and howling with laughter, on and on until way past dinner time. Then one after one, they formed piles in the street and lit them, each home with a little bit of smoke wafting high into the sky.

Chapter 18

After months of holding Mindy and Carly Mae hostage, Leon Ames finally let down his guard. He'd spent the previous night alternating between assaulting Mindy in her bedroom and forcing his victims to kneel on the cold kitchen floor while he waved his gun inches from their faces, pranced around them and let loose a barrage of accusations. This was nothing new. These assaults had become routine, but this time he was especially vicious because they'd run out of food. He'd been rationing canned vegetables, deviled ham and tuna from Mindy's pantry, along with stores from a freezer she kept in a shed half the size of her trailer. They'd just consumed the last chicken pot pie, split in three: half to Leon, a quarter each to his victims, and he was still ravenous.

His final assault began when Mindy stood to clear the dishes. He blamed her for his condition and forced her into the bedroom again, where she submitted to his advances in the hopes he would continue to leave Carly Mae alone. But afterward, he hauled the teen into the bedroom, too, and ranted well past noon the next day, threatening the whole time to take the frightened girl next and then kill them both. Finally, he badgered them into the living area, where Mindy plunked down on the couch. Carly Mae sat at the table and rested her head on her arms. He sank into a chair. There, he dozed, gun in his lap but not in his grip.

After studying his slow breathing for several minutes, Mindy pulled out the knife she'd hidden between the cushions, tiptoed to Leon, lifted her arm high, and stabbed at his neck, grazing him. Blood trickled from his flesh."

"Wha, what?" Leon touched fingertips to wound, opened his eyes, then grabbed the gun.

Carly Mae jerked up, alert in every cell, despite the lack of sleep.

Mindy raised the knife again and thrust it into his chest.

He lurched forward. "You bitch! I shoulda killed ya." He kicked Mindy away before she could pull the knife out of his body.

She stumbled backward and shouted to Carly Mae, "Run, kid! Run!"

Carly Mae sprang from the kitchen chair, knocking it over behind her, and stepped toward Mindy, not the door. She tried to speak but could not make a sound, not even a grunt.

Leon got a good grip on the gun and pointed it toward Carly Mae. "You, stay put." Then he aimed at Mindy and shot. She screamed. He fired again, then stumbled toward the exit, red oozing through his shirt where the knife was embedded.

He motioned for Carly Mae to follow.

She glanced at Mindy, who gave a weak wave and mouthed, "Go!"

"Open it," he said when Carly Mae reached the door.

She did as instructed, and he pushed her through, followed her down the stairs, shoved her to Mindy's Jeep and forced her inside. When they were both seated, he turned the key in the ignition and pressed on the gas, but the vehicle wouldn't start. He tried several times and flooded the engine.

"Jesus," he cried. "Jesus. Okay, okay." He looked from Carly Mae to the Jewel Tea truck. "Go on," he ordered.

Wondering why he'd even tried the Jeep, knowing it hadn't started when he'd attempted to get it going several times before, Carly Mae walked, knees wobbling, to the truck and got into the passenger seat. Leon climbed into the driver's seat, knife still planted in his breast, and got the van started on his first try. He drove away, muttering curses and threats. He continued his flow of obscenities as they bumped away. The bloodstain on his shirt grew gradually larger, and Carl Mae marveled at his stamina as he drove on. After sunset, on a dirt lane far from lights, laughter or other indications of human activity, the vehicle shuddered and slowed. Leon Ames coughed up blood and made a feeble fist to pound on the steering wheel, but his hand dropped, open, to his lap. "Goddamn … fuckin' … thing," he uttered between wheezes. "Don't … quit … on."

Carly Mae gripped the door handle; the truck drifted off the road onto the narrow shoulder and sputtered to a stop.

"Shit!" Leon cried out, then slumped over the wheel.

Jumbled and jittery head to toe, and fearing he might wake up if she moved, the teen sat motionless for a long time. She heard an owl hoot in the distance and rustling in the bushes at the side of the road. She gazed into the night and saw movement. Two pairs of eyes peered from undergrowth, then disappeared. She glanced at Leon. His eyes were closed; his wounds dribbled crimson; his chest rattled and heaved. She teased open the glove compartment, pulled out a small spiral notebook and pencil, and scratched out words in the dark. She ripped out her note, and left it on the dashboard next to a few receipts and a flyer for an August 1968 car wash at Old St. Michael's to raise funds for a new heating system in the rectory.

Carly Mae saw eyes peering from the roadside again. She reached for the gun between her and Leon on the seat. His hand moved on top of hers, but he remained slumped, eyes closed. Dreading what would happen no matter what she did, she jerked away, opened the door and jumped. Heart beating fast as a finch's, she shot down the road, oblivious for the moment to the ankle she'd twisted upon landing. Glowing eyes followed.

Carly Mae rubbed goose-bumped arms as she limped along a dirt road so overgrown it was more like a path. She'd been unable to track time passing since she'd limped away from Dusty's truck. And though she'd left Leon Ames behind, she saw his sneering face every time she closed her eyes, felt his gun at her back at the slightest unusual sound, heard his voice when she curled up on the ground at night unable to sleep. She feared every shadow behind a tree was his. Her formerly quick thoughts were hobbled by doubts, and her vision remained blurred, rendering the world like an Impressionist painting.

Ahead, a family of raccoons, one full grown and three juveniles, waddled from the brush alongside the forest, each one clamping an apple in its teeth. First the mother, then the youngsters dropped the fruit in the road and scurried back to the trees. In addition to apples, the raccoons had dropped carrots, peanuts, cabbage and pears in Carly Mae's path several times on her journey.

She was now so thin, two of her could have fit into the T-shirt flapping against her gaunt frame. She trudged to the fruit and bent forward to pick it up. "Thank you," she called, then bit through bitter skin of deep red into crisp, juicy apple. "You know I thought you were rabid the first time I saw you come onto the road. Raccoons just don't do that. But now I wish you'd come out and visit."

The raccoons remained hidden. As the day wore on, gray clouds conquered the sun. Carly Mae approached a creek that dissected the path. She stepped onto a log that served as a bridge. It wobbled. She almost fell in but regained her balance and inched across. The raccoons peered at her through reeds at the bank. Veering from the road was a path lined by fir trees with purple needles like none she'd ever seen. She continued along and reached a clearing, where a weathered house was surrounded by a picket fence broken in several places. She stepped into the open space and was immediately buffeted by strong winds. She hesitated, then continued toward the building. Hanging from a trellis supporting yellow roses still in bloom at the gate was a faded sign with ornate lettering that said, "Welcome to Windy Wood."

As Carly Mae studied the sign, the front door opened. A bent woman dressed in deep purple from her sturdy lace up ankle boots to the bonnet on her head stood in the doorway and called out, "Well, now, don't dawdle. Come on in. I've got some tasty pea soup on the stove."

Carly Mae entered the home, and the raccoons followed.

"Hello babies," the woman of the house said. She ambled to her refrigerator and pulled out a small fish for each masked animal, opened a door off the kitchen and threw the treats down a set of stairs. "Off you go now," she said as the raccoons skittered into the basement. She winked at Carly Mae. "They're like my kids. Been raisin' 'em since I found a pregnant mom wounded in the woods long, long time ago. That's how I knew you was comin'. They've been takin' food to ya, haven't they?"

"How did you know?"

"It happens once in a blue moon. They chirp and spin in circles outside there, and I know it's time to put out extra tidbits. Not too many folks come by these parts. I've been lookin' forward to your company. Snow's a comin' tonight. Lots of it. You got here just in time." The spinster dished out two bowls of soup and placed them on the table, where she'd already set napkins and spoons.

"I've lost track of time, but it's got to be too soon for snow." Carly Mae sat down as wind whistled and rattled the windows.

"It's the first of November. Too soon for snow in most parts, but not here. Winter comes early and stays late in Windy Wood."

Carly Mae took a sip. "Mmm. This is good. Thank you so much ... um, what's your name?"

"Most folks call me Aunt Truly, or they used to. I don't get many visitors these days."

"Pleased to meet you, Aunt Truly. I'm Carly Mae."

"What a lovely name. It rings a bell. Don't know why."

A shiver of hope ran through Carly Mae as she caught Aunt Truly's eye. "Maybe you heard people are looking for me?"

"Hmm. I don't recall, but my memory isn't what it used to be. Somethin' might come to me."

Hope fading, the teen looked down and took another spoonful of soup. "Well, thank you for this meal, anyway. It's really, really good."

"Just a traditional pea soup, I'm afraid. Nothing special. I believe you're just hungry and tired."

"And eager to go home." Carly Mae put down her spoon and looked out the window above the sink. "Wow! It's blowing even harder out there."

"It's one of those, what do you say, anomalies. The clearing's gonna fill with snow tonight. Drifts high as they sky, as they say. There'll be no gettin' out of here probably till springtime."

Carly Mae put her spoon down and frowned. "How do you know?"

"That's just how it always goes in Windy Wood. Don't worry. I've got plenty of food and supplies to get us through."

"Oh, I won't impose on you for that long. I just need to phone home and let everybody know I'm okay."

"No phone here. Got a TV there in the living room—it gave up the ghost some time ago—and there's a little radio in the kitchen. Reception's spotty during good weather. For the next five months or so I expect we won't even have that, sorry to say."

"You mean I can't get home for almost half a year?"

"I expect so. It'll clear up fast as it came come April."

Disappointment settled like a rock in her stomach as Carly Mae stirred her soup. "At least you have electricity," she finally said, trying to brighten her spirits.

"My friend Mindy had a generator installed years ago. Great gal. She comes by a few times a year and brings me supplies, bless her heart. It's been a while since I've seen her. I expect she'll stop in soon as the weather clears. She can help get you home."

"Mindy? Does she know someone named Leon Ames?"

"That scoundrel!" She stared intently at Carly Mae. "The less I think of him the better."

"We were at Mindy's trailer. That was after he kidnapped me—"

"Oh, I remember now. You were taken last summer. I heard your name, Carly Mae Foley, on the radio. People have been searchin' high and low for you. How did you get away? And where's Mindy?"

Carly Mae looked down at her dirty, calloused feet, not knowing how to tell the kind woman in front of her that Mindy had been shot. Aunt Truly furrowed her brow, bracing for what she expected would be bad news.

Finally, Carly Mae blurted, "Mindy stabbed Leon and he shot her. I don't know if either of them is still alive. I'm sorry."

Aunt Truly gave Carly Mae a look so tender it could have softened a badger's heart. "Honey, it's not your fault. I know that."

"He left Mindy behind and forced me into the truck. He was scary, even with a knife stuck in his chest. He passed out after a while, though, and somehow I made my way here."

"Do you know where he hit her?"

"He didn't strike her head. I know that much."

"Oh, dear, I hope the bullets only grazed her and that she had something on hand to treat the wounds. ... I'd better send a few homing pigeons over with some of my special ointment. I have a bunch of them birds in the attic. Better send the messengers off before the snow gets so thick it's blinding." Aunt Truly opened a kitchen cabinet and withdrew a jar of ointment, scooped several spoonsful into three plastic bags, folded them closed, secured them with a rubber band and headed toward a set of stairs.

"Can I help?"

"No, no, you stay there and finish up. This won't take but a second."

Carly Mae savored the rest of the soup, and feeling weary, she stretched and leaned back in her chair and dozed until she was awakened by Aunt Truly's steps coming down the stairs. She opened her eyes and saw a blur of white outside the window.

"Well, that's done," Aunt Truly said. "Brace yourself for one heckuva storm."

Just then, there was scratching at the door.

"All the coons are inside. Who could that be?" The old woman shuffled to the door and opened it.

In bounced a tricolor husky-sheltie cross with a lopsided grin and only one ear.

"Buster!" Carly Mae knelt as her dog raced across the floor and into her arms. "Oh, Buster. I knew you'd find me."

The dog licked her face. Raccoons climbed from the basement and peered at the scene, then came over to sniff Buster.

"Your friend, I presume?" Aunt Truly smiled.

"Isn't this something? He made it just in time."

"The critters like him, too. Wonders abound in Windy Wood, I'll tell you that."

As day turned into evening, the blizzard continued, covering Aunt Truly's stairs and front porch with layer after layer of pure white. By the flickering light of an oil lamp, Aunt Truly showed Carly Mae and Buster to a room just big enough for a twin bed, desk and dresser. The linens were clean and fresh. A pair of flannel pajamas was on the bed.

"You didn't have to do this." Carly Mae's blurred vision gave the room a softness, making it seem even more inviting.

"I've got many good things left behind by others over the years. Makes sense for you to use 'em. There's clothes in the closet and dresser, too. Might even have boots and a coat in the attic. We can check on that another day. Oh, and you'll find drawing paper and charcoals in the desk. All I can do are stick figures; art supplies are wasted on me."

"Thank you so much." Carly Mae blinked her eyes in an attempt to hold back tears, but they flowed anyway. "I don't know how much longer I could have lasted." She had the urge to crawl immediately into bed, clothes and all.

Aunt Truly sat on the mattress and patted the spot next to her. "Come here, now, and don't you worry about a thing."

Carly Mae joined her, with a rush of longing for comfort she hadn't known she needed. Velda and Missy had plenty of love in their hearts, but in times of stress, they froze up and displayed about as much physical affection as Madam Tussaud's wax figures. Aunt Truly pulled Carly Mae close and held her as the teen sniffed, then sobbed, then wailed full force and raged about all that had happened since she'd stormed out of Missy's door, especially Dusty's death.

"There, there," Aunt Truly said over and over while stroking her hair.

Carly Mae's sobs gradually ebbed and her breathing became calm. Aunt Truly gave her a last pat and stood up. "Time for some warm milk?" She backed toward the door.

"That sounds wonderful."

Aunt Truly busied herself in the kitchen while Carly Mae changed clothes and got into bed.

When Aunt Truly returned she handed a cup of steaming liquid to her guest. Then she pulled up a patchwork quilt that had been folded at the foot of the bed. "There you go."

"What are these?" Carly Mae put the milk on a stand to her side and rubbed a finger over a square with a castle and crescent moon in the sky above it."

"Those are scenes from some of my favorite stories. Shall I tell you one? It's about the origins of your companion, Buster. See, there's a dog here that looks just like him, except for the missing ear." She pointed to a square near the middle of the quilt.

"Yes, I see. I'd like very much to hear that story." Carly Mae lifted the mug, blew on the milk and took a sip.

"Very well then." Aunt Truly sat up a little straighter. "In a time that now dwells in the realm of legend, a trapper's husky broke loose, jumped a fence and overpowered a widow's prize dog. The bitch was in heat and of a breed resembling the modern-day sheltie. Hearing the ruckus, the woman grabbed her slingshot and rushed outside, cursing. But the canines had already mated by the time she took aim and let a stone fly, nicking the intruder as he bounded away.

"She bred the sullied female with a suitable male from her pack the next day and hoped for the best. Her family had grown a reputation up and down the Mississippi and its tributaries as excellent breeders of farm dogs, and she counted on trading puppies for food and other necessities to keep her through winters so bitter they withered the brain. But when the litter arrived, three looked like their mother; three clearly pulsed with husky blood, which she considered inferior.

Carly Mae took a few gulps of milk and put the mug on the stand. Then she closed her eyes and sighed.

"I can tell you the rest in the morning."

"No, no, please go on. I want to hear it. Plus your voice is so … soothing," she said through a yawn.

"Okay then, I'll continue." She patted Carly Mae on the knee and continued. "Incensed by the threatened lineage of two small herding dogs her Scots grandfather had brought across the Atlantic and then overland to a strange and wild world, the widow gnashed her teeth as she watched the pups grow. Finally, before daybreak one morning, she stuffed a brick and the three she didn't want into a burlap sack, tied it closed, slung it over her back and slouched to the banks of what would eventually be called the Bendy River. She tossed the writhing sack as far as she could, watched it splash and sink, and trudged back home.

"To this day, nobody knows how the pups got out. Over the years, sightings of this curious tricolor mix of speed and spunk were recorded all along the Bendy. And stories of encounters with them proliferated. Families even befriended them from time to time and trained them just like any other dogs. However, sightings gradually tapered off and eventually became so rare, most people believed stories were all that remained.

"But you know different, don't you, my young friend."

Carly Mae didn't answer. She'd already fallen asleep, with Buster, one eye open, curled up at her feet.

Chapter 19

*D*amon closed his eyes and saw multicolored swirls of agony circling every cell in his body. Eyes open, he squinted at a room that looked like a three dimensional fun-house mirror in hues of gold, orange and red. Pain pulsed up and down his spine. His hands were crawdad claws, then boxing gloves the color of acrylic yellow, then violet and scarlet sea anemones opening and closing. Around his waste a rope gripped like a python. He sat across from a man wearing a black suit jacket with lavender pin stripes, pink shirt and mustard-colored tie.

"Hello, Mr. Ames. I'm Dr. Ned Burton, interim director." At the bridge of his nose, he tapped on the metallic, copper-colored frame of his glasses, then brushed deep brown bangs from his forehead and ran his fingers down to the ends of his thick, shoulder length hair. "I guess you've seen a lot of us come and go in the time you've served here."

Damon looked into Ned Burton's eyes and saw miniature spinning pinwheels. He looked away.

"I want you to know I may be young and lacking in experience, but that can be an advantage," Ned continued. "I don't take anything for granted. Now, it took me a while, because we're way over capacity here, but I've reviewed your case, and, quite frankly, I see some discrepancies—the first being that your intake fingerprints and photo are missing." He looked down at a file opened on his desk and then at the prisoner seated, facing his desk.

Damon gripped the arms of his chair but was otherwise immobile.

Ned studied the inmate while chewing on the eraser end of his pencil. Then he wrote something in the file, brushed a piece of lint from the cuff of his sleeve and looked up again. "My predecessors were all convinced that could easily be explained by all the chaos back when the twister leveled the office building. Records were strewn all over the grounds, some lost entirely. But I like to dot all my i's and cross all my t's, so let's see here.» He glanced at the file, then back at Damon. "I know you've told your story before, many times, but let's start from the beginning here, so, well, what do you say your name is?"

The python tightened around Damon's waist; bile rose as he cleared his throat. He forced it down and, gasping, said, "My ... na, name is Da ... mon Fo ... ley." I, I ... I am a hu, hus ... band, fa ... ther of thr, thr, three a,a, and mah, muh, math tea ... cher fr, from Ki ... mi ... ney, Illi ... nois. I have a, a, a, suh, summer j, j, job deli ... ver ... deli ... vering ma ... il. The la, la, last th, thing I re ... mem ... ber wuh, was be ... ing li, li, lifted high in ... to th, th, the air in a roh, roh, roar ... ing cl, cl, cloud." He slumped, eyes closed, in the chair and fell to the floor, enveloped in a molten maroon sea.

Ned stood, bumped his chair back with legs clad in indigo jeans, stepped around the desk, and ran to the prisoner. He checked Damon's pulse, then took off his jacket and put it under his patient's head, before returning to his desk and picking up the phone.

"Hey, Georgia. Yes, Ames passed out in here. Get Sheldon—quick. And I'm adjusting his meds, starting this evening. Yes, I'm noting his chart right now. ... No, no, the opposite: we're going to wean him off the chlorpromazine, then the other two."

He kicked the side of his desk with the toe of his desert boot. "Of course I know what I'm doing ... Oh, and, Georgia, what do you know about a place called Kiminee? Yes, Kiminee, Illinois. ... Never heard of it? … How can that be? It's mentioned in his file. He claimed that's where he's from. … Several times. … Of course you have a lot to keep track of. … I understand."

He hung up as Sheldon, the orderly, entered with a gurney.

"Get him to the infirmary right away," the doctor said. "His drug regimen is enough to light a Christmas tree. I want to know what he's really like, whether he really is the monster he's cracked up to be."

On the floor Damon groaned and opened his eyes.

Chapter 20

*O*n a piercing February morning, 1969, Barb tightened the blue woolen scarf at her neck and, with gloved hand, locked the door to the Good Luck Café. She put the key in her coat pocket, stepped backward a few feet and looked up. Icicles extended from the weathered sign with coffee cups painted at the beginning and end of a name that had encouraged travelers for decades. Gray-green snowflakes the size of fifty-cent pieces fell from the sky.

"Come on, hon," Jeff called from the Dodge Sportsman camper van he'd been warming up. "Old Man Winkler's waitin' on us."

She turned and crunched through snow to the van. "I sure hope we're doin' the right thing. Those weird snowflakes bother me. They look like big globs of mold," she said as she settled into the passenger seat.

"It's a smart move. We held out as long as we could after they rerouted the highway." Jeff backed the van from the cafe lot and onto the road.

"Who makes those decisions anyway? Never mind people like us left high and dry. Progress. Ha! Frank's gas station's gone. Mel's grocery's kaput. I don't know how long Marge will keep her little curio shop open. She's the last holdout."

"Look on the bright side. Old Man Winkler's paying way more for the building and land than we could have ever dreamed. We bought a new home with cash and made a tidy down payment on the old Binsack building right on the Kiminee town square. We're not closing shop, baby, we're expanding—The Good Luck Cafe and a hotel."

"I'm a little worried about the hotel part. Between us we have zero experience in that department. We got carried away with the idea when we saw that wonderful old building, and made kind of a snap decision."

"Maxine and Velda worked at the Warren hotel in downtown Indianapolis. They know the ins and outs."

"I sure hope so. It's a big leap taking them on as partners."

"Did you forget Maxine is my cousin? I've known her all my life. She is reliable to the core."

"I just have the jitters. I've lived in Bright Corners my whole life."

"It'll be fine. Home is where the heart is, as they say. And your heart's with me." Jeff slowed the truck and pulled onto a gravel road leading to Heart's Desire Adventure Camp. The acreage was dotted with a stable, barn, dormitory, arts and crafts building, gymnasium, cabins, and more.

"I just hope things don't get too complicated." Barb climbed out and made her way through quickly falling snow to the door. When Old Man Winkler opened it, she handed him the key. After they exchanged a few words, she shook his hand and spun around to see the ominous oversize snowflakes had burst apart and formed swirls of tiny flakes twinkling in kaleidoscopic colors.

"Look at those!" Barb said when she climbed into the van.

"A good sign." Jeff gunned the engine, backed up and pulled away.

In Kiminee, the world had been frozen for so long, even the most optimistic residents felt bleak. Abby Louise Chute meandered around town sunrise to sunset most days, coming indoors only when neighbors took her by the arm, sat her near a heater and gave her a cup of hot chocolate or tea. Tam-Tam Parlo looked out her cabin window while knitting a scarf day after day, filling the floor with a multitude of heather hues. It grew longer and longer, but she didn't stop. Missy Lake huffed her way to the police station to staff the Carly Mae Foley hotline each morning, but no calls came in, and she doodled black-eyed Susans with blue ballpoint, filling pad after pad of pink message forms. In the afternoon, she baked oatmeal cookies, batch after batch, filling her kitchen table and counters with more chewy bites than she, Blanche and Ray could ever eat.

Then on Abe Lincoln's birthday, a school holiday, the children of Kiminee bundled into car coats and parkas, hats and mittens, grabbed their ice skates, and congregated at the river. They took to the ice and sailed along, bright scarves streaming behind them. As they glided and spun, they sang a round they had composed to the tune of the "Make New Friends" camp song.

We will glide with all our might
For Carly Mae our shining light
Won't you help us find a way
To bring our friend back home to stay?

As their voices carried over frozen fields, through barren woods and into every room in town, scores of brilliant red cardinals alighted on tree branches along the river banks, rabbits poked out from their holes and twitched their ears, fox and wolf loped side by side to the river's edge. Woodpeckers stopped drilling and craned their necks toward the sound, badgers and beavers ambled together to the source of the sweet music, where they nestled with all manner of other creatures.

At the sound of the angelic harmonies, Abby Louise, Tam-Tam, Missy and everyone else in town drew to the river, where they joined in the song. Grant Modine brought a giant pot of hot chocolate and gave cup after cup away. Missy set down platters of her oatmeal cookies for all to enjoy. Tam-Tam finished the scarf and draped it over the crowd.

Just then, Barb and Jeff pulled into a parking space near their new building right next door to Suzette's. They got out of the vehicle and walked, arms entwined, to the double doors and hugged. Then they peered into what soon would be the entrance to the combined lobby for the inn and waiting area for the cafe. To the right was a former drug store and soda fountain, already equipped with a counter and kitchen. Straight ahead at the back of the lobby area a staircase led to a landing, then turned sharply right and rose to the second floor. A spacious closet beneath the stairs could be opened up and be incorporated into a registration area. To the left was a smaller storefront that Barb and Jeff had no plans for yet.

"I think we've come to the right place," Jeff said. "There's something special here."

Barb agreed. "Listen to that enchanting song. Where's it coming from?"

Jeff took her hand, "This way, toward the river."

As they strolled into the crowd, they introduced themselves to Grant and accepted his hot chocolate. Then they sampled Missy's cookies.

"I like this spot—and these convivial people," Barb said.

"What do you think about naming the hotel after the Bendy River?" Jeff gestured toward the frozen water. "Maybe the Bendy River Inn?"

"Bendy River Inn. I love it." She stood on tiptoes and kissed Jeff on the lips.

A few feet away, Abby Louise smashed a cookie in her mittened hand and glared at the couple. "Bendy River Inn. Who do they think they are?" she grumbled, then reached into her coat pocket, took a swig from a flask and stumbled toward her home.

Chapter 21

News that Barb and Jeff were partnering with Velda and Maxine on the Good Luck Cafe/Bendy River Inn venture soon ricocheted like shrapnel throughout the community. Some, like Varnie Welch and Tempest Binsack, learned new words: lesbian and bisexual. That's because while shopping at the Five 'N Dime, they overheard Grant Modine and Race Burlington arguing over which term applied to Velda and Maxine. Folks got so riled, the wind kicked up, sending howls that echoed down the streets, rattling windows along the way. Finally, Abby Louise Chute and Tam-Tam Parlo, the ringleaders of this discontent, wrote a petition to stop the project on the grounds that deviants shouldn't be flouting their ways anywhere let alone smack in the center of things. A meeting was called in the town's ramshackle community center, a structure so unsound that Jasper Skrillpod had blueprints drawn up for a new building that could serve as gathering place for both the town and the academy.

Maridee Pratt, president of the Suzettes, took charge, since her husband and Kiminee's mayor, Bill, said he felt a cold coming on and didn't want to spend time in the drafty building. Maridee insisted the center wasn't drafty; it was merely haunted by the ghost of Gerald Pye. He died in bed the day before he planned to join the Confederacy. Most folks think his brother Francis, a Union backer, poisoned him.

Nobody investigated since most everyone in town was on the brother's side, so that's why Gerald has refused to pass on. Maridee told Bill the kind of chill Gerald brought to a room couldn't harm anyone, but Bill wasn't convinced.

Maridee stepped to the podium and grew flummoxed because Velda and Maxine, who held hands in the front row, regarded her with so much affection she wished she could call the meeting off. She scanned the crowd, knowing she had to continue, cleared her throat and said, "It seems we've had formal complaints about the proposal to open up a cafe and inn next door to Suzette's, and this here's a petition to stop improvements to the building from going forward." She held up the petition. "First, now, I know some of you don't want to hear this, but I have to say it anyway: everything has been done so far by the book, with permits and within exiting laws. This project will go forward whether you support it or not. But, we do have to live together peaceably. We'd best hear each other out. So, those of you opposed, please speak up. Why shouldn't this business go ahead?"

Folks squirmed and shuffled their feet under squeaky chairs. Maxine and Velda's hands gripped tighter as they dreaded what might come next. Finally, a female voice from the back said, "These folks, um, that lie woman to woman, or man to man, it's jus not, not natural, seems ta me."

The room grew quiet as a mausoleum. Maridee searched the faces of people she'd known and loved her entire life. "Who's that speaking now? Abby Louise, is that you? Come on now. Stand up so we can hear you."

Abby Louise stood, wobbling. "Sets a bad zample." She slid back into her seat, pulled a bottle of hooch from her pocket, took a quick chug and wiped her mouth.

Several "Yeah!" and "Right on, sister!" comments were heard.

Then Tam-Tam stood and said, "It's a scourge, goes against the Bible."

To this, Missy shot up and replied, "What would you know about the Bible? I could count the number of times you've entered a church in the past thirty years on one hand. You can't speak for the religious among us."

In response, there were even louder "Yeah!" and "Right on, sister!" comments, some by the very folks who had called out in support of Abby Louise.

"It's one thing for them to do what they do behind closed doors, but to be runnin' a business downtown? I've got problems with that," Race Burlington, a local farmer, said. "My Dora, who couldn't come tonight on account of she caught that flu that's goin' around, is dead set against it. And it's so close to Grant at the Five 'N' Dime, and him and Velda—"

"Nobody said Velda's perfect, but who here is?" Missy countered. "Velda should have been faithful to Damon and not gotten all involved with anyone else, man or woman. I admit that. But she is part of our community, just like all of you. And that Maxine—there couldn't be a sweeter gal, and she sure has a sense for business. Then there's Jeff and Barb. I can't believe any of you would turn on them. Sure they come from Bright Corners, which is a good ways away, but let's not forget all the people they welcomed over at the original Good Luck Café. They offered so much more than food, and you know it. If you didn't experience their hospitality yourself, you know somebody who did. It would be an honor to have them carry on that tradition here."

"That may be, but I don't want to see women kissing women right by Suzette's. It's unseemly," Tempest said.

Velda shot up. "Does anybody in Kiminee go about smooching in public? No. What makes you think Maxine and I will? We're not trying to upset you. We're just following our hearts." She stood taller, thrusting her chest out in defiance. "And the right word is bisexual for those of you who've been dissecting our private lives for sport lately." Velda eased back into her seat.

Race stood and pointed a finger at Velda. "Doesn't matter what you call it. It's just plain wrong. And I think it's them others pullin' you off course. You shouldn't be mixin' with them people. Strangers. We let that Skrillpod fella in, and, sure, it's been good for business folks like Grant at the Five 'N Dime, Cole at McDuggin Market and Chester at the hardware store. And the kids are gettin' some good book learnin', but how far are we goin' to let this go? I'm talking about the soul of Kiminee."

Race took his seat and several people spoke at once, creating a snarl of voices, nobody hearing anybody.

Then Randy Tarr rose and said, "Listen up everyone. I have a confession."

To this all grew silent, for they loved to hear a confession, the juicier the better.

"Remember that rumor about Carly Mae being taken by hippie squatters on the old Kiminee place?" Randy said.

Several people nodded their heads.

"When I heard that, I grabbed my shotgun and huffed over there, intending to scare the pants off of 'em." Randy blushed a deep red. "I accused 'm of bein' degenerates livin' like slobs, and takin' our dear Carly Mae."

"Sounds 'bout right to me," Abby Louise yelled.

"Shhhh. Let him speak," Tempest said. "For goodness sakes."

"Well, I sure made a fool of myself," Randy continued. "They weren't squatters at all and had nothin' to do with Carly Mae's abduction. They are livin' in a peculiar way in that commune thing, but Willie Holt inherited the place fair and square, and he has every right to live as he pleases. I hightailed it out of there in a hurry. Hurt my ankle, too, on the way. Anyway, those folks are contributin' to our community. Some of them bring stuff to sell at Suzette's. And they have a garden. You should see all the stuff they grow. The home is neat and clean, and there are lots of books, all kinds of books."

"Books ain't necessarily a good thing. Can put strange ideas in yer head, if you ask me," Race said.

"Those folks up at the Kiminee place have big hearts just like us down deep." Randy reached into his pocket and pulled out a piece of notebook paper and unfolded it. "One of them wrote a poem. It's called 'Welcome.' They have it posted by their front door, where they leave messages for each other on a bulletin board. I saw it when I went to apologize a few days after I barged in on them. Willie said I could copy it. Here's how it goes:

Welcome all who come our way
On this unique and wondrous day
We've known joy and sorrow, too
And know that's also true of you
So come inside and set a spell
Tell us what's been going well
And if a care is on your mind
No better comfort will you find

The room was silent again till Abby Louise said, "Words, words, words. What's the point?"

"The point? You're seriously asking what the point is?" Randy replied. "I made a judgment about those people because they didn't come from here, and they seemed odd, I guess, but they are much better than—"

"What does this have to do with the price of tea in China?" Tam-Tam interrupted.

"Let him finish," Maridee said.

Randy took out a handkerchief and wiped his brow, then continued. "When I heard the gossip about Velda and Maxine, I thought, my gosh, the same goes for those two. We're makin' judgments about 'em. You mentioned the soul of Kiminee, Race. Let's talk about what that is, exactly. What makes us who we are, like nobody else? I think it comes down to this: when push comes to shove, we're not small minded. We find a way to take the high road. What would our founders, Fleur and Charles, think of this petition? And all our ancestors for that matter, that strange and wonderful mix of people who settled this little section of river long ago. They were an accepting, blending sort of people, like the French who settled Louisiana, not like the rigid English colonists—no offense to anyone who has English blood, mind you. We're all the same here: French, Indian, Irish, Scandinavian, German, English, African. It doesn't matter. We are of a part. Now, we don't have to agree with them, but we've known Velda all our lives, and we're coming to know Maxine. They are part of us. And, I'll tell you this: no matter how much they might rattle us, we love them. I believe that, and I know down deep you do, too." Randy sat down, trembling. This was the longest he'd ever spent talking to a group.

Silence settled the room again as people considered Randy's words. Then Maridee spoke. "This is America, after all, is it not? We have principles, do we not? Those of us who went to Bentley Elementary back in the old days should remember how well Miss Egan guided us, not just in learning but in how to be good people. We've got children now getting not just book learning, but a top-notch education. They've got resources at the academy that we'd never dreamed possible. On any ordinary day, when we might be planting daffodils or baking a compote or fixing a lawn mower, they're encouraged to follow their dreams and do and be their best. They're not just bored to death staring out their classroom windows. What kind of example do we want to be for them? Think on that."

Another pause followed. Finally, Race said, "I guess there's no harm in having a live and let live approach to this project. I mean, I won't object anymore."

Others voiced similar opinions.

"Okay, then," Maridee said. "Those in favor of considering this petition business finished raise a hand."

All shot their arms up, that is, all except Tam-Tam and Abby Louise, who leaned toward each other, whispering.

As winter 1969 bumped toward spring, the search for Carly Mae wore on, needling folks like flies bouncing against a windowpane. People prayed for their lost girl before bed each night, and during the day found ways to cheer each other up however they could. Kitchens across Kiminee filled with the scent of cookies baking, chocolate chip and peanut butter being the favorites. The Suzettes were revved up, preparing weekly care packages for Mick Deely's grandson, Dave Deely, and two other local boys who had shipped off to Vietnam. Cookies were the main thing they requested in their letters home, so cookies they would get, the club decided. They also posted a basket outside of McDuggin Market, with a sign requesting donations of non-perishables. Soon it was overflowing with Spam, deviled ham, fruit cocktail, condensed milk and all manner of other canned goods folks thought would appeal to young men roped into war in far-off Asia.

Despite supporting Kiminee's own, the Suzettes came out unanimously against the war. They taped an anti-war poster in their storefront window. This incensed Grant Modine, who slapped together a poster that said, "We support freedom wherever we are needed." He installed it in the window of the Five 'N Dime, along with a display of Civil War memorabilia—something he knew would tug at everyone's heartstrings—and encouraged all who dropped in to never shop at Suzette's again.

Jeff, Barb, Velda and Maxine were busy restoring their building in advance of the combined grand opening of The Good Luck Café and Bendy River Inn. They kept mum about the dispute between their neighbors, fearing if they took sides, the whole town would turn against them before they even opened their doors.

Most folks, however, not only kept going to both Suzette's and the Five 'N Dime, they couldn't wait for the grand opening of the café and inn. There was precious little action in the town or in the farms and fields surrounding it, and worry over the fate of Carly Mae weighed heavily on them. Plus, due to their multicultural ancestry, a source of pride for most, an undercurrent of acceptance was ever present. They encouraged Grant to remember how important a live-and-let live attitude was. "Just agree to disagree," Race replied when Grant tried to enlist him in his anti-Suzette's campaign.

A laissez-faire sentiment extended to Willie Holt and his friends whose novel lifestyle had no ill effects as far as anyone could tell.

"As long as you don't pull up Fleur's black-eyed Susans, you're fine with me," Tempest said, pointing out the one act that could turn everyone against them when a young weaver living in the commune stopped in at Suzettes. She wanted the shop to carry some soft, earthy shawls and ponchos she'd designed. Tempest accepted the garments, which sold well.

Through that, new friendships developed. This led to a weaving club that met every Thursday afternoon up at what folks still called the Kiminee place, even though the owner was a Holt. Tam-Tam and Missy, both eager novice weavers, sat on opposite sides of the room. Their rift had grown even stronger because the Suzettes, swept up in the magnanimous spirit of the day, had voted to sell Tam-Tam's dolls, figuring Missy would get over it soon enough. Missy, already weakened like a couch with broken springs due to worry over Carly Mae, now felt betrayed. She pulled her own handiwork from the shelves and hadn't set foot in the store since.

Chapter 22

Doris perched on a window seat in the apartment above Jasper's art gallery. Legs outstretched, she leaned against a fluffy paisley pillow and watched people stroll by below. No dirty wrappers, flattened styrofoam cups, or other trash cluttered the gutters; no stray papers tumbled down the sidewalk. Flowers bloomed in windowsill planter boxes across the street. "I can't believe how clean everything is here," Doris said to her three calico cats.

Emily carried two cups of coffee from the kitchen into the living room. "Here it is, cream with two sugars, just how you like it."

Doris swiveled and held out a hand to accept her drink. "You and Jasper are too good to me. This place must rent out for a good penny. I don't know how I'll ever repay you."

Emily put her coffee on an end table, shoved a large shoulder bag aside to make more room and sat down next to Doris. "There's nothing to repay. Seeing how well you're doing after a little rest and some good food is reward enough. … And for the record, we never rent this apartment out. You can stay as long as you like."

Doris surveyed the selection of furniture and knickknacks in the room. "How did you know what to keep and what to toss?"

"The rest of your things are stored in the basement. I can help you sort it sometime."

"The shards of my wasted life."

"Sister Ann Marie always said the past is the past; nothing can change it. All we can do is change how we feel about it. God can help us with that."

Doris put her mug down and scratched the side of her nose. "I know that's true—and don't take this the wrong way because I'm glad you were born—but I often wish I'd never met your father, whoever he really was." Doris picked up her drink again and took several gulps.

"What do you mean?"

"He said his name was Jim Palmer, but that turned out to be just one of his many aliases. I found that out when I got out of the hospital after he almost killed me and ran off with you and Lolly—"

Emily jolted, sloshing coffee over her hand and onto her lap. "He what?" Color drained from her face.

She and Doris both grabbed napkins. Emily wiped her hands while Doris dabbed at her daughter's skirt.

"You're white as a sheet. I shouldn't a just blurted that out. I wasn't thinkin'." Doris shrank back in shame and chewed on her bottom lip.

"No, don't feel that way." Fearing nausea might soon overwhelm her, Emily closed her eyes and breathed in with her nose and out with her mouth.

"Are you okay?" Doris leaned forward and rested a hand on Emily's knee.

Emily opened her eyes and massaged her temples. "I'll be fine. It's just a lot to take in, like being force fed or something. I mean my father almost killed you and ripped your daughters away from you? I've always wanted to know about my past, but I never imagined that."

"As far as I'm concerned, we don't need to talk about any of it."

"I might not want to face it, but I think I need to know the truth about my father, all of it." Emily reached into her bag and pulled out the envelope from Sister Ann Marie. "This might help us piece some things together." She shook out the contents and spread them on the coffee table.

"Oh my!" Doris pointed to the beaded coin purse. "Is the ring still in there?"

"I didn't see a ring." Emily handed Doris the purse.

Doris unzipped it, reached a couple fingers inside and pulled out a ring with a Celtic trinity knot design. "I put it in that secret flap I made. Made one just like it for Lolly, too, after I had Joseph the jeweler make matching rings for you."

"It was a stroke of luck he's still in business. We never would have found you in time."

"Thank the Lord for that." Doris slipped the ring on Emily's finger. "Look, it fits!"

Emily lifted her hand to get a better look, then she sifted through Sister Mary Margaret's notes. "I used to talk about Lolly—and a baby, too. Did you have a baby after me?"

"I lost one from that last beating. I was four months along. Wrecked my insides good. No more babies for me. Just memories."

At this news, Emily's eyes welled with tears. "I'm so, so sorry to hear that."

"No use cryin' over split milk, right?" Doris' voice cracked.

"It really must have been a doll Lolly had. I thought she was real. We called her Daphne Sunshine. They said at the orphanage it was just a doll."

"Lolly was fourteen, too old to play with dolls." Doris felt dread brewing in her belly.

Emily clasped her hands together. "I could have sworn she held a real baby in her arms, all wrapped up in the softest butter-yellow blanket."

"Sh … she mu.. must …. have had hi .. his baby," Doris sputtered. "My poor, poor girl. She was getting a little chubby. … I thought it was just one of those growing phases." She sucked in several breaths, trying to stave off tears, but soon she succumbed, body heaving like a downshifting big rig.

Emily wrapped her arms around her mother. "It's just a vague memory. Maybe there never was a baby, like the sisters said." The words rang hollow to Emily, and she sensed the same was true for Doris. Tears dribbled, then flowed down Emily's face,

Doris grew quiet, calmed herself and said, "I should have protected my Lolly, seen it coming."

Emily shifted position and fidgeted with her ring. "Do you want to stop talking about this?"

Deep in thought, Doris scratched her chin, leaving faint red marks, then replied. "Now that we've gone this far, we may as well get it all out." She took both of Emily's hands in hers and shared the worst memory of her life. "One day, you know, an ordinary sort of day, so I thought ... I came home early from work and caught him messin' with Lolly in the hall outside the bathroom. He had her pinned against the wall and was pressed up against her, kissing her neck, and she was struggling to get away."

"How horrifying." Emily took a napkin from the coffee table and dabbed her eyes.

"I was so shocked I plum dropped the groceries I'd bought for supper, and they spilled all over the floor. I pounded him and pulled as hard as I could to get him off of her. He was in some sort of crazed state—enraged, I guess, that I'd come home unexpected—and he shoved me smack into a little table there in the hall. I fell hard on it, and it broke into a few pieces. I pulled one giant sliver out of my leg while I got up and went after him again, because he was still trying to assault my Lolly. I bit him, drew blood, too. That's when he threw Lolly to the floor and dragged me by my hair into the kitchen, where he beat me on the head with a welded trivet. It had this lovely rose pattern. I always kept it on the table for hot casseroles and things right from the oven. I was bleeding something fierce, but I made a dash for the kitchen stove. I was gonna brain him with my cast iron frying pan, but he got me from behind with your old high chair, which I'd never gotten rid of even though you'd outgrown it. That knocked me down, and I don't know how many blows I took after that. I was on the floor, still conscious when you came home from playing with your friend Suzy next door."

"You mean I—".

"The last thing I saw was your little feet in black patent leather Mary Jane's and little white ankle socks. Your entrance saved my life. ... I never saw you again till last month, when you rescued me again."

"I don't remember any of this."

"What could have happened to my Lolly?"

Reeling at the thought of having a memory like this locked deep inside, Emily put both palms on the seat at her sides and braced herself as waves of nausea rose from her gut. "I .. don't ... know."

Doris searched Emily's eyes. "You look awful, awful. It's the nausea, right?"

"Yes, it is." Emily fished a pack of Tums from her bag, popped one into her mouth and crunched furiously. She swallowed with a swig of coffee, then popped another into her mouth. "This will help. I wish I remembered even a little bit, something, anything to help find out what happened to Lolly."

"Could be clues in that Kiminee place or maybe Kankakee. He came from one of those places, or another place down state that sounds similar, that is, if he was even telling the truth. That's what got me so upset the day we met, just hearing you say Kiminee."

"Could it have been Cahokia maybe?"

"I'm not sure. It doesn't sound as likely as Kiminee or Kankakee.»

Emily took another Tums and stood up. "I need to get some fresh air. Do you feel up to taking a walk?"

Doris blew her nose in a napkin. "I don't think so."

"I'm sorry to go so abruptly, but I really do have to get outside. I could pick up something for you to eat while I'm out."

"There's plenty of food you already bought me that I can cook."

"Okay, then, I'll be back soon." Emily grabbed her bag and made a quick exit.

On the sidewalk, she maneuvered through the crowd until she reached a corner phone booth. Inside, she pulled out a business card and dialed. "Hello? Dr. Blake? It's Emily ... yes ... I need to see you. ... Do you have any openings this afternoon?"

On a turquoise brocade couch in Dr. Blake's office, Emily clutched a handkerchief and dabbed her eyes. Then she blew her nose, folded the damp cloth and tucked it into the pocket of her salmon-colored cardigan. "Thank you for squeezing me in, doctor."

"Of course, I wish we could do a regular session, but unfortunately we only have about fifteen minutes."

"I know. I just need help getting grounded, I think. You've helped me so much over the last several months. You helped me be strong for Jasper who fell apart when Carly Mae went missing. And I don't think I'd ever have looked for my mother if I hadn't sorted out some of my feelings here first. But this is about Kiminee—what brought me here in the first place—or I think it is. I wanted to figure out ... oh God, I'm just ... I want to figure out ..." She gazed at the wall clock and smoothed her skirt with her palms.

Facing her from across a magazine-covered coffee table, Dr. Blake gave a nod of encouragement. "Go on." She rubbed her bottom with thumb and index finger. "You have made progress with the nausea. It's milder now, isn't it when you go there—more manageable?"

"Oh, yes, that's true, but today, Doris, my mom, that is, I mean, she said my father, who it turns out was a violent man, might have come from there, from Kiminee. She's not sure. It could be Kankakee or some other place with a similar name." Emily winced and clutched her midsection. "It hurts just to think about it. I've got cold fingers and toes, literally, right now just thinking about what it could all mean." Emily squirmed and knocked the table with her foot. An issue of *Time* slid to the floor. "Oops! Clumsy me." She reached down, picked it up and thumbed through it. "More on that awful war." She tapped a picture of flaming jungle, closed the magazine and put it back on the table. "That would be a whole other line of whatever you call it to explore here, right?"

"In time, yes, but right now let's try to get you settled. Remember how to breathe slowly and pay attention to the breath in and out, in and out?"

"Yes, and I think I'm starting to get the hang of it."

"Good, good. Close your eyes, then, and I'll walk you through another deep breathing exercise."

For the next several minutes Emily followed Dr. Blake's soothing voice, and her anxiety slowly subsided.

When the therapist stopped speaking, Emily opened her eyes, feeling only a slight hint of nausea. "It's like magic, isn't it."

"I wish we had more time to get to the root of this today, but I do have an opening Friday morning, eleven o'clock. Will that work?"

"Yes, it will."

"In the meantime, I'm writing a prescription for anti-anxiety medication to take only in a crisis, not routinely, and I'm giving you the address of a yoga center just a few blocks down Michigan Avenue. I want you to start taking classes."

"Yoga? I thought that was just for hippies," Emily said.

Dr. Blake laughed and handed Emily the prescription and referral note. "I think you'll be pleasantly surprised."

Emily tucked the papers into her purse and rose from the couch. "Thank you, doctor." Pulling the bottom ribbing of her sweater down she shuffled to the exit and opened the door.

"Remember, you can call anytime."

"I will." Emily stepped out of the office, paused with her palm on the wall, then proceeded through Dr. Blake's waiting area toward a bank of elevators down the hall.

Chapter 23

From Waukegan to Cairo, Quincy to Danville, and Galena to Allendale, buds burst across the state of Illinois in mid-April 1969. Leaves rustled where, only days earlier, barren branches had craned toward a distant sun. Gardens and fields popped to life with crocus, forsythia, daffodil, iris, hyacinth. People in Kiminee whistled while tucking away snow tires and storm windows. Even Tam-Tam and Abby Louise, inveterate pessimists, couldn't help pausing to smile as slapping winds shifted to caressing breezes along the Bendy. In Windy Wood, however, a light snow fell. Carly Mae and Aunt Truly, bundled in wool, sat in rockers by a wood-burning stove.

Aunt Truly reached down to pull out an embroidery project from a wicker basket near her feet. "I reckon it'll just be another day or two, and winter will be gone."

Carly Mae pushed with her feet to set the rocker in motion. "And one way or another Buster and I will set off for home."

"I'm hoping my salve worked for Mindy and that she'll be at the door as soon as the weather clears."

"Me, too. The time has gone by quicker than I thought. I think it's because of all the stories you told. Where did you learn them?"

"Well now, there was a time before radio and TV when folks had to entertain themselves." Aunt Truly flattened a denim jacket on her lap and resumed stitching a border of violets at the hem. "We'd gather by candlelight and lanterns in the evenings and tell stories, sing songs, play instruments, a lot of them homemade. It was surely a lucky family that had something as grand as a piano. We read, too, those of us who had book learnin' anyway. And there were always games. But I guess the storytellin' is what captured my imagination most."

"I can't wait to hear how things turn out for the frog."

"How's that?" Aunt Truly brushed some lint off the jacket, then looked up.

"You know, the story about the trapper and the golden frog."

"Oh, yes. I'd love to hear you tell it, dear. *The Frog Who Wouldn't Budge* one of my favorites."

"Well, I can try. I won't be as good as you, but here goes." Carly Mae took in a breath and let it out slowly, collecting her thoughts. "It starts out that this trapper built a cabin by what he thought was a quiet pond, but a gleaming golden frog that croaked and chuck-chuck-chucked lived there, too. In fact, the little frog had called that pond home for a long, long, long time. This mattered not to the trapper, who couldn't stand the noise. He decided the frog had to go. So, first he stood up tall by the water, puffed up his chest, stomped his feet, waved his arms and yelled at the frog to go away. He was a fearsome sight, but the little frog wasn't cowed. He went on about his business, croaking and chuck-chuck-chucking the whole time.

"The trapper stormed off and returned with a shotgun. He aimed at the frog and pulled the trigger. Buckshot sprayed everywhere. Some landed on the little frog, giving him spots of deep greenish brown. But this didn't bother him at all. He went about his business, croaking and chuck-chuck-chucking away. The man returned to his cabin, where he sulked and sulked—until a new idea struck. He bent low to the ground and slinked toward the frog inch by inch. It took half the day because he crept so slowly, but at last, the unsuspecting amphibian was within reach. He lurched, wrapped his fingers around the poor creature and cackled, his face contorting into a sinister smile as he reveled in his victory. But, again, the little golden frog wasn't cowed. He wiggled and croaked, jiggled and chuck-chuck-chucked, tickling the man's hand. The captor giggled and loosened his grip while the prey squiggled out and hopped away. And … um …I'm not sure what comes next. My memory isn't as good as it used to be."

Aunt Truly looked up. "Just relax. You'll remember. You've got a knack for this." She resumed sewing.

"Let's see. I'm thinking. … Oh, I remember!" Carly Mae bounced once in her seat and continued. "The trapper gave pursuit, but the frog was too fast, so the man gave up and slumped on home. Soon he heard the frog's croaking and chuck-chuck-chucking on and on. He went to bed that night fuming about his nemesis. He couldn't sleep at all. But in the morning, he remembered his fish net. He grabbed it and snuck up on the frog again. This time, he captured and held his mark with ease. The trapper pranced off with glee, wondering what to do with the noisy golden frog and decided the best thing would be to bury him deep, deep in the ground. This the man did, certain he'd never hear from the frog again.

"Back inside at day's end, he drifted off to a much needed, contented sleep, but in the night, he was awakened by—"

"Yes, yes, the croaking and chuck-chuck-chucking. Delightful!" Aunt Truly smiled while continuing to work. "Keep going. You're doing a fine job."

"He stomped outside and realized the croaking and chuck-chuck-chucking was coming from underground—right where he'd buried the frog. Enraged, he dug up the hole and pulled out his victim. The poor thing wasn't the least bit golden anymore; he was tan with greenish brown spots, but the animal was alive as alive could be and was not the least bit cowed. So the trapper—"

Just then, a knock came at the door. Carly Mae leaned forward, putting weight on her feet, but Aunt Truly motioned for her to stay where she was. "Rest easy. I'll get it." The old woman rose from her rocker, shuffled to the door and opened it.

Mindy wobbled at the threshold. "Need more salve ... had to get here come hell ... or ... high water. I'm burning up." Splotches of blood on her jeans grew as she stepped inside and lost her balance.

Aunt Truly grabbed her arm. "There, there, I've got you now." But Aunt Truly swayed and stumbled under Mindy's weight.

Carly Mae reached Aunt Truly just in time to keep her and Mindy from falling.

Footing regained, Aunt Truly asked, "Get the door, will you?"

Snow fell so rapidly Mindy's Triumph convertible was almost buried in white when Carly Mae pushed the door closed.

From a rickety chair at Aunt Truly's kitchen table, Carly Mae took a last bite of oatmeal and watched snow melt rapidly outside. "Finally, the thaw," she said.

"A few days later than I thought, but once it comes, winter's gone in a flash." Aunt Truly took a swig of hot tea.

Carly Mae pushed a drawing along the table toward Aunt Truly. Due to the teen's blurry vision, the lines were fuzzy, giving it a dream-like feel. It showed the old woman in a rocker, mouth open, eyes alight. "This is for you."

The old woman looked down. "Thank you, darlin'. Oh, my, you flatter me. "

"That's exactly how you look to me when you're spinning tales. I should have written them all down. I don't know how I'll remember them."

"Just tell 'em to yourself on your journey home. They'll come back; it's like riding a bicycle."

"How is Mindy this morning?"

"A bit worse, I'm afraid. I've done all I can do." Aunt Truly wiped gnarled hands on her apron.

Carly Mae strode to the bedroom. Mindy was in a deep sleep, her skin pale and breath shallow. The girl dropped to her knees and grasped Mindy's hand. Aunt Truly followed and stood by the bed, Buster at her heels.

"Oh, Mindy, you didn't deserve this. It's all my fault," Carly Mae cried out. "I feel so bad."

"Stand up, young one, and look at me."

Carly Mae rose and faced her friend. The two searched one another's eyes.

"Never, never blame yourself for this. Never. This is strictly the fault of Leon Ames. He woulda gone to her home and raised hell with or without you." Aunt Truly looked away. "Now, let's get you packed."

"Maybe I shouldn't go just yet. If Mindy—"

"You've got a family waiting. Every day without you is torture for them. And you'd be of no use to Mindy here. Go on up to the attic. Pick out something—a backpack or duffel, perhaps—whatever you want to carry your clothes and such."

Carly Mae bent down and kissed Mindy's forehead. Then she followed Aunt Truly to the attic stairs, where the old woman motioned for her to go up. "Take what you like. I have so much more than I need just collectin' cobwebs."

"What if she doesn't—"

"The day's a wastin'. Get a move on, or I'll throw you out the door right now."

Carly Mae bolted up the stairs two at a time. She returned to the cabin's main living area about twenty minutes later and placed a bulging backpack on metal frame by the door. "I know I have to go, but I'm not sure which way." She took a Navy peacoat from a hook on the wall and put it on.

"Just follow Buster. He found the way here; he'll lead you home along paths no human has trod for ages."

"You make it sound like an adventure."

"Look at life like an adventure every day, and you'll do just fine." Aunt Truly rested her palms on the girl's temples, fingers on top of her head. "Hold still for a minute here." Under her breath, she counted, slow as a waltz.

Carly Mae felt a sense of peace flow through her. At the count of thirty, Aunt Truly removed her hands. Carly Mae blinked and was floored to see the world more clearly. "How did you do that? I mean I can see so much better. Not quite like before, but really good."

"It's just a little something my grandmother taught me long ago. I wasn't sure it would still work." Aunt Truly winked and handed her guest a small canvas tote. "This is jerky and trail mix, full of powerful nutrients to last you, so you don't need much. Just nibbles 'ill do."

Carly Mae folded the tote and tucked it in the backpack, hoisted the apparatus onto her back and kissed Aunt Truly on the cheek. "Oh, about the frog story ... How does it end?"

"Ah, that's for you to figure out, my dear." Aunt Truly tightened the pack's belt around Carly Mae's waist, then took both of the girl's hands and squeezed.

Carly Mae returned the pressure and noticed that instead of being stiff and useless, the pinky and ring finger on her left hand could bend and grip. "Another trick from your grandmother?"

"Shhhh." The old woman put a finger to her lips, then opened the door.

Carly Mae stepped onto the porch. Mindy's green Triumph, gleaming in the sunshine, was parked less than a yard away in a puddle expanding by the second with snow melt. All across Windy Wood sprouts of violet grass poked up; scattered patches of white were the only remaining hints of winter. Buster raced ahead toward the bumpy road lined with fir trees with purple needles. Carly Mae proceeded beneath the trellis, then turned and blew a kiss to Aunt Truly, who swayed at the doorsill and waved.

Chapter 24

A family of four saddled up at Huckleberry Stables and followed Dirk, their trail guide, into a forest preserve about ten miles east of the Mississippi. It was a perfect April day. Birdsong filled the air; tender baby leaves tested the new warmth. Color adorned the landscape; it seemed the whole world was unwinding and gulping air that was fresh and energizing as a new Beatles tune.

Dirk was in the lead, followed by the mother, wearing black stretch pants, sneakers, and one of her husband's white dress shirts under a windbreaker. Her French twist was protected by a lemon-yellow chiffon scarf tied under her chin. Behind her rode the children, a boy and girl. Each wore a madras shirt, jeans, fringed leather jacket, and western style hat and boots. The father brought up the rear. Except for his seersucker shirt, his clothes matched his children's. Everyone sang "Home on the Range" as they clopped along.

An hour into the ride, they stopped for a break. Dirk dismounted and tied his reins to a post near the trail. "You can hitch right up here, too, and then get some of this new stuff we call trail mix. We make it ourselves at the stables." He reached into his saddlebags and pulled out a Baggie for each of his riders.

"I'm thirsty," the girl said after she dismounted.

"Help! I can't get down," the boy cried out, his boot stuck in a stirrup.

The mother dismounted and hurried to help her son. The father handed a canteen of water to the girl.

"Is this all we have?" she complained while accepting the drink. "Can't I have a Coke or 7 Up?"

"I gotta pee!" The boy ran toward bushes at the edge of the trail.

"Not here, right out in the open," the dad said. "We can find a better spot."

Father and son meandered down a path and relieved themselves well out of sight. When turning back, they noticed an old dirt road ran parallel to the path. They clomped through a break in the trees to have a look.

"Sure is dusty," the boy said. He peered up the road. "Daddy?" He pointed. "What's that?"

The man's eyes followed the line of his son's finger. Seeing the colors of Jewel Tea Co., he drew his fingers into fists. "Looks like a delivery truck or van."

"Like the guy who sells dishes to Mom?"

The dad wrinkled his brow. "Maybe."

"Can we go see?"

"Might not be safe." He put both hands on his son's shoulders and swiveled him toward the trail. "Go tell Dirk I need him. And, you, stay there with your mom and sister."

In the waning days of April 1969, Missy continued to man the mostly inactive hotline in the police station's reception area every morning, including Sunday, while Earl devoted himself to contacting his cohorts throughout the state and across the country. One morning, he placed so many calls he could barely talk.

Missy made him a cup of tea with lemon and brought it into his office. "You gotta slow down. It won't do Carly Mae no good if you wear yourself out."

Just then the phone rang. Earl picked up the receiver. "Alvin, how are you?" he rasped. "Yeah, I've been spouting off too much. What's up? Got another book recommendation for me? … Huckleberry Stables? … Why are you there of all places? You don't ride."

The caller was Alvin Aldridge, police chief in Mighty Oaks, Illinois, the closest town to where a body in a Jewel Tea truck had just been found. He and Earl had struck up a friendship during Earl's many outbound calls. They'd discovered they both loved detective novels, especially those by Raymond Chandler.

Earl scribbled on a pad near the phone. "Oh, oh … yes … I see. You're sure it's a Jewel Tea truck?" He threw the pencil down and stood up. "I'm leaving now." He hung up the phone, tore off his page of notes, pulled his gun from a drawer, put it in his holster, and grabbed his jacket.

"What's going on?" Missy asked.

"I'm heading to Mighty Oaks, you know, that pretty town on the Mississippi in Adams County southwest of here a ways. Alvin says they found the truck, well, a Jewel Tea truck near a stable, and there's only one Jewel Tea truck missing as far as anyone knows." He dashed out of the office.

Missy rolled her chair back and shot up, chasing Earl. "Carly Mae? Did they find Carly Mae?"

"Alls I know is there's a body inside—"

Missy caught up to him and yanked his arm, "No!"

"Hold on." He rested his hand over hers, light as a butterfly. "I was about to say it's not female. That's all I know. I'll call as soon as I find out more."

Missy shook a finger at him. "You darn well better!"

Earl got into his cruiser and drove off, tires screeching. His swift exit caught the attention of neighbors, who congregated at the station. Missy got on the phone and called friends and neighbors one after another. Soon the area around Missy's desk was crowded with people passing information on to one another and to those lining up outside. And, as these things typically go, bits and pieces of the news got distorted, so some people were beside themselves thinking Carly Mae was found dead in the truck, had been run over by the truck and all manner of other horrible things.

Late in the day, Earl called to confirm it wasn't Carly Mae's body in the truck and that there would be a search of dental records to see if they could identify the body. They suspected it was the same person who killed Dusty and abducted Carly Mae. A pistol was recovered. Plus, there was additional evidence on the dashboard.

"What evidence?" Missy demanded.

"Hold your horses. I haven't seen it yet, but it seems to indicate Carly Mae made it out of the truck alive. It looks like he didn't kill her. That's all I can say now."

"Wow! He didn't kill her. She's alive! She's alive!" Missy jumped up and down by the hot line, and others in the office did the same.

"We sure hope she is," Earl said. "Folks are searching right now. I've gotta go now and join them.»

After bidding farewell to Earl, Missy hung up the phone and exclaimed, "Carly Mae's alive. I'm sure of it." She filled townsfolk in as best as she could, then shooed everyone out and went home to have a piece of pecan pie.

That evening, after another episode of *Bonanza*, folks savored the tail end of Sunday before a new work week began. Blanche and friends swooned for Little Joe Cartwright in her room, Mick Deely pulled out a Jew's harp and played on his porch, Tam-Tam stitched clothing for a new set of dolls, Missy dialed Maridee at her kitchen wall phone, parents cajoled their children toward bed, and Abby Louise slugged scotch and prayed for a better tomorrow. Then the sky lit up, and everyone except the most feeble of the feeble at Touch of Kindness Rest Home ran outside to see shooting stars sail by and explode into brilliant colors before twinkling like citrine gemstones and drifting to the ground. The display lasted seven minutes, and each and every person big and small took it as a sign that Missy was right. Their beloved Carly Mae was alive.

Chapter 25

Maridee Pratt and Missy Lake sat at Missy's dining room table, embroidering decorative pillows destined for the lobby of the Bendy River Inn. Designed by Missy, they featured two of Kiminee's botanical anomalies: black-eyed Susans fashioned with tiny red beads to resemble the ones that glowed at 5:05 p.m. daily from June through September, and lilacs inspired by the flowers in Missy's front yard that bloomed year round. While the women worked, their Maxwell House coffee cooled in china cups, and a chocolate-vanilla smell of Tollhouse cookies wafted from the adjacent kitchen.

Missy took a sip of coffee and looked at Maridee. "Thank you so much for helping with these. There's only two more to do after this, so we're on track to have six ready for the grand opening of the cafe and restaurant this Sunday."

"Aw, it's nothing. That's what friends are for." Maridee tied a knot and snipped a thread.

"I'm hoping Earl comes back in time for the opening, and with our Carly Mae on his arm, too. Wouldn't that be something?"

"That would be fantastic, especially since opening day is Mother's Day." Maridee held up her work. "These are gorgeous, you know. I think they'd make great ambassadors for our town."

"Ambassadors? What are you talkin' about? My Velda's part of a grand business venture. I'm just helping her pretty up the antique bench and chair she pulled out of my attic for the inn."

"Customers are going to admire them; some will even want one for themselves. You could make extras and sell them at Suzette's. Velda could refer people to the shop."

"I'm not steppin' one foot inside Suzette's. Them dolls of Tam-Tam's, they're smack dab in the front window." Missy set back to work furiously, jabbed her thumb with a needle, winced, but kept going.

"Don't be that way. You're being unreasonable. … Besides, it's no fun without you."

"Seems you've done just fine without me there.»

"Tam-Tam's new dolls don't look the least bit like you or any-one we—"

Missy slapped her embroidery on the table. "One doll is still wearin' my weddin' dress in miniature in every detail, down to the lace on the bodice and pansies embroidered on the inside of the hem. She copied my veil and bouquet, too. The face isn't mine, but everything else is. She continues to make dolls she knows full well will upset me."

"She did make adjustments; you have to cut her some slack, living all alone the way she does by the river, nobody to care for her."

Missy took a long draw of coffee and patted her lips with her napkin. "I can't help that she's got no family left."

Maridee pursed her lips. "You were once like family to her."

"I went steady with Juke for a time. That's all." Missy raised her voice. "You can't possibly be blaming me."

"I haven't a clue what happened. You never said.»

Missy shook her head and tousled her curls in an effort to remain composed, but tears eked from the corners of her eyes. "He made me promise never to talk about it, and I never have."

"Who?"

"Uncle Maurice."

"You've kept a promise to that ogre all these years? Oh, you poor dear." Maridee reached over and squeezed Missy's hand. "What was so bad that you weren't supposed to tell even your closest friends?"

"I wish that day never happened." She wiped her tears and blew her nose.

"You and Juke were supposed to go fishing. I remember 'cause I helped you pick out your outfit."

"Oh, those times, those times. Us girls used to have so much fun. I was feeling lucky 'cause we'd heard of a new spot where the walleyes were bitin' like crazy. So, all excited, I dug up some really fat worms and pranced on over to Juke's. It was a gorgeous day, you know, one of those when the sun is just right and a fresh, warm breeze is blowin'. I was feelin' absolutely divine. But as I got closer, a snappin' sound got my attention. I couldn't quite place it. Then, when I reached Juke's yard, there was his dad, Harlan, with a jug of hard cider in one hand, and in the other, a whip. Oh, what a fearsome sight! He was crackin' it in the air and then whippin' the ground. Little blades of fresh green grass and clumps of dirt was flyin', and all the while, he was takin' swigs of his homemade brew and yellin' at Juke, 'Go ahead, do it, do it! Show her who's boss!' Juke was taller than Harlan by a good three inches by then. He coulda challenged his dad and won. I'm sure of it. But it was like Harlan had him under a spell. Juke had his own sweet sister, Gracie, pinned to a tree, and he ripped her blouse right open." Missy's voice cracked.

Maridee sucked in a breath.

Missy took another sip of coffee and continued. "She was cryin' and pleadin', 'No, Juke. No, not you, not you, too.' Their brother—you remember Bram, don't you?"

Maridee nodded. "Of course, sweet, sweet Bram. Abby Louise's first and only crush."

"He was peekin' from behind a rain barrel. He looked terrified. And Harlan kept yellin' at Juke, 'Go on, take her, take her. It's the only way to keep her in line.' All the while he kept lettin' loose with that whip, and Juke was rubbin' up against Gracie and his hand pulled up her skirt. And I froze. I tried to cry out, but couldn't even peep. Then my hands started shakin', and I dropped my rod and worms. Them things just started slitherin' all over the ground, and my voice broke loose. I screamed and screamed. I couldn't stop." Choked with emotion, Missy paused to wipe tears away and then blew her nose again.

Maridee put a hand on Missy's arm. "If it's too much—"

"Oh, I gotta finish what I started now, after all this time. ... That Harlan, he spied me. He had madness in his eyes and let out this evil laugh. I turned and ran. I was fast, but Juke was faster. He came up from behind and grabbed me. I tried to fight him off, but he dragged me toward the tool shed. Gracie raced to the porch, Harlan right behind her, whippin' her legs. She banged on the door. It was locked. She cried out, 'Mama, Mama, please let me in. Let me in!' Tam-Tam was at the kitchen window, lookin' out, like it was an ordinary day. She didn't move one muscle to help. I almost broke free, but then Harlan came over to help Juke. I'll never forget the sour smell of alcohol on their breath. They reeked of it when they forced me behind the tool shed. Then Harlan went and dragged Gracie over, and what they did to us, what they did to us, I can't, I—"

"You don't have to," Maridee said, sweat beading on her forehead.

Missy leaned back and took another gulp of coffee. "All the while, Tam-Tam sat by the window, still as a lizard, watchin'."

"Oh, my God. I had no idea." Maridee shifted weight from side to side in her chair.

"When they finally let me go, they cackled and chugged more of that devil drink. I stumbled and limped home as fast as I could—straight to my mother. I had to tell her."

"Of course you did. I would have done the same."

"I couldn't have known Uncle Maurice and my dad were in the next room. I couldn't have known what they would do, that the two of them would bring me back there—the last place I wanted to be—that my dad and Gracie would end up dead, that Harlan and Juke would become fugitives wanted for double murder, that Bram would run off and get himself killed in the war."

Maridee hugged Missy. "It's not your fault what happened."

"Try telling that to Abby Louise. She's never been the same. She just drinks her sorrows away and cuts me every chance she gets."

"Tam-Tam should set her straight."

"She'd be the last to do that, what with those dolls. It's not just the wedding dolls either. I saw some wearin' the exact same outfits we had on that day. My white shorts and red-and-white gingham blouse, Juke's brand new indigo jeans, Harlan's frayed flannel shirt unbuttoned and wide open, Gracie's' s light blue skirt and matching blouse, each with white piping; Bram's tan slacks, fringed brown-leather jacket and cowboy hat. How could she? It's diabolical."

"I have half a mind to drive her out of town right now."

Missy stared out the window and took in a breath. "Oh no. The cookies! They're burning!"

"Don't get up. I'll take 'em out."

"Thanks, I'm plum wore out."

Maridee hastened to the oven, pulled out the trays and called to Missy. "They're only a little singed around the edges. They'll be fine." She put the crispy treats on top of the stove, then returned to Missy and kissed the top of her head.

The two sipped coffee in silence for a few moments. Then Missy said, "You know, it took me a long while to trust Grover on account of what happened. He must have asked me to marry him a hundred times before I finally accepted." She shook out her pillowcase and held it up to admire the red beads glowing in the sunlight.

"We all wondered why it took you so long to warm to him. We knew it was a match made in heaven." Maridee threaded a needle and got back to work.

As she stitched, Maridee vowed to herself she would remove all of Tam-Tam's dolls from Suzette's. But a few days later, she arrived at the shop shortly after it had closed and was surprised to see the dolls were no longer in the display window. She unlocked the door, entered and checked the shelves to no avail. She looked over receipts for the past several days and found only one doll sale, so she picked up the phone and called Tempest, who had worked the cash register that day.

"Last I saw, Tam-Tam's dolls was still in the window," Tempest told Maridee.

Chapter 26

Mother's Day 1969, Barb, Jeff, Velda and Maxine sipped their new coffee blend in a back booth of the relocated Good Luck Cafe. They agreed the pinch of chicory, added at the suggestion of Tempest Binsack, gave the drink a pleasing woody flavor. The partners went through their opening-day checklist, and it appeared all was in order. Laminated menus were stacked at the counter, silverware and dishes in their places, and the refrigerator and freezer well stocked. The tables sported the standard salt, pepper, sugar, ketchup, mustard and napkins, with all surfaces clean and gleaming. A jukebox was plugged in and ready to play, and a mural on the opposite wall created by students at the academy depicted the old Kiminee home and field of black-eyed Susans.

Outside, a green-and-white striped awning shone in the morning sun; above it the Good Luck Café's sign was securely in place. Across the front window a string of red, white, green, blue and gold flags hung above a Grand Opening sign taped to the glass. On the sidewalk, young and old, townies and farmers, hippies and businessmen, decorated veterans and draft dodgers, friendly folks and curmudgeons formed a line that stretched to the corner and around the block. Rumors had spread about how the cafe could help heal whatever might ail someone.

Barb and Jeff never claimed anything remotely along those lines, but even the shrewdest skeptics secretly hoped it was true.

At last, the four owners ambled toward the entrance, stopping here and there to straighten a napkin holder or brush away a bit of lint. They opened the doors, stepped across the threshold, and locked arms. "We're open for business. Come on in!" Barb hailed to cheers from the crowd.

The stools, booths and tables filled quickly. Some people stood at the end of the counter and ordered food to go. Barb and Jeff cooked and manned the counter. Maxine tended to the tables and back booths. Velda covered the window booths and the cash register.

Jasper and Emily pulled up in their Willys wagon, both smiling. He killed the engine, reached over and patted Emily's thigh. "You look the picture of health."

Emily smiled wide. "Not one little bit of nausea. I had no idea therapy would help this much. Dr. Blake has done wonders."

They joined the line on the sidewalk and chatted with their friends, who all remarked on how vibrant Emily looked. Meanwhile, a man in a black suit with lavender pinstripes, brown hair touching his shoulders and glasses with metallic frames the color of copper approached Velda, who was straightening a stack of menus at the register. "Excuse me, ma'am." He cleared his throat. "Do you know a man named Damon Foley?"

The question jarred her like ketchup on ice cream. She glared at the stranger and said, "Who wants to know?"

He handed her a business card.

She scanned the card. "Dry Gulch Asylum?"

Before the man could answer, Earl Wiggs walked in. Everyone in the cafe stopped talking and looked up. The stranger leaned against a wall.

Missy gulped down a half-chewed bite of cinnamon roll and burst out of a booth she was sharing with Maridee and Tempest. She ran so fast she smacked right into Earl. She tried to speak, but gasped from a surge of emotion instead.

Earl embraced her. "I'm sorry," he whispered into her ear. "I know she's out there, but I don't know where."

At the sight of Missy's crestfallen face and sunken chest as she backed away from Earl, all the joy of the cafe and inn's grand opening whooshed out the open door in one big gust. The festivities had for a little while put Dusty's death and Carly Mae's abduction in the back of their minds. A microphone had already been set up in a small raised area in one corner of the cafe for the Kiminee Academy String Band, which was set to play in a few minutes.

Mild-mannered, good-natured Earl went to the mic and did his best to brighten people's spirits as he filled them in on the investigation. He affirmed for the community that Carly Mae had indeed escaped from her abductor and left behind a scribbled note, stating she'd been taken at gunpoint by one Leon Ames, who was later stabbed by a former girlfriend. "We haven't been able to find Carly Mae yet, but we all—"

"So, you basically have nothin' new to tell us," Abby Louise taunted from a corner stool.

"Don't go attackin' Earl now." Tam-Tam swiveled on the stool next to Abby Louise and nudged her in the ribs with her elbow, which was enough to cause her friend to lose her balance.

"Hey!" Abby Louise slid off the stool.

Maxine stepped in to help Abby Louise up while heated conversations broke out around the cafe about whether Earl was doing a good enough job.

He stuck his shivering hands in his pockets, looked down and, with tears in his eyes, said, "Our Carly Mae's a smart girl. She found shelter somewhere. I'm sure of it."

The crowd quieted, most of his accusers realizing he wasn't some enemy keeping things from them. Earl Wiggs was one of them.

Earl stepped away from the microphone, approached Missy and said, "See you at the station tomorrow?"

"You bet," she replied.

Can you bring the kids and Velda, too? I'd like to talk with the whole family."

The little string band began to play. The tunes leaned toward the slow and melancholy at first, but then picked up, and the nimble danced down aisles between tables. Other folks nibbled on their meals, as Barb walked around offering free slices of banana crème pie. When they paid their bills, the good people of Kiminee left extra large tips, then drifted away. Along with them went the stranger with shoulder-length hair and glasses with copper colored frames.

While neighbors yawned and stretched in the morning light and slid their feet from beneath covers into cozy slippers, Velda, Blanche and Ray tromped with Missy to the police station. Once inside, Missy sat at her usual spot by the hot line while Earl brought folding chairs over for the others.

"So what's up?" Missy said to Earl. "This is sure a heap of suspense."

"People are gonna think we've gotten up to mischief," Blanche said, situating herself right beside her grandmother.

"Not a chance." Earl ruffled the flaxen hair on her head. "I just didn't want to say what I have to say to a crowd."

"That doesn't sound good," Ray said. He settled in at Missy's other side.

"It's not so much bad as curious. Anyway, the corpse hasn't been officially identified by family yet, but Alvin knew the guy and said Leon Ames was his name."

"Is that helpful to us in finding Carly Mae?" Missy asked.

"Not exactly, but in the note she left in Dusty's truck Carly Mae said Ames' old girlfriend, Mindy, had been shot. Alvin, who knew

Mindy well and said she'd dumped Ames years ago and turned her life around, went to her place right away. Mindy and a little Triumph she kept hidden were gone. It's odd because the evidence indicates she was seriously hurt, but wherever she went, it wasn't the local hospital. Nobody's seen her."

"So what does this have to do with finding Carly Mae?" Velda asked. She kicked the leg of the table.

"The search for Mindy is ongoing, and I think she'll be found. When that happens, Mindy might know something that will lead us to Carly Mae."

"Might, might, might, it's all speculative," Missy said. "This Mindy person could be dead for all we know."

"There's something else. Alvin took me to Mindy's, and I found this on the kitchen table." He sidestepped to his desk, lifted a sketchbook and handed it to Missy. "You'll see likenesses of Mindy and that Ames fella, but then flip through the pages and you see Buster, and all of you and me, and scenes from around town, you know, the Five 'N Dime, the river, the statue of Fleur and Charles down at the square, Damon in his favorite fishing hat. I wanted to give these to you in private, not with the whole town watching. Alvin gave the okay, said he didn't need them."

Velda rose and moved around the desk to hover over Missy's shoulder.

"Oh, my, my, she's captured us exactly," Missy said, tapping a picture of herself wearing a bonnet she'd worn to church last Easter.

"Oh, look, it's Dusty standing at his van, by the willow." Blanche's eyes filled. "She was wanting to remember, even Dusty's last day."

"Do you think she knew Dusty, you know … " Ray asked.

"My guess is she did, because Mindy's TV and radio are working just fine," Earl said. He put a box of tissues on Missy's desk so Carly Mae's kin could wipe their eyes and blow stuffy noses as they looked through the drawings.

When they reached the end, Missy closed the book and looked up at Earl, who stood nearby. "I'm just so worried. Where could our girl be?"

"I honestly don't know," he replied. "I'll tell you one thing, though, we're not going to stop looking; that's for sure."

They sat in silence for a few moments, each lost in private thoughts. Then Missy said, "Well, I suppose we should get goin'. The kids have final exams comin' up."

Velda picked up the book and thumbed through the drawings again. She paused at one of Buster and saw the dog wink. She shrieked and dropped the pad.

"Watch it. These here is precious things," Missy said, grabbing the sketchpad and holding it to her chest.

"What's wrong, Mom?" Blanche asked.

"I swear I saw Buster wink in that drawing. I need to get on home." She rose, unsteady.

"We'll walk you there," Ray said.

"But you'll be late to school," Missy complained.

"Oh, Grams, you worry too much." Blanche took one of Velda's elbows. Ray took the other and they helped their mother ease toward the door. Missy followed, still clutching her granddaughter's artwork.

"You can hold on to those," Earl said to Missy. "And, you know, that wink …" Earl smiled as all four of them looked over their shoulders at him.

"What?" Missy asked.

"I saw it too."

Chapter 27

*C*arly Mae and Buster meandered alongside a stream that smelled increasingly of root beer as morning transitioned to high noon. She paused and spied a row of sassafras trees up ahead, along with scattered patches of sarsaparilla blooming close to the trail. She took in a deep breath. "Oh Buster, doesn't it remind you of summertime at home? Ice cream floats in the afternoon? Before the twister? When we lived in our own home with Mom and Dad and Blanche and Ray? When I had no inkling what bone tired really means?"

The dog nuzzled her hand and licked her fingers before he danced ahead.

"I'm trusting you, my friend. I don't know where we are or where we're going next," she said before pressing on. Soon she heard birdsong in the distance. It filled the forest in stereo, growing louder as she plodded after the dog, who trotted at a good clip, circling back often and always staying within her sight. A soaring symphony of harmonies surrounded them by the time they approached a bend where a menagerie of birds—warblers, tanagers, monk parakeets, greater prairie-chickens, cardinals and bobolinks—parlayed in the branches and underbrush to the syncopated hammering of foraging woodpeckers.

"Buster, listen, they're singing 'With a Little Help from My Friends'; I'm sure of it. It's from that crazy Beatles album. *Sgt. Pepper's.* They aren't singing actual words, of course, but it's that melody. It is. It is!" Carly Mae halted in the path and surveyed the surrounding trees. "This is like Christmas, or a birthday or Fourth of July, don't you think?"

She scratched the sweet spot between her dog's shoulders. Then, spirits soaring, she pranced like a filly to the waterside, took off her backpack, flattened against the bank, and leaned in to gulp clear, chilled water before dunking her head. Buster dove into the current and swam upstream. Thirst quenched and refreshed, Carly Mae pulled out the last of Aunt Truly's homemade pemmican and trail mix as Buster swam back, climbed onto the bank and shook like a washing machine agitator, sending beads of water in all directions.

Holding her arms out wide to catch the spray, Carly Mae said, "I hope we get home soon, 'cause once this is gone, it'll just be berries we pick along the way for me."

After she savored the last morsels of food and eyed a beaver on the opposite bank as it chomped through a supple willow trunk, Carly Mae zipped up her pack, slipped it on, and moseyed off with her intrepid scout. In the late afternoon, white rose petals with edges of mauve exactly like ones that grew in Missy's backyard fell through the sky and filled the path. Buster sailed through, but Carly Mae stopped and sat down in the middle of them, remembering how Missy's roses had enchanted her when she was small. She grabbed handful after handful, inhaling their sweet scent, then throwing them into the air and watching as some landed in the current and floated away.

Buster paced a few yards ahead, circled and yelped before turning onto a new trail. She rose, brushing petals from her clothes, and dashed off. When she reached the fork, she saw Buster speeding down a path lined with sunflowers the circumference of garbage can lids. Her father, Damon, once grew sunflowers almost that big. It seemed so long ago now. Carly Mae caught up to Buster and trotted beside him as the stream gradually lost its root-beer scent and the forest became an ordinary place where sun-dappled leaves danced in the breeze and birds called to their mates.

A road came into view in the distance. They picked up their pace, crossed what turned out to be only an overgrown lane, then saw a car whiz by on another far-off thoroughfare. They kept going till Carly Mae, flagging like a punctured tire, settled in just off the trail on a patch of ground bordered by budding rhubarb. Buster leaned against her shoulder and licked her face. She looked up as evening closed in and stars winked in the sky. "It's starting to feel like home," she whispered into the dog's only functioning ear. The two curled into each other as water burbled by, lulling Carly Mae to sleep just before dark clouds blew in, tossing rain like myriad tiny water balloons to splatter the earth.

Damon Foley followed Ned Burton outside and was immediately pelted by raindrops big as gumballs. Ned opened an umbrella, but gusts blew it out of shape and tore fabric from frame. Damon covered his face with his hands and cowered like a beaten dog against the thick metal door that had just closed behind him.

Ned touched his arm. "It's okay, Damon. It's just a little storm. We'll be fine."

Damon opened his eyes to a world that felt slimy as a banana slug and smelled of flowers—too many flowers, a hundred funeral parlors' worth of flowers; and spilled gasoline running from pump into gutter; and grease—old rancid grease—used repeatedly to turn potatoes into French fries. Damon gagged.

Ned urged him forward. "Let's go to the car now. I'm taking you to Kiminee. Today's the day, remember? We're going to see your friend Earl Wiggs. He's chief of police there now."

"Earl?" Damon muttered as he crept along the asylum's front walk, then rushed to the grass and vomited.

Georgia Webb, head nurse at Dry Gulch, emerged from the building and spat out, "Don't do it, Ned. Can't you see he's no good for the outside? Look at how miserable he is." She grabbed Damon by the back of his belt.

Damon slipped on slick pavement. Ned caught him before he fell. "Let go of him at once!" Ned commanded.

"Who do you think you are, some young hippie doctor trying to set the record straight? Any discrepancies you have found are honest mistakes. You're stirring up things better left alone." She gave Damon a good yank.

"I said, 'Let go!'" Ned pried her fingers away. "Keeping this man locked up all these years when you knew all along he wasn't Leon Ames," he spat. "I don't know how you can live with yourself."

Damon trembled as Ned hooked elbows with him and ushered him toward the car.

"You don't know what you're doing," Georgia called.

Ned opened the front passenger side door and helped Damon in.

"You'll get this place shut down. Is that what you want?" she railed. "For what? He's lost. Can't you see that? He's better off here."

Ned walked toward the driver's side. "Damon is no longer your concern."

"That's Leon Ames you've got there. You're about to drive off with one of the worst criminals ever. You're not safe, not with him and not with this storm brewing. You'll get stuck on these roads. Mark my words."

"I'm plenty safe with him, and I'm not concerned about the storm. It's you I'm worried about. Get back to work while you still have a job." He slid into the driver's seat, closed the door and started the engine.

"Damn you, Ned Burton!" Georgia stormed toward the car, water peeling off her body as she ran.

"Ready?" he said to Damon as he backed out of the driveway.

Damon remained quiet, hands squeezing his knees.

Georgia gave chase, kicking the bumper just as Ned drove through a puddle. Splashed in the face by muddy water that sprayed up from the wheels, Georgia backed away coughing, swearing and wondering how much Ned Burton had figured out. If he thought it was a negligent but basically innocent case of mistaken identity, she still had time, she reasoned. If he suspected she had harbored Leon Ames, had, in fact, masterminded the whole thing, that was a different story, and she had no plan.

Ned steered the car onto the road and picked up speed.

Damon leaned his head against the window, closed his eyes and saw yellow ocean waves with chartreuse caps battering a shore of blue-black sand.

Driving eastward, Ned spied charcoal-colored clouds swirling above. "Hold tight, Damon," he said. "Looks like we're in the middle of some film noir movie."

Chapter 28

A deluge tore in after Mother's Day 1969 like an enraged giant on the hunt. Lightning crackled low in the sky, sending shivers down the trees. Thunder roared through buildings, slamming doors, rattling windows, and knocking both cherished possessions and inconsequential clutter from shelves.

"Seems it's the Devil movin' furniture upstairs these days, not God himself," Missy said when looking out her dining room window with Blanche and Ray on the third day of battering.

The three chewed their lunch in slow motion. Fried Oscar Mayer bologna sandwiches with dill pickles and Lays potato chips on the side weren't as compelling as wind so strong it caused Missy's prized flowers to twist and stab like dancers contorting to dissonant, avant garde music composed by John Cage. The twins sat close together, wide-eyed, knees touching. This slowed their hearts, which had grown wild and fearful in the months since Carly Mae's abduction. Missy worried about this. Before she fell asleep each night, she prayed for Carly Mae's return and for the twins' bond to loosen enough for them to live a normal life.

On the fourth day, gales ripped branches from trees and smashed them into buildings and cars. All Kiminee denizens huddled inside, their doors locked against the relentless rain and howling wind, hoping the onslaught would end soon. But it kept on, and the river rose with ferocity. Folks living near the banks rushed to friends or relatives situated on slightly higher ground—all except for Tam-Tam. She wouldn't budge.

As night descended on the fifth day, Abby Louise Chute braved the journey from her home to Earl Wiggs' place and banged on the door. When he answered she blurted, "Tam-Tam won't leave. She's soaking wet, rocking on her porch, smoking her pipe and watching the water rise. It's like she's been hypnotized. She can't swim. You gotta help me get her out!"

Earl put on his rain slicker and tall, fly-fishing boots and walked Abby Louise to the cruiser in the driveway. He navigated the roads to Tam-Tam's, but visibility was so poor, he drove at five miles per hour. When they arrived, the river covered the bottom two porch steps. Earl waded through swirling water toward Tam-Tam.

"Get yourself outta here, Earl Wiggs. I din ask for no help," Tam-Tam growled.

He sloshed up the stairs, leaned down, and got a good grip on her. She tried to beat him off.

"I'm gonna lift you up now. You may have your reasons for not wanting to save yourself, but this is no way to go. I won't let you die here, so stop your protesting.»

As he took her into his arms, she spit, sputtered, and for the first time in anyone's memory, Tam-Tam Parlo broke down and cried. She was sobbing full force by the time Earl placed her gently in the cruiser's back seat. Abby Louise sat with her, calming her down, as Earl drove toward Abby's. On the way, they passed Missy's home. In rain thick as Niagara Falls, they did not see a teenage girl and her dog, battered, soaked and shivering, at the door.

As the great deluge continued to pummel and rip Kiminee's tattered homes and fields, Ned pulled up in front of the police station, weary from all the times he'd gotten stuck in potholes and had to rely on strangers passing by to help push his car out. Drops splattered on his rain gear and hammered his face as he made his way from the car to the door. Inside, he approached Missy. She was manning the hotline and leafing through a copy of *The Whole Earth Catalog* that Willie Holt loaned to her last time she was up at the old Kiminee place for a meeting of the weaving club. Ned waited quietly, water dripping from his body onto linoleum.

Missy startled when she looked up. "Oh, my, hello there. When did you come in?"

"Just now, ma'am," Ned replied, tipping his cap, releasing a little stream of water that splashed onto the desk.

"Watch it," Missy scolded. She lifted the catalog with one hand and reached into her desk for a paper napkin with the other.

"Sorry about that." Ned removed his fogged-up, wire rim glasses, pulled a handkerchief from his pocket and dried the lenses.

"Oh, don't worry over it." Missy wiped the surface, put the catalog back down and peered at the man standing before her. "So, then, I guess you didn't come to talk about this fool book. I'm Missy, by the way. Missy Lake.

He replaced his glasses and tucked a wayward strand of wet hair behind his ear. "I'm Ned Burton, and I'd like to see the chief of police if I may.»

"You wouldn't happen to have a tip about Carly Mae's whereabouts, would you?"

"Carly Mae Foley?"

She clasped her hands over her heart, turned her head toward Earl's office and called, "Earl, come quick; it's about our Carly Mae."

Earl burst into the reception area. "What did you say?"

"Hold on a minute, " Ned said. "I didn't say that. I have news about her father, Damon."

"Damon? Oh no, no." Missy rose and lurched to Earl. "Damon. Did you hear that? Our Damon."

Earl's chest heaved as he wrapped his arms around her. "I knew this day would come. I guess we can have a proper funeral and burial now." Earl stroked her salt and pepper hair.

Missy pressed her face against his freshly ironed uniform.

"Why do you assume he's dead?" Ned asked.

"It's been eight long years since that awful twister swept him away." Missy returned to her desk, grabbed a tissue and blew her nose.

"So where did you find his remains?" Earl asked, eyes downcast.

"He's alive and well in my car."

Missy cocked her head, perplexed. "What … what are you saying? … How can that be?"

"As far I can tell, he's been at the Dry Gulch Asylum for the Criminally Insane all this time. I'm the director there, just took the post not long ago, and found myself in a helluva mess. There's been malfeasance up the wazoo I'm bound to report."

"Damon in an institution for criminals?" Earl asked. "That doesn't make sense."

"Damon's no criminal," Missy said, marching toward a coat rack by the door.

She lifted her rain slicker, put it on, opened the door and stepped into the storm. Earl threw on his raincoat and followed with Ned.

"Where is he?" Missy demanded.

Ned pointed to his car parked a few feet away. Missy bolted forward. Ned took her arm and pulled. "Um, ma'am, he's been through a lot and might not be the man he once was—not that I know who he used to be."

Missy shook him off, jumped over a puddle to the car and opened the passenger door. A spray of water blasted a skeletal man with pasty, almost translucent skin and white hair. He stared straight ahead and shrank away from her.

Earl came to Missy's side and peered into the car. "Damon? What on earth did they do to you?"

Damon leaned his head back and howled like a wounded wolf abandoned by his pack. When that was done, he let out another and another, each more woebegone than the last. The car shook; the earth trembled. Then the police station and every structure from the Good Luck Café to the Five 'N Dime to Touch of Kindness Rest Home to the Academy shuddered. Damon's misery spread like the stench of Gerald McDuggin's new pig farm. Soon the whole town was on alert, holding tight to a piece of furniture or wall to keep from weeping and crashing onto shuddering floors.

Ray and Blanche emerged from their respective rooms and held on to each other while the house gave one last heave. As Blanche caught her breath, she noticed mud on Missy's carpets and said, "Ray, how could you make such a mess?"

"Wasn't me. Must have been you." He jerked away from her.

"When have you ever known me to track in mud like that?"

"I swear it wasn't me."

"We'd better clean it up before Missy comes home."

"Let's do it later." Ray headed down the stairs. "Don't you want to know what all the commotion is about?"

"Okay, but Grams won't be happy."

The twins were walking down Missy's front stairs as Damon gave one last yowl that reached to the clouds and back. The rain turned to a fine mist. Inside, Carly Mae dreamed of Mindy finding a golden frog hopping in the woods, while Buster curled against her legs, his sole ear perked, listening.

By the time Damon quieted, a crowd had surrounded Ned Burton's vehicle. Missy, Earl and Ned attempted to pry him from the passenger seat but had no luck.

"It's like trying to bend stone," Missy said to people who had drawn so close, they were bumping into her. She elbowed them to make room for Blanche and Ray, who were pushing through the crowd toward her. "Back away now. Back away. Here come the twins," she said.

The twins were so close together they appeared fused when they reached the car and stuck their heads in.

Blanche gasped at the sight of a man who barely resembled the father she remembered. "Oh, my God, his hair is white!" She touched Damon's shoulder. "Daddy?"

Damon turned his head, but his unfocused eyes appeared to look inward, not at her.

The teenagers were both momentarily speechless at their father's vacant gaze. Finally Ray said, "Dad, Dad, it's us, Ray and Blanche. Remember?"

Damon leaned back and stared at the ceiling. Ray and Blanch shrank back, hearts thumping in unison.

Missy put a palm on the lower back of each grandchild and pushed. "Keep goin' kids. Keep at it. He may not seem to be responding, but I know he hears you." Her voice, laced with a desperation she tried to mask with enthusiasm rang through the crowd. Nobody was fooled. Everyone shuddered, fearing Damon might be there in body but lost forever in spirit.

Then Blanche got inside the vehicle, sat next to her dad while Ray worked his way through onlookers to the other side of the car and slid in, too, so Damon had a twin on either side. They pressed close to him, and the strength of their love spread through Damon, and then out to the crowd. Gradually, the three inched as one toward the door on Blanche's side. She slid out, then came Damon, then Ray.

When Damon stuck his first slippered foot outside, people on the sidewalk cheered.

"Shhhh!" Missy commanded. "You might scare 'im."

A hush came over the friends and neighbors gathered under umbrellas in groups of two or three. Even the birds stopped ruffling their feathers, and ants stopped burrowing as Damon stood once again on the ground where he was born and raised. But then he slumped like a sapling uprooted. Ned helped the twins prop him up. Once supported, he looked from the ground to the sky, to the faces in the crowd to his hands, faded clothing and slippers. But he didn't make another sound, not even when Velda bounced up, clutching Maxine's hand, something a few folks whispered might have been insensitive of the two of them.

Hearing these comments, Velda let go of her lover's hand. Maxine gritted her teeth, face flushed.

"What now?" Earl asked of no one in particular.

"He needs care, obviously," Ned said.

Randy Tarr stepped forward to block Velda. "Now I don't expect Velda and Maxine are gonna want to bring him home to their double-wide, and unfortunately, his dear parents, Jim and Mary, succumbed to injuries suffered during the terrible twister, so I have an idea. I got a spare room with a new color TV complete with one of them remote controls. Damon is welcome with me as long as he wants. And folks can come visit anytime they want."

Not to be outdone by a Tarr, Tom McDuggin said, "Heck, I've got a whole apartment above my shop. We could fix that up. He'd have privacy and everything he could need."

"We've got a whole community up at my place," said Willie Holt, who, everyone agreed had done wonders with the Kiminee property he'd inherited. "I mean, we've got plenty of room, sure, and we've also got healers and great thinkers, and acres of love. I can't think of a better place for him."

"Yeah, but he don't know you, Willie. Did ya consider that?" Varnie Black called out.

Volunteers kept coming forward with passionate pleas for why they should be the ones to care for Damon. Arguments erupted over who would do the best job. At last, Earl stepped in. He looked at Velda and said, "Well, you're still married to Damon, so he's your responsibility, legally, I expect."

Maxine stiffened at this and pulled Velda aside, where the two had a heated discussion after which Maxine broke away and ran off, purposely stomping through puddles as she went. Velda's knees buckled, and she would have fallen had Tempest Binsack not caught her just in time.

"Buck up, dear. You can handle this," Tempest said. "Nobody ever promised life would be easy."

Seeing Velda pale and shivering in her friend's embrace, Missy said, "That's it. Blanche and Ray are already with me. I have room for Damon. We're family. My home is an extension of Velda's, really. I am her mother, after all."

Velda blinked and rubbed her eyes while nodding at her mother. "You'll take him in? You really will? Like we'll all be together but in two homes?"

"Somethin' like that," Missy said. "I'll put him in Carly Mae's room, for tonight and get them twins workin' to clear all the junk out of the spare room, where he can settle for as long as he needs," Missy said. "Forever would be fine with me."

"He'll require psychological help after years of being incarcerated," Ned said as he helped Ray and Blanche escort Damon, still mute, to the sidewalk.

Missy bristled. "Love's what he needs now."

Ray, Blanche and Missy coaxed Damon toward home, one twin on each arm and Missy in front. Everyone followed close behind that is, except for Velda, who walked in the opposite direction, and Earl and Ned, who went into the station because Ned wanted advice on what to do about Dry Gulch.

When she reached her front gate Missy said, "You know I'd love to invite y'all in, but Damon needs his rest. Heck, he can't even stand on his own yet. Go on down to the Good Luck. Tell Barb I'll buy everyone a coffee and a piece of pie. She knows I'm good for it."

Barb's pies had already become legendary, so the crowd swept like a school of anchovies toward the cafe.

As soon as Missy opened her front door she pointed to the tracks on the carpet leading upstairs. She motioned to Blanche and Ray, who struggled through the doorway with Damon. "Shame on you for, one, sneaking out in the rain last night and, two, for tracking in this mud, and three, for not bothering to clean it up."

"We didn't go out last night. I swear we didn't," Ray said.

"Honest to God, he's right," Blanche added.

"Well, I've got bigger fish to fry right now. We gotta get Damon to bed."

Slowly, one shaky step at a time, the family coaxed Damon up the stairs. When they reached Carly Mae's room, they opened the door. Buster jumped off the bed and ran to them, tail wagging.

"What on earth?" Missy bent down to pet the dog. "Where you been anyway? I thought we'd never—"

"Look! Look!" Blanche stood at the bed. "It's Carly Mae. Right here."

Time slowed in that moment for Missy and the twins as joy bubbled up through them like hundreds of Fizzies tablets dissolving in water. Only Damon stood like a mannequin, unmoved, as Carly Mae's eyelids fluttered and a smile flitted across her face. Buster returned to the bed and licked Carly Mae's face, but she did not wake up.

Overflowing with exuberance, Missy grabbed hold of Damon and gave him a big hug. He received it, arms limp at his side. "You and Carly Mae back, both of you at the same time. Glory be. What a blessed day this is." She helped Damon to the edge of the bed. "Here, sit by your daughter, your baby." Damon plopped down and stared into his lap.

A flash of resentment dampened Ray and Blanche's spirits as each wondered whether Missy would refer to them as Damon's babies. They embraced, each knowing the other's thoughts and each forgiving the other for being less than perfect.

Missy plopped in a rocker, rubbing the back of her hand across her forehead. "Oh my, my, what a wonder, what a day." She rocked and hummed nursery rhymes, filling the entire room with peace as the last, weak gasps of the deluge drizzled down the windows.

Her grandmother's soothing voice eased into Carly Mae's dreams until she stretched, opened her eyes and saw Damon. "Daddy? Daddy, is that you? Your hair's all white." She looked around the room. "Am I dreaming?"

Damon reached out and grasped Carly Mae's hand as sunshine broke through cracks in the clouds.

Chapter 29

ord that Carly Mae had been found sleeping in her very own bed blasted through town faster than Wile E. Coyote in pursuit of Road Runner. Folks were so ecstatic about not one, but two of their own coming home that they set about cleaning up after the deluge with relish. They pitched in to help clear downed trees, retrieve salvageable items, pump out flooded basements and offer words of encouragement, along with food, clothing and supplies to those who suffered most in the storm and its aftermath.

The hardest hit was Tam-Tam. Along with her own belongings, her property was strewn with uprooted trees, boulders and all kinds of stray items. A stroller and front grill of a Mustang now rested on what remained of her roof. Volunteers, including members of the Tarr and McDuggin clans, came forward to help remove debris, repair extensive damage to her home and rebuild the shed, which had washed away. Waters had engulfed Tam-Tam's porch and filled her basement, while the little house itself, a shack really, had creaked and swayed until more than half the home had broken off. Some of Tam-Tam's belongings in the portion still standing were serviceable. Most of her craft supplies, including doll-making materials, were ruined; her mismatched dishes were smashed; her clothes and books had probably washed into the

Mississippi, including a cherished collection of family recipes started by her grandmother.

While helping with cleanup one afternoon, Randy Tarr waded to the opposite side of the river to retrieve lumber he thought could be used in rebuilding Tam-Tam's toolshed. There, he spotted something that looked like a skull. It was jammed between a tree stump and a slab of granite at the water's edge. Then, just a few feet away, he saw what looked like a rib cage. He splashed across the river calling to the other volunteers, "Get Earl. Quick! We got a situation here."

After Earl arrived, he waded to the remains and then called in help from experts in Joliet, since he'd never before encountered what he was certain were human remains. He wasn't sure what to do. People milled about for a couple hours while they waited, and the Kiminee grapevine ensured that a crowd was there to greet Earl's reinforcements when they arrived.

The first thing they did was take the names of all the volunteers and then ask them to leave. As folks grumbled about suspending work on Tam-Tam's home, Earl overheard a member of the forensic team say the bones looked like those of a female, probably a teenager. This perplexed Earl because no teenage girls had gone missing ever in Kiminee except for Carly Mae, who was now home.

When Abby Louise heard that work at Tam-Tam's had come to a halt, she had a wheezing fit while preparing a tuna casserole in her kitchen. She became so flustered she used Campbell's celery soup concentrate, not mushroom. Then she blended the ingredients with an electric mixer instead of layering them, guaranteeing supper that evening would be a bland, sprawling mush. It was Tam-Tam, not the bones that disturbed her most. She was committed to providing her friend and surrogate mother a home, but the old woman's pipe smoking and penchant for collecting more odds and ends for crafts projects than Abby Louise had room to store, and leaving parts of half-finished dolls all around the house, were causing her to blink and fidget nonstop.

At the Bendy River Inn's registration counter on Memorial Day weekend 1969, Velda hung up the phone and reached for a stack of paperwork. Before she even read a full sentence, the phone rang again. She'd expected an influx of antiquers over the long holiday weekend but nothing like the swarm of curiosity seekers overwhelming the town. Kiminee's joy at the return of Damon and Carly Mae and hopes for a speedy and private recovery had been short lived due to strangers who buzzed about everywhere and sucked up information like ravenous mosquitoes.

"Good morning, Bendy River Inn. How can I help you?" Velda said. "No, I'm sorry. ... We're all booked up ... for the next two months, I'm afraid. ... I don't read that magazine. ... No, I'm running an inn here, not a public utility."

A man and woman carrying matching blue American Tourister suitcases entered and paused looking from the cafe, which was abuzz with activity, to the reception desk. The man had a copy of *True Detective* tucked under his arm.

Velda waved them over to her while continuing her conversation. "I don't know, ma'am. ... Well, of course, I know them. No, I don't want to talk about that. ... I'd try the Old Mill Hotel just outside of town. ... Yeah, it used to be a working mill, grounds are real pretty, right on the river. ... I don't know a thing about any old bones. I can't help you there. Sorry. Bye." Sweat beaded on her brow and upper lip as she hung up the phone and looked at the smiling couple.

"We're so excited to be here," the woman gushed. "Do you think we'll be able to see Damon or Ned or Carly Mae?"

"Uh, hello. Do you have a reservation?" Velda tapped a pencil on her guest log.

The man pulled out the dog-eared copy of *True Detective* from under his arm. "Oh, we're Amy and Andy Rhodes. We called you right after we read the article in here." He plopped the magazine on the counter and tapped a picture of Georgia Webb in handcuffs snarling at the agent escorting her out of Dry Gulch Asylum for the Criminally Insane.

Amy peered at the picture. "We devoured it. How could that woman keep poor Damon locked up all that time? And they trusted her so much nobody else found out.»

"Or did they?" Andy winked at Amy. "We're here on a fact-finding mission."

Velda looked at her registration book. "Hmm, I see your names right here." She reached over to a pegboard with room keys and pulled one off a hook.

"Even if nobody else was in on it, there were plenty of signs. I mean the fingerprints didn't match, right?" Amy squeezed Andy's arm. "And photos were missing. They should have known."

"That Ned Burton guy is a real hero if you ask me," Andy said.

Velda counted to ten to calm herself before offering the key to Amy. "You're in the River Room upstairs to the left and down the hall. It's got the best view of the water."

Amy put the key in the pocket of her pedal pushers. "Is it true that Ned's going to work here now at Kiminee Academy? And what about Damon and Carly Mae? Are they doing okay?"

Velda slapped a leaflet with a brief history of Kiminee, along with pictures of the old Kiminee estate, Suzette's, the Five 'N Dime, cheese co-op, and the Charles Street Bridge. "You might want to take a river walk. It's right pretty, and you'll find some fine fishin' holes, too."

Andy leafed through his magazine and stopped at a picture of Blessed Heaven cemetery. "Oh, and Dusty. We're going to have to go there and put some flowers on his grave, poor young man. All that potential lost."

"Do they do tours of Dry Gulch, since it's closed and all now?" Amy asked.

Velda shrugged. "As far as the asylum goes, I have no idea. That's a long ways from here. And, well, the people who live here, nobody asked for this article to come out. We're all private citizens. All this gol darn interest is downright—"

"But the events, they're so, I mean, that Georgia Webb woman, she kept Leon Ames at her home, and her neighbors had no idea that monster was there—for years." Amy gazed at the wall behind Velda. "I wonder why he finally left her."

Andy puffed out his chest. "Helping a criminal who then killed someone might be enough to get her fried. I sure hope so."

"And what she did to poor—" Amy noticed Velda's name tag. "Oh, my God, you're … Damon's wife?"

"I've got nothin' to say to you about that." Velda pointed to the Good Luck's door. "There's a bunch of folks from out of town just like you gathered at the cafe. After you get settled, you can join in the tomfoolery."

"Oh, Andy, let's go in now, shall we? We can take our stuff up later."

Andy turned to Velda. "Can we leave our suitcases here for a little while?"

Velda cracked her knuckles and then gestured toward the side of the counter. "I'll keep an eye on them."

After dispensing with their luggage, Amy and Andy entered the cafe, where they began an animated conversation with a family waiting to be seated. They simpered and quivered with joy upon learning they were speaking with the very people who had discovered the Jewel Tea truck.

At Velda's elbow, the phone rang again. Fearing she might scream into the receiver, she ran outside, where several cars circled and filled the few remaining parking spaces in the square. She continued to the Charles Street Bridge, where she sat on the rail, dangling her legs over the side. She pulled out a Virginia Slims cigarette, lit it, took one puff, then threw it down and watched it disappear like stolen dreams into the flowing water.

The streets of Kiminee were so clogged with belching automobiles and pesky people poking their noses and cameras where they didn't belong that the Memorial Day parade was called off, much to the disappointment of the Scout troops, veterans, clubs and school bands that had planned to march, along with denizens who had looked forward to waving miniature flags as their loved ones pranced by in uniform. Everyone stayed indoors, knowing better than to gather by the river or in the square for a picnic. This was especially true for Missy and her family. For the first time in her life, Missy locked her doors. Strangers with a bizarre sense of entitlement had been trampling her yard, picking lilac blossoms for souvenirs, tromping on the porch, ringing the doorbell, and peeking in windows at all hours. A few had even waltzed right inside when no one answered their incessant demands for attention.

Missy, Blanche and Ray played Monopoly at the dining room table, lamenting the lack of festivities, when they heard a gentle rapping at the front door. Missy ambled to the living room and peeked from behind a curtain to see who was there. "It's Jasper. I was wonderin' when he'd stop by to see our girl." Missy stepped to the foyer and opened the door. The twins followed.

"Afternoon, Jasper," Missy said. "Good to see you. What cha got there?" She motioned for him to come in and follow her and the twins to the living room.

He bounded over the threshold, books in hand. "I thought the kids would like *The Left Hand of Darkness* by Ursula Le Guin—it's science fiction—and *Sounder*, a novel by William H. Armstrong." He handed the books to Missy, who thanked him and put them on the coffee table.

"We're trying to get Armstrong to read from his novel at Riverwood this summer. It would be a coup. I thought you all might want to go if he agrees.»

"Good luck with tryin' to pry Carly Mae away from Dad," Blanche said.

"Yeah, she hasn't set foot out of the house since coming home," Ray added.

"I'd like to go up if I may—if she's ready. Emily and I are going to Chicago in a few days, and, well, word got out that she's been drawing again. I'd like to see her sketches and maybe sell some at the gallery."

"She's not keen on seein' anyone, but you can give it a try," Missy said.

Jasper thanked Missy and bounced up the stairs. He paused at Carly Mae's door. She and Damon sat in a window seat. She was reading *Wind in the Willows* aloud. He turned the pages. Neither noticed Jasper.

"Excuse me. May I come in?"

Carly Mae looked up, frowned and lowered the book. "I suppose," she said.

Damon turned his head and gazed at the front yard. Blanche and Ray snuck up the stairs and stood on either side of Carly Mae's door, their backs to the wall.

"I'm so glad you and your dad are home. You mean the world to Emily and me. If I can be of help in—"

"I don't want your help," Carly Mae snapped, causing Buster, who'd been lounging at her feet to sit up, ear twitching.

In that moment, Carly Mae wanted to have never entered the library and overheard Jasper speaking with Dr. Croll and Miss Henchley. She was certain she wouldn't have been as upset about the twins' not sharing their doubts about Damon being their father. Jasper wished he'd invited Carly Mae to spend last summer with him and Emily in Chicago; then she would never have been abducted by the monster at the old willow tree, and Dusty would still be alive. Damon wished he had heeded the warning signs in the sky the day of the terrible twister instead of continuing to deliver mail. Now he could barely think straight let alone make his family a home. Silence enveloped the room as each person there felt the full weight of their respective regrets. Blanche and Ray both wished fervently they'd spoken with Carly Mae before pestering their grandmother until she became so frazzled she let the truth slip out. Then the quest to learn the truth would have brought them together like the Three Musketeers instead of driving them apart.

Carly Mae interrupted the lull. "I'm sorry. I shouldn't have spoken to you like that, no matter what you've done."

Jasper cocked his head, baffled. "Whatever are you—"

"I trusted you. We trusted you." Carly Mae choked, then coughed.

Reaching for words that would not come, Damon clutched Carly Mae's arm.

"What's going on?" Jasper asked, his eyes full of warmth and concern.

"Dr. Croll … Mrs. Henchley …" Carly Mae's voice cracked.

"What do they have to do with us?"

"I heard you talking with them, and I was trying to figure out how on earth to tell everyone what a fake you are. I loved you so. Everybody else still does. I didn't know what to say. Then I was kidnapped." She squinted at Jasper. "But I'm back now, and when the time is right, I will expose you."

"Jasper, a fake?" Blanche whispered, incredulous.

"That can't be," Ray added.

Carly Mae addressed her siblings. "He practically promised my soul to Lily Park Academy in return for enrolling me there. I was supposed to be their great big success story. They want to trot me out like maybe an academic version of Miss America—and Jasper went along with it. On top of that he's paying them money—for what I don't know—and he's in default, or something like that."

Jasper put a hand on his forehead briefly. "Oh, my dear, no, no, no. Croll and Henchley thought they could take advantage of me because of my failed investment in packaged lettuce, but they couldn't."

"You signed an agreement. Dr. Croll was waving it in your face. I saw."

"They altered the contract, put things in there I'd never seen before."

"You didn't say that," she challenged. "You were acting like a boy caught with his hand in the cookie jar."

"I was buying time so I could think of the best way forward.»

"I wish Aunt Truly were here. She'd know if you're telling the truth."

"Who's Aunt Truly?"

"She took me in over the winter. She saved me and healed me." Carly Mae held out her left hand and flexed and wiggled her fingers."

"My God, look at that!" He gaped and stretched out his arms, palms up. "She did what the finest doctors in the nation couldn't do. It's a miracle."

Carly Mae looked into his eyes and softened when she felt a love she'd missed flowing between them. "I appreciate all that you did, really," she said. "And I've been thinking about Mrs. Henchley and Dr. Croll since I've been back, about how wrong it was for them to try hold it over your head, but it was wrong of you to make promises about what I would and wouldn't do for them."

"I didn't, not really. We talked early on about how good it would be for the school if you went on to do great things, but I never made promises, certainly never put anything about your role into a contract."

"You said in the library—"

"I really was just buying time. I never would have pestered you to return to school there, nor would I ask you to do the promotional stuff they wanted. And now it's all taken care of. They actually thought I wouldn't realize they'd slipped new language into the contract. If anything, I'm holding something over their heads now. Doctoring a contract is illegal. Anything they think they might have dug up from my past is moot."

Carly reached over, scratched Buster between his shoulder blades and recalled Aunt Truly telling her that her instincts were good and to to trust her gut.

Jasper sprang closer and squatted so he and Carly Mae were eye to eye. "You must believe me."

Damon winced, hunched his shoulders, drew his legs up and hugged his knees.

"Fast movements frighten him," Carly Mae said.

"I wish you had come to me." Jasper sighed as melancholy compressed his heart.

"You aren't going to manipulate me into going back there somehow? You're not going to close Kiminee Academy and abandon the town?"

Her mentor pulled a handkerchief from his pocket and wiped his forehead. "Not now, not ever."

"And the bagged lettuce? They thought you'd put everything into that?" Her eyes twinkled with amusement.

Jasper laughed, relieved. "It did cause me a bit of trouble, but I've since hired someone with a better head for investment opportunities."

Carly Mae broke into a grin. "I might be daft for believing you, but my heart says I should, and I've missed you so very much." She looked over at Ray and Blanche. "You may as well come closer," she said to them.

Damon uncurled, sat up and surveyed the room. Carly Mae took Damon's hands. "Daddy, I believe Jasper is who we thought he was."

Damon gave a half smile.

"Oh, Daddy." Carly Mae squeezed his hands.

Pulsing with relief and happiness, Jasper moved toward the door, then stopped. "Ah, I almost forgot. I heard you've been drawing again, and I'd like to take a look and see if I can sell some of your work at the gallery this summer."

Carly Mae went to her bed, bent down and pulled a stack of charcoal drawings out from beneath. "I have plenty. Dad likes to watch me draw. Sometimes he sketches with me." She handed the papers to Jasper.

"Thanks. These could start your college fund. Not that you'll need it. I'm sure all three of you Foley kids will get full scholarships wherever you want to go. MIT has already offered Ray a free ride for this coming year." He nodded toward Ray. "I'm so proud of you, son."

Blanche's eyes widened. "Why didn't you tell me?"

She jabbed Ray in the upper arm; he flinched, ears reddening.

"I can't imagine shipping off to some school far from everything I know and love, far from Dad the way he is," Carly Mae said.

"Given everything you've been through, Miss Carly Mae, that sentiment is perfectly reasonable, " Jasper said. He headed for the door, stopped at the threshold and looked back. "See you soon, Fourth of July if not before." Then he proceeded downstairs, where Missy added a fresh peach pie to the top of his pile of drawings.

Ray sat on Carly Mae's bed, looked from one sister to another and said, "We have to talk."

"Not now. I can't do it now," Blanche said, and stormed out, ran to her room and slammed the door.

Ray chased after her, and Carly Mae sat next to Damon again. "Why did I have to run off that day, Daddy? Why couldn't I have run to my room like Blanche just did?"

Damon continued to gaze out the window at strangers milling about the front yard.

Chapter 30

A few days after Jasper's visit, Carly Mae, Blanche and Ray tromped down Missy's back stairs, across the lawn and to the garage.

"Close your eyes," Ray said to his sisters."

They obliged as he lifted the creaking door.

Carly Mae kept her eyes scrunched tight. "What's up? I thought we were just going for a walk, you know, to talk some things out."

"You'll see," Ray said.

"Dad will wonder where I've gone," Carly Mae complained.

Blanche reassured her. "Grams is with him; he'll be fine."

"Okay, you can open them now," Ray said.

They peered into the garage and saw their deceased grandfather, Grover's, 1940 Nash, which Missy had never learned to drive. Beside it were three Schwinns—one green, one red and one black—clean, gleaming and with tires patched, full of air, ready for the road.

Squealing with delight, Carly Mae rushed to the green one with white wicker basket and white streamers dangling from the handlebars. Blanche grabbed the red one with basket and streamers to match.

"When did you fix these? We haven't ridden them in ever so long." Carly Mae mounted her bike.

"I never even saw you come in here," Blanche added.

Ray hopped on the black one. It had saddlebags over the back tire. "I have my ways." He pedaled down the drive. "Catch me if you can!"

"But Dad—" Carly Mae said.

"Forget Dad for a while and just enjoy what Ray's done for us, will you? It's almost Fourth of July, and you haven't gone out once," Blanche said, rolling her bike out of the garage. "Look, Grams and Dad are at the window right now."

Carly Mae rode out, looked up and grinned. "I think he's smiling." She did a mock salute to Damon.

"The sisters sped to the corner, where Ray waited, along with Buster, who was yipping and spinning in a circle.

The three teens and one dog with a lopsided grin and only one ear zipped along streets crowded with cars parked willy-nilly by strangers who had descended upon Kiminee, eager to find out all they could about Damon, Carly Mae and the town they called home. The siblings sped around the square, making a game of navigating around clumps of curiosity seekers studying the menu pasted to the window of the Good Luck Cafe, peering at the goods on display at Suzette's and pointing at trinkets showcased at the Five 'N Dime. The trio went faster and faster around town until folks saw only a colorful blur as they whizzed by. Then they zoomed uphill to the academy and raced down campus paths and around the buildings. They zipped by workers finishing the new community center. They paused at a drinking fountain and giggled about past episodes of mischief: the night they and their classmates TP'd the administration building; chickens they raised in the school's climate controlled barn that were so big the judges at the county fair thought they might be a new kind of poultry; an experiment gone awry that caused a mini explosion in the chemistry lab. Thirst quenched, they pedaled to the river and followed its curves from one end of Kiminee to the other, stopping at their favorite swimming hole to splash with the trout. Well past lunchtime, they parked their bikes near a table in front of the cheese co-op. From his saddlebags, Ray pulled out three brown paper lunch bags and handed one each to his sisters.

Carly Mae peeked into one. "Wow, Ray. This is really something. Thanks!"

Blanche pulled out the contents of another bag. "Ooh, ham and cheese and chips ... and peanut butter cookies ... and potato salad. Yum!"

"You even remembered forks," Carly Mae added.

"Not me. Grams prepared our lunches, but I am going to treat you to drinks from the vending machine. Cokes, I presume?

The girls nodded.

Ray trotted to the co-op's store and returned shortly with three Coke bottles already opened. They settled in the shade of a beech tree, and when they finished eating, Carly Mae took their trash to a can close by. She returned, skipping.

"Sure is good to see you goofing," Ray said. "The way things were when you left—"

"She didn't leave. She was taken," Blanche said.

"I meant when she ran off all upset."

Carly Mae leaned against the tree's trunk. "You didn't tell me we have different fathers. You knew and didn't tell. If Grams hadn't blurted it out by mistake, I still might not know."

"We didn't plan to keep it from you. We'd only just found out ourselves, really," Blanche said.

"Yeah, we were still digesting it," Ray added. "But I'm sorry we didn't tell you right away. I really am."

"I'm sorry, too," Blanche said.

"So am I, for running off like a great big fool," Carly Mae said.

"I should have told you about MIT, too, Blanche," Ray said. "And you," he said to Carly Mae. "Here we've just all gotten reunited, and in a couple of months, I might be going clear across the country."

"I guess maybe I'm jealous that you've got something you're passionate about. Something that doesn't include me. Computer science just leaves me flat. All those 0's and 1's. Boring," Blanche lamented.

"But, you know, someday computers are going to keep track of everything. I mean everything from everybody's bank balance to who has what book checked out of the library. I want to be part of that. It doesn't mean I'll love you any less."

The three sat in silence, each one thinking about what the future might hold.

"Well, since we're apologizing and stuff. I have a confession to make," Blanche said.

"Do tell," Ray said.

"You know Tam-Tam's missing dolls?"

Ray and Carly Mae both nodded.

"They're under my bed."

"What are they doing there of all places?" Carly Mae asked.

"It's kind of a long story ..."

"We're not in any hurry, are we Carly Mae?" Ray asked.

"No, not really," she replied. "I mean, I'm a little worried about Dad, but I know he's in good hands with Grams."

"Okay. Here goes. I heard Grams and Maridee talking. This was before you and Dad got home." Blanche nodded to Carly Mae. "They didn't know I was there. I only caught parts of the conversation, but something big went down at Tam-Tam's a long time ago that ruined Tam-Tam's whole family, something awful having to do with Grams and one of Tam-Tam's sons. And those stupid dolls—"

"The ones everybody thinks Grams stole," Ray interjected.

Blanche puffed up her chest. "She would have had every right to take them, the way Tam-Tam was taunting her with them. You see, the outfits the dolls are wearing are exact replicas of the clothes everyone wore the day Grams and Maridee were talking about. The day something awful happened. Tam-Tam was getting even with

Grams for something with those dolls. Hurting her. One of them is holding a whip, too."

"Why did you take them?" Carly Mae said.

"I was going to put them back, but then Maridee reported them missing. I panicked and put them under my bed, and then we got overrun with all these true crime enthusiasts. Things have been crazy. I haven't even been able to think. I didn't mean to keep them this long."

"You have to take them back," Carly Mae said.

"I can't."

"Yes, you can, after closing time today. Nobody will know," Ray said. "We'll go with you."

"Gobs of strangers are milling about, snooping into everything. They'll see us go inside. Word will get around," Blanche protested.

"Nobody will be paying attention. It's not like we'll be breaking in. You have a key," Ray said.

"But the ladies have already searched the whole store, up and down and down and up."

"Things have a way of turning up. We can tuck them under some quilts or something," Carly Mae offered.

"This is why I love you both," Blanche said.

"It'll be like old times," Ray said. "The three of us up to mischief, palling around together.

The siblings stretched out in the shade, each chewing on a blade of grass while watching clouds go by in the blue, blue sky.

"I want to go back." Carly Mae gazed off into the distance.

"Where?" Blanche asked.

"To the old Kiminee place, the willow," Carly Mae said.

"Are you sure?" Blanche asked.

"I need to go." Carly Mae went to her bike and mounted. "We can meander first if you want."

The twins got on their bikes, and with Buster racing ahead, the Foley siblings pedaled on through pasture trails and woods, along cornfields and apple orchards and finally out to the old Kiminee place, where they parked their bikes and stood by the willow.

"I wish Dusty were comin' down the road right now," Carly Mae said.

"We all do," Ray said. "All of Kiminee wishes he could come back."

At that moment, the black-eyed Susans brightened, lighting up the entire field.

"They're like rubies. Must be 5:05," Blanche said.

The three locked arms, and Buster dove into the flowers.

"I have a confession to make, too," Carly Mae said.

"Oh?" Blanche raised an eyebrow.

"I'm not as smart as I once was. It's like I used to just tap into this source or something, and I'm cut off now. I'm afraid to return to school, to disappoint Jasper, to disappoint everyone." She bit her bottom lip. "I've been hiding out with Dad for his sake, for sure, but for me, too. I'm scared everyone will find out."

Ray and Blanche wrapped their arms around her and hugged her tight.

"You've been through so much," Ray said. "It takes time to heal."

"And even if you don't, and I'm not saying you won't, but even if you don't, we'll still love you just the same, maybe even more," Blanche said.

The three Foley teens held tight to each other for a long time, watching the blooms twinkle and sway and send up periodic bursts of colored light until the field settled down and returned to normal.

"There's something else. … I found out how to get back to Windy Wood," Carly Mae said, breaking away to pick up a flat skipping rock. "I want to take Dad there. He's lost more than I have."

"How?" Blanche skipped a rock, too.

"Yesterday, Earl came to visit Dad and read aloud the directions he got from Alvin Aldridge. I pretended to be drawing and wrote them down." Carly Mae pulled a paper from the pocket of her cutoffs, unfolded it and handed it to Ray. "We can find Aunt Truly. She healed my fingers. She restored most of my eyesight, which got all fuzzy for a while. She can heal Dad, I'm sure of it."

Blanche held out her hand to Ray. "Let me see."

He gave her the paper and sighed. "Directions are all well and good, but we don't have a way to get there."

"Yes, we do," Carly Mae said. "Gramps' old Nash. It's waiting for us, big as you please, in the garage."

A summer's day that was muggy as a boiler room turned suddenly dark as a windstorm kicked up. It blasted leaves against the windshield of Gramps' Nash, forcing Blanche to turn on the wipers. In the front passenger seat, Ray looked back and forth from the directions in his hand to the road. In the back, Damon hunched his shoulders and stared out a window.

Seated next to her father, Carly Mae gripped his hand. "It's okay, Dad. It's just some stuff blowing around."

Damon didn't respond. The vehicle pressed on battered by the storm until, as quickly as it had arisen, the tempest dissipated. Carly Mae looked out the rear window as a riot of leaves, sticks, dust, gum wrappers and other debris receded.

"Look!" Ray called out. "There's the stand of birch and three boulders just like it says here." He pointed to the directions Carly Mae had scribbled. "The turnoff should be close.»

"I think I see a dirt road." Blanche said.

"Time to turn," Ray advised.

Blanche steered the car off the pavement and immediately hit a bump, jostling everyone inside. Damon's bottom lip quivered.

"Slow down, okay? Dad's getting freaked out." Carly Mae said.

"Okay, okay." Blanche braked and proceeded like a sloth for a good ten minutes.

"It shouldn't be too far before we reach the driveway. Does any of this look familiar?" Ray asked Carly Mae.

"Not yet," she replied.

Blanche kept driving. "Look! Over there—the pine needles are purple." She pointed to the right.

"I see the path!" Carly Mae bounced in her seat. "We'll have to walk from here because a creek dissects the road, and this old jalopy can't make it through."

Damon pulled away from Carly Mae.

"Don't worry, Dad," she said, patting his arm. "We're going to a good place, though, not like that awful asylum."

Blanche pulled the car into a grassy spot between two pines with plenty of branches to provide shelter. Carly Mae and Blanche coaxed Damon out while Ray pulled a tarp from the trunk and covered the vehicle. A family of raccoons peered from the underbrush, then stepped into view and scurried ahead.

"Wow! It's the raccoons, just like you described," Blanche said.

Ray and Blanche scampered after the animals while Carly Mae attempted to hasten Damon along. After a few minutes on an over-grown trail, they rounded a corner, and a broken-down fence and weather-beaten home came into view. Parked in front was Mindy's gleaming Triumph TR3A. The raccoons skittered up the front stairs, where the largest one stood on hind legs, turned the knob, opened the door and led the other critters inside.

"This is it?" Ray pointed.

Carly Mae nodded. "But everything is so … different. … I'm really confused." She moved forward with steps more tentative than before.

"It's like a ghost town if you ask me," Blanche said.

They all proceeded toward the home in silence, crossing a field of tall grass full of tiny spotted frogs that weren't visible until, like synchronized swimmers in a water ballet, they hopped up and away.

When they reached the convertible, Carly Mae stopped and patted its gleaming hood. "At least Mindy's car looks normal.

Blanche approached the porch. The bottom stair creaked when she put weight on it. Damon backed away at the sound, but Carly Mae and Ray each took hold of an elbow and escorted him up.

"It's like a hundred years have passed since I was here," Carly Mae said. She tapped on the door, which the raccoons had left ajar. It swung open with a screech. "Something's off. I don't get it. The home was cared for, warm and cozy. I swear." Carly Mae hesitated at the threshold.

"Let's just go in and find out what's up." Ray brushed past her and into the home.

Carly Mae and Blanche helped Damon inside.

" Truly? Aunt Truly? Are you here?" Carly Mae called.

"Did you really spend the winter here?" Blanche surveyed the decrepit interior as the door banged closed behind her. "The place gives me the creeps."

Ray sneezed. "There must be an inch of dust on everything."

"It wasn't like this," Carly Mae said. "We just need to find Aunt Truly. She'll explain."

Just then, a woman stomped inside, carrying a bushel basket full of carrots, lettuce and corn. "What the heck is—Carly Mae is that you?"

Carly Mae turned her head. "Mindy?"

Mindy maneuvered around everyone and placed the produce on the kitchen table. Then she faced Carly Mae. "You're a sight for sore eyes."

"Mindy! You're alive! Aunt Truly healed you, too." Carly Mae rushed forward and gave Mindy a long hug, then turned to her family. "Everyone, this is Mindy. Leon Ames shot her before he dragged me off. And the last time I saw her she was in a really bad way."

"Don't remind me." Mindy pulled a handkerchief from the pocket of her overalls and wiped dirt from her fingers. "Sorry, I was just in the garden. It's good dirt, though, real good." She shook hands with Blanche, then Ray. She extended a hand to Damon, but he didn't lift his. He looked up, moving his head in a circular motion, appearing to eye the molding where ceiling met wall.

Blanche picked up an ear of corn. It was almost twice as large as a typical ear. "You grew this?"

Mindy nodded. "Aunt Truly gave me full instructions."

Ray strode to the table and pulled out a carrot. It, too, was extremely large.

Mindy took a few carrots, walked to the basement stairs and tossed them, tops and all, to the animals. "The 'coons can't get enough of 'em."

"Where is this Aunt Truly person anyway?" Ray asked. "We've heard so much about her."

"And how did Windy Wood deteriorate so much?" Carly Mae walked over to the rocker where Aunt Truly had entertained her with stories through the winter. She gave it a little push, setting it in motion.

"It's just one of those things," Mindy replied. "Whenever she's gone for a while, the place falls apart. It's sort of like *Paradise Lost*, only it's the person, not the place that keeps the ravages of time away."

"Where is she now?" Carly Mae asked.

"I don't know. Sometimes she's gone a few weeks; sometimes it's a couple of years. Who knows where she goes? She left on the first of May. It was after I'd turned a corner, and we knew I was going to recover."

"You have no idea where she went or when she's coming back?" Carly Mae asked.

"I'm afraid not. You yourself know how time works differently here."

Carly Mae clasped her hands together and paced the room. "But I need her right now to heal my dad. We need her." The raccoons watched from the top of the stairs as they nibbled, craning their necks to get a good view.

"I'm sure she'll want to help once she returns."

"You don't understand. Dad needs her now." Carly Mae spun around, gasping, and shot out the door, down the rickety steps and into the field in front of the home, where she stopped abruptly and plopped down in the grass.

The others watched through the window. Blanche wiped dust from the cracked glass to get a better view. "I'm so glad she didn't keep on going," she said.

Meanwhile, Damon shuffled with stiff limbs out of the house, limped to his daughter, plunked down like schoolbooks tossed into a locker, and pulled her close.

"Well, will you look at that," Ray said.

Blanche, Ray and Mindy lingered long at the window, watching father and daughter snuggle while brilliant sunset colors filled the sky and infused Windy Wood with a warm golden glow.

The day after visiting Windy Wood, Damon held scissors borrowed from Missy's kitchen and surveyed the backyard flower garden. Lured by the profusion of colors and scents, he clipped several sprigs of snapdragon, then moved on to claim an assortment of black-eyed Susans, cosmos, marigolds, iris and Missy's signature white roses with mauve edges. With a fist full of blooms, he returned to the kitchen, where Carly Mae and Missy were at the table, nibbling on walnut coffeecake. They watched him arrange a bouquet at the sink, wet a paper towel, wrap it around the stems, and cover that with a strip of aluminum foil.

Carly Mae shot up and followed him to the foyer, where he donned his favorite cap.

"Uh, Dad, what are you doing?" she asked, worried because he'd been more relaxed since their return from Windy Wood, but he still was far from the father she remembered.

He didn't respond.

"Dad?"

"Let him be." Missy came from behind and put a hand on Carly Mae's shoulder. "It's about time he went out."

"But he's not talking yet. I'd better go with him."

"You'll do no such thing. I said all three of you kids are grounded for that stunt you pulled, and I meant it."

Carly Mae stormed back to the kitchen table. Missy was at her heels, scolding her for the umpteenth time for taking the Nash out without permission on a misguided mission to find Aunt Truly, someone Missy suspected did not exist. Carly Mae took a bite of coffeecake and chewed furiously.

Meanwhile, Damon pranced out and headed toward the town square, whistling "You Are My Sunshine" as he went. His step was so light people watching him pass by marveled at his Fred Astaire grace. It was the first time since his return anyone had seen him leave Missy's house alone. A few intrigued denizens followed him all the way to the entrance of the Good Luck Cafe and Bendy River Inn. They leaned against the windows and peered into the lobby as Damon approached Velda, who was at the registration counter talking on the phone. When she hung up, she saw Damon and realized he looked even more handsome to her with white hair than he had with brown. He smiled and offered her the bouquet.

She stood silent. Damon leaned on one foot, then the other, back and forth. People came and went from the diner, and a crowd gathered at the window, counting the number of times he shifted his weight. Maxine, who has just finished making beds in the inn upstairs, stopped with an armload of sheets and towels on the landing and peered down at Velda and Damon.

Finally, Velda reached for the flowers. Her fingers touched and lingered on Damon's hand, while the two gazed into each other's eyes. Some onlookers swore they could see bolts of red passing like lightning between them.

"Why, thank you." Velda grasped the flowers as Damon let go. "It was sweet of you."

Damon grinned.

Velda looked up and noticed Maxine, who had resumed her descent down the stairs. "I'd better get these in water. They'll look real nice and inviting right here." Velda regarded her lover, who was now crossing through the reception area. "Don't you think so, Max?" Velda asked.

Maxine said nothing as she kicked open the laundry room door. It squeaked closed behind her.

Velda turned her attention back to Damon, whose smile had become rigid, reminding her of *Mad Magazine*'s Alfred E. Neuman. "Thanks again for the flowers, but you shouldn't have. I mean, I hope you don't have any expectations about you and me, because Maxine and I, we're together now."

Damon searched her face, a twinkle in his eyes.

"Oh, never mind. I gotta get back to work." She sorted a few papers on the desk and then picked up the phone.

Damon hunched his shoulders and shambled, head down, to the café. From a table by the window, Earl spotted his childhood friend, waved him over and ordered him a steaming cup of coffee. As they disbursed, onlookers were evenly divided over who would win Velda's heart in the end.

Chapter 31

Missy placed a basket of dinner rolls on the table in the meeting room at Suzette's and straightened a stack of napkins, while Blanche removed plastic wrap from a plate of deviled eggs she'd made that morning using a new recipe containing Dijon mustard.

Emily struggled in with a huge sheet cake, which wobbled in her hands until she managed to put it next to the rolls. "Whew! I almost dropped it."

"Gracious me," Missy said. "How did you ever fit that thing into your oven?"

Emily dropped her purse in a chair in the first of three rows facing the podium. "I baked it at the Good Luck. I got there at sunrise, and you know what? Jeff and Barb had already made cinnamon rolls for the breakfast rush."

Missy nodded her approval. "Them's hard-working people, that's for sure."

"I'll say. And they instantly clicked here, unlike me," Emily replied. "I'm finally feeling well enough to participate instead of hanging on the periphery, you know? But my heart's pounding about making my debut here. I know people have been talking about me, saying I'll never fit in."

"Oh, don't pay that no mind. Gossip happens here, sure, but it don't run deep. Comin' up front and gettin' your black-eyed Susan pin will be easy peasy. Isn't that right, Blanche?" Missy said.

"Sure. You get the jitters sittn' in your seat beforehand, but you don't even have to give a speech or anything." Blanche picked up a flyer announcing an upcoming sale on egg cups and other knickknacks that hadn't sold as well as other items at Suzette's.

"I'll do my best." Emily said. "Therapy has really helped with my nausea and jittery nerves. I'm finding my way."

Missy primped at her salt-and-pepper locks. "I wouldn't know about that mumbo jumbo, but I am glad you're feeling better. You'll be able to enjoy some of that cake you made."

"Drat! I forgot to bring a knife." Emily put both palms on top of her head.

Missy motioned to a built-in cabinet behind the podium. "There's one in the right-hand drawer, and while you're there, get some straws. They're down below, in a white box."

Emily stepped to the drawer, pulled a knife out and put it on top of the counter, then squatted and opened a cabinet door to search for the straws. "I see one here, actually it looks like several boxes." She grabbed a box. A brown paper shopping bag that had been stuck beside it fell forward. "What's this?" She stood and peeked into the bag. "I think it's those missing dolls everybody's been worked up about." She lifted a doll dressed in red-and-white gingham blouse and white shorts. "This is absolutely charming. She looks—"

"Gimme that thing." Missy hustled over and snatched the doll and the bag.

"Careful, you might break it," Emily said.

"That's just what I should do—"

The front door opened, and women's laughter carried to the back room. Missy puffed up her chest as Maridee Pratt and Tempest Binsack entered, each carrying dishes whose sweet and savory smells permeated.

"What's up with you standing there like the Queen of England herself?" Maridee joked.

Tam-Tam hitched into the room on the arm of Abby Louise, whose inebriated state made her less than sturdy.

Missy slammed the doll in gingham back into the bag, stomped over to Tam-Tam and shoved the bag into the old woman's hands. "There! Turns out these horrid things were in here all along. Ask Emily if you don't believe me."

All eyes turned to Emily, who said, "That's right. I found them in with the straws."

Blanche grinned briefly, then sighed with relief, knowing her impulsive theft of the dolls did no lasting harm.

"Now are ya gonna sell 'em?" Tam-Tam asked.

Maridee approached, put an arm around Missy's shoulder, and said to Tam-Tam, "I expect you've got your reasons for wanting to torture our Missy, but I'm telling you right now, it has to stop."

The temperature rose noticeably with each word she spoke. Tempest opened a window.

"You can't make me," Tam-Tam challenged.

"We aren't going to sell them, and, come to think of it, we can stop carrying all of your crafts," Maridee said. "That would put a big dent in your income, I expect, especially now that we've got so many curiosity seekers poking around. Business is booming, but it can be bust for you. Remember, you're not even a member."

"Don't be s-s-so petty" Abby Louise said. "I'll pay 'er back dues myself, for goodness sakes."

"It's twelve year's worth, and at five dollars a year, that's sixty whole dollars. You shouldn't have to bear that," Tempest said. "I'll pitch in." She turned toward Tam-Tam. "That is, if you'll agree to stop this infernal game you're playing."

"I'll contribute, too." Varnie Welch called from the back of the room. She pulled five dollars from her wallet and waved it in the air.

More members arrived, settled in and dug into their purses. Soon almost everyone was waving a five-dollar bill. Tempest went around the group collecting the money, and with each bill she took, the temperature in the room rose. She counted the money. "Looks like you're paid up for the next four years, Tam-Tam, if you agree to our terms."

Blanche noticed her grandmother's hand trembling and gave her a hug. "Don't you worry, Grams. Those dolls will soon be history, forgotten," she whispered.

"Golly, I'm feelin' like a possum. I wanna disappear." Tam-Tam scanned the room, then looked down in her lap. "Oh, I guess I got my pound of flesh." She smirked at Missy and Blanche. "I'll stop with the dolls—no outfits anybody we know wore, no familiar faces."

"That's settled, then," Maridee said. "Let's get rolling. We've got to welcome Emily and then decide who's doing what for the new community center dedication, which is just around the corner, July fourth to be specific. We volunteered to decorate the hall in case you don't remember."

Members grumbled about the heat while Maridee called the meeting to order, and by the time Emily was inducted and a pin placed on her blouse, everyone was sweating profusely and loosening clothes. And when the business was concluded, nobody lingered to nibble and chat at the table. The food had become so ripe, it was not even fit to contribute to Touch of Kindness. They dumped all of it into the trashcan outside.

Missy chalked up the heat wave in the building to Charles and Fleur looking down from above, disapproving. "They know somebody in the club is puttin' somethin' over on us."

Blanche knew right away she was the culprit and vowed never to steal again, even if she thought it was for a good reason.

With fingers sporting coral-colored nails, Doris puffed up her newly styled hair at the full-length mirror on her bedroom door. She smiled at the strawberry blonde waves, a color that hadn't framed her face in decades. She tucked a mauve blouse into a black Evan Picone pencil skirt, donned a matching suit jacket and slid into black leather pumps—all gifts from Emily. She grabbed a tattered, brown shoulder bag from the bed, leaving behind two purses with price tags still on, then strutted from her apartment and down the stairs to open Jasper's gallery.

She unlocked the door, made sure everything was in place and stood at a counter at the back of the room. She was sorting bills when Jasper and Emily entered. He carried a small portfolio of Carly Mae's drawings under his arm.

"Well, hi there," Doris said as the couple approached.

Emily and Doris folded into an embrace sweet as sugar and cinnamon on buttered toast. Then Emily held her mother at arm's length and said, "You look glorious. I still pinch myself whenever I see you. I feel so lucky."

Doris shook her head. "No, it's me who's lucky. To have my daughter after all these years, and a home. And on top of that, this job that you're paying me way too much to do."

Jasper wrapped his arms around mother and daughter and kissed the top of each woman's head. "I hardly think $500 per month is too much for managing this place day to day, especially when we're out of town, which is most of the time these days."

"I don't know why you have to spend so much time in that place." Doris turned her lips down, feigning a pout.

"Say, why don't you come with us? We're only here for a couple of days, so we can get back to help plan the new community building's opening celebration," Emily said. "It's on Fourth of July weekend. Kimineeans really know how to celebrate. Once you get to know everybody, you'll probably want to move there."

Jasper laughed. "Then we'll have to open a gallery on the town square for you to manage."

"I wouldn't want to uproot myself now. This is my first real home in the longest time." Doris shuddered as she recalled stacks of unpaid bills, shelves as empty as Old Mother Hubbard's, eviction notices taped to her door.

"We'd never force you to move," Jasper said reassuringly. "Seriously, you do a better job here than anyone else of sensing what our customers will like. Speaking of which, what do you think of these?" He placed the portfolio on the counter and pulled out several charcoal sketches. He handed two sheets to Doris.

She studied them, then closed her eyes, overwhelmed with memories. "Oh, they take me back; they take me way back."

"What do you mean?" Emily was curious but, sensing her mother's pain, hesitated to push hard for an answer.

Doris hoisted her bag from a cubby and plopped it on the counter.

Emily stiffened at the unsightly purse. "I thought you were going to switch to one of the purses we bought yesterday. That thing looks like a dead dog." She pretended to scold, but her tone was kind.

Looking like a child who hadn't turned in her homework, Doris said, "I just need a little time. It feels like my whole life is in this purse, you know? It's what's inside, but it's also every little crack and scrape on the leather." She dug through until she pulled out a spiral notebook slightly larger than an index card. "This is what I mean by my life being in here. Lolly used to sketch like crazy. These are the last drawings she did, the only ones I have left. I know they're no good being on lined paper and all, but that's all we had. There's one of you in here, and me, too, and Jim or Joe or whatever your father's name really was."

"Oh, something of Lolly's," Emily said. "A real treasure."

"It's uncanny how similar these are to Carly Mae's," Doris said.

Emily leaned in for a closer look as Doris flipped the pages. "You're absolutely right. It is uncanny."

Jasper looked over Emily's shoulder. "I see a resemblance. Definitely."

"I wish I remembered more about her," Emily said.

"You was thick as thieves, despite having different dads and being a decade apart in age. She's the one who came up with the name, Ellyanna. Did you know that?" Doris didn't wait for an answer. "She was all kinds of creative. I like to think Lolly could have become a great artist, or anything for that matter. She was the best at whatever she did. Leagues above her classmates."

"Wow! You could be describing Carly Mae," Emily said. She turned to Jasper. "Don't you agree?"

"A compelling coincidence, for sure," he replied.

Doris' mind flooded with memories of her eldest daughter. "The teachers were always telling me to take her here and there for some enrichment thing. Of course, I couldn't afford to follow through with that stuff, but the Art Institute did offer her a scholarship for some Saturday classes right before ..." Doris chewed her lip and looked back and forth between Lolly's drawings and Carly Mae's. "It's like the same person drew them."

Emily tapped her mother's arm and caught her eye. Chills ran up their spines.

Jasper broke the spell. "Lots of artists have similar styles. I wouldn't read much of anything into it." He collected Carly Mae's sketches and put them back in the portfolio. "I'll get to work framing so you can see if anyone wants to buy these," he said to Doris.

Emily flipped through Lolly's sketchbook and stopped at one. "Do you mind if I Xerox this sketch of whatever his name was?"

"Go ahead, I guess. ... I mean, he was your father, bad as he was."

"Good, 'cause I've been too chicken to face this, but, you know, Kiminee is a small town. If he was from there like you think he was, then somebody will recognize this drawing, don't you think?"

"Are you sure about this? Do you really want to know? Do I?"

"I believe we do." Emily blew her mother a kiss and took the sketchbook to the gallery's combination office and workshop.

A jingle sounded as the door opened. Doris crossed the gleaming floor to greet the first customers of the day.

Chapter 32

Barefoot and dressed only in a flannel nightgown, Velda caught up to Maxine in the Bendy River Inn lobby, which doubled as the waiting area for the Good Luck Cafe when the restaurant was full. Velda grabbed a suitcase Maxine was carrying and yanked so hard Maxine stumbled and almost fell to the floor.

"Let go!" Maxine wrenched the luggage from Velda's grasp. Her face flushed, green eyes flared, and red locks, akimbo, appeared ablaze. Maxine's beauty had drawn gasps from several observers when she'd emerged from Jeff's truck the day he brought Velda home. Now, despite the long hours working at the cafe and inn, she had grown so beautiful that many residents felt she even put famous actress Maureen O'Hara to shame.

Velda lunged for the suitcase again, but was unable to grab hold. "You can't move in here."

"I sure as shootin' can, and nobody can stop me. Not even you."

"I've told you every way I possibly can that I'm not going back to Damon. Why don't you believe me?"

"There are things I see that you're hidin' from yourself. Your heart might not be with Damon. That could be true. I don't know. But one thing is certain: your heart's not with me. I ground you; that's all. I help keep you steady, and maybe I don't want to do that anymore."

The two glared at each other like boxers in a punishing round. A few folks who'd been enjoying the day's breakfast special—two eggs any style, bacon strips, grits, hash browns, toast with marmalade and all the coffee they could drink—stopped chewing and craned their necks to see what the commotion was all about.

Barb came out of the cafe. "Ladies, ladies. What's going on here? We are fortunate the curiosity seekers have gone off to Dry Gulch for the time being. They would have gotten a big kick out of this. But we do have our regulars left from the breakfast rush, you know, and well—"

"She's leaving me." Velda's voice rose to a wail. "How could she?"

"Calm down." Maxine scowled at Velda. "Didn't you hear what she said about diners. You want them to get indigestion?"

Velda ran her hands through her brunette waves and appealed to Barb. "She said last night she was leaving come morning, but how could I believe her after all we've been through? And then, she slipped out quiet as death. It's only by chance I got up to pee, looked out the window and saw her running across the field. I was fit to be tied."

Maxine clutched the suitcase to her chest, chipped, ruby-red fingernails drumming against leather. "I'm not going that far, for goodness sakes. I'm not cutting you off, not at all. Why can't you understand?"

In her signature calming voice, Barb said, "Come on. Have some coffee and set a spell at our favorite booth." She ushered them into the cafe.

Stragglers from the breakfast rush glanced at Velda as she passed, but they quickly dug into the remainder of their meals, appetites intact, knowing Velda was one of Kiminee's more eccentric people. So what if she was wearing her nightie and screaming at Maxine? She was their Velda, the miracle baby brought in from the cold one long ago winter's night — so the latest lore went. If that turned out to be a tall tale concocted by a dying priest, they didn't care. She would always have a soft spot in the town's heart.

Barb served Maxine and Velda steaming mugs of coffee, along with thick slices of Good Luck's special pecan coffee cake fresh from the oven. Then she and Jeff, moving with the synchronicity of lovers who know each other so well there is no need for words, settled up with the last diners at the cash register; cleaned up the tables, counter and kitchen; and joined Maxine and Velda, who were in the middle of a conversation so heated steam was rising from the booth. Barb refilled their coffee before she sat down next to Velda. Jeff perched by his cousin.

"It's the beginning of the end. It always is when one person moves out," Velda lamented. She put a hand over her heart.

"I've been all alone in our trailer ever since Carly Mae and Damon came home," Maxine spit out. "You spend all your time at Missy's. You used to go there a lot on account of Blanche and Ray, but now, you spend almost every night with them, probably with Damon for all I know. It's given me a whole lot of time to think."

Velda sobbed and blurted out, "Oh, I guess I deserve this. The way I treated Damon, always cheating on him. What's that they say about chickens coming home to roost? Plus I've told everybody Blanche and Ray don't live in the trailer with us because there's no room, but all the while I've known Missy would get us a bigger trailer if I asked, but I never have. You want to know why?"

Maxine opened her mouth, but Velda held up a palm to stop her. "Because they don't want to live with me. I could build a Beverly Hills-style mansion, and they'd never come. They may love me, but they don't trust me."

Maxine's eyes flashed with realization. "That's exactly the way I feel." She grabbed her coffee and took several gulps, then coughed because it went down the wrong pipe.

Jeff patted Maxine's back. "It's okay, cuz. It's okay."

Maxine glared at Velda. "You still love Damon, and you don't even know it." Maxine leaned forward, hands on the table, her rear end rising from the seat. "And not only that, everyone knows he loves you, too—absolutely, unconditionally. That's not something to dismiss, nor is it something I can do. You require too much. I see that clearly now. We travel to the beat of a different drum, like that song Linda Ronstadt sings. In fact, you travel to a drumbeat all your own. Go back to Damon. I'm done." Maxine plunked back down and tapped Jeff's shoulder. "Move over. I need to get out."

Jeff slid out of the booth so Maxine could exit. Then, instead of sitting back down, he took her bag and walked with her to the inn.

Velda looked at Barb. "Here I am again. Back at the Good Luck Cafe on my own."

Barb cut a bite of coffee cake with a fork. "Open up," she said, stabbing the cake. "Come on."

Velda opened her mouth, and accepted the morsel and chewed. "Mmm, that is good."

"Yes it is. And so is life, my friend."

"But what am I going to do?" Velda sipped her coffee.

"Nothing yet. You're overwhelmed. Think about all that's happened in the last few years. Take your time. You'll get over this."

"I just want to disappear. I really do. There's nothing left for me here. I never really belonged anyway. I've always felt out of place."

"Don't talk that silly talk." Barb got up. "I've got to prep for lunch now. Take the day off, hon. We'll manage without you for a day. We'll need you back tomorrow, though, to start prepping for Fourth of July."

Barb set back to work, and Velda ran home, overcome with the same mix of sorrow, guilt and dread that had driven her away in the aftermath of the terrible twister. Convinced she was holding Damon back by leading him on while also failing to commit to Maxine, she cursed her fickle nature. Inside the doublewide, she dumped money from her purse and wallet on the kitchen table, then, pawed through drawers, in dishes and between couch cushions for spare change. She dumped that on the table, too. She counted the haul, mostly pennies, looked up a number in the Yellow Pages and dialed. "How much for a ticket to California? ... Los Angeles, San Francisco, San Diego. ... I don't much care. ... Yes, definitely one way."

When she hung up the phone, she sank into a chair, crestfallen, wondering whether her lack of funds was a sign she should stay in Kiminee. It would take more than a month to save money for a bus ticket and a small cushion to stake her while she settled into a new life. And she wasn't about to hitchhike again.

The next morning, when most of Kiminee was still asleep, Velda walked through the same field Carly Mae was crossing when the terrible twister of 1961 carried her up to the heavens and back. She then walked the quiet streets at a brisk pace, traversed the town square and trotted half a block to Bendy River Inn. Randy Tarr, who suffered from insomnia and eagerly took the night shift at the registration desk whenever asked, was attempting to engage Damon in conversation when Velda entered the lobby.

At the counter was a bouquet in a slender vase. Velda recognized it as one she and Damon found when they went antiquing with Emily and Jasper in Southern Illinois back when Carly Mae was still painting acrylics of Buster.

She scowled at Damon. "More flowers from Missy's backyard?"

Damon just smiled, as usual.

She walked behind the counter, put her purse in a cubby and looked over Randy's notes from the night. "Looks like it was pretty quiet," she said to Randy. "Can you work the night shift tomorrow, too?"

"I'll check with the wife; should be okay." Randy walked toward the cafe and turned to Damon. "Want to get some breakfast?"

Damon hesitated, looking at Velda, his body listing toward her.

Velda took off her sweater and put it over the back of the chair. "May as well go now," she said to Damon. "Save your love for someone who wants you."

He stroked the vase with his finger.

"I don't know how many ways I have to show you before it finally sinks in. I love you, but I don't love, love you." With her elbow she knocked the vase off the counter. The sound of shattering glass reverberated throughout the building. "If you don't stop this foolishness, I'll ask Earl for a restraining order or something. This has to end."

Maxine came out of the cafe, broom and dustpan in hand. "What happened here? Velda fly off the handle?"

"You'd better stay away, too, you deserter," Velda growled at Maxine. She then ran into the cafe, sat at the counter and lit a cigarette.

Maxine swept the glass. "It hurts to love that one," she said to Damon.

He bent down and picked up a sprig of lilac. He brought the flower to his nose, took a deep breath, trudged out of the lobby and toward the banks of the Bendy.

Chapter 33

*L*eaning on a cane, Tam-Tam limped from Abby Louise's guest room, where she'd been staying since the deluge. She immediately encountered a stack of dirty dishes and silverware. Beyond that were piles of yarn, cloth remnants, bags of thread, pin cushions and other crafting supplies strewn about. She made her way past the obstacles into the kitchen, where Abby Louise was at the table, sipping coffee and reading the latest Suzette's newsletter.

"Mornin'." Tam-Tam stood at the doorway.

Without looking up, Abby Louise pointed toward the counter and said in a voice sour as a glass of vinegar, "Coffee's ready, as usual."

"You got a problem with me?" Tam-Tam pulled her lips into a pout.

Abby Louise, head throbbing because she hadn't yet taken a nip, looked up. "As a matter of fact, I do. I've asked you time and time again to pick up after yourself. I'm tired of doing it for you. It's no way to live."

"You wrecked all my stuff. It's all jumbled up now all over the hall." Tam-Tam railed.

"Don't blame me if you don't take care of your things. I'll not be responsible for damage to your junk."

"Junk? That's how you really feel? Junk?" Tam-Tam inched back around and struggled toward the front door.

Abby Louise followed her down the hall. "Listen, you know I love you. I'm just tired of picking up after you. And I'm not even the world's best housekeeper, you know. It's not like I have impeccable standards. It's just too much pickin' up after you all the time."

"It's not my fault it's takin' so long for them to fix my home. And I can't even walk right yet." Tam-Tam put her hand on the front doorknob and turned.

"Wait! I didn't mean to drive you off. You can't go out without having somethin' in your stomach."

"I gotta go check on them hippie kids, see how they're progressin'. They had a time yesterday. The Tarrs and McDuggins wanted to take over again. Lost a whole afternoon's work over that—not that you'd care." Tam-Tam stepped onto the porch.

"Let's just stop dickerin', okay?" Abby Louse motioned toward the wicker love seat to the right. "Sit down there, and I'll bring you some coffee and a roll. Just made 'em this morning. Cheese with apricot on top. My best ever, I think."

Tam-Tam sat down. Abby Louise went to the kitchen and returned with a tray loaded with rolls and coffee and sat next to Tam-Tam. They ate in silence, Tam-Tam on her first meal of the day, Abby Louise on her third.

When the rolls were consumed, Tam-Tam said, "Thanks. I best be goin' now. Them Tarrs and McDuggins might return to harass the hippies again."

Abby Louise laughed. "Too many folks wantin' to donate their time. What a problem."

Tam-Tam rose, leaning on Abby Louise's shoulder for support. "It's hard for an old lady to change her ways, you know." She made her way to the stairs.

"Just try a little bit, will you?" Abby Louise stood and lifted the tray.

"Maybe I will; maybe I won't." Tam-Tam wobbled to the sidewalk and tottered to the square. She paused in front of The Good Luck

Cafe, breathed in the smell of coffee and cinnamon rolls and saw Velda sneak from the Bendy River Inn lobby to a recently vacated table, grab the tip, and return to the registration desk.

Tam-Tam hobbled inside and confronted Velda. "I saw you take that money." She jutted her chin out, a smug smile on her face.

Velda stuffed the bills and change into her back pocket. "You saw no such thing."

"Let's just call Earl over, then." Tam-Tam pointed to the police chief, who was at the restaurant's counter, finishing off the breakfast special: Denver omelet, three strips of bacon, short stack of blueberry pancakes and toast.

"Your word against mine, and everyone knows you're daft," Velda challenged.

"That money ain't yours to take." Tam-Tam shook a scolding finger at her.

"I took nothing that doesn't belong to me." Velda raised her arm toward the ceiling and made a sweeping motion from corner to corner. "I'm part owner of this place, I've helped build it, but I won't be around to cash in."

"Oh?" Tam-Tam leaned toward her.

"Maxine doesn't love me anymore. My children hate me. My husband—in name only, mind you—messed everything up with Maxine. It's all too much."

"You're stealing money so you can run away? Well, I'll be."

"I only need enough money for travel and to tide me over till I get situated somewhere—not that it's any of your business."

"How do you know you're not my business?" Tam-Tam threw the statement out like bait on a hook.

Velda didn't bite. "That's some crazy talk."

"You wouldn't understand, no, not at all, but I suspect you've got some real bad in you from your father and you must have gotten some sweetness from your mother."

Velda pointed to her ear and made a circular motion. "Like I said, crazy talk. Everyone knows you hate my mother."

Tam-Tam nodded toward Velda's chest. "Ever since findin' out about that ring, I been wantin' to know where it came from. I got my suspicions now. Don't you?"

Feeling probed like a lab specimen, Velda clutched the ring, which dangled on a chain around her neck. "I don't care since they just discarded me on the steps of St. Michaels like a piece of trash," she snapped to discourage what she considered to be Tam-Tam's aggressive tack.

"Suit yourself, then." Tam-Tam backed away, sulking. She struggled out the door, and crept toward her home.

Relieved when the door closed behind the old woman, Velda pulled the tip money out, counted it and put it back in her pocket.

Earl smoothed the lapel of his uniform as he approached Abby Louise's mustard-yellow bungalow. When he reached the porch, he cleared his throat and rang the bell.

Abby Louise opened the door and leaned against the frame. "Why, hello there, Earl. She's been expecting you." She waved him in.

He followed her to the living room, where Tam-Tam rested on the chartreuse brocade couch. Abby Louise kicked aside a few spools of yarn and removed a Kroger bag full of felt from a chair so that Earl could sit down. Then she shambled out of the room. He situated himself and pulled out a postcard-sized spiral notebook and stubby pencil from his pocket.

Tam-Tam wiggled her feet, which rested on the coffee table between them. "Hope you don't mind. I'm plum tired from marchin' back and forth from here to my place every day, just to keep an eye on things."

"Get as comfortable as you can."

Abby Louise reappeared with two mugs of coffee, along with cream, sugar and spoons on a silver tray. "Here ya go. I've got some chocolate chip cookies fresh from the oven, too, if you'd like."

"Oh yes." Earl rubbed his stomach. "My mom used to make them."

"All righty, then." Abby Louise tottered back to the kitchen, touching the walls every few steps to keep her balance.

Earl put two teaspoons of sugar in one of the coffees, stirred and offered it to Tam-Tam.

She brought her feet down and sat up to accept the mug. "How did you know that's how I like it?" She sniffed the brew, exhaled audibly and took a long sip.

"I'd say we all know almost everything about everyone here, wouldn't you?"

Abby brought in a plate of warm, chewy cookies and swayed as she tried to put it on the table.

"Thank you." Earl grabbed the plate just in time to avoid a spill. He took a nibble, then finished it off in one big chomp. "Delicious."

"Have another." Abby Louise stepped back and bumped against the archway between the living room and foyer.

"Don't mind if I do." He handed one to Tam-Tam and took another for himself.

Tam-Tam coughed. "Is she gonna stay here while we talk?"

Earl lightened his coffee with cream, stirred, took a sip and smiled at Abby Louise. "This is good, real good. But me and Tam-Tam need a little privacy right now. Sorry to impose like this, but it seemed easier on Tam-Tam to talk here than at the station."

"Of course." Abby Louise's face reddened as she turned and slunk down the hall into the kitchen, where she swerved and crept back toward the living room. She stopped inches from the doorway.

"Work on your home has been keepin' you busy enough?" Earl flashed a smile.

"I s'pose you heard things came to a head between them Tarrs and McDuggins. They wound up tearin' down a chunk of what remained of my poor house instead of repairin' it, then blamed each other, as they always do, and walked off the job. I was at my wits end till them hippies from the old Kiminee place saved the day. They've been learnin' as they go, but they all get along, and they're movin' real fast now. The new garden shed they's workin' on is bigger than the one that got washed down river."

"Speaking of things being washed away." Earl shifted his weight, and the chair creaked. "I have to ask you about those bones. You know that's why I came."

"Don't rightly know much about 'em."

"Here's the thing. I've known you all my life, and I think you do."

She scowled and put her coffee cup down, sloshing some of the drink on the table. "Why, Earl Wiggs, what are you … what are you gettin' at?"

"I just can't figure out why you're not tellin'."

She groaned and rubbed her temples with her fingertips. "I'm gonna faint if you keep this up."

"Oh, go on," he chided, eyes twinkling. "You're the toughest person in town, and I mean that as a compliment."

Flustered at his persistence, she looked away from him, trying to maintain her composure. "Like I said. I don't know nothin'," she muttered.

Earl took a sip of coffee, put his cup down and studied the old woman. "Tam-Tam?"

"You think you know so much."

Earl leaned back in his chair. "I'm in no hurry. We can pass the time nice and friendly till you get whatever it is off your chest."

Tam-Tam clutched a napkin, twisted it in her lap and stared at Earl for several moments as the urge to get things off her chest swarmed up like water in an overheated engine until she finally spoke. "This stays between me and you, ya hear? You wasn't the chief back then. It was the time of Missy's uncle, Maurice T. Brewer, who had it in for me."

"He had dementia real bad by the time I met him. Don't know why the town kept him on as long as they did." Earl bit into another cookie.

"He got it in his head that my Harlan—that'd be my husband in case you didn't know, since he left before you was born—so anyways, he said my Harlan murdered Gracie, our very own daughter, mind you, and he pinned the shot that killed Missy's dad, Foster P. Brewer, on Harlan, too. ... Now, there was some evidence pointin' to Harlan. No denyin' that, but it was never proved, 'cause there was no investigation. No investigation!" Tam-Tam felt her pulse quicken, and she paused to slurp coffee before continuing. "Whew! I gotta simmer myself down, here. ... So, you see, there was evidence pointin' straight at Maurice, too ... and ... I can't talk more about it. ... Just know that with gunshots and mewlin' ringin' in our ears, Harlan and Juke—he was my first born—ran into the forest, which they knew like the back of their hands. Maurice gave chase, but he warn't no woodsman. It's like the woods plum ate 'em up. They was gone, gone for good."

"I heard stories about them as a kid. People told all kinds of things, like how they'd sneak into town in the middle of the night and steal babies and eat them."

"And how do you suppose that was for me?" Tam-Tam pursed her lips.

"I never thought about it at the time." Chagrined, he looked away, eyes half closed, then back at Tam-Tam. "I'm so sorry."

"Oh, stop lookin' so guilty; you wasn't responsible. If that Missy hadn't been such a blabbermouth, and if that trigger-happy Maurice hadn't stepped out brandishing that old rifle, none of it would have happened. It's them I hold responsible."

"What does all this have to do with the body?"

"I'm gettin' to that. Hold yer horses." Her nostrils flared as she flounced her skirt.

He put a palm up, fending off her ire. "Okay, okay. Nothin' to get worked up about."

"How would you know? Think on it for a minute. Since Maurice couldn't get Harlan, who do you suppose he went after?"

"I don't rightly know."

"He made my life a livin' hell, led everybody to believe I was aidin' and abettin' Harlan and Juke, made me a pariah, he did." She lifted the napkin to catch a tear that leaked from her eye. "What do you suppose he'd have done if I came to him some years down the road and told him, 'Oh, say, I just found this body thawin' at the riverbank.' Do you think he woulda left it at that?"

"You found the body when, exactly?" He held his pencil up, ready to take notes.

"It was the spring of 1936, I'd say. A thaw came after a bitter winter, and I was out for a walk when I came upon her. I couldn't tell Chief Brewer. I just couldn't. And I couldn't leave her there, so I made her a nice grave across the river, planted flowers and tended it all these years till the storm washed that gal right up, or what was left of 'er."

Head down and still scribbling notes, Earl asked, "Who was she?"

"Beats me."

He looked up. "You don't even have a hunch?"

"Nope."

He leaned forward, tapping his pencil on his pad. "What do you suppose she was doing in these parts?"

"I don't suppose anything."

"There's nothing you can add, to maybe help me find her family, to let them take her home?" He closed his notebook.

"That was a long time ago." She sniffed, indignant. She clamped her mouth shut and jutted out her chin.

"Well, okay. That's it—for now," Earl said, knowing she was holding back. He stood, put his notebook and pencil in his pocket, grabbed one more cookie and popped it, whole, into his mouth.

Abby Louise bolted back to the kitchen, pulled out a fifth of whiskey and took a quick glug.

Earl strode to the archway, then turned to face Tam-Tam. "I'm not right sure what to do with this information now after all these years. You should have gone to Maurice."

"Easy for you to say," Tam-Tam muttered, both hands clutching her coffee mug.

"We're done now, Abby Louise," Earl called when he reached the door.

"Hold up." Abby Louise stumbled out with a small paper bag of cookies. "For you."

"Why, that's right kind of you. Thanks." He opened the bag and took a sniff. "Mmm." He folded it closed, pushed the door open and stepped outside.

After watching him tromp to the squad car, Abby Louise joined Tam-Tam.

"You'd better not breathe a word to nobody," Tam-Tam said.

"I don't know what you're talking about." Abby Louise grabbed the last cookie from the plate and took a bite.

Emily entered Suzette's and waited by the door while Tempest rang up a purchase. It was one of Varney Welch's patchwork lap quilts, which had been selling extremely well ever since a photo of one had accompanied a glowing article about Suzette's in Peoria's *Journal Star* newspaper. The woman acquiring the quilt giggled as she accepted her new prized possession and made her way toward the door.

Emily opened it for her and said, "Enjoy your quilt."

"Thank you kindly," the woman said. "I can't believe I got the last one." She stepped outside and pranced down the sidewalk toward the Good Luck Cafe.

Emily looked over at Tempest. "The last one, eh?"

"Yep, and it'll be a while before we get another one, takes a long time for Varney to make one of those." Tempest bent down low, pulled out a cardboard box and put it on the counter. "I expect you came for this. I combed through all the cabinets in back, and this is all the Fourth of July-themed stuff we've got. Crepe paper, a couple of honeycomb Uncle Sam-style hats and a nice banner—all in red white and blue, of course."

"I really appreciate this," Emily said when she reached the counter. "The kids who volunteered to decorate for the community center's grand opening are chomping at the bit to get streamers up. I have to keep reminding them how quickly they droop." Emily lifted the box a few inches, but then put back down and opened her shoulder bag.

"You must be doin' somethin' right at the academy to get 'em to help out in the summer." Tempest rubbed a dust cloth over the cash register keys. "Whew! I can't believe how much work it is keeping this place clean," she said.

"If only we all had genies at our beck and call." Emily pulled the spiral notebook of Lolly's drawings out and flipped to the sketch of her father. "Say." She put the book on the counter. "Do you know who this is?"

Tempest clucked as she scanned the page, then gaped as recognition hit. "Why that there looks to be Juke Parlo."

"Parlo? Hmm. Would this person be related to Tam-Tam?"

"Indeed he would."

"How?"

"I'd rather not talk about it if you don't mind." She clucked some more and wiped the sides and top of the register.

"I really need to know."

A group of giggling tourists entered, and Tempest slid the book toward Emily. "This would be one heckuva long conversation, one I'm surely not prepared to have. Danged if I even know whatever happened to him. I expect that's what you'll hear from most everyone else, too."

She stepped out from behind the counter and greeted the group of eager shoppers. "Welcome to Suzette's. I'm Tempest. Just let me know if you need help. Each one of these things in here has a story."

"Maybe not as good as this," Emily said under her breath as she put the book back in her purse. Terrified she'd opened a Pandora's box that would upend her life, she felt a wave of nausea strike. She winced, grabbed the decorations and rushed toward the door.

Chapter 34

The Fourth of July fell on a Friday in 1969, and while strangers still mucked about, wanting to find out more about the Foley family, Leon Ames and Georgia Webb, they were no longer clogging the streets, so the town went ahead with a parade and fireworks on the Fourth and the opening of the new community center the following day. Race Burlington and Randy Tarr, who always designed and managed the fireworks display, asked Willie Holt to join them, thinking some young blood would enhance the show. The three of them created such a profusion of shapes and colors and sounds exploding across the night sky that everyone was still wonderstruck the following day when making their way to the glistening, new building. They imagined the dedication ceremony would be enjoyable but bland by comparison.

Tempest Binsack waddled and huffed in an effort to keep up with Maridee Pratt, who strode up Kiminee's only significant hill toward the academy campus. Other members of the Suzettes followed at a more leisurely pace, each carrying her signature casserole, salad, snack or dessert, toward the school's new community building. The gleaming structure had been a bone of contention for some and a source of pride for others from the project's inception all the way through construction—completed only four days prior with the installation of washroom fixtures, cabinet nobs and whatnot. As anticipated, it was the strangest structure anyone had seen for hundreds of miles: a geodesic dome inspired by the work of Buckminster Fuller, an architect and inventor Jasper met in his youth at the 1933–34 Century of Progress World's Fair in Chicago.

"Slow down, will you?" Tempest pleaded. "There's plenty of time. Everybody's still picking out what to wear, shaving, shining their shoes."

Maridee paused. "Sorry. I'm just excited to get inside that thing. My Bill was there yesterday, and he says it's out of this world, like being in a space ship."

Tempest caught up to Maridee at the entrance. "I can't wait to see it."

Jasper opened the double doors for them. "Welcome, ladies. Thank you so much for your help. We've got a table all set up for you in the hall." They thanked Jasper and hurried inside, bumping into each other and almost tripping in their excitement.

Jasper greeted several more Suzettes as they straggled in. The friends chittered and gaped once inside, mesmerized by the spherical design itself, as well as the views on all sides, except for two places where corridors connected the dome to two traditional brick structures. They arranged their potluck contributions on the table and then stood at the see-through walls instead of seating themselves in the rows of chairs arranged for the occasion. As more residents, their friends and relatives, and a larger number of outsiders than anticipated arrived, students scrambled to haul in additional classroom chairs, but no one sat down. Everyone stood at the enormous window panels and gained new perspectives on the layout and personality of what many boasted was the finest little river town in all of Illinois.

People let out gasps of awe as they pointed out their favorite spots. Velda said she could see all the way to the wishing tree at the old Kiminee estate, as well as clothes on the line behind the refurbished home, something most folks thought was far fetched until they looked in that direction and saw those details for themselves. On one side, some pointed out a curious congregation of fox, raccoon, bluebirds, rabbits and squirrels sitting peaceably at the edge of the wood. Missy exclaimed at the sight of the wind chime on her porch and bees buzzing around her roses. "They're as clear as if I was right in the garden," she said.

Just as Jasper stepped to the podium and told everyone it was time to get the dedication ceremony started, Abby Louise's sweaty hands were shaky because she hadn't had a swig of whiskey all day, and when she got a glimpse of her home from above, she dropped her plate of blond brownie squares, which scattered with shards of broken china on the floor.

"Oh, no!" she cried out.

Tam-Tam, patted her arm. "Not to worry. There's plenty of other treats."

"You are a godsend," Abby Louise, still shaking, said to her friend.

Old Bill Deely, who doubled as the academy's music instructor and maintenance man, was on hand with a broom and dustpan to sweep up. Tam-Tam and Abby-Louise stepped around the mess and found seats in the back row. Finally, with everyone seated, Jasper stepped to the podium to say a few words about the unique qualities of this structure and geodesic domes in general. Then he introduced Missy.

"Without her, this project would never have begun," he said. "She's a pillar of the community who reinforces positive values in so many ways, and we all know she's a grandmother for the ages."

Missy walked to the podium, but everyone cheered so much, she could not begin to speak until the noise died down. Everyone, that is, except Tam-Tam, who fidgeted and rocked in her chair. She tried to sit still, but she'd barely slept since Earl had come to question her. He'd been kindly enough but she felt stained by his visit, like the whole town felt she was a bad seed, always in the wrong. The more she thought about it, the more riled up she became. Her agitation grew more pronounced as Missy greeted the crowd.

"Why, thank you all for the warm welcome." Her voice wobbled with emotion. "I hardly know where to begin, but I guess it all comes down to family. We're individual families, but we're all one big family, too, and no place on earth lives that better than we do right here.»

More cheers burst forth from the crowd, and at that, Tam-Tam leaned toward Abby Louise. "I gotta get out of here. I can't stand any more of that connivin' liar. It never ends." Tam-Tam lurched up from her chair. "Don't follow. I'll be right outside." And she marched out.

Abby Louise, still flustered from dropping her brownies, didn't move.

Tam-Tam paced by the door while people listened to Missy's remarks, followed by short speeches by a few other boosters of the school. She fought off hunger pangs when everyone crowded to the tables to heap paper plates full of food and then stand at the floor-to-ceiling windows to admire the views some more. Tam-Tam picked up a hoe left behind in a flower bed freshly planted with marigolds and tapped it on the ground. Then she leaned against the building, humming to herself. Finally, her neighbors, full and content, filed out.

Missy emerged, arm in arm with Varney Welch. Tam-Tam stormed from behind the door, shoved Varney aside and exclaimed, "You think you're such a fine citizen? Well, take that, Marcie Brewer!" She whacked Missy on the head with the hoe.

Missy cried out in pain as she fell and rolled down the hill toward a steep, rocky ravine. People already outside were momentarily frozen at the shock of what had just occurred.

Tam-Tam chased after Missy and whacked her on the back. "Take that, too, you uptight, self-serving, wretched excuse for a human."

The exit became clogged with too many people trying to get out at once to see what was causing the ruckus. Finally Missy's family and friends charged out and raced to save Missy as she rolled down, screaming and picking up speed. Tam-Tam, feeble as she usually was, threw down the hoe and sprinted. She handily outran everyone and grabbed Missy's arm just as she was about to tumble over the edge.

"Not so fast," Tam-Tam barked. "I'm not done with you yet. I'll just let you dangle here a while so you can contemplate your fate before you fall." She sneered at Missy, who was now reduced to muttering incoherently, teeth chattering.

Velda caught up and grabbed hold of Tam-Tam's legs.

"Unhand me, you, you, or I'll let go of your so-called mother," Tam-Tam growled.

Fearing Tam-Tam would follow through, Velda released Tam-Tam's legs and backed away.

"That's more like it," Tam-Tam spat.

Carly Mae arrived, and in the most commanding voice she could muster, said, "Stop torturing my grandmother. Pull her up!"

Ignoring the girl, Tam-Tam continued taunting. "I think maybe I'll count to three and let go, or maybe ten. Yeah, ten will draw it out some."

Missy twisted and tugged, trying to break free. Seeing Velda and Carly Mae's faces, she regained some coherence. "Unhand me, you, you—"

Earl arrived and, in one fluid motion, rushed Tam-Tam from behind, gripped Missy's arm and pushed Tam-Tam away. Tam-Tam cackled as she stumbled backward. "You ain't no match for me, even in my final years," she jeered at Missy.

Earl pulled Missy up to safety, and drew her close. "It's okay; you're all right now," he said. Blood gushed from her head onto his shirt. Straining for breath, she held tight to his sleeve as her family gathered around.

Carly Mae and Blanche, now more angry than shocked, conferred briefly before Carly Mae went back inside in search of Doc Redfield.

Meanwhile, Tam-Tam attempted to slink off along the ravine, but Earl saw her and said, "Not one more step, Tam-Tam." He handed Missy off to Ray and trotted after Tam-Tam.

Missy's eyes closed. She swayed and went limp as Ray lifted her into his arms.

"I've got you, Grams," he said. "You're safe."

Missy opened her eyes. "What happened?"

Velda squeezed close to Ray. "Mom! Mommy! Are you okay?"

"What happened?" Missy asked again.

Carly Mae returned followed by Doc and Della Burlington, who assisted him a few afternoons a week at Kiminee's clinic. While Della ran ahead to open the medical facility, Carly Mae handed Blanche a damp washcloth, so she could wipe blood from Missy's face.

"Tam-Tam whacked you real hard, but Doc is here now," Carly Mae said to Missy.

Doc stepped forward with his little black bag, which he carried wherever he went. He briefly assessed Missy's condition while Ray held her. "She's gonna need stitches," Doc announced, then turned to Ray and said, "Follow me."

Ray proceeded toward the clinic with caution, knowing his arms held an irreplaceable treasure.

Just a few yards away, Earl put handcuffs on Tam-Tam and led her toward his cruiser. Abby Louise catapulted toward them and whacked Earl with her purse. "What are you doing? Leave Tam-Tam alone. How can you treat a frail old lady like that?"

"You can come along to the station," Earl said to Abby Louise, "but you'd better stop beatin' on me or I'll arrest you, too."

"What did you do?" Abby Louise asked Tam-Tam as the three proceeded toward Earl's cruiser.

Tam-Tam let out a piercing cry.

Emily, who was standing next to Jasper, clutched both hands to her sternum. "I've heard that awful sound before," she managed to croak. "It's all coming back to me." She leaned against him and scrunched her eyes closed. "It feels like I'm being split apart."

"What can I do?"

"Get me to the nearest phone. I have to call Dr. Blake."

The wrath Tam-Tam directed at Missy left everybody in town jumpy—more inclined to startle if a door opened suddenly or if a strong wind rattled windows. Otherwise healthy people lined up at the clinic, complaining of shortness of breath, heart palpitations and vertigo. Some suffered from debilitating depression, remaining in bed until friends and family coaxed them out with promises they could not keep of miracle cures and happy days ahead. Desperate people who didn't believe in seeking psychiatric help knocked on the door of the old Kiminee home at all hours, asking to speak with Ned, the one who had rescued Damon. When Ned was overseeing the transfer of patients before Dry Gulch was closed in the wake of the Georgia Webb scandal, Jasper had offered him a teaching position at the academy. He'd gladly accepted and was now one of Willie Holt's many housemates.

Still upset about Tam-Tam's assault on Missy several nights later, Carly Mae, unable to sleep, slipped out of her grandmother's home, fiddle in hand and Buster by her side. Streetlights flickered and stars twinkled as she made her way to the town square, where she sat on a bench by the statue of Charles and Fleur Kiminee. Though Missy wasn't seriously hurt by Tam-Tam's attack, the thought that someone wanted to harm her grandmother made Carly Mae queasy. It also brought back the horror of the day Leon Ames shot Dusty and the trials that followed until Carly Mae happened into Windy Wood and was cared for through a bitter winter by Aunt Truly.

She looked up at the faces of Fleur and Charles shining from dim floodlights that came on at sundown each day and remained lit till dawn. She lifted her fiddle and bow for the first time since her last lesson with Mick Deely eight years ago, and played for them. Haltingly, at first, she tried to alleviate the sorrow she saw in their eyes, the never-ending grief over losing their girl. She imagined Suzette being sold into slavery but breaking free of her so-called masters, finding safe houses along the underground railroad, finding love and happiness in a new life somewhere safe.

As she played, the Kiminees, though merely stone, closed their eyes and moved an inch or so closer together. Carly Mae played on, growing more confident with each stroke and she imagined Suzette bringing grandchildren home one sunny day to her mom and dad. The couple opened their eyes, and they regarded Carly Mae and their surroundings with peaceful eyes that conveyed a sense that they remembered life can be good as well as bad.

Carly Mae played on for Missy and Tam-Tam, her mom and dad, for everyone she loved, especially Dusty, for everything he was missing in life that she wished he could have, for the choices he would never be able to make, the laughter he wouldn't share, the football games he wouldn't watch with his buddies, the children he'd never have. She played on and on, her music increasing in beauty and enchantment with each measure. It permeated the dreams of everyone in Kiminee. Her melodies reached Emily in the throes of a nightmare where the father who abandoned her was wrenching her arm. As the music continued, Emily breathed easier and fell into a deep, restful sleep. The tones also touched Missy and penetrated the lump formed after the hoe struck her head. It shrank just a little more than it would have on an ordinary night.

Carly Mae continued creating music until she fell asleep on the bench, with fiddle and dog tucked in and her arms wrapped around both. Her sleep was deep and peaceful, too. And in the wee hours, Damon, who had been sleep walking until Carly Mae's music reached him, came upon his daughter. He leaned down, kissed her forehead. "Sleep well, my daughter. Daddy's here. You brought me back," he whispered. Then he lifted her, Buster and the fiddle as though they were light as a pillow, and carried them home.

In Dr. Blake's Chicago office, Emily fidgeted on the turquoise couch. With hands on her knees, she pressed her thighs together and released them repeatedly in time to her hammering heart. "Thank you for squeezing me in again." She met the doctor's eyes, then glanced at the clock. "How much time do we have?"

"I had a cancellation today; we can do a full session."

"In that case, can we begin with some deep breathing? My heart's beating fast as a rabbit's. I think my ears and nose will start twitching next. I don't quite have the hang of the deep breathing on my own when I'm upset."

"I'll be happy to guide you. It's an excellent idea. Start by closing your eyes and paying attention to your breath."

Emily did as instructed and immediately grew calmer. When the therapist told her to open her eyes after ten minutes of guided meditation, she felt much more herself.

"Are you ready to talk now?" Dr. Blake asked.

"Yes, I think I am." Emily rubbed her eyes, blinked and offered a shy smile.

"What happened?"

"I've pieced a lot of things together, especially since Tam-Tam—I've mentioned her in sessions before; she's an elderly woman who lives in Kiminee, pretty eccentric—she's had it in for Carly Mae's grandmother for what seems like forever, and at the grand opening of the new community center, Tam-Tam actually attacked Missy with a shovel, no, it was a hoe."

"Witnessing something like that would upset anyone."

"It was a shock, but that's not what set me off. It was this piercing, otherworldly scream Tam-Tam let out just as Earl, the local police chief and a really nice guy, was leading her to his cruiser. Her voice went through me like lightning." Emily pulled a handkerchief from her pocketbook and kneaded it.

"What was it about that sound in particular?"

Emily shook the handkerchief open. "I realized I'd heard it before. The memory grabbed me like a mugger out for blood." She leaned down, brought the cloth to her face and breathed in the scent of Joy perfume.

"When, when did you hear it before?"

Emily withdrew the handkerchief and looked up at Dr. Blake. "It was a long, long time ago. In Kiminee, not Kankakee or some other place. Kiminee. I'm sure of it now. ... I was a little girl."

"Before the orphanage?"

"Yes." Emily leaned back on the couch and spoke for the first time about what she'd recalled the day of the Wallop and Roll. "It all makes sense now ... why I become so nauseated ... everything. ... Juke Parlo was or is, I don't know if he's alive or dead, was Tam-Tam's son, and I was there with him in Kiminee. I was maybe four years old." She threw her head back and groaned.

"Take your time. Remember to breathe," Dr. Blake said.

"Juke was my dad. Whoo! There, I said it. Juke Parlo was my father." Emily felt bile rising from her gut, but she forced it down and continued. "Doris showed me a drawing of him done by her other daughter, Lolly. I xeroxed it, thinking I'd show it around Kiminee to see if anyone recognized him. If not, I thought it would be safe to assume my father was from some other place, like Kankakee, because Doris couldn't recall for sure. So it wasn't long before I showed it to Tempest Binsack, she's one of the Suzette's in Kiminee. She recognized him and told me his real name. See, Doris didn't know it. She thought he was named James Parker, but then found a bunch of licenses with different names, all with his picture. So, I finally learned his name, but Tempest refused to say more. She said nobody else would want to talk about him either. I was worried what I'd find out once I found someone who would open up, having second thoughts, but then it all came back to me when, like I said, Tam-Tam cried out that day."

Emily's throat tensed at the thought of the sound. She took a few deep breaths and continued. "She was voicing absolute, unconsolable pain, just like when Juke wrenched me from her grasp. That's what came back to me. Being pulled away with a cruel force." Emily's voice cracked. She made eye contact with Dr. Blake and felt reassured she could persist. "She held on as long as she could, but he was stronger. He shoved me into the truck, where Lolly was screaming out in pain." Emily's bottom lip trembled as she scanned the room.

"Lolly. You've mentioned her before," the doctor said.

Emily nodded. "Lolly was real. She was my sister, my half sister. She was real as this." She squeezed the brocade cushion. "She was and might still be as alive as you and me." Feeling empowered, by speaking the truth aloud, Emily continued, her voice stronger than before. "Juke Parlo wasn't her dad. She was his stepdaughter, and he ... well, when our mom, Doris, found out what he'd done to Lolly, he beat Doris nearly to death ... and ran to hide out in Kiminee. Tam-Tam, who I now know is my grandmother, noticed that Lolly was gaining weight, but Juke said she was just eating too much. Then on that awful night, that terrible night, Lolly went into labor. I didn't know what was going on at the time, of course. I just knew she was in so much pain she woke me up. But my dad knew. He gave her a rag and told her to bite on it and keep quiet. Then he tried to sneak off in the dark while Tam-Tam was asleep. But Tam-Tam woke up, came out running and begged him to stay. He had already shoved Lolly into the cab of a pickup truck and was about to lift me in, but Tam-Tam grabbed on to me, and the two of them almost tore me in half. Lolly was there biting on the rag and trying not to scream. Finally he yanked me away, and the last I saw of my grandma, she was running as fast as she could, but she grew smaller and smaller in the distance as we sped away." Emily let out a long breath and nodded to Dr. Blake. "It feels uncomfortable but good to get this out."

"You're doing really well. Go on."

"My dad turned onto a bumpy road leading to a little shack not too far away. And it was there that little Daphne Sunshine was born. She was real, too, just like Lolly."

"Do you know what happened next?"

"Parts of it are clear; some stuff is really vague."

"That's often the case when dealing with traumatic memories."

"I do know that when the sun came up Lolly was burning with fever. She couldn't feed the baby, and my dad said she was gonna have to give Daphne Sunshine up if she didn't get better real quick. She got worse, though. That night he wrapped the baby in a little yellow blanket. Lolly begged him not to go, but he wouldn't listen. When he was at the door, Lolly stumbled over, took off her ring, pulled a safety pin from her pocket, and pinned it to the blanket. And then she collapsed onto this bare mattress, the only bed there. She stared at the ceiling, didn't talk more than one word at a time. And her voice was really soft. I had to lean in close to hear her."

"That must have been frightening for such a little girl. You were so young."

"I was afraid right then but also scared of what Juke would do when he returned. I wasn't even sure he would return. He was gone a long time. Lolly grew hotter and hotter. I didn't know what to do other than give her sips of water. Eventually, I fell asleep. I was nestled against her, one arm around her. When I woke up in the morning, she was gone. I cried and cried. I don't know how long it was before Juke came back without the baby. He didn't seem upset at all that Lolly was gone. He dragged me into the truck. I was sobbing. He told me to shut up, but I couldn't. This went on for what seemed like hours. We meandered. I don't know where. And the next thing I knew I was on the steps of the orphanage. I couldn't remember much of anything except that I had a sister named Lolly, who had a little baby, Daphne Sunshine. But the nuns didn't believe me."

"And you don't know what happened to either or them, or Juke."

"There may be some answers in Kiminee."

"Are you prepared for what you might find there?"

"I've already learned how cruel my father was, and I'm still standing. I think I'm ready to face whatever comes of this now."

Chapter 35

The fact that Carly Mae could create extraordinary music once again and Damon had begun conversing with relative ease spread through Kiminee, Illinois in the same spirited way news of a child's birth always did. People and animals alike set aside their differences to celebrate as one joyous whole. Mothers and fathers jigged around kitchens. Children cartwheeled around the town square. Farmers belted show tunes in their fields. Pigs played kick the can with bobcats; chickens dined with hawks; rabbits napped with coyotes. And once again, the Bendy River got in the act. The tune it burbled this time while crawdads marched in formation along its banks sounded a lot like the Beatles' "With a Little Help From My Friends."

Magnanimity spread to Missy, who declined to press charges against Tam-Tam after "The Wallop and Roll," as the attack had been dubbed. "After all," she said. "Who knows how I would act if my home had been ruined in the deluge and I'd been forced to live in a friend's tiny spare room all this time."

While some folks thought the failure to prosecute Tam-Tam was a travesty, others thought if Missy was willing to give her a pass, they were, too. It was, after all, the first time Tam-Tam had done anything violent in her long, long life. This was a relief to Earl, who hadn't had the heart to house Tam-Tam at the police station even one night. He feared the old woman, who was sputtering nonsense and shuddering like an overheated engine, when he brought her in, might expire, so after the mosquitoes came out in full force and the streetlights went on, he quietly drove her back to Abby Louise's and told her to stay put and keep out of trouble, which she had done, as far as anyone could tell.

The joy over Carly Mae and Damon's healing, along with a renewed sense of community, was also glad tidings for folks preparing for the annual Founders Day festival. The town established the holiday to honor Charles and Fleur and give them a little zip during the long, languid summer days between Fourth of July and Labor Day, when people tended to wilt like water-starved flowers. People now pranced about, energized. And when they learned Damon had accepted a position teaching math at the academy starting in the fall, even non-believers among them genuflected and gave thanks. Everyone expected Carly Mae would return to school and take every prize if she wanted to. She, however, had her doubts. She shied away from any sort of display of intelligence, like solving intricate math problems her dad gave her at the supper table, fearing she wouldn't be able to solve them. She threw herself instead into Founders Day preparations and found she loved working with Blanche and Ray just as much as she'd once loved doing math with her dad. They worked hours on paper mache busts of Fleur and Charles to adorn the new community center where quilts, paintings, woodworking, baked goods and other items made by local residents would soon be on display.

At her kitchen table, Missy was afraid that entering her signature blueberry pie and attending the awards ceremony would be too much for her. But when she tiptoed to the garage, where her grandchildren were hard at work, she gasped at the beauty of the busts, which were hauntingly lifelike, except that they were three times normal size. Seeing this made her decide she, too, could participate, and she pulled out her pie tins, washed them and put them in the sun to dry, something she believed was part of her formula for success in baking.

When the teens emerged from the garage and saw Missy's tins in the sun, they whooped for joy, knowing it meant she'd decided to enter the contest. They galloped into the kitchen, where they each hugged their grandmother in turn and made plans with her to go to the blueberry patch just outside of town, the one locals kept secret from outsiders because the berries were the plumpest, most flavorful any of them had ever tasted.

Facing sunrise hues of purple, pink, orange and gold penetrating a navy blue horizon, Jasper, Emily and Doris sat on a blanket at the beach and chatted while unpacking a picnic of bagels and cream cheese, yogurt, orange juice and coffee in a thermos.

Doris eyed the food skeptically. "I never had a bagel before, no yogurt either."

Jasper handed her half of a bagel spread with a thick layer of cheese. "I think you'll like this. Living in a great metropolis like Chicago, where people have settled from all over the world, there are so many cuisines to sample. Why stick with the same old things day after day? You know, bagels are boiled first, then baked."

"You don't say." Doris took a nibble. "Hmm. Not bad."

"It was the Jewish people in Poland who first made them," he continued. "They shaped them by hand, but nobody has the time to do that anymore." Jasper pulled out the yogurt. "I've got raspberry, blueberry and peach. Fruit on the bottom. You stir it up."

Doris selected peach, Emily blueberry. Jasper dug into the raspberry, his favorite.

"So where's this yogurt stuff from?" Doris asked.

"Scandinavia, maybe. I'm not sure," Jasper replied.

Doris stirred her serving and took a spoonful. "Well, it tastes pretty good. I'll give you that."

Emily looked out across Lake Michigan, then turned her head toward Jasper. "What made you so adventurous today? You never want to come to the beach."

"It's you, actually," he said to Emily. "When I think of all you've endured when we've spent time in Kiminee, how you've faced it and all the progress you've made, it makes me think I can learn to enjoy a picnic on the beach with my lovely wife and mother in law."

"Even with seals approaching? I see them bobbing out there." Emily eyed the water. "I think they're coming our way."

"All the experts in the world can't figure out what brought them here, it seems." Jasper swallowed hard. "But let's talk about your big breakthrough, shall we?"

"I was going to fill you both in on the ride to Kiminee today." Emily patted Doris' knee. "I'm so glad you're coming for Founders Day."

Doris fingered her spoon. "We'll see how Donny does while I'm gone. He's only been helping out for three weeks. It's a lot of responsibility to put on him," Doris said about the young man who would be managing the gallery in her absence. "But be that as it may, what's this about a breakthrough?"

"Yes, now's an opportune time to tell us," Jasper said. "It'll be harder to talk in the wagon. One of us will be in the backseat."

"I guess you're right." Emily poured orange juice into a plastic tumbler and guzzled it down before recounting what she'd realized about Juke and Tam-Tam Parlo, Lolly and baby Daphne Sunshine.

All three were choked up when she finished. Jasper pulled extra napkins from their wicker basket and passed them around. Meanwhile, the seals had swum closer and were hovering in shallow water at the shore. Then one of them waddled onto the beach, its big brown eyes on Jasper.

"Uh, should we be worried?" Doris inched back on the blanket.

"The animal doesn't look aggressive," Emily said.

Jasper sat rigid, tongue rubbing the back of his front teeth. The seal came forward, barking, and stopped about five feet in front of Jasper.

Doris clutched Emily's hand. "What if it's rabid?"

The pinniped advanced, barked again and nudged Jasper's foot.

He laughed. The seal maneuvered backward, barking intermittently at him. When it reached the water, it dove in to join the rest of its pod.

Jasper stood up. "I believe it wants me to follow.»

"Do you really think that's wise?" Emily asked.

"You gotta be nuts to do that," Doris added.

"Well, you only live once. I want to face my fears like Emily. What's the worst that could happen? It's women who turn into seals, not men, right?" He winked at his companions, then sprinted to the lake and dove in.

"What on earth is he talking about?" Doris pursed her lips in worry.

Jasper surfaced and stood in water up to his chest while the animals cavorted around him.

"There are some things I need to tell you about my husband. Brace yourself." Emily then shared all she knew about Jasper's childhood.

"I'll be a monkey's uncle," Doris said when Emily finished. "I'm kind of, I mean, he's not quite the solid guy I thought … um … should I be worried? He could fly off the deep end anytime, couldn't he?"

"He's as right as a sweet April rain," Emily said. "It's heartbreaking the way his dad treated him. There's no denying that. And by what's going on with him and those seals at this very moment … " She pointed toward the lake. "You have to think there's something to his story."

The seals swam one last circle around Jasper then dove off. He stood still watching for a few moments before returning to the picnic.

Emily handed him a towel. "What do you think that was about?"

"I don't know." He rubbed his skin vigorously with the terry cloth. "It's all unsettling, but I'm glad I went in. I can't deny there's some connection there."

"Could those animals really be your relatives?" Doris asked.

"I don't know, honestly, but we can talk about all of this on the road."

"Oh, you're right. We'd better get going." Emily reached down, put some used napkins into a paper bag and held it up. "This is for garbage."

Doris and Jasper joined in packing up, and soon they left the beach, morning sun warming their backs. A couple blocks from Jasper and Emily's co-op building, a stand holding a stack of the *Chicago Reader* newspaper caught his eye. He stopped and tapped the glass. "Look, it's a photo of Mrs. Henchley and Dr. Croll. He leaned closer and squinted to read from the page. "They've been charged with embezzling from Lily Park Academy—thousands upon thousands of dollars over the past decade."

"No wonder they tried to squeeze more money out of you," Emily said. "They'd already wrung the poor school dry."

The Wednesday before Founders Day, which always fell the second Saturday in August, the berry patch was busy as an anthill. Missy, Blanch, Ray and Carly Mae situated themselves in the row farthest from the road. Blanche set up the ladder and then climbed, bucket in hand, while her siblings and grandmother fanned out to pick lower branches of bushes that were unusually tall at twelve feet and loaded with plump fruit. Engrossed with picking and nibbling, the family didn't notice Tam-Tam and Abby Louise round into the row and lumber toward them.

Blanche spied them first. "I can't believe this," she warned from her perch. "Of all the places in this patch, those two have chosen this one."

Abby Louise yanked Tam-Tam to a stop a couple yards from Missy, who was so startled she clamped her teeth down and bit her tongue. "Ouch," she cried out.

Tam-Tam slipped away from Abby Louse and moved closer to Missy. "Well, well, I leave the house, on account of this knuckle-head," she pointed to Abby Louise, "to get some blueberries for my award-winning muffins, and what do I see, but you stalking me."

Attempting to ignore Tam-Tam in the hopes she'd move to another row, Missy faced a bush and picked with trembling hands.

"Look at you, Marcie Brewer." Tam-Tam huffed. "High and mighty, thinkin' you're too good to talk to me, too good to tell the truth about what you did."

"She says Grams' maiden name like she's digging in a knife or something." Ray whispered to Carly Mae as the two moved closer to their grandmother.

"Yeah, it's strange, especially since nobody else calls her Marcie. She's either Missy or Grams," Carly Mae muttered.

Tam-Tam inched closer so her nose was almost touching Missy's ear.

Carly Mae squeezed between them, moving Tam-Tam aside. "Leave Grams alone!"

Hearing the raised voice, berry pickers in other rows trickled, then surged toward the source. Among them were Maridee and Tempest. Jasper, Emily and Doris arrived shortly thereafter. Earl approached with a bucket of berries he'd picked for Abby Louise, whose blueberry cheesecake he'd been craving.

"Well, ain't this a fine kettle of fish," Tam-Tam said when she spied Earl. "You gonna arrest me again?"

"Not if you behave yourself," he replied, "which it doesn't' appear you're doing right now."

Tam-Tam pointed to Missy. "It's her. She's the one. She's the troublemaker."

Missy spun around to face Tam-Tam. "I've had enough of your accusations and assaults. Can't you just appreciate that I didn't press charges?"

"Bah!" Tam-Tam hoisted herself onto an upside down bucket so she could see more of the gathering crowd.

"There she is in the flesh," someone called from the back of the group, which now comprised almost one-third of the town, crammed into the row and field beyond. "You ought to be in jail, not stirring the pot here."

Some folks said, "Right on" and "Yeah, quit attacking Missy." But others were of a different persuasion. "Go, go Tam-Tam," one of the McDuggin children called out, and soon a sizable number of people were calling out, "Yeah, go get 'um, Tam-Tam" and "Speak up, old girl."

"Don't mind if I do." Tam-Tam chuckled, then let loose. "Most of you don't know Marcie Brewer over there was going steady with my son Juke." She pointed at Missy. "She was also best friend to my daughter, Gracie, and like a sister to my other son, Bram. Yes, Marcie Brewer, whose family was livin' just up river with her no-good father, Foster P. Brewer, brother of the town's corrupt and long-time chief of police Maurice T. Brewer."

"How dare you say those things about my family. What about your murdering husband, Harlan?" Missy challenged. "I—"

"You hush up!" Tam-Tam growled. "Sure, Harlan was mean as a hornet and had a devil's soul, but everybody knows that. I'm talkin' about what they don't know."

Missy turned to Earl. "Stop her!"

"Let her have her piece and get it over with. We won't allow her to hurt you again," Earl promised.

"Well, I never!" Missy turned to the bush again, grabbed berries and threw them into her bucket with such ferocity that they broke open and splattered, causing some stain-fearing folks to back away.

"Like I said, my Juke and Marcie were going steady, and she came over one afternoon, all dolled up 'cause she'd gotten a job at the old soda fountain and could order things from Sears that she never had before. So she strutted up all cute and flirty in her little checked blouse and white shorts, and the two of them went behind the toolshed. I supposed it was to neck. And then there was a whole lotta screamin' and yellin', and pretty soon young vixen Marcie comes runnin' out all disheveled, buttoning up her shorts as she was runnin' away. Juke chased after her, tried to stop her. He said, 'Marcie, doll, what's the harm? We'll be married soon, anyway.' But she ran off, and—"

"That's enough!" Missy commanded. "She didn't tell it right. For one, she left off completely how Harlan wrestled poor Gracie behind the shed." She climbed partway up the ladder, stopping a few rungs below Blanche. "Sure I was dressed up in my new catalog clothes, and I might have strutted like Tam-Tam said, but I stopped short at the edge of the yard when I saw—"

Tam-Tam stomped on the bucket. "You—"

"Let her talk now," Earl said to Tam-Tam. "You had a good turn."

"Go on, Grams." Blanche leaned down and patted Missy's shoulder. The ladder wobbled, and Ray and Carly Mae each grabbed onto a leg to hold it steady.

Missy then recounted, for only the second time in her life, the attack drunken Harlan and Juke had perpetrated on her and Gracie, Harlan's own daughter. Some people in the group gasped, backed away and muttered about how things like this shouldn't ever be spoken of, especially not in public. Indignant parents rounded up children and escorted them to a row at the opposite end of the patch. Many, however, squeezed in closer so they could hear better. Maridee, the only one in the crowd who'd heard the story before, felt as raw as when Missy had first confided in her. Tam-Tam raised a fist and lost her balance. Earl caught her just in time and held her steady on the bucket as trembles rippled through her body and grew so strong the vibrations caused berries to fall from nearby bushes.

When Tam-Tam's shaking subsided, Missy continued, "There was nothing willing on my part or Gracie's about what Juke and Harlan did to us that day. And I'll never forget the look in Juke's eyes or the moonshine in his breath and oozing from his pores. I saw the true Juke, and he was bad as his father." Missy sobbed. Earl handed Tam-Tam off to Abby Louise and handed Missy a tissue.

"Never happened," Tam-Tam challenged. "Never!"

"You!" Missy glowered at Tam-Tam. "When I finally broke away, I ran past the house, and you were there in the window. You saw. You may not have seen every little thing, but you know he dragged me behind the toolshed. You know I did not go willingly. You heard our screams. You saw Gracie pound at your door, begging for you to let her in. You saw your husband drag her off the porch, whip cracking, and pull her behind the shed. And you, you did nothing. Nothing. You let it unfold."

The entire patch grew quiet as a sleeping dog. Color drained from Tam-Tam's face as she cowered against Abby Louise

Finally, she spoke, "What was I supposed to do? I was sittin' at the window with a broken arm, busted pelvis and dislocated shoulder from a beatin' Harlan gave me just that mornin'."

"You could have yelled for them to stop," Missy accused.

"So I could get another beatin' come suppertime? Get myself killed?"

Silence ensued as folks digested all that had just been said and feared what might be revealed next. Missy's chest heaved. Tam-Tam buried her face in Abby Louise's ample chest.

After another long pause, Missy muttered, "I'm just lucky Juke didn't follow me."

"Speak up. Nobody can hear ya," someone called from the back of the crowd.

"I ran all the way to my mama." Missy's voice quavered, and tears streaked the makeup she'd patted onto her face earlier in the day. Tempest took a handkerchief from the pocket of her flowing, flowered dress and handed it to her.

Missy blotted her face, then revealed what happened next, something not even Maridee knew. "I told Mama everything. I didn't know

Papa was home. He heard the whole thing, and he stormed off and got his brother, the police chief, and they went to the Parlo's all set to arrest the two of them. They dragged me along, too. I didn't want to go; I was so rattled, but they forced me, said I might be needed to coax Juke out. But as soon as my dad and Uncle Maurice got out of the patrol car, shots came at them. Juke and Harlan had rifles raised by then, and my dad got hit in the chest. I got out of the car to help him. Gracie raced toward me, and she got hit, too, in the neck. After that, Harlan and Juke ran into the woods. … Gracie and my dad didn't make it, and nobody ever saw Harlan or Juke again."

"It was your uncle killed my girl. He shot an innocent girl in cold blood," Tam-Tam rasped.

Missy threw the handkerchief to the ground. "That's preposterous! He wouldn't have done that."

"You saw him do it, too." Tam-Tam said.

"I saw no such thing. I was with my dad, beggin' him to stay with me, beggin' him not to die."

"You said in an official statement it was Harlan killed Gracie. You remember that?"

"I, I thought it was. Uncle Maurice said it was." Missy rubbed her forehead and temples hard enough to leave red marks. "I never doubted him. He, he was a good man—and the law."

"A real investigation woulda showed the bullet that hit my Gracie came from your uncle's rifle. He killed my girl, and he knew I knew, so he, Maurice T. Brewer, made sure I suffered till he finally limped out of office. The old sourpuss turned me into the town pariah—poor Bram, my youngest, couldn't take it. He lied about his age, ran off to join the Army, be a hero in World War II, and lost his life.

At this, Abby Louise burst into sobs so forceful they spread like falling dominoes. Soon the patch was crowded with people clutching their chests and wailing like they'd just lost everyone and everything near and dear to them. Knowing Bram was the love of Abby Louise's life, Maridee took hold of the long-grieving woman and held her in a full-body embrace until she gradually calmed down, which caused the crowd's distress to subside as well.

Tam-Tam dried her eyes on the hem of her skirt and gave Missy the evil eye."I lost my whole family, and it's all because of you."

Missy swayed. Carly Mae pulled an empty camp chair over and helped her grandmother down from the ladder to take a seat.

A number of people thought this was the end of it. Secrets long buried had come to light and painful as it was, things would settle down, and maybe even be a bit better in time. But Tam-Tam wasn't done. "You ain't off the hook here, Marcie Brewer. You've kept Velda from me all these years," she claimed.

"What are you talking about?" Missy sighed, exhausted.

"The ring. The ring pinned to Velda's blanket."

"Grover and I didn't even know about that ring when we adopted our sweet baby girl. Velda and I only learned about it when Father Ahern moved to Touch of Kindness. And I'm not sure what to believe about that. He was havin' trouble keeping his story straight."

"You must have known she was my family."

Perplexed, Missy didn't respond.

Maridee spoke up. "How could she be? When Velda was born, Bram and Gracie were dead. Juke was on the run somewhere, probably dead, too. How could she be connected to you in any way?"

"And we didn't keep anything secret. Velda even had identical rings made for the kids," Missy added.

"That's when I realized it, when I saw them rings on Blanche and Ray," Tam-Tam said.

Emily pushed through the crowd. "Stop! Stop this hurting each other for no good reason," she cried out. "I know what happened. I was there."

"You don't have to do this," Jasper whispered, leaning in. "If it's too much."

Emily shook her head. "I want to go on. People ... need to know the, the truth. L- Lolly was real. Sh- she was my sister." Empowered by claiming Lolly as her own, Emily continued, her voice stronger than before. She told the people of Kiminee what had happened the terrible night Juke Parlo had wrenched her away from Tam-Tam, including the birth of Daphne Sunshine, Lolly's disappearance and Juke dumping her on the steps of the orphanage.

Tam-Tam jumped down from the bucket and ran toward toward Emily. "Ellyanna. My little Ellyanna? I never thought, I- I never thought I'd see you again."

"Get away from her," Doris growled. She looked like a leopard poised to strike. Tam-Tam shrank back, mouth open.

"It's okay, Doris." Emily held up a hand to signal Doris to stay where she was. "Tam-Tam was good to us. I swear I don't think she knew what Juke did to Lolly ... though she must have suspected deep down."

"I didn't realize she was pregnant till it was too late," Tam-Tam wailed.

"And the nuns never believed I had a sister named Lolly, who had a little baby, Daphne Sunshine."

"That little baby was Velda," Tam-Tam crowed triumphantly. "Ellyanna, you is my grand baby and so is Velda. My Juke fathered you both, though I admit his, well, his ... what he did to Lolly ... it wasn't right. I didn't see it then, but I do now."

Shock ran through the crowd like a buzz saw as people realized that Velda and Tam-Tam were of the same flesh and blood. And the notion surfaced that Tam-Tam, full of faults as she was, could have a real grievance here.

"And the bones that washed up during the deluge ..." Emily searched Tam-Tam-s face. "Those, they were—"

"Lolly," Tam-Tam whispered, then looked away.

Missy motioned for all three grandchildren to come close. Ray helped Blanche down from the ladder, and Carly Mae, stunned into silence, leaned in.

"It's a bitter pill to swallow, but I guess my Velda is Tam-Tam's grandchild. I swear I had no idea. Neither did Grover. We believed Uncle Maurice's story about her parents being killed in a car crash hook, line and sinker."

"So that means Tam-Tam's our great grandmother?" Carly Mae looked from Blanche to Ray.

"I guess you're right, by blood anyway," Ray said.

Missy and her grandchildren packed up their berries and ladder, while their friends and neighbors milled about, trying to absorb what they'd heard and figure out how they felt about it, not knowing quite what to do.

Seeing confusion on so many faces, Earl said, "Well, I guess we've all got a lot to chew on here, figurin' out who's related to who and all. Let's let the dust settle and give the family time to adjust to things. Tomorrow's a new day."

Abby Louise and Tam-Tam stood still, arms around each other. Earl picked up his overflowing bucket of blueberries and said, "Let's go, ladies."

"I suppose you're gonna lock me in the slammer, over them bones," Tam-Tam said to Earl.

"Lolly's bones, you mean." He tipped his hat. "I think you've suffered enough."

Abby Louise and Tam-Tam walked with Earl down the row toward his cruiser. Some people followed, heading to their own vehicles; others, needing more berries for their Founders Day baking, returned to picking.

Velda, who'd been listening from two rows away, slinked off. She was consumed with sorrow that her mother, a girl not even sixteen, had been buried right here her whole life and she never knew.

Chapter 36

*V*elda pulled a Radio Flyer wagon filled with empty quart-size yogurt containers, shovel and trowel across the Charles Street Bridge and along the far bank of the Bendy. Her stash of money was now large enough to pay travel and living expenses for several months, but instead of packing up and slipping away as she'd planned, she yearned for the black roses that grew at what used to be Lolly's secret grave. Since the deluge, the flowers had spread toward town, as well as into the wild wood beyond the river's edge, becoming much more than the little hedge Kiminee's eldest resident used to tend.

Compelled by a force she didn't understand, Velda stopped by an especially hearty section, pulled out the tools and dug into rich black dirt. She sang snippets of melancholy folk songs as she worked, pausing periodically to catch her breath, then continued singing and humming as she dug. After gathering twenty-four plants in plastic containers, she made her way home. Locals who were outside weeding or raking called hello when she passed by. She stopped and chatted with some. All admired the roses; none considered incorporating them into their gardens. Beautiful as they were, everybody who regarded them felt a stab of grief slice into their hearts. Velda, however, found comfort in them, a connection to the young mother she never knew.

When she arrived home, Emily was there, trowel in hand.

"What are you doing here?" Velda asked.

"I thought you could use some help when I saw you pass by. And, you know, Lolly was your mother, but she was also my sister, which makes me your aunt. But we had the same father, so I'm your half-sister, too, strange as that is."

"It is odd." Velda dug a hole in one of the empty flower beds surrounding her home, put one of the bushes in, and packed rich, black earth around the roots. "I don't know the first thing about her."

Emily carved out an adjacent hole, and Velda handed her a plant. "I'll tell you what I know; it's not much," Emily said.

Velda and Emily worked together, spacing the roses all around the house, six on each side, so once they took hold, Velda would be able to see them from every window. As they planted, Emily told Velda everything she could remember about Lolly and how much Carly Mae takes after Lolly in uncanny ways.

Planting done, the two stopped for a supper of tuna casserole on Velda's deck. When they finished eating, they gaped at the roses because they'd grown at least six inches in the last hour.

As the rose bushes climbed over her windowsill flower boxes, choking violet mums and grabbing windowpanes, Velda twisted and curled, straightened and rolled in her sleep. Black petals and darkest green, thorny stems soon blocked all moonlight from the room, and a translucent figure appeared in the corner. Clad in a sleeveless, cotton nightgown and slippers worn thin, the teenage mother was no longer running, no longer wild with fever, as she had been so long ago.

Arms outstretched, she glided toward the daughter she had last seen as a babe wrapped in a yellow blanket. She sat on Velda's bed and hummed a lullaby her mother used to sing in a city where coal dust muted the horizon. Her heart thrummed. She had no fever, nor was she cold. Tears flowed, but they were tears of joy at seeing her daughter.

Velda opened her eyes and saw the girl smiling at her. "Who? Who are you?" Her heart throbbed as the answer came to her. "Lolly?" Velda pinched her arm to make sure she was awake.

"Yes, I am your mother, Lolly, the girl who didn't want to birth you but who loved you nevertheless—still loves you with all her heart." Lolly reached out a cold hand and touched Velda's leg.

A chill went up and down Velda's spine. She shivered but didn't shrink away. "Okay, um … so I guess you're a ghost or a spirit?"

"It doesn't matter what you call me. I am your mother, and I was trapped, and now I'm free."

"So how is this going to work now that you're free? Are you going to stay here? Do you want me to stay? This is new territory for me." Velda had always wanted to know who her parents were, especially her mother. She wanted to feel close to the woman who had birthed her, but looking at the teenage specter before her, a girl younger than her own children, Velda thought of the old admonition to be careful what you wish for. She feared she might be haunted, and it could be worse than feeling like she didn't belong anywhere.

"I see worry in your eyes, sweetheart. Don't be afraid. I can be here only a few moments before I have to move on, and before I go, I want you to know, really know in your bones, that you don't owe anyone anything. I was robbed first of my childhood, then of you, my daughter, then my life was gone before I'd ever really lived. Please don't waste your life worrying about what is expected of you. You've always been different, a restless spirit who wants to call the whole world home. Take your adventure by the horns. Your loved ones will be fine. They might not understand, but they'll be fine." Lolly stood up and grew dimmer.

"But—"

"No buts. Listen to what I'm saying. Be true to yourself, live fully—not just for you, but for me, too. Do it for both of us." With that, Lolly faded into nothing.

Velda vibrated with indecision as she mulled over her mother's words in a room so dark it felt like a tomb. Then, at last, she resolved to leave, not to escape like she'd done before, but to fulfill her destiny—not just for herself, but for her mother, too. She rose from bed, turned on a on light and pulled out a suitcase. With the hem of her nightie, she wiped dust off its faux alligator exterior, then she pressed two golden buttons on the clasps, releasing them with a satisfying click.

Chapter 37

*M*issy added the last pinches of secret spices to her pie filling, stirred briefly and set the bowl aside. Then she set flattened dough for the crust on her "good luck" pie tins, the ones that had held many a prize-winning pie over the years. Daydreaming as her fingers worked, she thought of Tam-Tam. And it struck her how frail the old woman looked standing on an upturned bucket in the berry patch and how alone she must have felt after losing her entire family. It also struck her that she could have been kinder instead of turning her back on Tam-Tam time after time.

She shaped the crusts to perfection, poured in the filling and spread it around evenly. And when she rolled out more crust and sliced it into strips to crisscross over the tops, she vowed to turn over a new leaf as a few tears of compassion leaked out and plopped onto each pie.

In her kitchen, Abby Louise licked her fingers after drizzling a layer of graham cracker crumb mixture on the bottom of a pie plate and pressing it against the glass. Then she pulled her flask out of her robe's pocket, took a swig and thought of Bram, the love of her life. For the first time she felt a flash of anger at him for joining the Army at fifteen and getting killed at the Battle of the Bulge in Belgium. He ran off without saying goodbye, but promised in letters he would come home to her. "Shoot," Abby Louise said under her breath, "Missy didn't make him leave. He did that on his own." She took another swig of alcohol. She spooned her blended cheesecake ingredients into the dish, and a tear of acceptance fell from her eye onto her creation.

Tam-Tam hummed as she folded fresh blueberries into her muffin batter. While she worked ever so gently so as to not smash the berries, she thought of how Missy was only sixteen the day Tam-Tam's family fell apart. She was sweet and naive, and of course she believed her uncle's version of the shoot out, and truth be told, he'd been more likely correct than not. And as she filled her muffin tins, one sweet tear of possibility slid down her cheek and plopped into the batter.

Throughout Kiminee, people had similar thoughts as they baked and sliced and sawed and pounded in preparation for the coming Founders Day faire. Hands slowed down as teardrops of regret, reconciliation, compassion and newfound love peppered kitchens and workrooms around town.

While Missy's pie baked, the scrumptious smell filled the home, drawing Damon, Carly Mae and the twins to the kitchen.

Blanche squeezed her grandmother's shoulders and gave her a kiss. "Did you make an extra one for us?" Blanche asked.

"Of course. It'll be out to cool in about ten minutes."

The spirit of reconciliation infused Damon as he went to the cupboard and pulled out a box of Wheaties. He thought of the woman who had drugged him and passed him off as a convict so she could help the real criminal, Leon Ames, escape and hide him away in her home. "You know, it could be Georgia Webb was hoodwinked by that Leon Ames fella. He professed a love for her that he didn't feel. I mean what sociopath is capable of love? He charmed her, pretended to adore her until he couldn't keep up the facade any longer, then left her high and dry. That's what I think happened."

His family all stopped what they were doing and looked askance at him.

Fearing they thought he was not of sound mind, he said, "Not that she doesn't belong right where she is, but I had completely forgotten she's a human being, too."

Carly Mae ran across the room and threw her arms around her father. "Oh, Dad, I can't forgive her yet, but I also forgot she's a person with a story to tell. I've been gloating over her being locked away."

Blanche nuzzled in with Damon and Carly. "This line of thinking might turn out to be good for all of us. Isn't there some saying about grudges hurting the people who hold them more than anyone else?"

A wide smile spread across Damon's face. "Well, if there isn't one, there ought to be."

Ray and Missy followed Blanche, completing the little huddle around Damon, who laughed from deep in his belly. The others joined, and soon the kitchen was filled wall to wall with mirth.

The much-anticipated Founders Day parade, celebrating the town's birth on August 5, 1832, began at the foot of the statue of Charles and Fleur Kiminee. Participants dressed as pioneers and soldiers, chimney sweeps and nurses, cowboys and hunters. Some farmers came directly from their fields and marched in well-worn work clothes alongside the Kiminee Academy band, which helped maintain a brisk pace. Floats powered by tractors included the Suzette's traditional crepe paper black-eyed Susans; the Cheese Co-Op's styrofoam head of cheese; the Future Farmers of America's enormous ear of corn, made from dyed muslin and stuffed with myriad old socks; and, new this year, the Good Luck Cafe's giant paper mache coffee cup.

Carly Mae dressed as Rosie the Riveter, Blanche roller-skated by in a car-hop uniform, and Ray strutted along as an astronaut to great applause from people watching in lawn chairs and porches along the route, which wound around town, traversing the Bendy and back, and ended in front of the Kiminee Academy's community building—site of the infamous Wallop and Roll.

People filed into the building and rushed to the tables housing baked goods to find an enormous blue ribbon pinned in front of Abby Louise's cheesecake—a surprise to all, who thought the top prize would go either to Missy's pie or Tam-Tam's muffins. Further examination of the treats on the table revealed that Tam-Tam and Missy each won second-place red ribbons. Sporting a third-place white ribbon was Tempest Binsack's blueberry cobbler. Honorable mention was awarded to Willie Holt's bride, Sylvie, who entered blueberry-sour cream coffee cake.

"Not bad for a first time making cobbler," Tempest said to Maridee and Bill Pratt, as they strolled through the hall to admire the display.

A crowd gathered around the table housing the winning goods. Judges stood behind the table with Abby Louise and extolled the virtues of her cheesecake. Missy and Tam-Tam were in the group, standing close together.

Barb, one of the judges, said to Abby Louise, "We'd like to serve this in the cafe. Could you make one for us every week?"

Abby Louise's eyes were alight and her grin seemed wide as the Mississippi. "Oh, I don't know."

"That's the first I've seen her aglow since before my Bram died in the war," Tam-Tam said under her breath.

"I never meant for any of that to happen," Missy said.

Tam-Tam turned her head and nodded at Missy. "I know. We all just done what we could."

"I talk to Gracie sometimes," Missy confided. "She's my friend from beyond who comes to visit. Not often, just at times when I feel the weight of the world on my shoulders and can't sleep. She'll appear in the night and sing me lullabies in her fragile soprano, and pretty soon I'm off in dreamland, and in the morning I wonder if I've imagined it all."

"Nobody ever had a better daughter than her." Tam-Tam blinked to stave off tears. "She sings to me, too, at times just like you described."

Missy handed her a handkerchief with black-eyed Susans embroidered in the corners. The two lingered, smiling through tears, as their fingers touched until their attention was drawn back to Abby Louise, who was addressing the group.

"I want to thank our fine chief of police, Earl Wiggs, because he's the one who asked me to make this cheesecake." She cut a slice and put it on a plate and handed it to Earl.

He accepted the cake and took a bite. "Mighty fine. Better than the best anywhere." He took another forkful. "Mmm ... Why, Abby Louise, I think you should open your very own bakery."

"Oh, Earl, I ain't nothin' but a drunk." She fanned her face rapidly with a Founders Day program. "How could I do something like that, especially at my age? I'm not even sure I could really do one a week for the cafe."

"There's plenty of folks right here who'd help you."

Barb shouted out. "Yeah, like Jeff and me."

The thought of having a bakery in town made the sweets-loving crowd erupt into cheers so loud it made everyone's ears ring. After they quieted down, friends and neighbors lingered in the hall, viewing an impressive array of quilts and doilies, oil paintings and charcoal sketches, flower arrangements and bird houses—all entered in the hopes of winning ribbons. Then they filed out and headed for a picnic by the river. It was sponsored by the McDuggins and Tarrs, whose barbecue sauces had tied for first place. This kept resentment from seeping into the chicken and ribs on the grills, for which many people gave thanks as they bit into their grub.

At the riverside barbecue, Missy, the twins, Carly Mae and Damon sat on a red-and-white checkered blanket spread on the grass and watched youngsters zigzag around groups of chitchatting adults.

Missy pointed to a girl in a red dress whose brunette pigtails bounced as she darted through the crowd. "She's the spittin' image of Velda when she was that age," Missy said.

"I haven't seen Mom all day, have you?" Carly Mae said to Ray, who was next to her picking a scab on his knee.

Ray looked up, brushed his knee with his palm and said, "Nope." He turned to Damon and asked, "Have you seen her?"

Damon shook his head and motioned to Earl, who was talking with Mick Deely nearby. Earl finished his conversation and came over.

"Seems Velda hasn't shown up here yet," Damon said to Earl.

"I suppose you want to check on her?" Earl put a hand on Damon's shoulder.

Damon rose, and the two friends ambled toward Velda's. When they arrived, they gaped at the black roses, which had grown so thick and tall, they covered the entire doublewide.

"They're still growing. Look at that," Earl said. "I mean you can actually see them move."

"She could be trapped inside." Damon took a step forward.

Earl grabbed hold of his arm. "Let's be careful, okay?"

Damon pulled away, and ran toward the home. "Velda, you in there?" he called.

Silence permeated as Earl came up behind him. "How are we going to get through those bushes," Earl wondered aloud.

"She's got a little shed in back, should be some tools there," Damon said.

The two raced to the small wooden structure and found a hatchet and hedge trimmers. They returned to the front and hacked at the thorny mess covering the porch. The stems were tough and the thorns long. As they made headway, the roses closed in. The men chopped and clipped furiously, barely able to stay ahead of the threatening vegetation. Finally, they opened the door and got inside.

"Velda? Velda?" Damon called.

"It's like a cave," Earl said.

As the structure creaked from the pressure of the branches now wrapping around it and squeezing, the men walked from room to room. They looked everywhere—even in each closet and behind the shower curtain. Velda was not there.

As stems broke through several windows, Earl cried out, "We gotta get out of here!" He ran to the door, with Damon close behind.

The porch was covered again, so the pair chopped their way through and got away just as the home heaved and groaned and collapsed. Breathing heavily and sweating profusely, they threw down their tools and sank to the ground.

"What was that?" Earl mused.

"All I know is Velda's gone, gone with the river's flow, gone with our youth, gone with our love," Damon said.

Earl stretched out on the lawn. "When did you get so poetic, my friend."

Damon plucked a blade of grass, put one end in his mouth and sucked as he stared at what was left of Velda's home.

Chapter 38

August crept along in a steam permeating skin and bone and causing people to meander rather than proceed at a purposeful clip through their days. Workers refurbishing Tam-Tam's home hammered and sanded in slow motion; children on swings glided more than pumped; lemonade cooled in every refrigerator, causing a citrus shortage at the market for days on end. And during those desultory days, each resident old or young, visited the remains of Velda's doublewide to contemplate the black roses, which had stopped their aggressive growth and took on deep purple highlights when struck by the sun.

Sometimes alone and sometimes together, the Foley youths, Blanche, Ray and Carly Mae visited the spot, each trying to absorb a sense of the mother that had been gone more than present in their lives. One languid afternoon they sat cross-legged on Velda's front lawn when Blanche spied something near her knees. She separated blades of grass and clover with fingers moving rapidly and plucked. "Look!" She held a prize in her palm.

Ray and Carly Mae leaned in. "Wow! A four-leaf clover," Ray said.

"That surely means good luck for us all, our mother included, don't you think?" Carly Mae said.

The others agreed as they passed the clover hand to hand.

When Ray held up the cluster of leaves he said, "I think we should each share something important or make a wish, sort of like wishing on a star."

His siblings agreed, and Ray went first. "I'm all set to go to MIT in the fall, but …" He turned to Blanche. "You didn't apply there. You said you would, and you didn't, so I'm worried about you and think maybe I shouldn't go. Maybe it's too soon to leave after all that's happened. My wish is that we figure this out so I can make the right choice." He handed the clover to Blanche.

"I can't imagine life without you by my side," Blanche said to Ray. "But I- I didn't apply anywhere except Riverwood Community College. It comforts me that it's just up the road because something in me is telling me not to leave. I hate for you to go, but I don't want to hold you back either. I feel my heart will break either way."

Carly Mae reached for the clover. "I'd like to make a promise instead of a wish, I think."

"Go ahead." Blanche handed her sister the leaves, then hugged her knees to her chest.

Carly Mae looked Ray in the eyes, "I'm not ready to go anywhere just yet even though I've had offers for early admission from all over the place. I'm still not back to normal and probably never will be, so I'm going to say put, and I promise to stand by Blanche when or if you go to MIT. I will be her confidante, her best friend, everything I can possibly be for her. I mean, I can't be her twin, but I think I can ease the pain of your leaving, especially since we can write letters and talk on the phone, and you'll be coming home for Thanksgiving and Christmas, right?"

"Of course I'll come home for the holidays—and for all of next summer, too," Ray said.

"I'd like the clover, please," Blanche said to Carly Mae, who promptly returned it to her. "I want to make a promise, too. I know you're scared about returning to school," Blanche said to her sister.

"You've mentioned your memory isn't what it used to be, and I know how high everyone's expectations are for you and how much you don't want to disappoint anyone. I promise, dear sister of mine, that I will love you no matter what. If you can't ace those math tests anymore or remember who conquered who in 1520, or whatever, I will love you just the same. You will always be beautiful and brilliant in my eyes."

A rush of emotions clogged Carly Mae's throat; it took a few moments before she could respond. "You mean the world to me, both of you." She moved in to put an arm around each twin. "Our mom may be gone, but we still have each other. Even when Ray goes all the way across the country, we'll still have each other. And we have Dad, whose love for us never wavers. And we have Grams, always Grams."

Blanche tucked the four-leaf clover behind Carly Mae's ear, and the three hugged in silence as the sun beamed gently down, and the teens, along with the ruins of Velda's home, sparkled as though sprinkled with glitter of gold, silver and green.

Shortly before Labor Day, the rag-tag group of volunteers refurbishing Tam-Tam's home declared the work was finally done. Much discussion had gone on among the populace about how Kiminee's eldest resident should be dealt with after the Wallop and Roll. A small faction believed she should never be fully accepted back into the fold. However, while sipping lemonade during languid August days, chatting by notions at the Five 'N Dime, selling wares at Suzette's or savoring Abby Louise's blueberry cheesecake now sold at The Good Luck Cafe, most folks came to the conclusion that Tam-Tam deserved a break, especially since Missy's feelings for her had softened so much. Tam-Tam didn't know any of this on Labor Day, which fell on a Monday, the first of September and was the day she'd decided to move back home.

Tam-Tam and Abby Louise packed meager belongings she'd salvaged after the deluge, along with numerous odds and ends she'd acquired in the months since, into paper bags and boxes, and hauled those outside just as Earl pulled up in his cruiser and parked at the curb.

He stepped out of the car and picked up one of the bags. "Today's the big day, eh?" He opened the trunk and a rear side door. "You wouldn't believe how big my trunk is. If we fill the backseat, too, we just might get all of it in one trip. Come on, ladies. Let's pack 'er up."

Tam-Tam was dumbfounded at Earl's arrival. "Wh- why, thank you kindly, son, for helpin' an old pariah like myself," she finally choked out before dumping a bag into the trunk.

Earl chuckled and tossed in a bag of yarn. Soon, with cruiser packed, the three took off. The town square was empty when they passed through.

"Look," Abby Louise said. "The Good Luck's closed. I wonder what's wrong."

"And the folks from Touch of Kindness ain't feedin' the pigeons by the statue of Fleur and Charles like usual," Tam-Tam said.

"Maybe everybody's just getting off to a slow start this morning," Earl said, as they traversed the square and turned onto the road leading to Tam-Tam's, where Earl hit the first of many potholes and braked to slow the vehicle down.

They turned a corner, and Tam-Tam's yard came into view. "Oh, my! Everybody and their second cousin twice removed is here," Abby Louise exclaimed.

Applause broke out when Tam-Tam emerged from the car. Several academy students held up a banner that said, "Welcome Home, Tam-Tam!"

The shock of seeing a yard full of well-wishers made Tam-Tam dizzy. Shuddering head to toe, she leaned against the cruiser for support as she surveyed the crowd. She tried to speak, but the words wouldn't form. Almost everyone was holding something wrapped in paper of various designs available at Grant Modine's Five 'N Dime.

Earl took her by the elbow. "Come along. We have all kinds of surprises for you." He led her to the home and up the stairs, Abby Louise right on their heels.

On the porch, Tam-Tam lifted a card from a new swing near the door, and paused to read. It was from Damon, who wrote that he had made the swing himself and hoped Tam-Tam would enjoy it. She spotted Damon at the back of the crowd, made eye contact and nodded, then entered her new home.

"Whoo whee, this … this is a veritable palace." She looked down at her scuffed shoes and darned socks and shook her head. "It's fit for a queen, not for the likes of me."

"Nonsense," Earl replied. "Check this out." He walked across the room and opened a sliding door that led to a storage area as big as the rest of the home, with built-in shelves and cabinets already half full.

Tam-Tam hobbled over and peeked inside. "My God, look! Them's some of my craftin' supplies. I thought they'd all been lost. And look, my trunk's in the corner." Her eyes teared up.

Abby Louise came to the doorway. "How can this be so big? You don't see it from the outside," she said.

"Could be some sort of optical illusion. I don't know. You'll have to ask the hippies; they built it," Earl said. "They're right outside along with everyone else."

Tam-Tam left the supply room, peeked into the bathroom and gasped. "Look at that beautiful stained glass." The window was a pattern of black-eye Susans, violets, lilacs, sunflowers and salvia. "Must have cost a fortune."

"Damon made that for you, too," Earl said.

"Damon? A swing and a window? When did he learn to do all that?"

"I guess it was one way he passed time in that asylum."

Abby Louise brushed her hands along the kitchen cabinets, which were cherry wood with a Celtic braid pattern carved at the edges. "They just might be the most beautiful cabinets I've ever seen," she said.

"Carly Mae took charge of that project." Earl puffed up with pride. "She got other kids at the academy involved. They made all the furniture you see here, except for this." Earl went over to a recliner upholstered in royal blue. He spun it to face the door. "Now, sit here, and prepare to greet your public."

"Why? What?" Tam-Tam asked.

"You're Kiminee's Queen for a Day." He took her trembling hand and guided her to the chair.

Abby Louise tittered as she rubbed the back of the chair with her fingertips. "Oh, goodness, goodness. They didn't tell me about any of this, not one word." Her eyes scanned the room. "I would have done something, too."

"We couldn't tell you, Abby," Earl said. "You know you wouldn't have been able to keep it secret from Tam-Tam.

Abby Louise sat in a straight-backed chair near Tam-Tam and fingered the flask in her pocket.

Tam-Tam settled into the chair. "Dang. This might be the most comfortable seat I ever set myself in."

"I'm glad to hear that," Earl said. "I found it on a trip with Alvin Aldridge, a fellow keeper of the peace, and reupholstered it myself."

For the rest of the day, friends and neighbors filed in, each person or group carrying something for Tam-Tam. The residents of Touch of Kindness gave her potholders woven during their twice-a-week crafts period. The McDuggins brought her a new set of pots and pans they'd gotten by redeeming S&H Green Stamps. The Tarrs donated garden tools ordered from the Sears catalog. Grant Modine gave her silverware and dishes he bought wholesale through the Five 'N Dime. Jasper and Emily brought in several paintings by up-and-coming artists in Chicago. Members of the Suzette's, led by Maridee Pratt and Tempest Binsack, carried in what amounted to an entirely new wardrobe, sewn and knitted by hand and tailored to Tam-Tam's slight frame.

Mick Deely, his grandson Dave, who had just returned from Vietnam, and several students from the academy serenaded Tam-Tam with original compositions and then gave her a tape player and several tapes of their music. Missy came in carrying a quilt she'd made. It was solid green on one side. The other was festooned with the same flowers as those in Tam-Tam's new bathroom window. Missy kissed the top of Tam-Tam's head as she laid the quilt on the elder's lap. The two now shared a growing bond of worry over Velda, who hadn't been seen for weeks. But they didn't mention their worries just then. Days like this were for celebrating the best things in life, and they greeted each other with good cheer before Missy stepped aside to let more people present their gifts.

Maxine brooded over Velda, too, thinking perhaps their breakup had driven Velda off, but she was determined to enjoy the day, too, and swiftly joined the musicians in song after presenting Tam-Tam with beer she'd brewed herself in the basement of the cafe. Members of the cheese co-op provided an assortment of their finest cheeses, along with a cutting board and knife. Barb brought a pecan coffee cafe baked that morning, along with a box full of recipes donated by dozens of families in town.

Later, after almost every neighbor had bid Tam-Tam farewell and moseyed on home, she still clutched the recipe box while the last two party goers, Abby Louise and Earl, prepared to leave.

"I don't know how to thank you all," Tam-Tam blubbered.

"No need to," Earl said.

"I didn't do nothin'," Abby Louise muttered.

"You know that ain't so. You're my truest friend. Nobody else volunteered to take me in."

"She's right," Earl said to Abby Louise. "We all did our part, you included."

As the sun sprayed swirls of vivid colors across the sky, Earl and Abby Louise rode off in the cruiser, and Tam-Tam lowered herself onto her new porch swing. She lit up her corncob pipe and watched chickens, given to her by Mick Deely, peck away in their spacious new coop. "Life's a funny sort of thing," she said to the flock. "Here I thought I lost everything and everybody. Life's a funny thing."

Chapter 39

*F*ull of optimism over what the future might hold, Ray zipped downstairs and placed his bags by Missy's front door. Breathing in the familiar smell of bacon, coffee cake and lilacs, he moseyed into the kitchen, where he was startled by a room packed with people who cried out, "Surprise!" He'd already said goodbye to everyone in town during and after the housewarming at Tam-Tam's just two days prior. He thought he would slip off to college quietly. Missy had other plans.

Blanche grabbed him before anyone else could. "I'm going to miss you, my brother, my twin, my best friend."

"Whoa," he said moving her an arm's length away to get a good look at her face. "Are you having second thoughts about me going to MIT?"

"No, no, no." She grinned. "You must go, and I will be fine. It will test our mettle."

"Hey, stop hogging the star, will you?" Missy moved in for a hug. She gave him a quick embrace and peck on the cheek. "We're doing breakfast buffet style. It's all set up in the dining room."

She stepped aside to make room for Carly Mae and Damon; Earl, Jasper and Emily; Tempest and Maridee; Maxine, Barb and Jeff; and several students from the academy—all of whom wanted to give Ray a hug before joining the feast in the dining room, where Missy had set up card tables to augment the limited seating at the table. Ray was the last one seated. Still surprised at all the attention, he blushed repeatedly as people shared fond memories and embarrassing moments from his childhood.

When just a few crumbs were left on plates, Missy rose and took a cassette tape player from the sideboard and put it on the table. "This here is Velda's tape player. I found it in a cabinet yesterday when I went searchin' for my papa's Bible so Ray can take it with him to that dang fancy school he's gonna take by storm. It's got a tape inside with Damon, the kids and me, and Earl on the label, but I don't expect she'd mind other folks listenin' too."

She scanned the room, took a breath and pressed Play. First there was a little rustling, then Velda's voice began, "Dear, dear family, I just had the most amazing experience. I'm not sure I'll be able to describe it, but I'm going to try. ... You see, all my life I've deep inside longed for my mother, though I didn't have any memories of her. It didn't seem fair to Missy and Grover, my mom and dad who raised me and gave me a wonderful home, to feel like I wanted more than what they gave me, so I kept this longing deep inside for years and years. Then when Father Byrne gave me the blanket and ring after the terrible twister, the longing grew more intense. I felt more out of place than ever. Plus I was ashamed of myself for being such a bad wife to Damon, and I did the cowardly thing and snuck off, leaving just a note for my mother and children. Truthfully, if Jeff hadn't come to fetch me after Carly Mae was taken, I might never have come back. That sounds awful now that I said it, but it's true. I tried to make a go of it, partnering on the Good Luck Cafe and Bendy River Inn, but things were chafin' at me somethin' fierce. And then when it came to light that my mother was buried by our Bendy River all those years, well, that was a shock. I didn't know how to absorb it. I planted some of those black roses that grew by her grave. Emily helped me do it. Emily who is both my sister and my aunt, which still confounds me.

"And it was so strange the way the roses kept growing and growing. Then the other night, I couldn't sleep, and my mother, Lolly, came to see me. She said it was time for her to move on, but before she did, she wanted me to know I don't owe anybody anything. She was robbed first of her childhood, then of me, her daughter and her life. She never got to grow up and live the life she wanted. She told me not to waste my precious years worrying about what's expected of me. She said I've always been a restless spirit who wants to call the whole world home and to take my adventure by the horns.

"Whew! She said if I follow my heart, all of you will be just fine. And she said I should be true to myself and live fully—not just for me, but for her too. Then, just before she faded like morning fog, she said all will be well.

"So my dearest ones, I've made a choice. I'm recording this while all of you are getting ready for the Founders Day festivities. By the time Missy finds this, I'll be long gone. I don't know where my path will lead. I just hope you can come to understand as the years go by that I've done the best I could and will cherish all my memories of you. Please don't take it too hard, and know that I will always love you. Truly, Daphne Sunshine."

Missy looked out the window at her garden. "Looks like our Velda's gone for good this time. She's Daphne Sunshine now, travelin' with the wind."

"Heck, that's nothing new," Blanche said under her breath to Ray and Carly Mae.

Missy's face reddened as she gave Blanche a sour look. Uncharacteristically, she didn't stand tall and focus on something needing to be done to stave off dark feelings. "Please excuse me for a minute," she blubbered to no one in particular. She then rose, ran through the kitchen, out the back door, and sat on the grass. The others gathered at the window.

"Oops!" Blanche bit her lip.

Carly Mae took Blanche's hand. "It's okay; you didn't mean anything by it." Then she turned to Damon. "Should we go to her?"

Damon studied his mother-in-law as she gazed at the river burbling by at the far edge of the yard. "I expect she wants to be alone with her memories just now. Sometimes things build up to where you have to sink down and let it all go on your own. She'll come back inside when she's ready," he said.

"We could all clean up for her," Ray suggested.

"Yes, let's get to it," Damon said.

Everyone at the gathering got busy. Since there were so many hands at work, they didn't stop at merely washing dishes and wiping countertops. They dusted cornices Missy couldn't easily reach, fixed a broken fan and mopped floors that didn't really need mopping. Maridee and Tempest even set to work on a basket of sewing. When Missy marched back inside, wiping her face with her apron along the way, the house was empty of guests, dishes were done, counters cleaned, card tables put away, and dining room table polished. Missy's face flushed with a mixture of embarrassment and gratitude. She said a gruff thank you to her family, who were still inside the home, and then focused on the departure at hand. There was just enough time for her to give each of her grandchildren a long hug before they piled into Damon's recently purchased VW bus, which Willie Holt and his friends had converted into a top-notch camper. Damon closed the vehicle's door, and Buster jumped through the window into the back seat, where he settled into Carly Mae's lap. "Good old boy," she said. "You're gonna miss Ray, too, aren't you."

Ray leaned over from the front passenger side and patted the dog's head. "I'll miss you, too, buddy."

As they eased away from the curb, Earl Wiggs pulled up, his cruiser packed with academy students, and followed the van. Jasper and Emily were right behind in the Willys wagon. Next came the McDuggins in an old Chevy pickup, with the Tarrs close behind in a belching Buick sedan. Then came the Pratts and Tempest Binsack in an old Nash with no shocks so they bounced at every little bump in the road. Right on their tail was a slew of Willie Holt's friends from the old Kiminee place, all driving refurbished Model T cars. Longer and longer the queue grew, until bringing up the rear, were Barb and Jeff in his old red semi, which grew larger with every mile they traveled to the airport, where they would all bid a bittersweet farewell to Ray, the first child of the town to go to college out of state. He was living their version of the American Dream, the Kiminee Dream.

On a mid-September Sunday afternoon that warmed without burning, Jasper and Emily pulled into the Kiminee town square in their Willys wagon. They'd just returned from a weekend of antiquing in the Springfield area. In the driver's seat with the window rolled down, Emily inhaled and felt no nausea. "This is glorious," she said. "I feel fine, absolutely fine." She parked in front of the Good Luck but left the engine running.

"Are you sure you don't want to join us?" Jasper asked.

"She asked to meet with you, not both of us. Besides, I want to unload our new treasures right away."

"Okay, I'll see you later then, love." Jasper exited the wagon, waved to his wife as she drove off, then stopped to greet Buster, who was sunning himself on the sidewalk. He scratched the dog behind his ears and murmured, "Waiting for your girl, huh." He entered the cafe and strode to Carly Mae, who was already sipping a Coke at a window booth. "So, sweetheart, you wanted to see me?" He sat down across from her.

Barb came over to fill a mug with coffee for Jasper and take their order: two BLTs with fries, and, for later, one chocolate malt that Carly Mae had promised to bring to Blanche, who was working a shift at Suzette's.

"So I heard you and Emily are taking a big, long trip to Ireland, and school's barely gotten started."

"We're not leaving until the middle of October, and we'll be back before Thanksgiving. It'll be a little more than a month," Jasper said.

"Why do you want to go to Ireland anyway?"

"I have some research to do there."

"Research?"

"Of a personal nature."

Carly Mae tapped the ice cubes in her drink and watched them bob. "I was counting on you being at school. I'm, I'm not as smart as I was, and, without you there ... " She looked up at Jasper. "I guess I just feel uneasy."

"You might feel like you've lost some of your brilliance—"

"I don't just feel that way. It's the truth."

"It's too early to tell what's lost and what isn't," Jasper said. "Way too early. And Ned thinks maybe some of what we thought you had wasn't real. Maybe it was an illusion."

"Ned? He can't even see the black-eyed Susans when they turn ruby red and sparkle. He thinks we're all deluded."

"It's probably a delusion I'm going to chase in Ireland, too."

"You mean you agree with Ned? Don't you see them?"

"I've been awed by their transformation many times. Emily has, too."

Barb brought their sandwiches. "Me too. They sparkle at 5:05 like precious gems. I've seen it with my own eyes."

Earl walked in and seated himself at the counter. Jasper and Carly Mae waved to him, and Barb left to pour him a cup of coffee.

"I just don't get what could be so urgent in Ireland all of a sudden." Carly Mae bit into her BLT. "Mmm, this is good."

"Well, I hired a researcher, someone who specializes in genealogy, and it turns out my mother was born in Ireland." Jasper took a swallow of coffee. "I knew she was Irish, but, you know, a lot of Irish Americans say, 'I'm Irish.' I just always assumed she was full-blooded Irish but born here."

"What difference does that make, whether she was born here or there?"

"Do you remember how Henchley and Croll threatened to make private things from my childhood public if I didn't give them what they wanted?"

"What things?"

"Um … that I thought my mother had turned into a seal and swam off in Lake Michigan … that I almost pushed my father off of a ledge—"

"Go on, I didn't hear anything like that. I would have remembered."

"It was during the conversation in the library."

"I missed that entirely. You were still talking when I left. I was so upset I couldn't listen anymore. You thought your mom was a seal?"

"Yes and no, well sort of."

She shrugged her shoulders. "That makes no sense."

"I'll try to explain," Jasper said. And while he and Carly Mae consumed their meal, he shared memories of his mother and the sealskin, the long estrangement from his family and how he forced his dad onto a ledge. He filled her in on as much as he could recall and ended with his splashing with the seals in Lake Michigan.

"No wonder you came to us, Jasper," Carly Mae said, feeling even more kinship with her mentor that before. "We needed you, and you needed us, too."

Jasper poked his French fries, momentarily too overcome with emotion to meet her eyes.

"I sure wish Aunt Truly were back at Windy Wood. She told me a story about a fisherman in County Galway a long, long time ago who captured a seal woman. She said similar tales were told all over Ireland and Scotland."

"County Galway. That's where my mother's from, the Connemara region. Do you remember it?"

"Pretty much. It goes that the fisherman was all lonesome because he'd been unable to find a wife, and one day he heard beautiful singing coming from behind a rock at the shore. He peeked around the rock and saw several women more beautiful than any he'd even seen. They were singing and dancing in the sand. To the side were sealskins. He'd heard of women that shifted shapes from seals in the ocean to women on shore, but he'd never believed the stories until that moment. But instead of letting them be, he crept up, stole one of the skins and carried it back to his home, where he locked it in an old chest, put the key in his pocket, and stuck the chest high up on a shelf."

Barb arrived with the malt to go and the check. "No rush," she said. "Take your time." She rushed off and called over her shoulder, "I'll be back with a refill on that coffee, Jasper."

"You're the best," he said.

"I agree," Carly Mae said, and then continued the story. "The fisherman returned later to the beach and found a young women naked, shivering and weeping at the rock. He wrapped her in a blanket and took her home, comforting her as though he didn't know what could have happened to her skin. The two grew fond of each other and soon married. He always guarded the key. She always longed for the sea, even after she had children. Then one day, the fisherman was gone longer than usual and, out of curiosity, she decided to try to pick the lock on the chest. She stood on a chair, reached for the chest, and it came crashing down and broke apart, revealing her sealskin. She grabbed it, rushed to the sea, put on the skin, turned into a seal and swam away, never to return."

"Wow, that lines up with what I think happened to my mom, except for different continents, different kinds of seals, and, well, a whole different time in history."

Barb returned and refilled Jasper's cup. "Anything else?"

"No, we're all set," Jasper said.

Barb spun around and headed to a table where Race and Della Burlingtons had just seated themselves.

"That story makes me want to go even more to Connemara and other places in Ireland and Scotland. I want to know what happened to the children, and whether there are more threads to follow, and if maybe this sort of thing happened more recently anywhere," Jasper said.

"I hope you find what you're looking for," Carly Mae said. "I just wish you could find it here." She giggled and kicked him under the table.

Jasper grinned, marveling at her combination of uncanny wisdom and normal teenage fervor. "You'll be okay while I'm gone, you know."

Carly Mae took hold of the malt with both hands. "I think I should get this to Blanche while it's still good and cold."

"Of course, go along," Jasper said. "I'm going to stay a while and drink my coffee."

Carly Mae rose and left the cafe. Outside Buster greeted her with happy yelps, and the two ran to Suzette's. "Boy, do I have a lot to tell you," Carly Mae blurted when she and her dog burst through the door. "Jasper's mom might have been a shapeshifting seal from Ireland."

Blanche, who had been doodling by the cash register, looked up and laughed out loud. "Sure, and our mom is a rabbit."

Carly Mae chortled, but then grew serious and said, "Come to think of it, it makes me feel better about our mother. She's not the only one whose family couldn't hold her. It's been going on, like, forever."

Chapter 40

*A*t her stove Thanksgiving morning, Tam-Tam was aglow with joy as she prepared sweet potatoes to bring to the family dinner at Missy's later in the day. "To think I'd ever be invited there," she said to a squirrel perched on her kitchen counter. She'd found the critter with a broken leg and nurtured him back to health. When he recovered, he refused to leave, so he slept now in a wooden box full of rabbit bedding in her kitchen, coming and going as he pleased.

After she put the potatoes in the oven to bake, Tam-Tam went to a coat rack by her front door and slipped on her jacket. As she opened the door, the squirrel dove off the counter, skittered across the room and climbed up to her shoulder. She ambled across her property to the riverbank and crossed, careful to maintain her footing when she stepped on the stone that still wobbled. "I dunno why they couldn't a fixed this thing when they fixed up my house," she said to the squirrel. "But then beggars can't be choosers, they say." She chuckled and walked the path to the clearing that she called Lolly's Spot because even though Lolly's remains had been laid to rest, per Doris and Emily's request, at Blessed Heaven cemetery, something of her spirit lingered at the river.

"I had to come visit today even though I ain't got time for weedin' and such," she said. "I'll get to it in a day or two. I just want to tell you it's like a miracle what's happened in my life. I got family I never had, and a sort of understandin', even love. Who knows? Maybe you feel it, too. Today, I'll be seein' your grandkids, and my great grand-kids—all three of 'em, since Ray's back for his first visit home from college. Blanche and Carly Mae are making college plans, too. They're just the smartest—oh, I don't need to tell you, now do I. Oh, today's gonna be something, I'll tell you that."

When she finished saying her piece she returned to the river, and the squirrel hopped on her shoulder again for the crossing. When she stepped on the unsteady stone, she slipped and fell, cracking her head on a boulder jutting from the bank. The squirrel splashed into the water and swam to shore. Tam-Tam's head bled profusely, turning the river water red. She was pulled a few feet by the current, then caught by a root sticking out. The squirrel ran back and forth along the root, making shrill chirps of distress. In the oven the sweet potatoes burned to black.

Grant Modine was the first to see Bendy River run red on Thanksgiving Day. He'd been open from 9 to 11 a.m. just in case anybody needed a last-minute cardboard turkey centerpiece, the kind with an orange tissue tail that fanned out; a bag of orange peanut candy to put in a crystal dish for guests; or a can of pumpkin pie filling in case a homemade pie burned, which tended to happen more often on Thanksgiving than one might expect. That's why, when Grant locked up the Five 'N Dime at 11:03, he didn't think too much about the pervasive smell of charred food. He was just sad it was too late for the poor cook to start over.

It wasn't until he walked toward the river that he saw scarlet water burbling past. He beelined to the police station, knowing from a conversation he'd had with Earl that the chief would be at his desk till 11:30, when he planned to pick up Abby Louise and take her to Missy's.

Meanwhile, guests were already socializing in Missy's living room, catching up with Ray, living college dorm life vicariously through him.

The blend of turkey, stuffing, spices, warm pumpkin, and mulled cider wafted through the home, which was more packed than ever.

Missy Lake paused at the stove when Jasper entered and put two bottles of Jameson Irish whiskey on the counter. "Wow! Thank you, Jasper."

"My pleasure. Emily and I brought it back from Ireland." Jasper patted one of the bottles with pride.

Eyes full of merriment, Missy cocked her head. "Ah, yes, you went to research shape-shifting seals in them British Isles on account of your mother being a shape-shifter herself?"

"We had a great time, but we didn't find anything besides some hints of magic and several variations of the sealskin story. It could very well be my mother told me the story when I was little and somehow, with the trauma of her death, I just got everything confused. I expect I'll never really know. One good thing, though, is we are bringing a scholar on Irish folklore to the academy next semester. That's an exciting development."

"You don't say. … Well, I'm glad you're back. Carly Mae sure missed you. Don't tell her I said this, but she hasn't exactly been hittin' home runs in school, and people have been talkin', you know, sayin' we've lost our little star, even though she's right here in the flesh."

"She might not be light years ahead of everyone like she was, but she's still very much a star in my book. You have no need to worry about her."

"Thank you for that reassurance," she said.

He leaned down and kissed her cheek. "I should be thanking you and your wonderful family."

"Enough of that, Jasper. You're family now, too, so you're good and stuck with us. And imagine if you hadn't taken such an interest in Carly Mae's paintings way back when. Think of all we would have missed." She swatted him with her dishtowel and chuckled. "Now, go enjoy yourself."

Jasper went to the front porch, where Mick Deely and Emily sat on wicker chairs. Mick's grandson, Dave, and Carly Mae perched on a swing, Buster firmly in place between them.

"Emily's been telling us all about your trip. She said you didn't exactly find what you were looking for, but it was still worth the time," Carly Mae said.

"It's the quest that matters anyway, not the prize," Dave said.

Carly Mae eyed Dave with admiration.

"You've got that right, son," Jasper said.

Just then, Missy came out with a plate of Ritz crackers and Velveeta and asked Carly Mae to take the snacks around to guests. When the plate was empty, Carly Mae and Missy added another leaf to the dining room table.

"I saw you flirtin' with that Deely boy on the porch. He's six years older than you, pumpkin—and a Vietnam vet," Missy said. "Best stay away."

A tingle moved through Carly Mae's core as she looked down, tongue tied. She scratched the back of her neck.

Sensing Carly Mae's discomfort, Ray came to her aid while placing a tablecloth on wood polished to a sheen with Lemon Pledge. "Isn't it more the quality of the relationship than the years between?" he asked. "And he's not all that old. He went into the Army when he was seventeen."

Blanche helped smooth out the cloth and chimed in. "Look at Frank Sinatra and Mia Farrow. They had decades between them," she said.

"And how long did that marriage last?" Missy opened the case holding her special-occasion silver.

"How about Humphrey Bogart and Lauren Bacall, then? That one lasted," Ray offered.

"It was scandalous. She broke up his marriage," Missy retorted with a wink at Carly Mae.

Seeing her grandmother's expression, Carly Mae felt a wave of relief wash away her embarrassment. "Oh, Grams, you don't have anything to worry about. I'd go out with him if I could, but he says I'm too young. I play fiddle with his band sometimes, but he treats me like a kid sister."

"Now, that puts a smile in my heart," Missy said. "I shoulda known the Deely lad could be trusted to do right by you. Now, if Velda would just come home, I'd be worry free, except I always wonder if there'll be enough chairs—"

Ray laughed. "Or enough food."

"Or if the rolls will burn or something like that," Blanche added.

Just then Earl arrived, helped Abby Louise find a seat in the living room and then went directly to Missy. "I'm sorry, but I've got to check into something, so if you need to start dinner without me, go ahead. Hopefully, this won't take long." He turned and trotted toward the door.

Missy wasn't about to leave it at that. She chased after him. "What do you mean you've got to check into something? What could you possibly have to check into on Thanksgiving Day?"

Earl paused at the door and rubbed his upper lip. "There's something strange going on at the river." He turned to step out.

Missy grabbed his arm. "Hold on. What sort of strange?"

He lowered his voice. "It's running red."

Missy gasped and cried out, "The river's red? Red?"

"Shhh. Keep your voice down. We don't want to alarm everyone." He stepped outside.

Several people had already heard Missy, though, and word spread through the home like lava running downhill. Much as they all looked forward to Thanksgiving dinner, everyone followed Earl outside and to the Charles Street Bridge to see their very own river turned scarlet. And what a sight it was. It was chilling, but there was also something peaceful about it that was hard to peg.

"Maybe it's the birds singing in such beautiful harmony that makes it not scary," Carly Mae said, voicing what many others were thinking.

When he arrived home, Grant told his family about the river, and they told others, so by the time all of Missy's guests had filed after Earl, word had reached almost everyone in town. A gaggle of folks gathered on the bridge and elsewhere along the Bendy's course. Earl walked the bank against the current, seeking the source. Damon followed. Earl was soon greeted by a chirping squirrel that circled around his feet, darted ahead, came back and circled again, and so on, encouraging him to move faster. He was at a full run when he saw Tam-Tam in the water. He skidded to a halt and pulled the old woman out.

Damon approached, panting, behind him and asked, "Is she okay? What can I do?"

Earl unclipped a newfangled portable radio from his belt and handed it to Damon. "Call an ambulance," he said, then began mouth-to-mouth resuscitation.

Missy's guests and other townsfolk couldn't resist gawking as Earl and Damon tucked blankets around Tam-Tam, whose eyelids fluttered but did not open. Meanwhile, Missy and Doris entered the little home that had so recently been refurbished with love. Missy turned off the oven and opened windows to let smoke out. Doris scraped charred sweet potatoes into the garbage and filled the sink with soapy water to soak scorched baking dishes. Finally, an ambulance arrived and spirited Kiminee's eldest resident away.

A few folks drifted home; most rushed to the hospital, where they waited for what they hoped would be good news. But less than an hour after her arrival, Tam-Tam was pronounced dead.

"She fought hard, but just didn't have the strength to go on," said Doc Redfield to the tense group packed into the waiting room. "We must all remember, now, in this time of loss, that she had a good, long life."

"And she was happy in the end," Abby Louise said between sobs. "So happy. But now I got no one. She's the only one loved me, 'cept for her Bram—love of my life—lost too young in the war." Her pulse quickened as she sank into a chair and succumbed to a coughing fit.

Around the room other people broke down, too. Soon the walls reverberated with a mix of misery and sorrow, regrets and should-have-dones spreading from person to person, seat to seat, swirling faster and faster, making it difficult to breathe. Outside, Buster joined a gaggle of rabbits, wolves and chipmunks, mingling in the bushes.

This reminded Carly Mae of the state she was in when she arrived at Windy Wood. Memories of Aunt Truly filled her mind, particularly the old woman's weathered voice as she rocked in a chair and told stories. Carly Mae sat down next to Abby Louise, who was in the most distress. She took the woman's trembling hands and said, "Let me tell you a story."

Startled at the thought, Abby Louise sat up straighter. "A- a story? You … you … and me? N- now?" she sputtered.

"Yes, now," Carly Mae said, and began the tale of the trapper who built a cabin by the pond where a frog had resided in contentment for a long, long time. She told of the trapper's efforts to do away with the frog, because he couldn't stand the amphibian's croaking and chuck-chuck-chucking at all hours. As the teenager spoke, Abby Louise's breathing settled down, her sobs grew softer, her tears tapered off. The same happened to others in the room as they leaned in to hear what was going to happen next. Carly Mae continued until she reached the point where the trapper buried the creature, certain he'd done away with it at last—only to be awakened in the night by the frog croaking and chuck-chuck-chucking from beneath the ground. Realizing she didn't know what happened next, Carly Mae stopped. The room was silent as everyone waited for her to resume. She remained still.

Finally Abby Louise blew her nose into a handkerchief and said, "Go on, girl. You can't stop now."

Remembering Aunt Truly's confidence in her storytelling abilities, Carly Mae improvised. "Okay, so the trapper, blind with fury, lit a campfire, got it going strong, and threw the frog into the flames." Gasps echoed through the room as Carly Mae continued. "There was a sizzle and a pop. Then hundreds of sparks burst out and flew through the air toward the trapper. As each spark landed, it turned into a tan frog with dark spots. Each one croaked and chuck-chuck-chucked in harmony with the others forged in fire. And those were the ancestors of the leopard frogs living in these parts to this day."

Tempest Binsack, Race Burlington and several others let out murmurs of satisfaction at what would become local critter lore repeated at front-porch gatherings through the coming years.

"As for the trapper," Carly Mae said, "no one knows for sure what happened other than he left the pond, screaming while brushing amphibians from his face, hair and clothes. Some say he haunts the rivers and streams still, but I wouldn't know about that. I only know that nothing could defeat the frog in the end."

Abby Louise leaned into Carly Mae, and a sense of peace enveloped them. They didn't move until Missy tearfully invited everyone back to her house for what would now be turkey sandwiches instead of a traditional dinner. She wanted to give the community in which Tam-Tam had spent her entire life a chance to comfort one another before going home to face life without her.

Carly Mae placed a hand on Abby Louise's heart and said, "Nothing will defeat you in the end either."

Abby Louise felt a sliver of hope for the first time in years. "Maybe so. Maybe so."

While the first group of mourners emerged from the hospital into bright daylight, an elderly woman peeped through a hedge that bordered the parking lot. "Jasper's right," she said to a family of raccoon that was trekking with her westward away from town. "Our girl will be fine."

Inside, choking back a mix of sorrow and relief, Earl offered Abby Louise a hand. "May I escort you to Missy's, m'lady?"

She gripped his fingers. "Aw, if ever I'd had a son, I'd a wanted him to be just like you, Earl Wiggs."

He pulled Abby Louise up, and Carly Mae broke away, bidding them a quick farewell. She didn't see Abby Louise pull a flask of whiskey from her coat pocket and dump it in a trashcan on the way out of the hospital. She was already out of the building and running toward the Charles Street Bridge. When she arrived, Buster was sitting at attention, tail wagging.

"There you are, my friend." She bent down and ruffled his fur from neck to rear and back, and gave him a kiss on the muzzle. She then stood, leaned over the railing and watched the now clear water flow by. "You know something?" she said to her dog.

He lifted his one good ear.

"Aunt Truly was with me just now. I couldn't see her and might not ever set eyes on her again, but I could feel her. And you know what else?"

He cocked his head.

"I feel just like when I was a kid, only better, because I can see that sorrow is alchemy. It makes us strong as diamonds."

Buster trained his eyes on the gurgling water, tail thumping the pavement.

Acknowledgments

When I began what became *The Kiminee Dream,* I thought I was writing a short story. If it hadn't been for my critique buddies, who greeted each new scene with enthusiasm as the tale grew, I don't think this book would have come to life. Time after time, they cheered me on as the folks who populate Kiminee came to life and demanded attention. Thank you, Skye Blaine, Patrice Garrett, Marie Judson and Beth Ann Mathews. I also want to thank Greek poet, novelist and playwright Nanos Valaoritis, who traveled the world during his long literary life and landed at San Francisco State University for a time, where he championed his students and regaled us with stories during his office hours; and Ruth Stotter, a storyteller and mentor par excellence who continues to inspire me and many others on our creative journeys.

Editor Elaine Silver gave me advice on the book's opening chapters that I was able to apply to the book as a whole, and editor Rachel Lyn Solomon went through the complete manuscript, leaving notes and reminders about things I wouldn't have seen without her help. Early readers, Vicki Daughdrill, Julie Fadda, Mary Ellen Gambutti, Chris Predick and Rayne Wolfe, asked excellent questions and pointed out areas that needed shoring up. Plus Rayne noticed that on one page I had mistyped a character's name as "Aunt Truly" instead of "Aunt

Trudy." She suggested Aunt Truly was a better name for that enigmatic character. I agreed and changed it. I cannot thank these discerning readers enough. A great big thank you also goes to Jo-Anne Rosen and Stefanie Fontecha, who created the layout and cover design, respectively, for this book's advance reader copies.

And to my family: where would I be without you? Certainly not writing books. Day in, day out, you demonstrate your support in countless ways. Jim, Kathy, Mary Ruth, Ryan, Jackson, Moira, Roger, Ava and Reina, you are all dear to me. Extra special thanks to my husband, Jim, who endures my preoccupation with imagined places and people when he'd rather be spending time with me, and to Unc, who encouraged me to write this novel. He is no longer with us on earth, but I am sure he will find a way to read this book in Heaven.

Note to Readers

*T*hank you for taking time to read *The Kiminee Dream*. I sincerely hope you enjoyed it. I grew to love the town of Kiminee and its quirky band of residents while writing the book. Readers have expressed delight in the people who live there and how the connections between them unfold in surprising ways. They've also said they love to hate Georgia Webb and Leon Ames.

What about you? Are there characters you particularly like or dislike? As an author, I love feedback. Candidly, you're the reason I continue to write. So tell me what you liked, what you loved, even what you didn't much care for. I'd love to hear from you. You can write me at laura@WORDforest.com and visit me on the web at http://lauramchaleholland.com.

Finally, I want to ask a favor. If you're so inclined, I'd love it if you would post a review of *The Kiminee Dream* on your favorite online review site(s). Reviews can be tough to come by these days, and you, the reader, have the power to make or break a book.

Thank you so much for reading *The Kiminee Dream* and for spending time with me.

In gratitude,
Laura McHale Holland

Other books by Laura McHale Holland

Reversible Skirt: A memoir
Resilient Ruin: A memoir of hopes dashed and reclaimed
The Ice Cream Vendor's Song: Flash fiction
Just In Case: Twenty-one bite-sized stories

About Laura

I believe when we follow our fondest dreams, we open doors for other kindred souls. While this is rarely easy, and life wrenches without mercy at times, words well-crafted can enchant, mend and empower us to rejoice in our hopes anew. This quest and the friendships formed along the way are central to my life and writing, through which I plumb diverse emotions in memoir, fiction, poetry and plays. I hope you've enjoyed reading *The Kiminee Dream*, my first novel. To learn more about me, please visit https://lauramchaleholland.com, where you can read about my books, as well as join my readers group, which, along with giving you special offers and updates on my writing, will, I hope, encourage you reach for your own fondest dreams.

Made in the USA
Monee, IL
23 January 2022

89685674R00204